LIEUTENANT JACOB STARKE AND THE ANARCHISTS

Michael T. Ribble

Apalachicola Publishing—Dumfries, VA
ISBN: 978-1-7330842-1-5
Library of Congress Control Number: 2020906620
Title: Lieutenant Jacob Stark and the Anarchists
Author: Michael T. Ribble
Digital distribution | 2020
Paperback | 2020

This is the second book following a fictional navy officer just before the Spanish-American War; when the United States Navy and Revenue Cutter Service carried out now largely forgotten operations to prevent military supplies and fighters from illegally entering Cuba. While the coordinated effort described may not have occurred, it would have been possible. People from the period with political, military, and public roles were included, and actual events inserted as accurately as possible. All fictional events and characters are wholly imaginary and any likeness to actual persons, living or deceased is coincidental. Certain long-standing institutions, firms, agencies, and government offices are included and their activities taken from historical sources, or assigned tasks that could have occurred within normal operations.

The cover art is the work of Samuel Ward Stanton who was lost on RMS Titanic.

Dedication

To:
Lieutenant (junior grade) Bruce J. Orr,
Master Chief Engineman Arthur D. Hurd,
and most especially, Baerbel, my love and muse.

Other books by Michael T. Ribble:

Lieutenant Jacob Starke and Calypso

TABLE OF CONTENTS

Chapter One
A Captain's Dilemma

A navy officer detailed to Washington sipped warm coffee from a white china cup with its fading, embossed eagle as he stood gazing from his State, War, and Navy Building window. Captain Sydney Albert's east wing office was on the fourth floor of a massive French-inspired structure, called the Building by its denizens, and overlooked the Presidential Grounds, Treasury Building, Executive Mansion, and Lafayette Square. The early morning sun reflected off marble walls and teased the trees' flickering July leaves. Red and white striped awnings shielding the tall, four-pane window would soon be extended and shade well over half the glass. The lower frame was cracked open to snatch some of the morning's ephemeral coolness so he could hear Executive Avenue's horse-drawn vehicles and streetcars beyond the pedestrians passing inside or near the decorative fence below. Starting at the Treasury Building, he scanned through grounds, walkways, trees, and statuary to the Executive Mansion then northeast past its greenhouses to Executive Avenue and Lafayette Square to settle on a Capital Traction Company's yellow, white, and mahogany open streetcar. Several different lines moved an eclectic clientele around the city and riders of every stripe were stepping down from this one's side platforms. Although overwhelmingly men at this time of day, the capital's streetcars moved merchants, clerks, lobbyists, bankers, tourists, and various other customers. Most were on business, but some rode for pleasure, like House Speaker Thomas Reed, or to enjoy the breeze.

Captain Albert stood in this exact spot less than five months before, preparing to offer Lieutenant Jacob Starke the *Calypso*; an ex-merchant ship with a bark rig, modern steam plant, 4-inch rifles, and nominal crew of picked officers and men. She was his ferret, the single Navy ship permanently assigned to disrupt filibusters running weapons and fighters to Cuba. Filibustering to cleave areas and islands from Spain had a long history but the current iteration was effectively organized, well supported, and times had changed. Only Puerto Rico and Cuba remained, with the larger island suffering regular uprisings, including the Ten Years' War two decades earlier. Filibuster expeditions were run from New York City by the Cuban Revolutionary Party, or Junta, with an office in Washington's Raleigh Hotel, just four blocks beyond the Treasury Building and almost visible from Albert's window. José Julián Martí Pérez, known as Martí, began this insurrection less than two years before, fostered by endemic independence movements, persistent Spanish misrule, and an economy hurt by the Wilson-Gorman Tariff. He became an early casualty in 1895; along with the belief independence would come from a short, popular uprising. His successors calculated it was now possible only by ruining the economy, draining Spain's treasury, and bleeding the army through fighting and disease. Spain, in response, fortified cities then sent thousands of soldiers to the West Indies. The Junta's war of attrition was fed by illicit support from a sympathetic American population still torn from its own civil war, adjusting to the Reconstruction's demise, recovering from the 1893 Panic, and preparing for national elections. Business and political leaders feared greater involvement risked a war with Spain that could force European powers to take sides; and the

Junta's illegal filibuster expeditions smuggling weapons and fighters to Cuba could easily ignite it.

Revenue Cutter Service and Navy ships patrolled the Florida Keys for filibusters as a secondary mission, even between uprisings, but more ships were now required and more departments' attention. Captain Albert coordinated the Navy effort although *Calypso*, under the Special Service Squadron, was the only ship he controlled. Anything else was detailed from a North Atlantic Squadron trying to develop tactics to fit its modern additions. He also coordinated with a Revenue Cutter Service captain who liaised with individual districts for any cutter except *Vanguard*, temporarily under headquarters control. Albert also briefed the Secretary on related Europeans actions or reactions.

Having experienced blockade duty during the war, Albert understood they could never begin to match those numbers and this time would require all traffic from Maine to Texas intercepted to determine which ships were filibusters. He was also called to joust with frustrated Spanish diplomats, adversarial jingoes, passionate Cubans, and an irreconcilable press; so rather than play the Junta's game he conceived, proposed, persuaded, and negotiated for *Calypso*. She, unlike other ships, targeted Junta operations just as commerce raiders like *Alabama* had trade. Acting as his rat terrier or ferret, she was not pursuing individual expeditions but operating just within the law without any set routine or pattern. Albert calculated, if successful, worrying filibusters would prompt mistakes, make planning difficult, and raise their costs. Lieutenant Starke was now taking her from Norfolk, where she commissioned, through Straits of Florida to the Dry Tortugas for a final work up. The bark was last reported on her way south after a Port Royal coaling stop. Once working up was complete, Starke's roving commission covered the Caribbean and southern coastline; and Albert would learn if his scheme panned out.

Captain Albert was reassigned to Secretary Hilary Herbert after his recent promotion, with the same portfolio he worked for Assistant Secretary William McAdoo. He came to the Building in 1893 as a senior commander from the Port Royal naval station to await orders and expected a Bureau of Yards and Docks assignment. He was instead detailed to McAdoo, an official met while establishing the naval station as a shipyard. Orders to the Secretary's staff and promotion placed him in the line officer cadre controlling eight independent bureaus and five squadrons. Herbert and McAdoo relied on him to work filibuster operations but his immediate superior was Rear Admiral Francis Ramsay, Chief of the Bureau of Navigation; the most powerful bureau because it controlled most personnel assignments. Albert hoped becoming the most junior of fifty active duty captains would bring command of the second-class battleship *Maine* for a final sea tour but his ability to navigate national bureaucracy and politics made that less likely as months passed. This pleased his redheaded wife Abigail and their two daughters, despite what they said. It also meant his future lay in the Building, or a shipyard, since the opportunity for advancement to commodore or rear admiral was small and nothing senior existed. The national election might also bring a Republican administration that could eliminate his current position.

Albert ended his morning ritual by walking to the carved oak desk where he set the worn china cup, pulled back a rolling chair, sat, then scooted forward, bumping over a Persian rug. This caused sharp knee pains he attributed to shore girth and sea arthritis. Away from the desk, he walked with a rolling gait accentuating a short, stocky frame fixed to thick, powerful arms and legs made for climbing, casting the lead, or rowing a pinnace. His short neck melded this torso to a round head with close-cropped and receding, gray-white hair. He was clean-shaven, unlike most officers, and always wore an immaculate service dress blue uniform although civilian clothes were allowed in the Building. The blouse was trimmed with braided black mohair as were four new stripes on each sleeve. Peeking from the high blue collar with anchor and eagle devices was the upper perimeter of a white standing collar tightly clamping his neck and wrinkling the slightly reddened skin above. Since service coats were to end just below the hips and conform to the figure, his underscored a rounded paunch above smartly creased blue trousers, stressed at waist and thighs, which rose over and partly covered polished, black calfskin shoes, never patent leather.

While studying routine reports, he heard packs of government clerks, stenographers, and staff passing through the interior hall and glanced at the wall clock before surveying his desk. On its far right corner, beside the mahogany pipe stand and correspondence box, was a small desk calendar with four rollers displaying weekday, month, day, and year; set earlier to "THU JUL 09 96". The sun illuminated his desk and faintly reflected off a brass and white glass gas lamp hanging from an ornate ceiling medallion. He signed two reports before leaving for one of the small Department of Justice offices spread across the city since his contact, Arliss Spencer, had called an urgent, confidential meeting about filibuster expeditions.

Leaving through the east entrance, Albert walked past an ornate gate in a black, wrought iron fence surrounding the Building then headed north over bare ground. He quickly passed the Executive Mansion's greenhouses, heading for Lafayette Square's south side, and Capitol Traction Company streetcar line. After avoiding the scattered and clustered road apples, he crossed streetcar rails and power slots in the asphalt, then stood beneath a shade tree in the square; across from the Executive Mansion and south of the Metropolitan Company's rails, a large hotel, and imposing duplex mansion off the square's north side. His arrival was well-timed, so he soon boarded the second of two coupled Capital Traction Company streetcars running east on Pennsylvania Avenue, then to the Washington Navy Yard. While looking for a vacant bench seat, he noticed a young woman sitting alone; her auburn hair pinned in a loose pompadour and wearing a muted gray traveling suit with mother-of-pearl buttons. The Brussels carpet bag beside her was anchored by a light gray, kid glove. Brown eyes tracked him as he took the facing seat, gained time by settling in, then recalled they attended a dinner party four months before at Immanuel Starke's northwest Washington mansion. She was one of two unmarried women that evening, besides his daughters. The other was a British widow traveling with her brother but this one worked for a newspaper. He remembered because Starke was uneasy about including her on the guest list; but ultimately served as her escort and met those obligations almost too properly in Albert's mind. Since they were introduced at the dinner he moved quickly, "Captain Sidney Albert, miss. I believe we met at the Starkes in March?"

"Cassandra Evans; and yes we did. I hope Abigail and your daughters, Isabella and Olivia, are in good health. Are you still with the Assistant Secretary?"

Evans welcomed and exploited such opportunities to troll for leads but had only until 10th Street, where she would leave for the Times building. She enjoyed meeting the captain and his family at the dinner party but it was her nature to probe, deposit results in a phenomenal memory, and retrieve them later using short notes in small notebooks. This often lulled her subjects into thinking anything not written down would be forgotten. She also possessed a hunter's patience that was especially effective on reticent men. Evans would demurely take a seat, gaze at the quarry with pencil poised over a notebook, and silently wait for the void to fill with useful information. Since neither worked with this captain, she suspected he was well-practiced at keeping close what he did not want known and getting out what he did.

Adjusting to the hard bench seat, he responded, "I appreciate your asking. They're fine and I'm still in the Building although I prefer the sea on days like this."

Evans saw an opening, "Are Lieutenant Starke and *Calypso* at sea?"

"Yes, she left Norfolk on schedule. If I may ask, how's your work faring? Isabella and Olivia seem interested in university or a career."

"I write *The Evening Times* society stories as Boudica Brown and cover hard news when the editor wants a woman's slant. My father publishes a country newspaper in New York so I grew up in the business and learned early dues must be paid."

As Benjamin Franklin's statue near 10th street approached, she gathered herself to leave, paused, and then offered, "I'm available if Isabella and Olivia have questions."

Starke alerted Albert to Evans' capabilities but the captain was still impressed by her subtlety; and grateful *Calypso*'s commander was naturally taciturn. She was apparently undaunted by spinsterhood, poised, intelligent, and committed. He also suspected, as she rose, the attractive female worked every attribute, although by nature or design he could not judge. Soft flowing hair, appealing brown eyes, flawless eyebrows, and fashionable S-figure emphasized by a modest bustle must contribute to an already formidable arsenal. He was confident many in the Building would hemorrhage information, if exposed.

Evans navigated a street flanked by tall saplings planted in sidewalk tree wells as the streetcar rolled off. Mingling with people, wheelers, and horse-drawn delivery carts, she crossed the intersection, glanced at Benjamin Franklin's statue and recalled his commending the Paris maisons de tolérance as ideal venues to understand the French politics and language. It was, appropriately, near several newspaper buildings, the best bordellos, worst bawdy houses, and freelance prostitutes' hunting grounds. She once asked to work there undercover but her editor thought it risky and, she surmised, unladylike.

The brief conversation with Albert reignited suspicions of a lurking story that involved Starke, *Calypso*, and, most likely, Cuba. Without thinking, she looked up Pennsylvania Avenue at the seven-story Raleigh hotel's distinctive French Second Empire architecture that dominated red-brick structures surrounding it. Two blocks from the Times Building, it housed the unofficial Cuban legation where, despite or because of her sex, she pried two seemingly accurate articles from the Junta's Gonzalo de Quesada. It also convinced her that Cuba was where the reputation needed for a position on some New York City paper might be earned and was polishing her latest proposal when Albert boarded. This scheme consisted of traveling to Havana for a woman's perspective on reconcentrados; Cubans from the countryside forced into camps and buildings. She was also resolved to seek a different position if refused since the Times papers were being sold and staff changes inevitable. At the Starke dinner party, she discovered Jacob Starke, her reluctant escort, was a close friend of *The Sun* reporter Darwin Tyson; a man she already approached who proved more interested in refilling a silver hip flask before leaving for the Democratic Party convention in Chicago.

Evans entered the Times Building as Albert walked down the street to his meeting, frustrated at being slightly late. It was a discourtesy, except for very senior officials unwilling to embarrass their hosts, but adjusting his schedule to oblige Spencer was partly to blame, as was Department of Justice offices being scattered across the city. This one was behind the small door in a two-story, red-brick building sandwiched between a tobacco store and dry goods emporium. Inside, a steep, narrow staircase led to the second floor's long and equally confining hall. Climbing to the top, he opened the first door, passed through the small outer office, and entered a large room with its curved front wall conforming to the building's solitary turret. It was pierced by three double-pane windows overlooking the street that undoubtedly made the room pleasant during spring and fall but cold in winter and close during summer; even with its slow-turning ceiling fan. It was dominated by a large, circular pedestal table with eight oak chairs. Seated around it were Captain Gibson Fischer of the Treasury's Revenue Cutter Service, Clarence Newcomb from State's Diplomatic Bureau, and, facing the door with his back to the windows, their host, Arliss Spencer. A fourth man Albert did not know stood by a window, availing himself of a heavy drape to conceal his observation of those passing in the street below.

Albert apologized, introductions began, and Spencer's unknown guest introduced as Horace Green, a senior Pinkerton National Detective Agency operative. Reacting to Spencer's nod, Green began in a strong, precise voice, "Gentlemen, Spain's mission to our nation engaged my firm to obtain Junta gunrunning information but we disclose results to Justice, and other agencies, when loyalty or law require. In this case, our client is aware and agreed, but requests anonymity."

The overhead fan stirred, but did not diminish summer heat exacerbated by a rising sun and closed windows. Albert glanced furtively at a small corner table for a water pitcher, found nothing, and then resigned himself. Green seemed unaffected, "One of our operatives reported a filibuster expedition willing to fight any ship intercepting it."

Newcomb interjected, "That's always been a risk."

"Shooting to escape a Spanish gunboat; not looking to fight a warship or cutter."

Newcomb quickly responded, "Then, legally, they'd be pirates."

Albert was reminded State's man needed to appear the most astute present, regardless of subject or circumstance, then observed neither dress nor manner had changed since their March meeting. The brown-blond, center-parted hair still endured a liberal coating of Macassar oil and his body remained enveloped in a three-piece suit. He was doubtless there to gather information and his comment intended to provoke unguarded discussion. Albert was confident Spencer would return the compliment and induce the influential bureau's lawyer to contribute an equal amount.

Oblivious, the Pinkerton went on, "It appears some in the Junta think General Weyler is succeeding and want to take a major city, other than Havana or Santiago, to discredit claims there are safe areas. This means taking on blockhouses and fortified lines so they need artillery and gunners; which insurrectos are short on."

Before Newcomb could interrupt again Spencer coughed to alert Green, who quickly resumed, "Our sources report an expedition forming in Mexico, Veracruz to be precise, where the Junta has popular support and level of European trade using the port has caused instability and intrigue. This means President Diaz would find it ill-advised to act openly unless his government is targeted. Our resources there are limited but it was imperative you were informed of what was discovered."

He then distributed identical envelopes, "This is our culprit. The oceangoing, steam tug *J.W. Fawkes* was acquired and renamed *Rafael Riego*. She's 138 feet long has a twenty-five foot beam, fourteen-foot draft, and displaces 340 tons; with a steel hull, large cargo hold, and room for passengers. The superstructure was gray and hull black but the distinguishing features are two funnels approximately amidship, gaff-rigged masts of equal height, and deckhouse running about two-thirds her length with the pilothouse forward; just ahead of some ventilators and two whaleboats. She was designed for long distance towing and made sixteen knots on builder's trials. We've reports she's registered in Brazil, probably illicitly to conceal her owners, and said to have used Brazilian, British, and American colors."

Spencer sighed, "Another *Virginius?*"

Captain Fischer picked it up, "It's been twenty years. An ex-Confederate blockader runner illegally registered under our flag was boarded by a Spanish cruiser, seized, and taken to Santiago. The governor there started shooting crew and passengers; whether Cuban, British, or American."

Albert added, "There were rumors in Spain and Cuba that our navy was protecting her but Secretary Fish still settled it through negotiation and probably saved half our fleet."

Newcomb saw his opening, "A diplomatic success?"

Captain Fischer eyed him coldly, "Not for the poor bastards put against a wall, shot, then trampled with horses; and some signed articles thinking the voyage legitimate. Killing didn't stop until a British cruiser arrived and her captain threatened to sink the closest Spanish warship at the next execution."

Newcomb noticed a speck on his sleeve and carefully

brushed it away, "If what Mr. Green says is accurate?"

Spencer raised his hand slightly, "Later; please continue Mr. Green."

"While not widely known, or covered in the press, the Junta includes an anarchist faction. Whether from Russia, Germany, Italy, or Spain is less clear but our sources claim this expedition is theirs and intended to be what they call propaganda of the deed."

Albert became skeptical whenever anarchists were invoked because any suggestion of their involvement usually initiated an immediate response. The philosophy had many variants but some advocated propaganda of the deed, which included inciting, rioting, murder, and assassination but could be anything that disrupted order and brought attention. Besides the Chicago Hay Market bombing a decade earlier, they recently assassinated the French President, bombed public functions, and attempted to murder an American industrialist. Albert also suspected Green's source might be a senior Junta official since revelation of an anarchist faction would cost public support and they would likely campaign against any Cuban government after independence.

Green added, "Last month's Barcelona bombing suggests Spain is their real target, with Cuba the means to an end, although we've not identified any person or group."

Retrieving the worn pipe secreted in his small bag, Captain Fischer briefly fondled it, before observing, "Seems odd for anarchists; their style runs to coal torpedoes, arson, and murder. Ships require more than rhetoric and dynamite."

"True, but some received military education before becoming adherents, and many could have a maritime background. However, my role is only to provide what we uncovered to your respective departments."

Since Green had little more to contribute, they briefly

revisited several points, everyone offered obligatory appreciation for disturbing news, then Spencer walked him to the staircase. Albert and Fischer studied the packets until Spencer returned and distributed a bundle of papers held together with a Hotchkiss staple. While they read, Spencer began, "My apologies for the haste, but you needed to hear Mr. Green directly. However, since Pinkerton's employed by Spain through their legation, and to protect sources, we'll bill this meeting as one to discuss legal considerations when working with civilian firms, which is not altogether false."

Shifting in the chair, his expression dour, Spencer continued, "We might have dismissed this, except for Pinkerton's reputation and the Marshals Service unearthing comparable rumors. Our man in the South Florida District, Brian Fields, passed what information he gathered to captains Starke and Hunter. They recommended we bring it to this group."

Fischer lowered his pipe, looking perturbed, "Only *Vanguard* and *Calypso* know?"

"Correct, but they've no ship description and the anarchist information just arrived."

Newcomb leaned forward, "This could be planted to create an incident but if anarchists are involved it's probably accurate and the Junta wants someone else to take them out of play. Anarchist schemes to achieve utopia by destroying the existing order at any cost don't fit the Junta's need for recognition and support, or avoid a war that could leave Cuba with us. Cuban anarchists are a small faction they may want us to weaken or eliminate. If the *Rafael Riego* expedition is planned by an internationalist faction, they probably see it as a strike against the Spanish government and monarchy with an eye to toppling both and reviving the 1848 revolutions. To them, Cuban independence would only be a means to that end so success, failure, consequence, or casualties become irrelevant. Independence, however, is everything to the Junta so it's possible they don't want this expedition to succeed even if it benefits their cause."

Albert observed from behind pipe smoke that State's clerk just broke cover to join the other mortals then added, "Two other considerations. Navy and cutter patrols have not been warned, and intercepting *Rafael Riego* would require extraordinary luck."

Spencer nodded, "There's also her flag and registry. Justice and State agree boarding a Brazilian ship would be unhelpful with that government recovering from the mutiny and our southern neighbors still agitated by the Chilean incident."

Newcomb agreed, "Not just South America, President Diaz supports American investment in Mexico but his people favor the Cubans and are upset over our army crossing the border after Apaches. If *Rafael Riego* leaves from Veracruz, intercepting her just off the port could cause an incident and asking Mexico to act would be pointless."

Captain Fischer tapped his pipe on the ashtray, wrinkled his brow, and looked to Albert, "*Vanguard's* repairs are nearly complete. What's *Calypso's* status?"

Albert understood what was coming, "Underway off Florida. I'll cable orders to ports she might enter that divert her to Key West. Hunter can meet her there with *Vanguard* and new orders for Starke. *Calypso* won't know why she's held in Key West but that can't be helped. If this information is accurate, the anarchists can't suspect anything's in the works."

Albert later exited one of the open streetcars popular during summer months, walked past the Executive Mansion to the Building, and climbed to the Office of Naval Intelligence on the fourth floor. The Chief Intelligence Officer, Lieutenant Commander Wainwright, was new and the captain preferred his predecessor, Lieutenant Singer. He was not alone. Wainwright was exceptionally thin with dark, graying hair, large mustache, and extraordinary self-discipline. Albert also distrusted his office reorganization; something he felt was usually done by those trying to impress seniors, regardless of the disruption. Even so, it could be justified and Wainwright was entitled to the benefit of doubt since Albert never worked there. Another irritation was the man's constant attempt to develop naval strategy for the Assistant Secretary; despite never holding permanent sea command or involvement in any operation more violent than landing in Panama. However, relationships and access often carried great weight in Building politics so Albert greeted the officer two ranks his junior, related what occurred, and offered to assist briefing the Assistant Secretary; although Albert would meet with Herbert before Wainwright had a chance to reach the Secretary.

When he returned to his desk, Albert pulled a briar pipe from the rack to consider his best tack with Herbert. He needed more mature planning than saying *Calypso* and *Vanguard* would hunt together since two ships hardly improved the odds. If *Rafael Riego* was crossing the southern Gulf of Mexico, rather than Straits of Florida, they would be asked to intercept a tug transiting hundreds of square miles with visibility limited to the view from a masthead; twenty miles on a good day, but usually less. Besides, the Gulf had few points to waylay *Rafael Riego* off some port or navigation aid. Albert draped a chart over his desk, blanketing several items. These expeditions usually came from the States, so using Veracruz was a bold approach that complicated any interception by involving Mexico. It also removed Dry Tortugas as the final landfall before crossing to Cuba; which was almost certain if the tug left from a northern gulf port. Albert smoked another bowl, studied the chart, and kept returning to Veracruz despite placing *Calypso* off the port would cause a diplomatic row and be unsustainable.

He finally considered what he would do if organizing the expedition and settled on steaming along the Yucatan Peninsula's treacherous north coast to the Yucatan Channel. Although heavily trafficked, it was unlikely the Navy or Revenue Cutter Service would station a ship there; patrolling indefinitely to intercept a single filibuster that would probably cross at night with running lights out. While packing his third bowl, a tobacco strand fell on the rumpled chart beside Arrecife Alacranes, a large reef system about halfway to Cuba and just south of the major shipping lane between Veracruz and Straits of Florida. If *Rafael Riego* did not hug the Yucatan coast from Veracruz east, but cut across the southern Gulf, it served the same purpose as Dry Tortugas. If so, the odds just improved. Touching a match to the pipe, Albert considered the implications.

Stationing *Calypso* near the reef would pull her off more heavily trafficked filibuster routes. Asking other ships to cover for her would not be welcome and might raise questions regarding his ferret's value since *Calypso* was partly justified as freeing ships for squadron duties. It also compromised his intent to make the ferret's movements less predictable since greater communication with Starke was necessary and only possible because undersea telegraph cables had proliferated in recent years. With cable offices in more ports, major nations required fleets and ships to remain nearby or maintain contact using dispatch ships. European navies employed a large number but the Americans only built *Dolphin*; then made it their President's yacht. Albert accepted infrequent contact with Washington while commanding *Apalachicola*, even if his decisions were evaluated later from a safe distance. At the time, he saw this second guessing preferable to control by someone far away and not directly accountable. However, he now felt the impotence others endured during periods of silence. *Calypso* left Port Royal, the situation changed significantly, and she would be incommunicado for a week or more. Starke had not stopped at Jupiter Inlet because there had been no reason, it lacked a deep-water port, and messages were telegraphed after being sent ashore by boat or signaled using International Morse Code.

Albert briefed Ramsay, who suggested Secretary Herbert issue a carefully worded warning that provided *Rafael Riego*'s unique features and enough information to avoid being surprised. Meanwhile, Fischer did the same with the Revenue Cutter Service's senior captain, Charles Shoemaker, for cutters in districts the filibuster might pass. The alert reached First Lieutenant Boyd Hunter and his *Vanguard* in Jacksonville, where boiler work was finishing, then quickly followed by secret orders for both ships.

A relieved and elated Clarence Newcomb left for his south wing office after briefing Secretary of State Olney on *Rafael Riego*. The New York City transplant knew Olney wanted options or specific decisions but found he must continually resist a predilection to philosophize when comfortable, distracted, or unsure of his arguments. The Secretary's second story office was especially distracting because its three large windows opened to a panorama consisting of the shimmering Potomac River winding south to a greenish-blue horizon, the busy port, Long Bridge, and mix of business and residential buildings that included southeast Washington's Colored section. There was also the Near East-themed room's lavish interior with heavily stenciled walls, ornate fireplace, and splendid furnishings resting on Persian carpets. The Diplomatic Reception Room next door was no less distracting with its Persian carpets, crystal electroliers, dark leather furniture, oil paintings, mirrors, and superb view south over the Potomac River.

Newcomb walked to his Diplomatic Bureau office down a corridor of checkerboard floor tiles between off-white walls and dark wood doors with embossed eagle brass doorknobs. It was spacious and boasted a high ceiling, white walls, and small ornamental arch over a dark wood entrance that incorporated a transom window, slanted open for summer. After sitting in his high-backed leather chair, he looked over the pedestal desk's polished top. There was a black telephone on its right corner, mushroom-shaped light near the left one, and woven wire wastebasket beneath. A large oak bookcase with rectangular glass doors sat against the corridor wall, holding legal reference books with matched spines and John Jay's Parian marble bust centered on its top. Other appointments included a small fireplace, large floor clock, two leather sitting chairs, and, if he lifted his head, a pleasant view through two windows of the Potomac River, Lee plantation house, and national cemetery.

He was here more often than his Cairo Hotel lodgings, being unmarried and lacking such aspiration unless some advantage accrued. He came to State during Cleveland's first administration; assisted by family connections and a Harvard University law school degree. He felt a seasoned veteran after nearly twelve years but his position, even as professional staff, could be in jeopardy if Republicans regained the presidency and it was likely since Cleveland's two terms were the Democrats' only national successes in thirty-six years.

While considering his framed degree above John Jay's bust, Newcomb knew he must become indispensable; and Albert's project offered the opportunity. Regrettably, clerks such as himself were often tolerated more than accepted by the likes of Spencer, Albert, and Fischer. The Revenue Cutter Service captain seemed to have emerged from the sea fully grown, Albert enjoyed an enviable Building reputation, and Spencer served under General Thomas during the war. Their experience, honesty, and credibility meant security and power in the Building. However, he did contribute at the last meeting, saw an opportunity to do more, and had the Secretary's approval to cable Matt Ransome, minister to Mexico, asking for information on *Rafael Riego* and Junta or anarchist activities in Veracruz. Extracting off-white writing paper from the desk's center drawer, he uncapped a black Wirt fountain pen and began a note for coding and transmission to Mexico City.

Chapter Two
Key West

While Captain Albert waited for news, *Calypso* entered the Straits of Florida and was completing a full power run along the keys when the filibuster *John Gwinn Williams* departed Bahia Honda for a Sunday crossing and mistook her for a merchant. The tug turned back and ran for shoal water with *Calypso* in pursuit. Just as Starke was about to abandon the chase, one of the tug's propulsion boilers exploded and *John Gwinn Williams* sank. Her master, Fachtna Harler, survived; a man known as Captain Buff due to his buffalo-like manner and appearance. Burdened by survivors and corpses, *Calypso* postponed the Dry Tortugas work-up and raced for Key West where she found the battleship *Maine* under Captain Crowninshield. As senior officer, he passed on Department orders for the bark to remain in port. Later, legal peculiarities and authorities' disinclination to prosecute meant no one involved with *John Gwinn Williams* would face prison; leaving *Calypso* the only participant detained.

As a hot, still July passed without a Department cable explaining *Calypso*'s Key West detention, Starke understood all islanders' unquenchable urge to escape, if only for short periods, and some going mad for want of it. Meanwhile, *Calypso* became a wood and steel islet, anchored just off the ship channel and seaward of *Maine*. Day followed day in this purgatory, with each mirroring the last. The brilliant morning sun would light his cabin through its starboard windows opening on Fort Taylor, cross the sky, then dip below the blue sea beyond small, verdant keys. Ship's work began before colors then played out according to predetermined Day Orders. A Marine fifer bugled *Reveille* from *Maine*, and sunset's call to colors since *Hail Columbia* required a band. Starke sometimes went on deck to watch the western horizon's kaleidoscope and sunset's illusive green flash before the same bugler, who had a flair for the instrument, ended the day with *Taps*. Starke usually retired soon after, once work ended and daily observations in running letters to Katherine were complete.

Maine and *Calypso* were anchored south of Key West's small naval station established decades earlier to deal with pirates. It now centered on a large building serving as headquarters and warehouse behind a steel pier with iron pilings; and equipped with three small tugs, a modest machine shop, and new coal bins. A lieutenant, paymaster, boatswain, and small civilian staff supported the commander. There was no station ship but warships were often there on filibuster duty.

The city's commercial piers, wharfs, offices, warehouses, and horse-powered marine railway were just up-channel to its north and most everything on the island passed through this port, including building bricks and barges of drinking water when cisterns failed to fill. Passenger liner stopovers also created a brisk tourist trade, with carriages queuing on wharfs and streets for each arrival. The Plant Line's fast steamships *Olivette* and *Mascotte*, dominated the Cuba run by ferrying passengers, mail, and cargo between Port Tampa, Key West, and Havana. Three runs were made every week from January to March, then two during the summer months when yellow fever reduced riders to a trickle; and *Olivette* left for her summer route in the Northeast. Other liners running between New Orleans and Havana put in at Key West; often bringing passengers from Cedar Key, where the Atlantic & Gulf Central Railroad connected that port with Fernandina.

The sea supported most island industries, directly or indirectly. City Wharf's daily sponge auctions were supplied by a fleet of small sloops and schooners scouring Florida's west coast and northern Gulf. These mother ships would anchor or drift in some favored sponging ground, then launch two-man boats to snag the creatures with a long pole. The trade employed a devout jumble of black, brown, white, and mixed races, many from the Bahamas; with the predominant participant a Greek. Less often, live loggerhead sea turtles, stored on their backs, were sold to locals, restaurants, and the factory run by a French chef. Yamashita learned of this through John Bell, his Negro counterpart on *Maine*, added several cases of the canned meat to Starke's larder, and prepared veal-like fresh turtle streaks when available. Sea salt production, although small, was another industry with several ponds located southeast of the port.

The enterprise Key West was best known for on the mainland, and the Cuban community's mainstay, was cigar-making; since the climate resembled their homeland and the port made it easy to receive leaf tobacco then ship cigars from factories across the city. Skilled workers came from Cuba in trickles and waves, looking for a better life or escaping the current revolt, war, or insurrection. Not surprisingly, these factories regularly experienced labor unrest and were artesian funding wells for every planned or active Cuban revolt. The community was well-organized, with social and political life centered on the San Carlos Club fronting Duval Street; a small edifice exuding old Havana with its white, gold, and black arches; double glass doors; and twisted wrought iron railings. Cuban clubs not only used it for meetings and social functions, but their elected presidents held coordinating council meetings there; to look after the community's needs and support Cuban independence.

Local newspapers like the *Daily Equator-Democrat* and *Key West Herald* were small and short-lived, while the Spanish language paper *El Yara* was created to promote Cuban independence. Fighting in Cuba also brought an infestation of freelancers, stringers, and correspondents that holed up in stuffy hotel rooms or scurried about Key West looking for tidbits. Whenever a morsel did surface there were footraces to the cable office with every author demanding his creation be the first sent; usually to New York City where stories vacillating between rumor and fiction, with spasmodic bursts of accuracy, went to press under Havana datelines. Starke was more familiar with the press than many, due to a friendship since military school with Darwin Tyson, correspondent for *The Sun*; so he made a point of spending a few minutes with them, damped appetites with monochrome information, suggested *Calypso*'s mission was mundane, and collapsed the *John Gwinn Williams* affair to a three-line rescue story.

Although the city was fully electrified after its solitary gasworks failed, the streetcar line relied on mules; probably because the short distances involved meant its only attraction was not walking through the heat. Reasonable order was maintained by a police force of less than a half dozen, since the most threatening aspect of island life, besides yellow fever, was drinking water. The cisterns honeycombing the island were usually sufficient, but this summer was exceptionally dry so most drinking water was barged in from Port Tampa. *Calypso*'s surgeon, Sydney Conrad, distrusted the practice and advocated distilling their own, to reduce typhoid and cholera risks. The chief engineer, Lieutenant (junior grade) Adrian Osbourne acquiesced but disliked the additional equipment wear and worried about the plant's ability to produce enough to meet the need for feed and potable water during the summer heat.

Also at Conrad's suggestion, their crew swam regularly in the clear, translucent green water, guarded by sharpshooters placed on board and in whaleboats. *Calypso* also anchored far enough offshore to outrange black clouds of milling mosquitoes and other annoying insects, so her executive officer, Lieutenant (j.g.) Benjamin Watson, permitted hammocks to be rigged on deck at night. Despite being inappropriate, Starke nearly did so himself when the night breeze vanished and he was left awake in a sweltering cabin.

To prepare the ship, maintain morale, and distract sailors from the city's liquor supply, Watson increased training. Masts and yards were sent up then taken down, topsail yards and jibboom were shifted, sails bent on, furled, unfurled, and then unbent. Boats were operated, boarding parties mustered, and aiming drills scheduled weekday afternoons like the North Atlantic Squadron; while the black gang focused on training, housekeeping, and maintaining their steam plant. Boatswain Mate Chief Braddock Weaver requested they delay coaling to expose the waterline and permit sailors on floats to repaint wood sheathing worn raw by saltwater; then inspect and repair copper sheets along the sides and near the stem. A task that received mixed reviews was augmenting *Maine's* thirty-three foot steam launch patrolling harbor, shoreline, and small keys for quarantine violators and filibusters.

Sports became a welcome diversion after *Calypso* sailors heard *Maine's* crew boast about their baseball and singlestick prowess; and the chiefs talked their executive officers, Watson and Adolph Marix, into allowing competitions. The larger ship's practiced baseball team easily beat *Calypso's*, but singlestick was a different matter. Watson grew suspicious when the chiefs wanted him to ask their captain to provide coaching; since rumor correctly had Starke possessing a reputation with blade, singlestick, and cane. After several inquiries and a visit to Marix, he was certain some ill-advised bets were at risk and ignored the request; leaving Starke unaware of their scheme and the gamblers adrift.

Thaddeus joined during the crew's first run ashore when one liberty party visited a small waterfront bar opening to the street. While they drank and debated who paid for the next round, a nondescript gray and black cat with a dirty white belly jumped to the counter then slowly walked its length. While they watched, the scrawny but discerning creature sniffed and dismissed several foaming beer mugs before eagerly lapping the first shot glass of whiskey. The cursing bartender, tired of previous forays, snatched the freeloader by the nape of its neck, and then threw it spinning into the dirt street; where the recalcitrant feline rolled, stopped, shook off white dust, and then returned. Seeing its approach, the formidable barkeeper grabbed for a truncated, two-foot boat oar kept under the bar for unruly customers. The sailors sprung to action when it appeared this fellow spirit was about to receive a death blow. Afterwards, several well-lubricated debates produced the consensus their cat would be Thaddeus; a name the feline accepted as eagerly as he lapped several shot glasses of whiskey remnants. Just before liberty expired, five disheveled, bruised, and inebriated sailors, with a similarly impaired cat, staggered up the accommodation ladder to report their return. The sailors went below while their semi-comatose tomcat was cleaned and placed in a low wooden box filled with rags to recover. Thaddeus eagerly polished off a full breakfast the next morning, showing fewer aftereffects than his saviors; then spent several bad days inspecting every glass similar to those that contained his preferred nectar. After a week, he appeared resigned to a dry life afloat and settled in to quiet lounging, cat box visits, grooming with his rough tongue, and scrounging food. He was popular with all, except those with implacable hatred for such creatures, and even Starke, who disliked mascots, reconciled to a cat as preferable to goats, pigs, birds, or more exotic choices. Intermittently, the gray feline with faint black stripes and white belly would even pad noiselessly through his cabin for the adjoining pantry; to wait in quiet anticipation, long tail moving slowly, watching Yamashita prepare fresh-caught fish.

Starke learned two officers from his Academy class, Lieutenants (j.g.) George P. Blow and John J. Blandin, were in *Maine's* wardroom. His role as *Calypso's* commander limited their association, although they met twice for supper ashore. He did become well-acquainted with the station's commander, James McQueen Forsyth, the second occupant of a six-year old duplex housing the commander and paymaster. Their two-story building had wood siding, was encircled by ornate porches with blue-gray floors, incorporated three brick chimneys, and each residence was topped by a single gable. Located behind a seawall off the ship channel, it was convenient to the large stucco building housing the station's warehouse and administrative offices.

Starke's host had a large head, receding hairline, and oversize goatee that failed to obscure the complete absence of any chin; with every facial feature below the nose converging on a throat rising from broad, curved shoulders and rotund body. Like Starke, he sailed in merchant shipping; then volunteered as a master's mate during the war. Afterwards, he applied to transfer from volunteer to regular service, and beat out 880 competitors. Born in the Bahamas and familiar with the Caribbean, he was acquainted with Captain Albert and served as *Constellation's* executive officer during the Irish Relief Expedition, when Starke's Academy friend, Philo

McGiffin, was a cadet on board.

As with *Maine*, the officers were accepted in Key West's insular society as a source of new faces, mainland news, or eligible unmarried officers; and one Cuban club invited the wardroom to a San Carlos Club dinner. Neither Forsyth nor Starke welcomed the invitation since refusal might be received as an insult and accepting give credence to correspondents' speculation *Calypso* was waiting to convoy filibusters, rather than the competing rumor of sinking them on sight. Starke, Crowninshield, Marix, Forsyth, and Herminio Gonzales y Ochoa, a *John Gwinn Williams* survivor, finally agreed that Starke, Osbourne, and Conrad would attend in civilian attire and there would be no political speeches or correspondents.

The affair not only came off well but proved useful to Starke. Gonzales, their host, limited his speech to offering the community's appreciation for *Calypso*'s rescue and the care given survivors; while Starke learned how the community split between those wanting new lives in the States and others who saw their stay as temporary. Everyone supported some vision of Cuban independence but disagreed on form and how to achieve it. While most distrusted American involvement beyond recognition, some advocated a blockade and others autonomy under Spain. Although Starke did not doubt they wished to show appreciation for those saved and bodies returned to families, he suspected Gonzales also wanted to learn what precipitated *Calypso* sighting *John Gwinn Williams*; so his two officers were instructed to avoid discussing their cruise and mission.

While in Key West, the monthly ritual dreaded by officers and chiefs transpired. Payday meant those willing and able would have money for revelry ashore. A week before the crew was paid, every sailor "put down" the goods they wanted from small stores. These requests were assembled by pay clerks; then "serving out" was announced and crew called to Passed Assistant Paymaster Matthew Wiggs' office by division to retrieve and sign for their items. *Calypso*'s crew was small, so this usually took place once accounts balanced late that afternoon or next morning. The process was repeated to distribute cash and sign receipts, with their partial food ration issued the following day. Whatever else each mess wanted was then purchased from ship's stores, bumboats, or pier venders; depending on each mess' funds, what was available, and their cook's preference. Wiggs disliked the system and relentlessly argued for a general mess, but still went above what was required to make sure each mess had what it wanted and could afford.

Calypso's crew did not fare well during waterfront forays and several altercations took place with the police reluctant to interfere; being seriously outnumbered by both contingents and living on the island. When an incident did land participants in court, sailors were fined, locals warned, and everyone released. This prompted Watson to begin inquiries. He soon learned the tug's dead engineer was popular and watering holes were rife with rumors about *John Gwinn Williams'* demise that were likely started by Captain Buff or associates. When he received two proprietors' written complaints, demanding sailors cover all damages; their bars were quickly placed off limits, which ended several more claims in the pipeline.

Maine left for New York on July 13, 1896, since battleships were in demand and the Navy wanted them visible to the public. Observing *Maine*, Starke was concerned the 324-foot steel warship's 6,700 tons must be turned, then moved to the ship channel through unpredictable currents. A mistake could set the steel behemoth down on *Calypso*, allowing her twelve-inch armor belt or ram bow to crumple his bark's iron frame, wood sheathing, and wafer-thin copper. Although Starke did not want to suggest any lack of confidence in Crowninshield or *Maine's* crew, he had a propulsion boiler brought out of layup and placed on line; then detailed a party to pay out more chain or slip the anchor, if needed. With as little outward display as possible, the pilothouse and engine room were readied to get underway, steam pinnace sent to the naval station, and boat booms retracted. Although completely useless, rope fenders were placed discretely behind bulwarks.

Starke was on deck after breakfast for the event. The day was warming, its blue sky almost cloudless, and the sea a shifting palette of translucent greens, blues, and browns, with small white strings of bubbles. Ever present gulls glided overhead in large circles or bobbed on nearly flat water; while feeding fish left swirls or rough patches. As he watched, a brown pelican plummeted through the water surface then reappeared with a struggling catch in its pouch. Undisciplined formations of spongers under sail were outbound, their booms swung over one side to catch the light air, with dinghies lashed to the deck or towed astern. As they passed the naval station piers, three harbor tugboats trailing small columns of gray-white smoke joined the procession and Watson ordered sea and anchor stations. Starke was satisfied. *Calypso* was often astern and slightly west of *Maine*, but today more of the battleship's starboard side was visible; suggesting the capricious current flowing south between seawall, small keys, and reefs was condescending this brilliant morning. *Maine's* eight boilers were lit and smoke came from straw-yellow stacks while sailors disassembled her two accommodation ladders then lashed them under a line of shuttered windows on the aft superstructure island. She began recovering boats the previous evening, so pinnaces, barges, whaleboats, and launches were secured in cradles under round-bar davits or within reach of two massive midship cranes. For the moment, most visible activity occurred near her dark mahogany pilothouse, or anchor party on the forward superstructure island.

Starke, in the pilothouse, retrieved the new Bausch & Lomb binoculars bought before leaving Washington for Newport News. Their two-year old design, licensed by Zeiss, allowed for a short, light body, and powerful lenses that gave a sharp image and better view. The merchant boasted they made single or paired-telescopes obsolete; and spyglasses a curiosity. Starke left with the binoculars after handing over what most laborers took a month to earn. Looking through them now, he made out the battleship's small anchor buoy bobbing north of the ship; tethered to the battleship's stocked anchor worked deep in the sand bottom. A short smoke burst from the forward stack signaled her steam windlass had begun to slowly claw the ship to short stay, turning her stern to *Calypso*, then port side. During this, the sponsoned turrets stood out, as did a large, black searchlight aft on the steel framework between two small whaleboats. After reaching short stay, with the anchor almost directly under her ram bow, the three station tugs made up to starboard, near the stern. Her whistle erupted in a blast of white steam soon after, the ensign aft and jack forward came down at a run, and the American flag broke from the mainmast. *Maine* was underway.

With port screw spinning faster than the starboard, rudder over, and tugs pushing on the hull aft; she swung slowly right then eased forward, overcoming the current, increasing speed, and gaining steerageway. Clear of Fort Taylor, *Maine* cast off the tugs then plowed into the channel. Standing on the collapsible wooden bridge-wing extending from pilothouse to ship's starboard side, was a mustached figure, waving as the ship made its first turn. Crowninshield was taking the deeper and more direct South West Channel until he dropped the pilot just clear of Key West's shoals and then steered east to ride the Florida Current. Beyond the Straits of Florida, *Maine* would turn north and take advantage of Gulf Stream until it curved northwest to Europe. In three days she would drop anchor off New York City, leaving *Calypso* alone in Key West, Forsyth the senior officer, and all but ending Navy patrols to enforce the Key West quarantine and dissuade filibusters.

Chapter Three
Two Correspondents

The Plant Line steamship *Mascotte* from Port Tampa was nearing Key West, bound for Havana. She regularly passed *Calypso*'s anchorage on these stopovers, as did the line's second ship, *Olivette*; away for the summer on a seasonal route in New England. *Mascotte's* 210-foot black hull was near *Calypso*'s length, with a single triple-expansion engine, straight stem, overhanging counter, and prominent rudder. Forward, above staterooms running most of the main deck, was a half-round pilothouse, single black funnel amidship, with Plant Line markings, three ventilator pairs, and six white lifeboats under davits. Towards either end was a mast for signals, cargo handling, and navigation lights.

Her sparse passenger list included the rail-thin, balding Darwin Tyson. Since leaving Washington, he slept little, traveling day and night by train to Port Tampa's pier. Pressed for time and disheveled, he walked across its wood planking to *Mascotte* then watched Tampa Bay pass his stateroom window. As she slowed to enter one of the Key West channels, he was reclining in a canvas deck chair enjoying an occasional sip from a worn silver flask and making periodic extractions from his gold-trimmed, jade cigarette case. He seldom slept solidly more than three hours, so he was completely rested from the train and on deck before first light. Having his choice of deck chairs, he picked one offering a good view with few fellow passengers passing, before relaxing into it. The engine vibrations, morning sun, and atmosphere ripe with sea, coal, and steam, soon had him nodding off.

He had been summoned a week before to his editor's desk in *The Sun's* building on New York City's Nassau Street. With the Democratic Party Convention over, and paper supporting the Republican Party, he expected an assignment tied to the gold standard or ongoing 1893 Panic recovery. Instead, he was shunted to the publisher's office, received tickets for Key West, and encouraged to consider Havana. He was not enthusiastic, believing the assignment redundant with coveys, flocks, and flights of correspondents already nesting in Tampa, Key West, and Havana; all scratching for a seed that might sprout the rare honest story or passable fabrication. However, his editor heard rumors the Navy and Revenue Cutter Service were coordinating efforts to stop Junta expeditions and believed Weyler's reconcentration policy worse than reported. He wanted Tyson, or rather his passion for doggedness and accuracy, on scene.

The Sun's correspondents accepted whatever assignment given, but Tyson left the office quietly miffed since Caribbean summers were hot, miserable, and deadly; Florida largely vacant except for pestilence; and Cuba worse, even without the ongoing insurrection. He also had little time to recover from his recent Chicago assignment and now faced more than three arduous days on trains. There would be multiple transfers while they passed through Washington, Lynchburg, Danville, and Charlotte; before picking up the Savannah, Florida and Western Railway for a final leg south into and across Florida to Port Tampa; where he would board a Plant Line steamer for Key West. As always, his sulking mellowed into fatalism once he sipped a quick restorative from the silver flask and threw himself into the familiar routine of buying, packing clothes, obtaining a Kodak camera, arranging

Travelers Checks, and securing a two-bottle Scotch whiskey reserve for the silver flask. This was now allocated between his battered steamer trunk, a matching cabin trunk, and worn carpet bag.

As *Mascotte* glided up the ship channel into Key West, he watched passing buoys and small schooners towing dinghies, until, surprised, he rose, went to the rail, then shielded his eyes with a palm. Sitting placidly at anchor off Fort Taylor was a tall, black bark with white whaleboats tethered to booms and sailors moving about her deck. From the single stack between her first two masts, small wisps of light gray smoke lifted lazily into the cobalt blue sky resting on translucent green water reflecting a Caribbean sun's harsh rays. Light smoke meant only an auxiliary boiler on line, so she was not preparing to leave; and the scene excessively idyllic, even for a New York gallery. He suspected it was *Calypso*, commanded by friend and confidant, Jacob Starke, then confirmed it when her two 4-inch rifles appeared in the small spyglass carried for such occasions; that he began waving over his head like a talisman as *Mascotte* slipped past the red-brick fort.

As *Mascotte* neared *Calypso*, Starke was writing to Katherine Ledford, his aunt's distant cousin and British widow; now in Rhode Island at the family's summer cottage overlooking Newport's waterfront. Their correspondence resulted from an extraordinary meeting in the Starke mansion's library, following a formal dinner. He was caught off-guard and agreed out of courtesy, but any hesitation vanished after an evening of dance in Old Point Comfort's Hygeia Hotel; leaving him with conflicting perceptions and emotions. Each letter from her was slightly more amiable; and none fit a woman he found severe, remote, and indifferent less than six months earlier. The last bordered on an intimacy he would have thought improper for unmarried women, or widows; even one with a steadfast commitment. While distance seemed to strip Katherine's inhibitions, Starke could not explain his own desire to correspond with an eligible, but guardedly proper, widow who would return home and disliked the States. There was also Constance Starke, the aunt who raised him after his mother died. She was the widow's host in Newport, and gently persistent about him marrying well and soon; which gained precedence in his own mind after learning he would inherit the Starke fortune, shipping firm, and business interests.

Before returning to more immediate concerns, he went to the window then gazed across the main deck and over sparkling water towards the fort; watching *Mascotte* steam up the ship channel. Neither she nor *Olivette* attracted much attention beyond the city wharf since they were regular visitors but he noticed sun reflecting from a shiny object waved above some passenger's head as if signaling. Smiling, he marked it down to some deranged soul, which applied to anyone in the Caribbean without reason during fever months. After *Mascotte* passed, he went to his desk, sealed the letter for posting, and began reviewing expenditure reports.

The next day a boney, balding, clean-shaven man in light suit and straw hat confronted Ensign Carl Martyn at the top of *Calypso*'s accommodation ladder then taken to the day cabin where he was greeted by a pleasantly surprised Starke. Once Martyn returned to his duties, Starke took an armchair, Tyson spread himself over the small settee under a window, and Yamashita conjured two cool lemonades; since Key West was blessed with an ice factory.

Once they were alone, Tyson smoothly extracted his worn silver flask, fortified the lemonade, and then extended it to Stark who grinned faintly, "Navy regulations forbid hard liquor on ships and it'd be poor practice for me to violate that."

Tyson responded with perfunctory contrition, "Sorry. Never saw you going temperance, Jacob, but I'll destroy the evidence."

"That's appreciated."

"I couldn't believe my luck and waved when we entered. Exiled to Key West, I'll die of boredom unless some fever takes me first. Expect the mob's wiring anything north they sweep off the streets?"

"That's about right; I occasionally pass a few minutes with your more reputable colleagues."

Following a quick swallow from the sweating glass, Tyson grinned, "Ever get your ashes hauled, or are you still rutting over the widow?"

Tyson obviously remembered the raw advice offered in Newport News just before *Calypso* commissioned, "I see your tact's not improved. Mrs. Ledford has written."

"And you responded?"

"Yes, despite your sage counsel."

With that, Tyson again sipped the lemonade, already blessed with significantly more bite than Yamashita intended, started to reach for his flask, stopped short, then took a long swallow. Moving it slowly over his lap, he contemplated the swirling concoction several seconds, looked Starke in the eyes, then pronounced judgment, "Dammit Jacob, you should propose. She seems a tolerable woman. Besides, your aunt would be ecstatic, especially if there's a child. I'll wager she's orchestrating the union while we speak. Don't ever tell her I encouraged you, she'd lose all faith in her judgment."

Starke attempted a diversion, "Your take on Aunt Constance's accurate. What brings you here in the summer?"

"A couple of possible stories; but at the hotel bar last night a brusque gentleman was complaining about some Navy bastard anchored in the black bark sinking his ship."

Starke set his glass aside, "Coal-black eyes, clean-shaven, balding, short hair, and neck that collapses into his shoulders when agitated?"

"Neck had three rolls last night. He hates well and I assume you're the bastard. Says *Calypso* blew him out of the water, his engineer went down with the tug, and only two whaleboats were lowered; so sharks nearly had the survivors."

"He's a local filibuster known as Captain Buff. We were doing a full power run and saw his tug break for shallow water. He pushed too hard and a boiler blew. We never did see any sharks; and there wasn't time to lower the steam pinnaces."

"Well, be warned, Jacob. It's personal."

"I expected as much. However, I doubt *The Sun*'s interested in *Calypso*, so what brings you to purgatory?

"My editor craves an accurate account of filibusters and reconcentrados; in Florida and Cuba."

"Until *Maine* left a few days ago, she kept a steam launch patrolling for filibusters and enforcing the local quarantine. We supplied some sailors, but nothing unusual. I don't have the crew to continue and it's a bad business to keep boats out during yellow fever season, especially when filibusters seldom leave port with passengers and cargo. The city's upset about losing quarantine fees. Perhaps you'd like an introduction to one of the Cuban Club presidents, station commander, or customs collector. There's also the Spanish consul, Manuel Garcia y Ruiz."

"Appreciate that Jacob, but you're diverting attention from *Calypso*."

Knowing his friend possessed extraordinary tenacity when on the scent, Stark offered a little more, "Truth is, we saw *John*

Gwinn Williams acting suspicious while doing a full power run and went to investigate. He was running for the Bahia Honda shallows and just before entering, a boiler burst and the tug sank. Our two boats rescued survivors and retrieved bodies. Captain Buff's revealed nothing, the authorities lack an appetite to pursue the case, the Junta's unlikely to gloat over failure, her owners are content with the insurance money, and there's no benefit in any survivor talking."

"Then why's *Calypso* in Key West? I hear you arrived early this month?

"Yes, waiting for orders, maintenance, and crew liberty."

Tyson threw Starke a wry look, "In the summer? Well, either way, join me for dinner tomorrow. I'm at Hotel Key West. We'll meet and try a restaurant I've located. The food's supposedly good and I won't have to drink alone."

"I'll come in civilian clothes at seven."

Starke's friend avoided severing a limb between the accommodation ladder's lower platform and water taxi's gunnel, took a seat, and then settled in as the small sloop made for City Wharf. Once he was safely away, Starke left for his cabin to meet with Osbourne and Wiggs about coaling; to be followed by Conrad with his sick-list. He was grateful *Calypso*'s only loss was the seasick case Forsyth was employing at the naval station until convening a board since the Caribbean was rife with diseases that incapacitated, crippled, killed slowly, or extinguished life in hours.

Tyson's Duval Street restaurant was on the second floor of a wood building with its kitchen at the rear and dining room street-side. They arrived in lightweight sack suits with broad-brimmed hats; having mostly eluded swarms of voracious evening insects. After taking a center table, Tyson immediately ordered rum, and Starke, tonic water with gin. Besides a double-door main entrance, three sides of the dining area consisted of tall, rectangular windows with small strips of wall above and below; left open for evening air behind louvered shutters hinged at the top. The proprietor had not totally relied on mosquitos, or other pests, being content to stalk their prey at street level and installed screening between window and shutter; a northern product first used to keep sparks and cinders off railroad passengers. Further deterrence came from ceiling fans whose slow rotation spread warm air and cigar smoke. The fourth wall segregated eating and cooking sections, with a swinging door placed on either side. Between was a long, dark, and heavily carved, walnut bar set out from the counter. Three mirrors sectioned its six glass shelves that displayed liquor bottles of various shapes and colors. As Starke lit his pipe, Tyson pulled a cigar from his jacket, clipped one end, struck a match, and then looked at his friend, "Beats cigarettes for bugs. Let's hear about *Calypso*."

"We've been mostly under steam, except staysails to ease the ride, but will see how she does under canvas in the Gulf. What's bent on has been dropped for airing several times, but the stored canvas also needs pulling for inspection and air. We tested the 4-inch batteries on a dead whale off Port Royal, survived the station commander's garden party, coaled, and headed south for a full power run. It appears the conversion added at least a knot, and Osbourne's calculated our coal will last more than three weeks at cruising speed."

Tyson suddenly ended a small bug's existence after it landed too close to his glass' thick base, "Caribbean summers: heat, yellow fever, and pests."

"While in Montana, I heard people wore screening over their heads when mosquitos got bad during summers."

"Here, they wrap newspapers around their legs during the day, but night's a different story. I stay away from the mosquito netting. Little bastards sit on it waiting to bite; and I don't care to test my malaria immunity."

Starke smiled, "*Calypso*'s far enough out so breeze and distance discourage them; but our boat crews put ashore for training ran into clouds of mosquitos and biting gnats."

An unescorted woman entered while they waited. Starke noticed because restaurants usually served single women in separate rooms and she seemed familiar. Overcoming a bout of disbelief, he recognized Cassandra Evans, the Washington reporter that first caught his attention on a street car. They met and he was introduced when she interviewed his aunt; who then maneuvered him into escorting her to the same dinner party that ended with the widow's unexpected visitation. Evans' classic appeal still featured lovely auburn hair worn in a loose pompadour, although now suffering from gloved hands swiping airborne pests. Since Evans was immediately seated, Starke decided their host harbored an egalitarian streak or favored custom over convention; then drew from his pipe, expelled a small smoke cloud, looked over the table and said, "Miss Evans just arrived. Did she sail with you to Key West?"

Tyson's back was to the door, but he turned quickly, studied her through a rising smoke cloud, balanced the half-consumed cigar on the ceramic ashtray's rim, then rose, "No, I didn't know she was here. She's alone and you've been introduced, so a cold shoulder and confirmation of my bad manners is the worst to come from inviting her to join us."

Before Starke replied, Tyson was crossing the room, not in a straight line but threading between obstructing pillars, tables, chairs, diners, and two waiters balancing trays. The first attempt obviously failed, but the reporter regrouped and the second brought greater animation, head movements, and glances in his direction. She stood, placed her hand lightly on Tyson's arm, and returned with him as though he was giving the bride away.

Starke rose during their approach then bowed slightly as she extracted a gloved hand from Tyson's arm, "Good evening, Miss Evans."

"And you, Lieutenant Starke."

She adjusted her clothing, preparing to sit on a chair Tyson positioned, then slid onto it as he added, "Captain, Miss Evans; so long as he commands *Calypso*."

"The ship anchored off the fort? When we arrived from Cedar Key, several passengers claimed it wasn't any Navy ship they knew."

"Yes, *Calypso*'s been in port since early last month."

With that, Tyson regained his chair, lifted a smoldering cigar from the ashtray, looked at Starke, smiling, "Her father partakes and she prefers smoke to mosquitos," then took a long drag which revived the embers.

Evans sensed her circumstances just improved. Supper with *The Sun* correspondent who ignored her in Washington and the ship commander reporters thought was on some strange mission. These potential leads were welcome after her spirits were tested by a long, unpleasant rail and steamship journey from Washington through the South. They rose when her ship eased up the South West Channel, since its draft precluded North West Channel, then fell when she discovered the shimmering Caribbean offered a bright, exotic quality that did not last. Up close, the port was a rough, stifling hot waterfront swathed in various smells of decay, and beset by voracious mosquitos, impervious to all but hovering gnat clouds that chewed up anything breaching their dark swirling mass. After hiring one of the carriages lining adjacent streets, waiting to whisk arrivals off to a hotel, she decided Florida's glowing reports were concocted by unscrupulous speculators, tourists visiting during livable months, and well-heeled winter residents. The rest apparently dedicated the season to surviving heat, avoiding vicious insects, and sleeping under screens. The poor had even fewer choices: endure, leave, or expire from yellow fever, malaria, and other ailments. She also received a mixed reception from hovering Key West reporters lounging in the hotel lobby and taking pleasure in being loutish. By evening, she decided to stand away from a clique that was condescending at best and truculent at worst.

Evans deftly fingered her wine glass' thin stem, pondering how to exploit this change of fortune. Starke would never be one of Jane Austen's sophisticated naval officers, but was not unattractive in a roughhewn way; and probably reliable in tight situations. The thin and bony Tyson, who slouched in his chair, was more attentive and enjoyed a reputation for intelligence, results, and credibility. From rumors in Washington, both seemed inexorably drawn to events, or created them; and she was now with both, just ninety miles north of the war.

Tyson was studying the amber drink, whose consumption would raise an already impressive evening tally, while Evans contemplated how to politely scratch the puffed remnants of a raiding mosquito; acquired before understanding why local women favored heavy stockings and long, thick skirts. She was preparing to flout good manners when Starke asked, "What brings you here during the worst months?"

"I convinced my editor that women and children suffering under Weyler need their story told,"

She barely stifled an angry retort when Tyson observed, while sighting a shuttered window over his glass, "Opposed to old, young, and everyone else trapped between Spain and the Junta?"

Evans held her temper long enough to realize Tyson, like her father, challenged ideas and statements, not people. She caressed her glass, recently refilled with white wine, "Also, rumors are the Times will be sold, so I want to make the best of it. This was a story I could sell and deliver on; but if you can offer something better?"

Seeing Evans shared Tyson's repartee ability, Starke tried to shunt the pair to a different track, "What did you think of Cedar Key, Miss Evans?"

"It leaped from the wilderness beyond Jacksonville. One moment trees and clear-cutting, then we were crossing an embankment and trestle to islands filled with piers, stores, factories, and hotels. I ate fried mullet and stayed at the Schlemmer House until my ship arrived; so there was time enough to explore. There's the pencil factory, sponging, seafood, and shipping, but the merchants claim times were better before Plant and Port Tampa started taking business. Apparently, the city refused to give his railroad control of the wharf, so he built one in Port Tampa, ran a spur to it, and took their trade."

Tyson was impressed by her memory and eye for detail, particularly after a long rail trip from Washington, so they were soon discussing various New York City newspapers, their owners, and Charles Dana. This only paused long enough to eat their seafood before continuing. Starke listened, observed, and broke in a new briar pipe with several bowls; enjoying an atmosphere no longer centered on filibusters and *Calypso*. He also observed the pair spoke about everything without giving away any story lead.

Starke took advantage of this uninterrupted opportunity to study the woman illuminated by an electrolier over the table. Besides auburn hair coaxed into a pompadour, Evans possessed flawless eyebrows above innocently suggestive brown eyes with a hint of the make-up women used and ladies denied. A slight scent revealed she still used lemon or vinegar juice liberally. She had temporarily shielded her face from Key West's sun; but it was early days and that glowing orb could produce an unsightly burn in hours. Starke wondered if Evans would gain a dark working-class tan or, like Tyson, burn easily then tan lightly. While half-listening and enjoying the pipe, he considered Katherine, first in Washington, then on the Old Point Comfort pier; and recalled his friend's recent advice on *Calypso*, and wondered if love like his Uncle Immanuel and Aunt Constance's might be possible with her.

Calypso's steam pinnace was to meet Starke at the naval station pier so he did not want to leave its crew at the mercy of mosquitos and nearby bars but felt obligated to escort Evans to her hotel since they were formally introduced. Tyson resolved the dilemma by offering his services, which she happily accepted. Outside the restaurant, Starke watched her hand slip through Tyson's arm as they walked away and realized it was the first time he saw his friend in feminine company.

Chapter Four
Sailing Orders

Starke glanced at the mechanical desk calendar rotated to "MON AUG 10 96" earlier that day, then a draft cable to Albert requesting clarification. After receiving orders to remain in port followed by ambiguous messages suggesting a new mission, he needed to know what was coming. Albert's or his own removal was possible since *Calypso* cost the Junta an expedition; which would not sit well with their supporters and allies in the capital. He was attempting to convey the exact amount of urgency when a seaman knocked at the door, entered, and reported an unusual ship coming up the same channel taken by *Calypso* almost a month before.

No foreign warships were expected and, since Starke would undoubtedly be junior, any Navy ship could shift local command, restart continuous boat patrols, or disrupt *Calypso*'s routine. Setting the draft cable aside, he found the duty officer, Ensign Gideon Blair, on the collapsible bridge-wing off the pilothouse. Starke looked through binoculars, and recognized the vertically striped Revenue Cutter Service ensign as the ship turned to clear Whitehead Spit and Fort Taylor, before entering the northeast leg. Her silhouette shortened as she left South East Channel and came around Whitehead Point, growing longer as the cutter continued north, and passed between *Calypso* and Fort Taylor to moor near the customs house or in the quarantine anchorage.

Two figures waved from the bridge as she sliced easily

through calm water reflecting a brilliant sun. One wore light civilian attire topped by a broad-brimmed hat threatening to lift from its owner's head. He was certain the newcomer was *Vanguard*, a new cutter delayed in Jacksonville for boiler work. Her commander, First Lieutenant Boyd Hunter, and Brian Fields from the Justice Department's Southern Florida District visited him in Port Royal before *Calypso* left for Dry Tortugas. Since *Calypso* and *Vanguard* might work together, Starke asked about Hunter's command. She was no conversion but designed keel up as a cutter, second of the *Windom* class, and out of the builder's yard less than a year. The 170-foot white hull was twenty-seven feet at its beam and drew less than nine. She had a straight stem, overhanging fantail, and between, a single line of portholes just above the waterline. The main deck included a large work area aft of the deckhouse and its forward third hosted her foremast and one 3-inch gun just aft of the small forecastle bulwark that anchored lifelines covered with dense snaking. The old stocked anchor arrangement was used for ground tackle, which Starke thought dated for a recent design. The pilothouse was at the deckhouse's forward end, behind the foremast, with large ventilator cowls just off its rear corners. A slightly raked stack rose between the masts, just aft of the flying bridge's canvas windscreens. Two pairs of round-bar davits on either side rose above four white whaleboats. Twin screws spun by 800 horsepower triple-expansion engines gave her a reputed fifteen knots. With midship 6-pounders supplementing her 3-inch mount, Hunter's claim she balanced a useful armament, with speed, agility, and shallow draft seemed accurate. Starke thought the ships an excellent pair to work the Caribbean and Gulf of Mexico. *Vanguard* was well-suited for shallow water work, being shorter than *Calypso*, but nearly as wide, with half the draft and displacement, and twin screw maneuverability; while the more heavily armed bark would ride out rough seas better, had longer legs, and carried more than twice the cutter's crew of around fifty.

Starke saw the services operating together as a possible challenge. Besides different command and rank structures, the Revenue Marine, just reorganized as the Revenue Cutter Service, had a long-standing rivalry with the Navy, and their relations worsened the year after Starke's graduation. The Navy tried to force Academy graduates not offered commissions into Treasury's fleet, and temporarily succeeded in closing down its New Bedford School of Instruction as an economy measure. Although the school was reestablished by executive order, animosity lingered. However, he met Hunter twice, liked the man, and learned *Vanguard's* commander graduated from the two-year New Bedford school, was nearly the service's first officer sent to the Naval War College, and enjoyed a reputation for getting results.

Starke resolved to avoid beginning their relationship by attempting to establish whether a Revenue Cutter Service first lieutenant or Navy lieutenant was senior, so far as service etiquette was concerned, and directed a pinnace get steam up for a courtesy call. Despite the obvious discomfort created for Blair, Weaver, and O'Leary, he watched the boat crew lite off, then warm, its small boiler while tethered at the boat boom. Since crews picked and trimmed each lump by hand, the polished brass stack emitted a barely visible vapor, not much more than a shimmer for the moment.

Before it was ready for boarding, a steam launch left the naval station pier and headed for *Calypso* at something like full speed. *Vanguard* carried whaleboats, so it could only come from the customs house or naval station, but as it closed, Starke saw a white uniform standing at one of the poles supporting its overhead canvas awning. Knowing it could only be Hunter trying to avoid smudging his uniform; Starke guessed the cutter's captain was equally willing to shave decorum. When the launch was hailed, it responded *Vanguard*, and the steam pinnace could be released to practice landings.

First Lieutenant Boyd Hunter stepped onto the accommodation ladder's lower platform, trailed by Brian Fields from Justice. Climbing to the upper platform, Hunter saluted the flag and was piped aboard. When they met in Washington, Hunter had a mustache, and in Port Royal an emerging goatee. The result was a seamless combination on a tanned, otherwise clean-shaven face. His slightly curved eyebrows, trimmed hair, steady gaze, and other features created a professional image that fit name, build, and manner. Hunter was lean but solid, average in height, and moved in fluid, precise motions. The white service blouse or tunic covered trousers of the same material and rose to a standing collar overlapping another on the underlying shirt. Two sleeve stripes marked him as a first lieutenant and the white cap with polished black visor and knotted gold cord set him apart from Navy officers, despite a rough similarity in uniforms. Starke greeted the men with an outstretched hand, "Welcome aboard *Calypso*."

Hunter responded with a broad smile, "*Calypso* looks like a painting from the channel. Glad to finally get here; and we've something for you."

Fields clutched a leather briefcase tight against his three-piece suit with banker collar as they walked to the day cabin. Starke decided the man clearly favored the style since material and hat were the only variations between meetings; and his wide-brimmed straw boater an obvious change from Port Royal's bowler. Once they settled at the table, Yamashita delivered three tall glasses of iced lemonade; although Starke never understood his cabin steward's ability to conjure these cool drinks with little warning.

As Yamashita closed the pantry door, Fields set his leather case flat on the table, then looked at Starke, "May we close the windows, captain?"

Starke looked closely at him, "We could, but it would be stifling and attract crew interest, if avoiding it's your concern."

"It is."

"I'll ask Yamashita to make sure no one's listening."

"Can he be trusted?"

"Absolutely."

The crew was busily employed or concerned with rising heat and sunburn, so they took little notice in Yamashita quietly stationing himself to provide warning. Returning to the full table, Starke began, "Now, gentlemen."

A fully composed Hunter sipped from his sweating lemonade glass as Fields extracted a thick paper stack bound with Hotchkiss staples. Sliding it hesitantly across the table, he grimaced, "This additional information has surfaced since Port Royal, captain."

Starke's expression caused Hunter to cant his glass then slowly rotate its contents, "It appears what we heard in Port Royal was optimistic. It's no longer a filibuster willing to fight but apparently anarchists planning a propaganda of the deed. Which reminds, I would like to hear about *Calypso* putting *John Gwinn Williams* out of business."

While Starke sipped the tangy-sweet lemonade and paged through the document, Hunter continued "I've dealt with Captain Buff more than once. He's a superb seaman and known filibuster, but I doubt he favors either side; became something of an outlaw when his family was destroyed after the war. I hear *John Gwinn Williams'* engineer went down with her. If it's the man I think, he was well-liked on the waterfront and close to Captain Buff, although they argued constantly."

While swallowing, Starke remembered Captain Buff's barely controlled rage after his tug sank; and intimidating manner accentuated by a formidable physical presence. He was older than Starke, clean-shaven with coal-black eyes, and nearly bald; with whatever black or gray hair left cut short. Starke now understood the rage was exacerbated by his friend's passing; and empathized with the animosity towards what *Calypso* represented. One of his uncle's masters, never dipped an ensign to American warships, and his expatriated father was a navy officer forced to "go South" by Radical Republicans just before the war then Rio de Janeiro after. He now owned a Brazilian shipping line and had no desire to return or any residual loyalty to his birth nation. The war cost wife, career, and country; and some still wanted him tried for piracy. Jefferson Starke disowned the States, would not return, and possessed a resentment that probably differed little from Captain Buff's.

As he set the glass down, Fields rejoined with, "This is not *John Gwinn Williams*. Information received since Port Royal confirms an anarchist faction within the Junta's assembling an expedition to ship artillery to Cuba; and believes this propaganda of the deed will make the revolution and reconcentrados an international cause."

Recalling Herminio Gonzales y Ochoa at the San Carlos Club supper, and sophisticated Junta representatives in Washington, Starke observed, "The Junta will do anything for independence, but they've been successful using or circumventing the law. Most don't want the States involved and an anarchist link risks popular support."

"You're correct, captain. We have different sources giving us the same basic story so it's just possible Junta leaders could be undermining their anarchist faction for those precise reasons. They may believe international anarchists are more committed to destroying the Spanish monarchy and government than creating a different one in Cuba. Anyway, keep your copy close-held as it contains all we know, except sources."

Having delivered his package, Fields extracted a second brown envelope from his case, placing it on the first bundle, "This amends *Calypso*'s orders, captain. They were sent by courier to Jacksonville for *Vanguard* to deliver. Secrecy was the reason Albert did not cable you. Captain Hunter has his from Treasury. *Calypso* and *Vanguard* have been asked to locate this expedition, if it exists, then apprehend or prevent it from continuing. You'll find State's involved and contributed points of contact and letters of introduction."

Pushing his empty glass away, Hunter added, "I doubt Navy's more illuminating than Treasury. Some Junta anarchist cell is putting together a filibuster expedition to equip insurgents with 12-pounder Hotchkiss landing guns, a pair of dynamite guns, ammunition, and trainers. Gómez gets mobile artillery to use against a fortified city, or part of a trocha, if they succeed. An oceangoing tug was sold recently, probably to them, and renamed *Rafael Riego*. It's supposedly large, fast, and may or may not be in Veracruz. Your masters want a result, but can't be specific, and don't have the resources, so it's passed to you."

Fields nodded, took his first sip of lemonade, "A legal quagmire. She may be registered in Brazil but has been observed under American, Brazilian, and British colors. I don't need to point out the implications of boarding Brazilian or British ships, but any ship is thorny in territorial waters. We could officially warn Spain, but they're apprised through the Pinkerton agency. Besides, if they take *Rafael Riego* outside territorial waters and she's flying our flag, or American citizenship is claimed, the *Virginius* affair could be repeated. Besides, their local capability is mainly converted tugs and the like."

After pausing for questions, he resumed, "From what we've provided, you'll see *Rafael Riego* is fast, steel-hulled, and will seek confrontation. It seems the Posse Comitatus Act prohibits our army from interfering with civil matters, but doesn't address the navy; and Revenue Cutter Service jurisdiction is limited to territorial waters or vessels under American registry. Albert and Fischer believe it best to intercept her off Cuba or Mexico. State thinks a boarding off Cuba would see Spain react based on how and where it occurs; but likely follow international law and custom. They're more concerned about causing a diplomatic breach with Mexico since that public generally supports Cuban independence and is agitated by our recent border crossings. Newcomb, in State's Diplomatic Bureau, claims President Diaz will act to maintain his nation's stability and curb indigenous revolutionary groups, so they've unofficially confirmed *Rafael Riego* is expected in Veracruz but intend to ignore her presence."

While *Vanguard's* arrival explained *Calypso's* stay in Key West, Starke disliked the tasking. State wanted swift action that did not upset anyone, as did Justice, but neither had the leverage or jurisdiction. Treasury felt obligated to act so they contributed the only cutter not tethered to a district, and the Navy obviously chose not to divert ships on a speculative mission. He did not doubt Albert did all he could, but the bureaucratic consensus appeared to be passing it to *Calypso* and *Vanguard* without precise direction; the very scenario Admiral Brown cautioned him about in Norfolk, based on experience with a Chilean filibuster.

Starke fingered his pipe before realizing he picked it up, then, looking across the table, recalled his supper with two reporters scouring Key West for just such a story. If either learned of it, responsibility for the dubious and ambiguous mission would land back in Washington. Starke was tempted, especially since Tyson was a longtime friend, but instead looked at Hunter and Fields, scratched his sparse beard, began packing a bowl, and responded, "I'll study this today and we can meet tomorrow; customs house or *Vanguard*?"

Despite orders to seek out the filibuster, Starke and Hunter stood by in Key West waiting for State or Justice to confirm *Rafael Riego* entered a Mexican or northern Gulf Coast port. *Calypso* and *Vanguard's* crews became listless as August crawled past under the relentless sun. It was no consolation this misery was shared by half the nation as the most devastating heat wave in memory spread west from the coast to Chicago, bringing still, mostly cloudless skies, and record temperatures.

The hellish shroud included Newport, at the mouth of Rhode Island's Narragansett Bay, where British widow Katherine Ledford looked forward to Starke's letters. Although sun-scorched, the port city's location offered intermittent relief. Light winds frequently caressed it, including a daily sea breeze that flowed over dark boulders along the coast, lifting traces of their living and dead armor's pungent scent before continuing up the expansive dark-blue bay to Providence. Katherine was resolved not to complain; and spent her days walking ocean front cliffs or cantering across pastures overlooking a gray-blue ocean streaked with white. Even so, she longed for Brydian Grange, the family estate near Bridport, England and, despite locals claiming this was the worst summer weather on record, was committed to it being her last this side of the Atlantic.

It was endurable only because letters trickled in from Key West and Constance Starke, her host and Jacob's aunt, proved a welcome confidante with surprising insight, who willingly spoke to intimate subjects Katherine never raised with mother or governess. Jacob not only kept his promise, but the correspondence revealed someone beyond the stiff and formal man who met them at the train in Washington. Each page and every line brought *Calypso* to life, especially after visiting her in Norfolk. She could see the fantail and almost hear the coxswain called Melvin picking and strumming *Farewell Spanish Ladies* or *Brighton Camp* on his mandolin. Another favorite was Thaddeus the cat, a feline whose weakness for spirits became a continuous quest for food. Others she met briefly: a curious Japanese cabin steward, four enthusiastic cadets, and the indomitable Chief Weaver. While Katherine read less cheerful passages, such as the filibuster tug sinking and Key West's cholera outbreak with detachment, she felt an unexplained disquiet when Cassandra Evans came up; especially after adapting her behavior to avoid men attracted to wealthy young widows. She recalled the Times reporter from Constance's dinner party as attractive, intelligent, and ambitious.

Katherine contemplated this while sitting at the bedroom's small writing table looking out on Newport harbor, fidgeting with her mourning ring, and absorbing bay, sea, and city smells pulsing gently through an open window. She followed one boat or ship until another caught her fancy; then extracted a sheet of paper from the varnished mahogany lap desk with inlaid top, set the previous one aside to dry, and resumed imparting smoothly curved script across the page. There had been gentlemen callers since her arrival, including an awkward afternoon spent on one's naphtha launch, but none made headway against the husband lost with HMS *Victoria* or *Calypso*'s captain. Without competing for attention or affection, they regularly penetrated her thoughts; and she sometimes forgot only one read what was written, so every line was scrutinized and agonized over to preserve boundaries. This letter would be lengthy since Starke's last said *Calypso* would leave Key West and be at sea for a time; but she expected only a few paragraphs would finish today.

A letter from her older brother, Edward Curtis, also wanted answering. He was in New York City with Constance's husband, Immanuel Starke, exploring some opportunity for his British syndicate. He wrote that the heat wave's effect on the city exceeded description, especially in its tenements, and was struggling to keep pace with Theodore Roosevelt; a Republican official Edward compared to a minor British aristocrat who lacked business sense, but possessed an abundance of political skill and stature. The new acquaintance was police commissioner and part of the city machine who, when not stalking patrolmen having a beer on duty, introduced Edward to people at a breakneck pace that ignored the heat. Roosevelt, he wrote, reminded him of accounts regarding the late Major General Gordon's dynamic nature; which she thought an exaggeration given her brother's energy, political interest, and propensity to acquire acquaintances.

The same summer heat wave enveloped Washington, making life insufferable for those remaining in a low-lying city known for seasonal heat, humidity, and disease. Brutal days separated equally disagreeable nights, when the briefest brush against the one beside you in bed woke both. Excluding Sundays, saloons filled with men and boys crowding below ceiling fans to grasp sweating glass mugs with foaming heads. The women patronized drugstore soda fountains for alcoholic relief until Sunday, when saloons closed and men also came. Thriving ice firms worked horses to death, discarded them where they dropped, then bought more to continue supplying homes and businesses with frozen water blocks to splinter for cooling drinks and sucking. Residents collected under shade trees in parks or immersed themselves in public fountains and horse troughs; acts studiously ignored by police wanting to avoid unnecessary exertion. The wealthy fled to nearby high ground or more northern states as always but found less relief; while those left endured unrelenting heat and still days lacking the transient breezes or fleeting showers of past summers. As residents broiled, trying to adapt and survive, many believed Negro citizens suffered less under these conditions but the myriad of races and nationalities were all struggling to survive each oppressive day. Nights offered little relief, so many took to sleeping on rooftops. Those who fell were added to the newspapers' growing casualty lists, led by the elderly, infirm, poor, and laborers.

At the dormant Starke mansion, Joshua Altman, butler and manager, shifted staff from rooms under its gabled roof to makeshift ground floor accommodations. Darius Sutton, overseeing the stable, ensured their two large, bay geldings, Castores and Gemini, were watered constantly and seldom saddled or put in traces; since the streets' dead horse count was rising dramatically. Some blocks south, the Albert family endured with less complaining than might be expected because it was too taxing. Their patriarch, recalling periods spent becalmed off Africa on antislavery patrol, held to his early morning routine and white cotton uniform.

As the heat wave ground on, those with means chose lighter clothing, while others loosened garments or jettisoned whatever thought proper; and somewhat more as Captain Albert discovered. Returning early from the Building to their row house, he found Abigail, Isabella, and Olivia draped in clinging, half-damp shifts, sprawled over couches recently placed near open windows. Looking at his naturally vivacious spouse, he asked if the Albert bordello's madam was available. She would have risen to the bait under different circumstances and responded with a half-serious upbraiding while their daughters twittered in the background. Today it was a feeble hand wave and distracted, "Yes, Dear," as his daughters wearily rolled their eyes without missing a beat with either fan.

The next morning found Albert at his tall window overlooking the Executive Mansion, with steaming morning coffee that seemed to mask hot weather. As he slowly moved to his desk carrying the empty white porcelain Navy cup, he glanced at a morning paper predicting the temperature would surpass 100 degrees, humidity hover around saturation, and hope for a halfhearted breeze absurd. The white uniform's light cotton was already damp before he stepped from the open-sided streetcar filled with people riding for breeze as well as transport. Once in the Building, he found no relief, despite striped awnings over its windows and slow-revolving overhead fans.

Work slowed during summers when government clerks were forced on vacation, but meetings continued. Today's was with the Bureau of Navigation chief, Rear Admiral Ramsay, to obtain agreement on the *Rafael Riego* exercise. Selecting, charging, then lighting his first pipe, Albert enjoyed it until he saw the clock summoning him, placed his meerschaum in the stand, and left for the conference. He found the thin, nearly bald man with white walrus mustache behind a desk strewn with papers, books, sorting boxes, and other paraphernalia. Wearing a light civilian suit, and moving carefully to conserve energy, Ramsay motioned Albert to a wooden chair with dark framing and cane inserts worn to dull amber.

Mustering a halfhearted smile, Ramsay considered the stout, lightly perspiring officer in high-collared white uniform, sitting between his desk and tall bookcase partly filled with leather-bound references. Knowing Albert, Ramsay suspected he was resisting an urge to extract a nonexistent pipe from a uniform lacking space for one. Ramsay never wasted time on preliminary discussion, and was even less inclined with heat paring away sociability, so he began, "Good morning, Sydney. I've read young Starke's report and Crowninshield's endorsement. It seems fortune's with you."

"I believe Lieutenant Starke would agree, admiral."

"I suppose, but my concern's your recommendation regarding this other matter. Justice supported Starke's *John Gwinn Williams* actions, so *Calypso*'s instructions are with the Secretary and have my endorsement; but only because we cannot ignore *Rafael Riego* or send the North Atlantic Squadron into the Gulf of Mexico. If Commodore Bunce was successful, the press would claim a sledge squashed a gnat, but if not, the Navy could fall victim to election year politics. I see you've allowed your man a great deal of latitude. Can he deliver?"

"Admiral," Albert paused to consider and pull the uniform from where it clung damply to his skin, "Not without luck; but Revenue's added a cutter and *Calypso* can handle *Rafael Riego*. I'm confident Starke will be decisive but not impetuous. He's seen the elephant in Montana, Alexandria, and Korea; and knows merchant shipping."

"He also sails close to the wind, Sidney."

"He did inherit his father's sense of being where there's action but also seems tempered by greater discernment; from experience or his mother, I don't know. Still, I'm confident he'll be prudent, but remorseless should it be required."

"A somber appraisal."

"Perhaps, admiral. He's unusual, I'll admit, but his qualities fit *Calypso*'s role in the filibuster project and she fits him. I suspect he was about to resign in favor of his uncle's shipping firm, but was unable to forsake *Calypso*."

"Sydney, you know my feelings regarding unique officers."

It was well-known Ramsay believed all navy officers must be interchangeable, so Albert only agreed, "Yes, sir."

"Anyway, I take it you meant his uncle's firm, Starke Shipping and Shipbuilding, and not the father's Southern Caribbean and Atlantic Shipping Company?"

Since Ramsay had both names, Albert realized someone researched Starke for him, but only added, "Yes, admiral, although he'll probably inherit both."

"Well, Sidney, on your head be it. Should *Rafael Riego* be located and detained, it becomes a Justice problem and the Navy gets quietly left astern. If not, then others will go down with Starke, so I hope he justifies your trust."

Calypso's signed orders were already with Starke, and the cable to start the operation working its way to the Secretary. Albert allowed Starke relatively free rein in them, but could not ignore Ramsay's warning that he fully owned the operation, or, as the captain of his first ship often observed, his paw prints were all over it. Even so, Albert knew it was in everyone's interest for Starke to have enough leeway, rather than control this hunt from the Building; except he strongly suggested they consider Arrecife Alacranes. A day earlier, Newcomb provided confirmation the filibuster had entered Veracruz, so Starke would soon be loosed. Considering his next move, Albert rocked back in the chair, dredged a favorite pipe's bowl through his tobacco pouch, packed the moist, brown shreds, and passed a flame over the center. They were committed to pursuing *Rafael Riego* and her anarchists.

Chapter Five
Pursuit to Veracruz

Some days later, as Albert endured Building politics, *Calypso* was hundreds of miles southwest of the capital, sailing for Arrecife Alacranes off Mexico's Yucatan coast. With her fine bow slicing effortlessly through the Gulf of Mexico's blue-green water, she slipped steadily west by southwest with all plain sail set and a steady wind from her port quarter. The same air driving her replaced the light scent of burning coal with sea aromas, since only a donkey boiler was on line. One propulsion boiler's fires were banked and the other let cool to inspect boiler tubes and repack a feedwater valve. Taking a deep breath of sea, tar, and hemp, Starke paid homage to the designer who vented the galley's greasy exhaust through her stack rather than the lower stovepipe known as a Charlie Noble.

He was well satisfied with the bark under canvas, and this was not her best point of sail. Heeled to starboard, she held a slight, and desirable, weather helm while running true at near ten knots, with moderate wind, well-trimmed sails, and favorable conditions. She took the seas easily with the slow pitching movement of a well-sprung carriage traveling short hills on good road. Starke knew this superb weather was unlikely to hold during hurricane season, and a tropical storm could whip it to a vicious frenzy with little or no warning. He hoped *Calypso*'s first would be a lesser upheaval; just severe enough to acclimate the inexperienced and reacquaint those requiring it. Until then, seasoned hands must press shipmates to build the skills and habits needed to survive. Studying the undulating swells, Starke felt that reckoning's approach, since a hurricane already clawed up through Old Bahama Channel before *Calypso* sailed, but swung northeast to pass east of Florida and spare Key West, which had been in its path.

Arrecife Alacranes, Scorpion Reef in English, was familiar territory for Watson since his last ship completed surveys nearby after the States abandoned its claims in favor of Mexico. While reviewing charts with the navigator, Ensign Walter Dunbar, the executive officer described Arrecife Alacranes as five small islands, barely above sea level, with white sand beaches encircling slightly higher crests blanketed by rough, green thickets. They crowned a reef complex sixty or seventy miles off the Yucatan coast on Campeche Bank's northern boundary. Inhospitable and devoid of water, their value and hazard lay in navigation since the lethal mix of deep, shallow, and shoal waters, barely submerged the reefs and hidden coral heads lay just south of the main shipping lane between Veracruz and the Straits of Florida, Atlantic Coast, eastern Caribbean, and more distant seaports. Heavy passing traffic and numerous shipwrecks drove Lloyds of London to build a cast-iron lighthouse on the largest islet. Since then, losses declined and the lighthouse was employed by passing ships to fix position; the same purpose Dry Tortugas served for ships using northern gulf ports.

The sortie was part of a scheme conceived in Key West to intercept *Rafael Riego* off the reefs. Acting on Secretary of the Navy orders delivered to Starke by *Vanguard*, he was operating in concert with the cutter. Although planning was largely left to Starke's initiative and judgment, Albert offered three scenarios. If *Rafael Riego* took a southern route through the Gulf, interception in the Yucatan Channel was feasible, but the tug could bypass it or enter from three widely spaced directions, so her pursuers would need to know if the filibuster's rendezvous was on Cuba's southern coastline towards Santiago or Pinar del Río's north coast; and the tug would likely cross while mixed with other night traffic. A second possibility was for *Rafael Riego* to cross the central Gulf of Mexico north of the main shipping lane and avoid any common landfalls. Albert suggested this be excluded because two ships could not hope to cover such a vast area and it required the tug's master navigate to a precise Cuban landfall without a fix on Arrecife Alacranes or Dry Tortugas. The last, and in Albert's estimation most likely, was for the filibuster to cross Campeche Bank from Veracruz. Widely varying depths and numerous hazards would make piloting a challenge, but there were two possible routes to complicate pursuit. The first was to pilot along the largely uninhabited coast, assisted by a comfortable number of landmarks and lighthouses; but the master might also choose to remain offshore by heading first to Arrecife Alacranes before turning east for the Yucatan Channel or Cuba's north coast. This offered easier piloting since its hazards, besides Arrecife Alacranes, consisted only of the small, flat islands, Triángulo Oeste and Cayo Arenas, just out of Veracruz.

Starke and Hunter favored the Campeche Bank route, but split on the two possible tracks across. Hunter thought *Rafael Riego* would run Yucatan's north coast because Porto de Progresso, a small port and city less than twenty years old, was not only the north coast's solitary port, but had a lighthouse and direct rail line to the large city of Merida. There was also only eleven feet of water at its three small piers so most ships anchored three miles offshore and transferred cargoes by barge; allowing the tug to anchor for a short time with little attention paid. Starke found the logic sound, but favored the Arrecife Alacranes route; gambling *Rafael Riego*'s master would be hesitant to steam just off an unfamiliar coast for any time. In the end, during August's last days in the red-brick customs house, they compromised by using Arrecife Alacranes as a blocking point and location where *Calypso* could watch traffic on the shipping lane just north of the reef. She would sail to the reef and wait for the tug to come within visual range of the lighthouse. *Vanguard* would leave Key West first to prevent their departures being linked and make for Veracruz to confirm *Rafael Riego*'s presence, then follow her east to Arrecife Alacranes and *Calypso*; or trail the filibuster along the Yucatan coast. If the tug left Veracruz before the cutter arrived, *Vanguard* would rendezvous with *Calypso* off Arrecife Alacranes and sweep east together.

Once this was agreed, debate centered on what action could be taken if either or both hounds treed the raccoon. Hours of debate failed to produce anything, since they could not predict *Rafael Riego*'s reaction and were limited by law and custom. The tug would have a dubious registry, requiring courts to sort out, and skirt waters claimed by Mexico. Boarding any merchant ship without its nation's agreement was viewed as a hostile act; and especially between the United States and Great Britain since it sparked their last war, inhibited efforts to end slaving off Africa, and came with days of allying Britain with the Confederacy. Both captains agreed it would be best for their ships to join before either boarded; gambling this imbalance might induce *Rafael Riego* to accept her situation, or increase their options if she refused. For insurance, Starke sent a coded cable to Albert suggesting State pass a note to Consul-general Lee that loosely described the plan and could be provided to Spanish officials in Havana; to warn the captain general and block his office from claiming they were not informed should the interception fail. He also sent a detailed version to Lee using the clandestine courier, *Mascotte's* purser, who received the document from Paymaster Wiggs; visiting under the guise of researching Port Tampa ship chandlers.

The paymaster's inquiries also served to spread rumors she would travel up Florida's west coast; adding to those of her leaving for Port Royal to dry-dock, visiting Jamaica, and surveying a new ship channel in Port Arthur, Texas. Starke encouraged these speculations by enlisting Watson, Dunbar, and the ebullient Chief Quartermaster, Paul Owen, to lay out the track; while routes along the Gulf Coast to Texas and through the Yucatan Channel to Jamaica were developed by the ensigns, assisted by quartermasters and naval cadets. The subterfuge's finale was a two-afternoon open ship; outwardly to repay the port's hospitality, but primarily to convince those watching, especially press and Junta, that *Calypso*'s departure was unconnected with *Vanguard*.

While waiting for Albert's cable, *Calypso* shifted to the coaling pier, where she also took on water and provisions. Paymaster Wiggs arranged for anthracite to complement the bituminous coal on board and allow Starke to choose between power and smoke. The freshwater used to clean after coaling was taken off a Port Tampa lighter, rather than from the channel or potable water tanks filled by the ship's distillers when at anchor. There were also rumors coming from the Gulf Coast and Florida that a cargo consigned to Veracruz included obsolete howitzers, 12-pounder Hotchkiss guns, at least one compressed-air dynamite gun, and carriage-mounted Maxims; along with explosives, ammunition, and instructors. Starke conferred with Fort Taylor's ordnance officer, who believed the weapons mix well-chosen since its field pieces could be broken down for transport by two or three mules, the dynamite guns' effects were terrifying, a Hotchkiss gun's ammunition gave them firepower, and the howitzers, used since the Mexican War, could be fired with improvised ammunition and homemade powder. He was less enthusiastic about the Maxim guns; which he claimed were formidable but often jammed and had a voracious appetite for ammunition and cooling water.

Darwin Tyson and Cassandra Evans left separately for Havana before *Calypso*'s open ship and subsequent departure. Starke and Evans saw Tyson board *Mascotte* with carpet bag, silver flask, spyglass, and new straw hat. After enduring the swarming Key West reporters less than a week, he declared war and disease preferable to writing shoddy fiction; although still predicting the brief excursion to Havana would be of little value. Starke kept it to himself, but was confident Dana and *The Sun* would profit once their reporter reached Havana. His old friend was unlikely to join what Tyson called Inglaterra lobby lizards; and invariably dogged every story started to its end, no matter size, type, or direction. While grousing about nothing to keep him occupied in Key West, Tyson interviewed the Spanish consul, Manuel Garcia y Ruiz; a local Junta leader, Herminio Gonzales y Ochoa; the naval station commander; and often crawled through local watering holes. Most stories wired home were background, but one spoke to Charles Govin, a young *Equator-Democrat* reporter guerrilleros executed by machete in Cuba. That came closest to a tribute Tyson ever wrote; despite his belief the affair was a quixotic, needless, and naive tragedy.

Starke escorted Evans, who soon sported an unfashionable tan, to supper at the Key West Hotel several times; where her efforts to extract information through expectant silence failed. Instead, trapped by her own ploy, Starke discovered a more loquacious Evans fit his aunt's evaluation of her erstwhile protégé. She may have lacked Tyson's stature with the Key West mob, and familiarity with their labyrinthine customs, but was inquisitive, persistent, and accepted nothing at face value. She also found the à la carte diet of Cuban victories and

Spanish atrocities unpalatable; and became as frustrated with island's newspaper clique as Tyson.

Despite growing respect for a woman Starke thought might approach Tyson's ability in their profession, unless she married, he offered no special consideration and carefully avoided subjects related to *Rafael Riego*. He thought about giving her a wide berth to ensure nothing slipped, but decided against it, calculating it could work against him and stimulate a proclivity for subtle probing that came naturally, by virtue of her occupation, or some combination. An unspoken agreement evolved over years of friendship with Tyson that Starke would not lie or betray, but was under no obligation to reveal all. This did not exist with Evans, and experience with her sex convinced him most felt disclosure obligatory in all relationships and anything less a betrayal.

While completely open about Havana, he refrained from offering assistance for Evans' venture; one he believed too much like Govin's; or his own youthful decisions that put him on a Montana bluff surrounded by hostiles. When Evans understood he could not be coaxed, she reluctantly played the trump card by mentioning Constance Starke volunteered his assistance and the Starke firm's Havana office. His aunt could have approached her husband, so Immanuel Starke had avoided the request or his wife had other aspirations. Since she raised him almost from birth, Starke acquiesced, despite a plethora of misgivings. One being the possibility of it becoming common knowledge he helped arrange a correspondent's Havana visit, especially an attractive female with whom several evenings were spent. This was resolved using the personal code given him by Aron Sharett, the Jewish ship chandler in Norfolk. Acting swiftly, Sharett used the Starke firm's Havana office to arrange lodging at Hotel Inglaterra; known for its quality, reputation, and a cliental that included correspondents, Consul-general Lee, and other diplomats. He also engaged a reliable translator who might not be selling information to the Junta, government, other reporters, or a mixture. Starke also cabled Tyson, without Evans' knowledge, then escorted her to *Mascotte* where he truly wished the lady well then, as the liner passed Fort Taylor, considered the favor complete as he lacked capability or inclination to be the protector his aunt may have envisioned.

The *Rafael Riego* pursuit began with Albert cabling that the filibuster lay in Veracruz, loading cargo and passengers. *Calypso* cleared Key West's South West Channel for Arrecife Alacranes under bulging canvas on September 7, 1896; just as *Vanguard* crossed the rough coral reefs surrounding Mexico's largest east coast port after a four-day run from Key West. As the cutter anchored across from the low, gray and white silhouette of San Juan de Ulúa, Veracruz's prison-fortress, Hunter was impressed by the Diaz port modernization. After a break of more than ten years, the uncompleted construction to enclose the bay had resumed and new projects were visible along the waterfront. Hunter called for his gig and began courtesy calls soon after the cutter settled to her anchor.

The American consul's translator proved especially enlightening by offering information unfiltered by the American minister in Mexico City. It seemed local officials welcomed *Vanguard's* arrival, hoping it would speed *Rafael Riego's* departure; which was twice delayed to load additional agricultural equipment and mule carts with suspiciously small, fine wheels. They also viewed the expedition, which Mexico City turned a blind eye to, more anarchist than insurrecto and were growing anxious about its local effect. Foreigners attracted by construction work, seeking asylum, or other reasons had inundated the city and local Mexicans resented the lost work and accommodations made. Many Mexican anarchists also shared the authorities' desire to see the last of *Rafael Riego*, since Spain declaring martial law to purge that nation, and particularly Barcelona, of anarchists sent swarms to Veracruz. These émigrés supported the expedition as a strike against the monarchy, while indigenous anarchists, mostly in Mexico City and centered on the Magón brothers, saw the swelling Veracruz coterie as willing to risk a Mexican purge to strike Spain. Despite international rhetoric, the only anarchist consensus was for *Rafael Riego* to leave for Cuba; and the foreigners' appeal for direct support effectively neutered.

Hunter also attempted to pressure *Rafael Riego* to depart, by letting the expedition see *Vanguard* was interested. He rented a carriage, then spent an hour openly observing them load from a safe distance; accompanied by an armed cutterman. From a spot neither too far nor near the wharf, he studied the oceangoing steam tug *Rafael Riego* and confirmed the Justice reports. She was large, at least 140 feet long and twenty-five wide, with a black steel hull, gray deckhouse, two funnels, and identical gaff-rigged masts. Otherwise, the design was largely conventional, with her superstructure taking two-thirds of the main deck and large pilothouse, ventilators, and two whaleboats on the deckhouse. The current name was hurriedly painted over raised block letters on her counter that read *J.W. Fawkes*, with no homeport visible beneath. She also lacked a Plimsoll mark, ruling out British registry; leaving the United States, Brazil, or a third country as likely candidates. Draft markings were also absent, so he could not be certain of the fourteen feet reported, but it seemed right and gave *Vanguard* a shallow water advantage. The towing gear had also been removed in Veracruz or before sailing for Mexico to accommodate more cargo. As Hunter watched, lifts of narrow wood boxes or clusters of finely-made wheels left the wharf, hovered briefly over her aft deck, then disappeared through a large cargo hatch.

Hunter returned to *Vanguard*, convinced the cargo was not for farming. By then, his executive officer, Second Lieutenant Earnest Buck, had a watch set to raise the alarm if *Rafael Riego* headed to sea. Since rules of war did not apply, Hunter was only restricted by port regulations and possible government reaction should he choose to follow the tug out of Veracruz; so *Vanguard's* boilers stood ready with banked fires that could be quickly spread and her crew restricted to the ship. Although Hunter was often liberal when it came to liberty, he needed to avoid leaving cuttermen behind when the tug made its run; and Veracruz was known as a rough port so it sidestepped other complications.

Across the harbor that evening, Manuel Valencia y Gomis leaned on *Rafael Riego's* railing, still warm from the day, staring over the harbor lights' shimmering reflection on black water to the white cutter anchored off a barrier island. Earlier, while in work clothes, he spotted one of its officers observe them load the last crates of artillery and ammunition. *Vanguard's* appearance exacerbated a frustration that grew steadily since arriving on *City of Washington*, a New York and Cuba Mail Steamship Company, or Ward Line, ship. He left New York City when reports said the expedition was ready to sail, but found these extremely optimistic, recriminations flying between the Junta officials, the schedule in disarray, local authorities losing patience, and anarchist factions near fisticuffs.

Valencia threw himself into salvaging the filibuster expedition since *Rafael Riego* was his creature. He conceived, developed, and launched the plan after leaving Spain and joining the Junta's small anarchist cadre. After discovering artillery was accumulating in the States while the Junta struggled to gain belligerency status, he pushed, cajoled, debated, coerced, and appealed to wealthy anarchists, expatriate Cubans, and others to charter the tug. Convinced oppressors again triumphed over people, and the Junta's constant gymnastics to ignore or circumvent laws lacked boldness, he envisioned these artillery stores as the means to mount an epic propaganda of the deed. Cuban insurrectos lacked artillery and gunners skilled in its use. Filibusters left many ports to supply, equip, and replenish, but artillery only trickled in and few recruits were qualified to use it. An artillery corps could change everything, so he overcame Junta reservations, and launched the expedition.

Valencia reluctantly fled Spain before martial law was declared, convinced everyone, including Cubans, should be free; but his dream was a model anarchist state in Barcelona. He found the New York movement impeded by peasants, workers, and intellectuals ill-prepared for true anarchy, perpetually in debate, and split into factions with dubious philosophical loyalties. Valencia soon tired of endless single-topic meetings that mutated into formless debate before collapsing entirely. This would have been equally true for the Junta, except freeing Cuba set a common intellectual goal and Martí's spirit still prevailed. Valencia admired the organization, but his anarchism grew purer and more international; which often placed him at odds with Junta leaders. He was convinced people and causes must be risked or sacrificed; and heroic failures could prove more useful than quiet successes. The Junta aspired to Cuban independence, not world anarchy, so they refused to support activities that risked support or invited a purge. He argued every opportunity to end Spain's rule should be embraced, since the peninsula's rich aristocracy and big business willingly accepted obscene costs borne by others to keep the island subjugated. Consequently, the *Rafael Riego* project was finally birthed through logic, perseverance, and dedication; but only just since some in the Junta resolutely opposed it.

Mexico proved no different. *Rafael Riego*'s first master stormed from an acrimonious meeting after the ship docked in Veracruz and never seen again. This nearly finished the expedition and intensified Junta and anarchist factions' animus. The original plan to complete the trip to Cuba without sighting land also fell apart because that captain was an ex-Russian naval officer and expert navigator. Valencia grew desperate because he was unable to get underway without a master and Mexican authorities were about to act since the ship remained pierside with her cargo on board and a crew too large for commercial purposes. His unlikely champion, and only willing candidate, was Captain Buff who was neither an anarchist nor dedicated to the Junta but a tested filibuster who recently lost a ship and two comrades in the trade. While his vocal desire for revenge caused the Junta to avoid him, Captain Buff's reputation was excellent, his skill beyond reproach, and Valencia appreciated vengeance as a reliable source of purpose, drive, energy, and endurance. His working-class background would also read well in anarchist papers and journals after the propaganda of the deed. Captain Buff was stranded in Key West looking for a berth, saw this as his best opportunity, and accepted; despite many reservations and any idealist inclinations extinguished long before. Within days, he boarded *Mascotte* for Havana, transferred to the *City of Washington*, and greeted by Valencia on the same pier where the anarchist landed.

Valencia found a powerful man with little fat, other than lozenge belly, clean shaven, and bald; although curly black hair blanketed what else was visible. Mature, but not old, his skin was more a hide, damaged, burned, and tanned from a lifetime under the Caribbean sun; and both hands scarred from hard fishing, fighting, and work. Captain Buff struck Valencia as the beau idéal of a worker, although subtle overtures regarding anarchism, class struggle, or Cuban independence revealed no interest. Captain Buff also ended any discussion about the northern gulf route, after a perfunctory examination of the chart, by declaring its architect knew nothing of the Caribbean. Valencia countered it might be due to his withholding the final leg and landing spot until the expedition left Veracruz, but the new master summarily dismissed him, claiming night piloting to any precise location other than a city was absurd unless it was a short run from some fixed position; or they traveled along the coast moving from one landmark to the next. Taking a pencil, he touched the chart, with a surprisingly deft movement, just south of the Dry Tortugas, observed the American Navy used Fort Jefferson for coaling, then traced a light circle around Arrecife Alacranes, explaining its isolated lighthouse allowed them to fix their position just north of Campeche Bank; then placed a straightedge across the chart from it to the Yucatan Channel, and traced a line along it, gently rolling the pencil. Setting the ruler aside, he decreed *Rafael Riego* would leave Veracruz unannounced, make the reef, turn east to pass over Campeche Bank to the Yucatan Channel; then head for whatever landing site Valencia chose.

Before the anarchist could protest, Captain Buff demanded boiler repairs, port fees paid weekly, and anthracite coal. Valencia acquiesced because there was no time to replace him and further delay would finish the expedition; unaware his new master made these as a diversion. Captain Buff was convinced Junta leaks cost him *John Gwinn Williams* and anarchists were even less reliable, so *Rafael Riego* would leave just after midnight the following day; once word spread she would be a week for boiler work and completing pre-work testing. Those watching would expect her boilers lit-off during the day for tests, and taken offline to cool overnight. Instead, boiler fires would be banked until dark then reawakened using every contrivance to quickly build steam without a burst of sparks or stack fire. Should either occur, or any other problem, he would claim they started working nights on a boiler. If everything went well, the tug would slip mooring lines just after midnight. The cutter would not follow if in port on other business but *Rafael Riego* would gain several hours head start in any case while her pursuer raised a head of steam and recalled liberty parties.

Valencia was livid when Captain Buff informed him they were getting underway and abandoning several artillery instructors; since they were just told another week in port was needed. It was only because he resolved to confront Captain Buff the next morning that no warning went to Cuban insurrectionists about this sham delay. Although Valencia remained agitated about his usurped authority, the underway was smoothly accomplished.

The tug's two propulsion boilers were quietly placed on line by the engineer and oiler then, just before midnight, a seaman went on deck followed by another. They appeared to check mooring lines and make adjustments but were preparing to cast off lines made ready to slip without requiring anyone on the pier. When the plant had a full head of steam, Captain Buff went to the pilothouse, took the helm and engine order telegraph, or EOT, and waited for his night vision. After a last scan of the harbor, every mooring line save one was taken in, his rudder put hard over, and bow eased against the pier while holding the bowline. With his stem fixed, the screw was put slow ahead. Leverage and propeller wash against the rudder pushed her stern off, slowly pivoting *Rafael Riego* until the tug was perpendicular to the wharf. Captain Buff then put his rudder amidship, signaled deckhands to release the bow line, and backed rapidly into the harbor. Once he gained maneuvering room, the rudder went hard over as full ahead was rung up. *Rafael Riego* gathered momentum and steerageway until reaching the harbor speed limit then steadied on course. Night movements by tugs, even without pilots, were not unusual since they might be summoned from the harbor at short notice so Captain Buff gambled he would be seen as a tug getting underway for a call or going to anchorage. Ghosting through the dark port, *Rafael Riego* steered for Isla Verde, moving slow and deliberate. Clearing *Vanguard* at a comfortable distance, she continued east then turned northeast to pass between La Blanquilla and Anegada de Adentro. As the turn began, Captain Buff extinguished running lights lit to avoid suspicion when leaving the pier. He hoped this might disguise the turn and suggest the tug left the pier to anchor until morning, request a pilot, and recover excess port fees. Instead, he cleared the harbor and set the underway watch while Valencia watched the halo of Veracruz's lights fade, with no sign of pursuit.

Valencia woke their artillery instructors and prospective insurrectos before getting underway and instructed them to remain below. After clearing port, the men filtered on deck, gathered at the stern, and told they were steaming northeast towards Arrecife Alacranes then Cuba. He was exhilarated; the expedition was at sea and in less than three days field artillery that might bring an end Spanish rule in Cuba, and possibly the monarchy, would be ashore. After everyone returned to bunks or bedrolls, Valencia lingered on the main deck, feeling unnaturally alive as a smooth throbbing engine pushed *Rafael Riego* through the near-black Caribbean under a thousand stars, with a white bow wave and glittering phosphorescence trailing astern to mark their passage.

Several minutes later he climbed through the warm breeze to the pilothouse and heard Captain Buff's account. The man grinned, adding it was fortunate the starboard side was against the pier, there was little wind, and negligible current; since single screw ships were impossible to work away from piers on one side or the other, due to propeller rotation. A tug would have been required for *Rafael Riego* if her port side was against the pier; unless an anchor had been dropped in the channel as she moored. It was first Captain Buff explained anything to his young patron, so an emboldened, Valencia pressed him, "I see no pursuit, captain. Are we safe?"

Captain Buff's eyes and face hardened, "Not until cargo and passengers are ashore and we're outside Spanish waters. First, there's getting there; then a good chance your Cubans will cock-up landing cargo, even if they are waiting."

"I trust them, and these guns will free Cuba from oppression."

"So you say, señor, but the ship wasn't ready and your first master high-tailed it."

Captain Buff paused to offer the figure leaning against the chart table a chance to protest before continuing, "Look señor, I'm paid to get your cargo to Cuba, but will jettison everything in a heartbeat to avoid prison or a firing squad. This is no parlor game and any debate's fatal. That revenuer in Veracruz was *Vanguard*; arrived in Key West from Jacksonville just before I left. She's not only new and fast, but commanded by a First Lieutenant Hunter. He's no jacked-up Navy bastard, knows the Caribbean, and nearly had my butt on several occasions."

Before Captain Buff retreated to his customary demeanor, Valencia planned to reveal they would rendezvous with insurrectos under General Gómez off Bahia Cochinos, or Bay of Pigs, about forty miles west of Cienfuegos in Santa Clara Province. Instead, he asked, "Do you think the authorities know?"

"Dammit Valencia, it would surprise me if the Americans, Spanish, and Mexicans didn't; the question's how much. *Vanguard* must have steamed straight from Key West and Hunter's probably chasing us."

Vanguard was indeed astern, just below the dark southwest horizon, clearing Veracruz harbor under a black smoke plume. Hunter was called on deck three hours before to see his darkened quarry turn northeast then extinguish all running lights. When the watch separated *Rafael Riego* from the harbor lights and woke him, she was nearly abreast *Vanguard*, some distance off the cutter's port side, and running fast. Spotters thought the amorphous form moving through the harbor at two in the morning was a different ship, one that spent the day unloading and loading. When *Rafael Riego* turned, her two funnels ended all doubt. The handling and audacity also convinced Hunter they faced an experienced filibuster like Edward Murphy, Dynamite Johnny O'Brien, or Captain Buff; but, however skillful the exit, it would not disrupt the scheme developed before leaving Key West.

Unless Mexican authorities acted, *Vanguard's* role was to confirm *Rafael Riego* was in Veracruz, then, after *Calypso* was near or off Arrecife Alacranes, flush the tug and trail her to the reef. If all went well, *Calypso* and *Vanguard* would be there to board or block any escape. If the tug turned back or chose to follow the Yucatan coast, Hunter would determine what action to take. He anticipated something similar to what occurred so the crew was kept on board after *Vanguard* anchored, one Babcock & Wilcox boiler used for auxiliary steam, and the second's fire banked. The cutter was brought to short stay using the first while glowing embers were spread across the second's grate and coal added. By the time sufficient daylight arrived to distinguish the landmarks needed to pass safely through coral reefs surrounding Veracruz there was steam enough to get underway. Just before leaving, the pilot boat was hailed and a note sent to the consul; then the anchor raised and catted as *Vanguard's* white hull gained momentum and her crew went to breakfast.

Hunter made for Arrecife Alacranes at twelve knots since *Rafael Riego* was not in sight and he did not want to overtake their quarry. Two ships in sight when they met with the filibuster might prevent a fight, and if Justice's information was inaccurate nothing was lost. Hunter scrutinized *Rafael Riego* in Veracruz for any indication she mounted or could mount a deck gun and saw nothing, but this was expected since any suggestion would have forced Mexican authorities to search and seize the ship. Even so, it was possible to jury-rig a mount at sea; or another weapon might be on board.

Chapter Six
Arrecife Alacranes

The next morning, *Calypso*'s lead stoker for the oncoming watch, Delmar Kemp, stepped onto the main deck, glanced towards Arrecife Alacranes, then crossed to the port bulwark. He shielded his eyes with a coal dust ingrained palm to watch the orange-yellow sun lift from a shimmering eastern horizon as its rays became a vast array of colors passing through low clouds. The evening display in the west would be equally spectacular, but a Caribbean day's blazing start spoke to him more than the magnificent splendor of its fiery demise.

Large, muscular, and dark, with strong African features and taut, flat cheeks irritated with raised bumps from shaving, Kemp was off to the fantail for a pipe, since smoking was restricted to specific times and places. Pausing to brush dried salt crystals from the varnished bulwark cap, he thought of the family farm. Working hot, humid fields during a Virginia summer was grueling, but must be hell with the heat wave newspapers were reporting. Like his father, he read what was available, but preferred mechanics and the Bible over fiction, history, or politics. This drew him to Newport News and Norfolk where there was shipyard work, but his size, stamina, and farmer's acceptance of hard labor were more attractive to employers than desire or mechanical aptitude. Frustrated, he read a Navy flyer recruiting stokers and enlisted the next day.

Once in the boiler room, he would pour strong, grainy coffee from the blue-enamel pot warming on a boiler's flat spot and prepare to shovel; while supervising the port watch's trimmers, passers, and stokers. Coming from Key West under sail allowed the black gang more time above deck, especially after engineers used the long stay in port to maintain their plant and complete the odd repair; but it was time to restart and adjust to the backbreaking rhythm needed to steam a ship.

His starboard watch counterpart, Dylan Jones, would be there, waiting to be relieved. The two men met on *Franklin*, Norfolk's receiving ship, where their desire to learn about boilers proved a common bound. Jones, who enlisted in Pennsylvania, came from a family of Welsh miners, but detested working underground. It was a common friendship in Navy crews that mixed citizens, Indians, immigrants, foreigners, Whites, Coloreds, Negroes, Freedmen, Republicans, Democrats, ex-soldiers, Christians, Jews, sinners, and others. On the fantail, Kemp saw Yamashita speaking in what seemed gibberish to another Japanese steward, while the veteran Irish sailor, and Chief Weaver's leading seaman, climbed the foremast's windward ratlines. Two small, swarthy sailors steadied a large metal block while the tall, blond Swede worked a marlinspike to unjam its sheaves. Entering the deckhouse was their paymaster's clerk, a small German Jew who tailored Kemp's liberty uniform. Up forward, their seaman from the Sandwich Islands, nearly as large as himself, stood out from a deck force gang at work. When this medley blended under a good commander, sailors called their ship a home; even in the face of letters, newspapers, and recruits describing a social hardening outside the Navy. Most sailors were tagged with some descriptive epithet, but comradeship, especially on *Calypso*, came from interdependence, never being out of uniform, loyalty to ship, and common complaints, such as civilian establishments refusing sailors. As he left for the boiler room, Kemp glanced up to see Weaver's Irish sailor vanish over foretop's rim. The captain was also headed for the pilothouse, but too far away for a salute or greeting.

Starke was heading there after his eggs and rice breakfast; and enjoying a short escape from the day cabin to another morning at sea. He paused in the pilothouse before going up to the flying bridge; then checked the stack for excessive smoke as he ascended. Once settled, he scanned Arrecife Alacranes with binoculars. *Calypso* was steaming north and south, about three miles southeast of the roughly circular reef; a dozen miles wide and nearly twenty long. Using the black, cast-iron lighthouse for reference, *Calypso* patrolled a station affording lookouts an excellent view of traffic from the southwest, while merging the bark's silhouette with the low islands during part of each leg; and varying the pattern every three hours to continue the run north far enough for a quick scout of the shipping lane passing above the reef.

The morning lookout, Seaman First Class Doran Kearney, was content with not being on the flying bridge, where the watch was stood after sunset. With little wind, and *Calypso* steaming slowly back and forth, he would perch on the foremast's top yardarm because it equaled the mainmast in height and was forward of the stack. There was almost no wind, but he chose the weather shrouds anyway. Grabbing two, he swung himself over the side, began climbing, and felt ratlines press into calloused feet; with a big toe still sensitive after striking a metal deck fitting. The blue-green water below flowed down the side in a hissing stream of ripples and bubbles heard through the wooden hull at night as the bark slid easily through the sea.

Looking down, he noticed Kemp, the formidable Negro stoker, staring over the port bulwark, and the captain's steward Yamashita setting up to fish with his crowd. Within minutes they were likely to land several good-sized fish, and be joined by Thaddeus, the gray and black feline possessing an unnatural ability to sense when and where a meal might develop. Kearney found the tomcat napping behind a ladder just below the main deck on his way to watch. Pausing to stroke the curled mass, he felt warm, silky-smoothness lean into his hand and emit a rumbling purr with each pass.

Without pausing, he passed over the futtock shrouds to the foretop then continued to the fore topgallant yard where he wedged himself against the mast. Looking over the reef's broad disruption in the flat Gulf, he studied the largest island and lighthouse that clung to the southern section with four smaller companions. Each scruffy green island was ringed with white sand rising tenuously from a blend of dark blue, light blue, green, and crystal water; depending on depth, bottom, and sun. Flocks of white, black, and gray birds would intermittently rise, circle then resettle on land, sand bottom, or semi-submerged coral. Silver-blue flying fish broke the surface, skittered over it, then landed safely beyond some predator; and the gentle air caressing him as *Calypso* moved forward proved increasingly welcome with temperatures climbing under a light blue sky and only high, fluffy cumulous clouds to temper the rising sun.

The word from their chiefs and petty officers was they could spot the filibuster within a few days so Kearney was exceptionally attentive this morning. The crew knew they were off the reef to intercept a filibuster running from Veracruz to Cuba because Starke wanted them to understand what they were about and put the word out before *Calypso* raised the desolate lighthouse. While appreciated, most lacked strong opinions on Cuban independence and were far more interested in the next port, latest mess topic, or personal triumphs and trials. Kearney sailed with Cadet Starke on the steam screw sloop *Apalachicola* and went ashore with him into Alexandria's chaos after a British fleet shelled its forts and city. They had not sailed together since, but Starke seemed fundamentally unchanged, although more mature and even less expressive. He still looked out for shipmates, cautioning them about overconfidence and concealing concern, but Kearney also observed their captain had not jettisoned his capability to be damned harsh and detached when called for.

Shifting position slightly to fend off a brilliant sun, Kearney ensured his feet swung clear of lines; then quickly scanned the horizon for smudges or disruptions. After one pass, he used the lighthouse to adjust his paired-telescopes. When the navigator, Ensign Dunbar, was issuing them, he heard a quartermaster report *Calypso* was in better than 100 feet of water, possibly 200, but near shoal water measuring inches. He easily confirmed that by running his glasses over the reef, about three miles northwest. When the sun obliged, he could see crystal blue water turn black or the shallows marked by various hues. Near the beaches, it seemed possible to see the bottom when there was no reflection.

Around seven o'clock, Kearney picked up a faint smudge at the western horizon just above the reef, briefly placed his paired-telescopes on it, and then completed his pass. Once certain there was nothing else, he waited a moment then put the telescopes on it again. The anomaly was darker, and might be a cloud at the horizon, but the night orders encouraged lookouts and watch officers to risk a false alarm if uncertain. As *Calypso* was about to clear the reef, he decided, slid the crook of his arm around a line, cupped his hands, then hailed the flying bridge, where the captain stood alongside Ensign Martyn, "Officer of the Deck, ship on the horizon, just off the starboard beam."

Ensign Martyn just finished reviewing their track with Starke when they heard the lookout's hail. Since *Calypso* arrived off Arrecife Alacranes the previous day, he reported two false sightings, while Blair's starboard section had not. Although their captain seldom displayed frustration, and often warned of too much caution, or lack of it, Martyn was grateful he did not have to decide a third time.

Kearney saw Starke speak to Martyn then barely felt the turn as *Calypso* came slow and smooth to port. Because this was accomplished early, the islands rotated from starboard to port as though they turned around the ship, then, as *Calypso* steadied, the captain looked up at Kearney, cupped his hands, yelling in a strong, clear voice, "Good work Kearney, keep a sharp eye on her."

Starke sensed it was *Rafael Riego* as *Calypso* steadied on their northern leg; although there had been other sightings while they loitered east of the 100 square-mile, kidney-bean shaped reef. Using its five diminutive islands to remain clear of warm saltwater undulating over hard coral, their patrol was continued farther north towards the shipping lane on every fifth circuit. During the clear, nearly moonless nights, ships traveling above them appeared as a collection of lights that were often little more than a loom, but several did pass near enough to make out a shadowy silhouette. Most did not approach closer than required to fix position from the light flashing out of a dark tropical night with sky and sea indistinguishable except for thousands of stars. *Calypso* found few visitors of interest. North of the lighthouse, one turned out to be a small passenger liner and another, a freighter; while a promising tug crossing further south on Blair's watch finally revealed its single stack.

Starke felt confident because of the previous evening's discussions with Watson and Chief Owen. The chief began by unrolling a western Caribbean chart on the cabin table, then carefully placing cast-iron corner weights. Seeing the sharp mind behind a cherub-like countenance was debating whether to offer an opinion, Starke ruffled the perpetually optimistic and massive sailor with, "Take a seat, chief," then, as he lit his pipe, "Do you smoke? I'd offer brandy but couldn't get it past our master-at-arms."

"No thank-you, captain. Don't smoke and take only a glass of dinner wine or the odd beer. Smoked cigars before tying the knot, but now only chaw some. Wifey don't abide smoke or spittoons, and she's temperance, so going along eases the passage."

The chief was exceptionally competent and earned the wardroom's respect, for which Starke was grateful. Real proficiency in navigating, piloting, and their related skills required time, focus, and passion; whether quartermaster or master. It was a calling, and those deficient in understanding the intricacies were a burden, threat, and far too common. Apparently, the chief's family was the only thing he thought more important. While Owen's opinion was never taken lightly; Starke was unsure how the chief viewed his captain, so he moved first, "What's your thinking on this fellow, chief?"

Owen attempted to digest this as his bulk was planted on a wooden chair that protested by creaking until the burden pressed it to silence. He thanked Providence for calm seas when sitting on weak chairs, since his weight occasionally broke them, but only the engine's steady rumble confirmed they were not pierside. In response, Owen unrolled a second chart, using the interval to balance risk of souring his relationship with Ensign Dunbar by appearing to seek the captain's favor at his navigator's expense; or remain silent and gain a plodder's reputation through misplaced deference.

Lieutenant Starke seemed competent and decisive, but distant, leaving only Weaver's opinion to rely on; and few commanders posed open-ended questions without serving together for many years. Even then, in the chief's experience, most sought a confirming echo or minor suggestion. It was Owen's natural enthusiasm that finally tipped the scales, "Captain, I'd say catching any ship traveling off fixed routes depends on what's known and more than a fair bit of luck, but Arrecife Alacranes seems our best bet."

"And?"

"Well sir, depends on when the master leaves Veracruz, how long he wants the Arrecife Alacranes lighthouse visible to set his course, and whether he's concerned about being seen. Two-stacked tugs aren't common."

Starke leaned back in his chair, took a match, passed it over a pipe, then drew on the worn stem, letting the chief continue, "Night offers concealment but requires familiarity with the lighthouse, and daylight gets a better fix. If a master was to split the difference, passing near breakfast makes sense since the keeper's coming off watch, and likely eating or starting chores. Late evening's also good, since he can raise the lighthouse, have enough visibility to run a bearing, then lose anyone pursuing during the night."

Owen paused as Yamashita carried in a silver-plate coffeepot with black wood handle extending from its flank, quietly refilled Starke's cup, then left. When the steward was back in the pantry, Owen resumed, "In any case, it depends on when the master leaves Veracruz, and not many will at night. There's a direct course here, but it's not often run after dark because some reefs and two small islets need clearing. Either way, he'll keep to a speed that makes good time and helps piloting. Mr. Dunbar requested times and tracks to put him off the lighthouse early morning or evening; but I'd guess morning, if pressed.

Starke looked at the chief through light pipe smoke. Dunbar would probably learn of this request after Owen left the cabin, and the second marked up chart likely due to wagering. He extracted the worn pipe, placed its stem just above the chart, then traced a route from Veracruz to their position, "In other words, the betting favors a morning sighting."

Owen was caught and, relying on Weaver's opinion, replied, "Er, yes, sir. Favorite's arriving here at daylight then crossing the Yucatan Channel overnight, since most hazards lay between Veracruz and Arrecife Alacranes; then its deep water to the northeast Yucatan coast; unless he goes inshore."

"What about weather."

"I'm uneasy there, captain. There've already been tropical storms, and we'll see more, but this season's been kind. I'm watching barometer, clouds, and anything else, but would like a small blow so the crew gets a feel."

After Owen left, Starke added several lines to Katherine's letter as he sipped coffee amidst light-gray smoke and the choice tobacco's aroma. He was waiting for its India ink to dry when Watson entered with the night order book then sat across from him, waiting while his captain checked courses, reviewed entries, then added a line that false alarms were preferable to missing the filibuster.

Setting the pen aside, Starke had studied his executive officer, repacked his pipe, then asked, "Thoughts, XO?"

"If *Vanguard* arrives and there's no filibuster, *Rafael Riego* has taken the route captain Hunter suggested. If so, our only choice is to join the cutter and chase the filibuster to the Yucatan Channel; although the odds are bad. I'm still concerned about what happens if we find her. Boarding a ship filled with anarchists risks our sailors; and standing off to sink her won't go over well back home."

"We're forced to play the hand dealt, XO. Unfortunately, we're tied to rules *Rafael Riego* can predict and is unlikely to honor if under anarchists, since they advocate ending them. Even so, *Rafael Riego* can't be certain how much we know or entirely confident we'll stay within the law; so there's advantage for us in being only a little unpredictable."

"But we still can't sink her or watch arms land under an American flag."

"The hand changes with every deal and draw, XO."

"Yes, sir."

"Seen a bar fight? Rioting? Land battle? Fleet action?"

"No, sir?"

"There's no difference if you're a casualty. Be ready for anything from boarding to a fight. We know she's traveling from Veracruz to Cuba, belligerent, and dangerous; but they can't be certain about us. The steel hull is her best weapon close in but the light field artillery and machine guns on board could be jury-rigged and there's the dynamite gun to consider. I've not seen one fire, but those on *Vesuvius* are said to be a terror and firing into her could set off ammunition or high explosives."

Pausing while three bells were struck in pairs followed by a solitary stroke, marking two and a half hours into the watch, Starke continued, "Washington sets mission and rules from a safe distance then evaluates. I've seen this before and it often doesn't end well; but stay ready and we'll see what develops. Anyway, get the night orders to the first watch."

After he left, Starke recalled Watson's efforts and success assembling, molding, and training the crew; and that he nearly passed on the officer due to an ominous letter from the candidate's last duty station, the survey ship *Winston A. Capps*. Albert saw his ability and helped Watson write a response; then, soon after, *Winston A. Capps* went aground on Cay Sal

Bank and her commander blamed his crew. That incident required a second letter, reviewed by *Maine's* executive officer and posted before leaving Key West. Starke never learned what occurred on the survey ship, and less about its demise, but *Calypso* gained a first-class executive officer.

Shortly after finishing his pipe, Starke retired and was called to the pilothouse only twice during the night. He now stood on the flying bridge, enjoying a wondrous Caribbean morning lit by a yellow-orange sun. Beside him was a perplexed Ensign Martyn, who just ordered a turn north through the brass voice tube to the pilothouse. Realizing *Calypso's* lookout had height-of-eye advantage, Starke directed Martyn to turn north before the end of their southern leg. If it was the filibuster approaching, he hoped the islands might screen *Calypso's* hull until *Rafael Riego* was committed to turning east and passing south of Arrecife Alacranes for Cuba, rather than going north above the reefs; which meant a long stern chase. For now, he concentrated on not staring anxiously towards the western horizon.

Through binoculars, Starke traced the cast-iron lighthouse down to its cement base then across the yard. The keeper was climbing three board steps to a long wooden porch on the plain house situated between a white sand beach and green scrub at the island's low crest. Struck by the loneliness of weeks or months tending the isolated light, Starke shifted to the southwest horizon and its thin wisp of smoke. He suspected the ship was closer than the smoke column suggested, which meant anthracite coal, a costly choice for working tugs. It was too far south for passenger liners, but a filibuster wanting a low profile might bear the expense. Starke lowered his binoculars; nearly certain *Rafael Riego* was approaching with Hunter and *Vanguard* somewhere astern.

Calypso steamed roughly two miles, then turned south and

slowed to bare steerageway near the southern leg's turning point. With the ships closing, Starke thought a position southeast of the reef's three southern islands, and barely visible lighthouse, offered some advantage. Continuing further north would obscure *Calypso* a bit longer by keeping three islands between them, but place her too far north if their quarry turned east after raising the lighthouse. Starke studied the smooth blue-gray sea with an otherwise empty horizon under increasing clouds. He was comfortable that both courses a ship approaching Arrecife Alacranes from the southwest might chose were covered. If their new arrival turned due east after sighting the lighthouse, *Calypso* would pass down her port side at about three miles; but should she turn north, towards the shipping lanes, *Calypso* could do the same until clear of the reef, then close from the tug's starboard bow, albeit much later.

Captain Buff used what little anthracite remained in the bunkers as *Rafael Riego* closed Arrecife Alacranes, so only light gray smoke streamed astern as Valencia woke from a too-short few hours of sleep. It was the anarchist's first nap after remaining mostly awake for a long day and two nights. Outside, he embraced a light breeze caressing their deck and temporarily moderating the steadily rising heat. Months of solicitations, arguments, negotiations, and prodding finally seemed worthwhile. He was excited, alert, optimistic, and more alive than he could remember; it seemed like childhood's magic rushes were back.

Their expedition was days away from resurrecting the Cuban insurrectos' fortunes and freeing the island. As a propaganda of the deed, it would eclipse assassinations, strikes, and bombings. *Rafael Riego*'s hold, deck load, and passengers would provide the same Cubans a corrupt Spanish elite labeled mixed-race rabble the means to control their lives and land by force of arms. Such a thunderbolt could spread across Europe, freeing more people to rise against class domination, perhaps eclipsing 1848, but with anarchists leading them. Mexico also seemed restive, and Russia was always ripe under the Romanov dynasty. Even the United States might provide fertile ground, with labor finally resisting mine owners and anarchists determined to avenge four of their number hanged in Illinois for the Haymarket Massacre. This excitement was shared by most of the passengers; fueling debates between anarchists and Cuban nationalists until midnight passed and several self-described soldiers of fortune called a stop.

This euphoria did not infect the crew, and most certainly not Captain Buff, who warned Valencia the outcome could as easily be decided off Arrecife Alacranes as Cuba; so the revolutionary wanted to be in the pilothouse. Yesterday, Valencia failed to see the flat islet surrounded by reefs Captain Buff pointed out, even with paired-telescopes, but was assured Arrecife Alacranes was different and would be clearly visible in the blue-gray sea under billowing clouds that merged in the distance. When Valencia entered through the latched-open pilothouse door, Captain Buff's black paired-telescopes were pointing through an open window to something just off the bow. Valencia saw a climbing sun reflecting from wave crests and causing the far line dividing sea and sky to sparkle; while flying fish off the port bow launched themselves then glided over a smooth surface leaving water droplets along their path to reentry.

Lowering his paired-telescopes, Captain Buff turned, "You're up, señor."

"Yes, captain. I wanted to see Arrecife Alacranes."

The master responded, with a hint of irritation and concern, "The low smudges on the horizon are its three southern islands and that small flash to the left is the lighthouse. The spot beyond and further right's likely a ship."

"What kind?"

"We won't know for ten or fifteen minutes. She's hull-down with three topmasts just visible. They've the advantage if there's a lookout in one."

"What are we going to do?"

"Turn east as planned and see what develops. If we're being watched, any heading other than north or east, would be suspicious or unnecessary; and passing north of the reef would take longer and put them between us and Cuba."

"*Vanguard*?"

"No. She can't have overreached us and these masts were built to carry canvas."

"Spanish then? *Alphonso XII* or *Reina Mercedes*?"

"So you've looked up Spain's ships in Cuba. We're too far west. If not for the trace of stack smoke, I'd have thought it was some windjammer bound for Veracruz that's anchored or drifting."

After shooting a bearing to the lighthouse, Captain Buff turned *Rafael Riego* starboard, then headed due east over the northern Campeche Bank towards the Yucatan Channel. The three small islands moved down the port side as the dark ship, rising from the sea ahead, crossed to port. It appeared headed south, but they would still cross the bark's bow, some distance off. Maneuvering disoriented Valencia, but it helped to watch the frothing white wake astern as it curved, straightened, changed to blue-gray, before fading to a light surface etching. Captain Buff studied the young man, "We could hold off turning and run closer in, but I shot solid bearings on the lighthouse and coming east early means they won't get a clear look at us for a few more minutes. We'll know soon enough if they're after us; our two stacks are a dead giveaway."

Through a spare set of telescopes, Valencia studied the masts, hull, and stack as they grew clearer; relieved it wasn't *Vanguard*. The nautical terms escaped him, but the ship was too elegant for commerce; and smoke from her stack was increasing, despite the shimmering image's absence of movement. Turning to Captain Buff, he saw the man's knuckles whiten as powerful hands tightened around paired-telescopes protruding from his face. The bullet-shaped head reddened, and thick neck collapsed into three tanned rolls as Valencia asked, "Is she anchored, captain?"

"She's underway without much way on. That's *Calypso*. Bastard sank my last ship and killed the engineer; my friend. She should be in Key West. Her sailors on liberty claimed they were surveying the Gulf or testing engines, but I never believed it. Some informer or Junta traitor told the government about my last expedition; and now, after a long stay in Key West, she suddenly crosses the Gulf to Arrecife Alacranes where there's nothing but a lighthouse. We've been sold out. Maybe the master you ran off, or the rat that did in *John Gwinn Williams*."

Valencia's elation crumbled and exhaustion overwhelmed him. He almost pleaded, "Our cargo must get through, captain."

Captain Buff roughly hung the paired-telescopes on a hook beneath the window then shifted the dark cap back on his head, exposing a sharp boundary between reddened face and pale, translucent pate, "There's a slight chance it's a coincidence since the States did claim the place once. Until we're certain and clear, make sure your friends aren't on deck. Tell them to stay out of sight. It's too soon to jettison cargo, but if they come for us we might be able to stay ahead long enough to get it done."

"I'll tell them to remain below, but the cargo stays."

"We may not have a choice, señor. *Calypso*'s here, well-placed, near as fast or faster, and carries 4-inch mounts backed by Gatlings."

"We've guns and can fight."

"That's makes it piracy, señor. Besides, they'd just stand off and use deck guns. Even if you winged her and escaped, they'd know the ship. Piracy means the rope or garrote; firing squad if you're lucky. Besides, with the ammunition, guncotton, and dynamite on board, a single hit would turn us to chum."

Valencia did go below and tell everyone to keep the deck clear, but also pulled several reliable anarchists into a corner to plot an alternative. Sensing another small turn, he returned to the pilothouse to see Mexico's mercantile flag flying from the tug's mainmast, the three islets shrinking rapidly off the port quarter, and *Calypso* about six miles off, rapidly shifting from the tug's port bow to beam.

"We've come southeast a bit to pass clear, señor. Since we were about to cross his bow, opening the distance is just courtesy, and we're maintaining speed so there's no increased smoke to tell the bastard we're running for it. Had shallows off Bahia Honda and ran for them. Almost made it when the boiler went, but this time we don't even have that. They're getting a clear view, but she may still think we're a Mexican coastal freighter heading for Puerto Progresso and want to avoid an incident. We can come back to due east later."

"What else can we do?"

"Not much. There're clouds but no storm making, and it won't be dark for twelve hours or more. If she boards, Arrecife Alacranes is still close enough to claim we're in Mexican waters, but the nearest authorities are in Puerto Progresso, about sixty miles south, and *Vanguard's* probably been astern since Veracruz, so we're trapped."

"We can't just wait?"

Captain Buff resettled his cap, reached for the paired-telescopes, adding, "Nothing for it, señor, next move's theirs."

Starke observed the dark shape turn east and steady, then came further south. Confident it was *Rafael Riego,* he ordered enough turns to build momentum, without displaying a sudden speed increase that might provoke a reaction. *Vanguard* could not be seen from the flying bridge, but depending on the distance Hunter was trying to maintain after flushing her from Veracruz or trying to join *Calypso* after not finding the filibuster in port, he should be coming up fast.

Mexico's new maritime flag of three green, white, and red vertical bars without a crest flew from the tug's mainmast. It was the proper merchant ensign, she was outbound from a Mexican port, and had not done anything suspicious. Starke did not think the tug was registered in Mexico, but confirming that required boarding; and it could still be a legitimate voyage, or decoy using anarchist rumors to pull ships off the Straits of Florida. Almost no filibusters plied the trade full-time and most carried lawful cargoes between expeditions. If she just changed registry to Mexico, boarding meant diplomatic and political repercussions. That nation's president, Porfirio Díaz, would be forced to restore national honor or the American administration apologize during an election campaign. Díaz adroitly balanced foreign investment against Mexican nationalism but American cavalry entered Mexico two months before to fight Apaches, so another slight could not be tolerated.

If the filibuster resisted, as some informants claimed she would, a volatile situation could become dramatically worse; and *Vanguard* was not yet there to add her weight. They had reached the point and situation no one had an answer for in

Key West. After another look at the approaching tug, he called down through the brass voice tube, "Pilothouse, flying bridge; Mr. Dunbar, please ensure our log includes the smallest detail while in contact with that ship; and pass the word for Mr. Watson."

Martyn left for the pilothouse to be near the helmsman when Watson joined Starke on the flying bridge. They observed the tug work steadily east from Arrecife Alacranes as *Calypso* slowly increased speed south. When *Rafael Riego* began to cross their bow, right to left, Starke called down to Martyn, relieved his seniors were there, "Pilothouse, flying bridge; come right and aim for his stern. Stay on it until you think we'll pass about a mile behind; then head due south. Let's see if we can read anything on her transom."

Starke saw little risk passing a mile astern because it limited *Rafael Riego*'s ability to cause damage; and expected since the tug had right-of-way. It would also buy time and increase tension on *Rafael Riego* if she was filibustering. *Calypso* heeled slightly during the starboard turn until her bowsprit pointed astern of the tug, just behind where the spinning screw created a white-topped mound of aerated water at the spreading wake's apex. Martyn eased *Calypso* to port with small course adjustments while Chief Owen provided ranges with a stadimeter. Checking to ensure the bearing drifted left and it was time to steady, Martyn gave the order, just as Starke was about to coax him.

Rafael Riego's flag did not dip as the ships crossed within a mile of smooth, blue-green Caribbean; although it seemed nearer several hundred yards. Starke considered ordering the crew below *Calypso*'s bulwarks, but wanted them on deck acting normal; and taking shelter from a tug would not boost morale. Besides, he was quite sure *Rafael Riego* would not act until certain she was found out, or an irresistible opportunity was on offer. Like handling a viper, some fear improved concentration and sustained caution but Starke still found it difficult maintaining a casual appearance as the range closed since anarchists played by their rules and were notoriously unpredictable. He avoided continuously staring at the tug, but after a quick sweep of the horizon, put his binoculars back on her. Looking first for anything suspicious, since machine guns or Gatlings could easily reach out a mile, he caught two equally curious figures in *Rafael Riego*'s pilothouse and saw the deck cargo under tarps. Lowering the binoculars, Starke saw Watson wanted to do something and suggested, "Go ahead and wave, XO. It's appropriate since we didn't hail them."

"Yes, sir."

Watson raised his right arm and moved it back and forth. Starke shook off a momentary vision of bullets splintering the ship's bulwark, raised his binoculars, and tracked the tug's wake to a black transom slowly lifting and dropping in almost flat seas. Although he looked hard for the name and homeport, it required several attempts to confirm *Rafael Riego* in white block lettering; painted over raised letters he suspected read *J.W. Fawkes*. If there was any homeport below the name, it was illegible beyond a few yards; obscured or distorted by coats of thick, black paint. Starke lowered his binoculars after *Calypso* passed astern, then turned to Watson, "He's past, XO, let's go below."

The two officers entered the pilothouse, where Martyn had been joined by an expectant Ensign Blair. Watson tried not to smile. If Martyn's confidence needed nurturing, Blair's was in equal need of restraint. Blair was the more forward, wanting those present to hear and consider his contribution. Watson watched the young man struggle to avoid interfering with Martyn's watch when their captain asked, "Thoughts, gentlemen?"

Blair would have responded immediately, but Martyn waited for his executive officer to speak before committing. Starke shared Watson's observations regarding the junior ensigns. Blair was susceptible to premature, decisive action, while his opposite never did anything without support unless unavoidable. Neither trait was, in Starke's mind, more laudable. He hoped, between himself and Watson, the pair would mature towards some common point. Starke recalled Captain Wilkes nearly causing a second war by abducting Confederate emissaries from a British steamer; while Katherine's husband was entombed in HMS *Victoria*'s carcass because cowed officers failed to press their admiral about an impossible order. That unexpectedly started his thoughts returning to an evening on Old Point Comfort pier with the British widow, before checking himself to concentrate on what *Calypso* faced across the widening gap. Within seconds, Watson grew impatient with Martyn balking and Blair chaffing. They encouraged the most junior to speak first, forcing them to think, and insulate their conclusions from seniors' influence; but nothing was forthcoming so he turned to Starke, "It reads *Rafael Riego*, captain." Martyn parroted, "I saw the same, captain," just before Watson looked to the quartermaster, "Log everyone read *Rafael Riego*."

Once *Calypso* passed astern and opened the distance; Starke was forced to board, follow, or ignore the tug. Although he must act before dark, that was almost a full day off, so time temporarily favored *Calypso*; unless something reshuffled the deck or forced their hand. *Rafael Riego* must still be boarded; which could bring on a fight or reveal the Mexican flag flying from her mainmast halyard matched her registry and the cargo legitimate. This was what the Key West plotters could not resolve without *Rafael Riego*; and now she was less than a mile away.

Watson looked to his commander, who must break off contact by continuing on course or follow *Rafael Riego* and eliminate all uncertainty. Starke turned to the deck officer, saying casually, "Ensign Martyn, loop to starboard, bring us astern of *Rafael Riego*, then follow about two miles astern, no closer."

On *Rafael Riego*, Captain Buff and Valencia watched *Calypso* increase speed under a burst of smoke, pass a mile astern, continue another quarter mile, then swing starboard. If stars aligned, she would continue her turn north then return to Arrecife Alacranes, but Captain Buff did not expect she would and quickly proven right as the tall black bark continued turning starboard with fore and mizzen masts seeming to pivot on the main, then merge until all three lined up astern of *Rafael Riego*. When steadied, bowsprit, jibboom, and masts aligned over a stem that gently rode up and over long, undulating swells, with occasional water bursts showering out over a white bow wave.

Captain Buff saw Valencia's frustration as *Calypso* entered their wake. The young anarchist's sunburnt hands resembled a falcon's talons in the way they grasped the varnished wood cap-rails of *Rafael Riego*'s bridge-wing. He felt a brief flash of sympathy since the young man's expedition was clearly in jeopardy, but turned to the Spaniard, "That's it, señor. Starke didn't buy the flag and will signal they're boarding or put a shot across our bow; and the bastard's where he can see us dumping cargo. Until he does, we'll hold course and speed. Perhaps they'll not be able to keep up, something breaks, or we might shake them off tonight."

"We can fight."

"You may be that kind of fool, señor, but I'm not. Even if I was, the crew did not sign on to fight a warship and I won't risk their lives; as much as I'd relish plucking that jumped-up bastard from the sea. The odds . . ."

"Captain, more than a free Cuba depends on us. . . ."

"Not my fight or theirs, Manuel. Running guns is one thing; a hopeless sea fight with a rope for survivors is something else. Yankees, carpetbaggers, or traitors stick in my craw, but I saw that elephant on the river, standing by my ironclad's gun while a shell ricocheted inside. Didn't explode, thank God, but tore hell out of everything; butchered men, took off limbs, and filled the place with steel splinters. That's where I learned it's always a rich man's war and poor man's fight. Revolutions are no different."

"You were paid . . . ."

". . . to run cargo to a place in Cuba you've never seen fit to tell me; not fight a Yankee warship. It's not over yet, but shed that fight'n talk."

Valencia yielded field and pilothouse like he did when the man arrived in Veracruz. Captain Buff's predecessor seemed more eager to fight than land artillery; which provoked his angry departure. Valencia wished that fellow was in the pilothouse, relieved it was Captain Buff, and felt fear eroding his devotion to anarchy. It seemed a personal crossroads was approaching and the young anarchist began to doubt he had the courage to face death screaming, "Long live anarchy," as the gallows trap opened.

The young man's retreat cleared one distraction from Captain Buff as he watched the tug's bow slice through a swell and considered possible moves. Making a knot or two above the impressive fourteen *Rafael Riego* maintained since Veracruz might be extracted; but he already lost one ship to a boiler explosion, and Starke seemed content to remain astern while every hour brought sunset closer. *Vanguard* was still unaccounted for, so he could not write off Hunter, who could be closing fast after misjudging *Rafael Riego*'s speed. He could not be certain, so he studied the chart, tried to recall Hunter's habits, and concluded it was just possible that *Vanguard*, with a shallower draft than *Calypso*, was steaming east along the coast for the Yucatan Channel. If so, and she turned north to join the Navy ship near Arrecife Alacranes, the cutter might appear in the south and prevent *Rafael Riego* from entering Mexican water. He doubted *Vanguard* was that fast, but she was new, he could not be certain about her top speed, and it would explain why Starke seemed in no hurry to board. Captain Buff wanted time consider, readjusted his cap, glanced astern at *Calypso*, then went below for coffee; leaving the pilothouse to his mate.

Valencia needed help, since he was convinced Captain Buff would not act, and the person to provide it was the Italian Niccolo Salvaggi. The intractable anarchist was only allowed on the expedition because he was an explosives expert and Luigi Galleani intimate who helped that prominent anarchist orchestrate University of Geneva protests against Chicago hanging the Haymarket anarchists. Galleani was arrested, deported, and jailed in Italy; but Salvaggi fled to the communities of anarchists and communists in the northeast United States.

Salvaggi's journey to *Rafael Riego* began as a wealthy Florentine family's second son intended for the military. Even so, they accepted his plans to study physics, supported him at university, and continued after he announced his anarchist-communist conversion. Traveling through southern Italy and villages near his home, he found people whose natural abilities approached his own, but trapped in poverty by the wealthy and class suppression, and became an insurrectionist-anarchist. Once he advocated mass wealth re-appropriation and proclaimed just societies must come through violence, the

Salvaggi family had enough. Disowned, disinherited, and infuriated, he stormed off for the University of Geneva then exile in the United States; and joined Junta anarchists during the larger organization's May exposition in New York. He accepted their convenient alliance with the Junta to defeat and expel Spain since it would result in a fledgling government taking root; then the fight for real equality on the island could begin. Junta leaders also recognized this and feared a second Black republic so they undermined leaders like General Maceo. Once he understood and saw Cuban anarchists' unwillingness to act, Salvaggi tried to change minds through persuasion but was searching out new pastures when the *Rafael Riego* expedition surfaced. It not only had the potential to regain insurrectionist momentum and free Cuba but bring down the monarchy. If Spain's fell, Italy might follow, since its anarchists enjoyed periodic success, then other states in Europe. Convinced this could be a pivotal propaganda of the deed, whether or not it played out as envisioned, he overcame several objections, closely studied operating manuals, and boarded *Rafael Riego* as an explosives and artillery expert.

Captain Buff's demand for passengers to stay away from topside areas made sense, so Valencia ensured everyone remained below deck, except one or two at a time to get air. While passing through the large berthing space, forward of the hold and mostly under the deckhouse's aft third; he spotted the dark Italian sitting against a bulkhead with his flat laborer's cap lowered over the eyes. Valencia touched him, whispering, "Niccolo, the expedition's in trouble. A warship's following us and Captain Buff won't act."

The Italian rose with surprising authority and firmness, whispering, "Come with me."

They found an unused towing gear locker, entered, and Salvaggi closed the door, "What type warship?"

"Captain Buff says a steam screw sloop with two 4-inch guns."

"What else?"

"Gatlings and 3-pounders."

"We can't outrun it?"

"He won't attempt anything before dark but expects something before then."

Lifting the flat hat slightly, Salvaggi considered the problem aloud, "If they keep directly behind we could build a bomb then lower it over the back."

"Do we have what's needed?"

Salvaggi grimaced, "Not everything. And before dark they'd guess what we're about anyway. How close?"

"Captain Buff says two miles, just over three kilometers, and closing."

Salvaggi twisted his dark mustache, "Too far. Closer and our machine guns could take their Gatlings. The dynamite gun's good for a kilometer at most, probably less. The Hotchkiss cannons could reach, but wouldn't be fatal. Captain Buff's right; that ship's staying exactly where its 4-inch guns make the difference."

"He won't fight anyway; says its piracy."

"All laws suppressing the masses must be cast aside for real change, Manuel. We'd be ready if the committee kept the first master but it may still be possible to disable or sink them and get the guns through. Think of the propaganda. Anarchist tug sinks warship. If we rammed, then detonated the cargo. . . ."

"Cuba needs that cargo, and what about us?"

"We might get away in the whaleboats, but if not," he grinned, ". . . hurrah for anarchy."

"Would the rest join?"

"International anarchists will. Cuban anarchists might, but see independence as their first step and don't want to lose fighters. The soldiers of fortune won't, and the crew will follow Captain Buff."

"Let's gather the most reliable and consider what's needed."

As though patiently dissecting a physics problem for eager students, Salvaggi explained, "If you insist Manuel, but bold action's needed. Think of the propaganda of the deed achieved by sinking that ship."

"We must get the cargo through, Niccolo."

"Of course, brother, of course."

Valencia and Salvaggi moved quietly through berthing, gathering supporters while Captain Buff finished his coffee and returned to the pilothouse. Once there, he studied a chart, looking up periodically. The scene astern seemed more painting than pursuit with the elegant black-hulled bark cleaving an empty blue-green sea, her single straw-yellow stack releasing a translucent gray blemish against a pale-blue sky filled with tall cumulus clouds.

Ensign Blair assumed the forenoon watch from Martyn, saw *Calypso*'s quarry continue unmolested, and shifted to the flying bridge. He was standing beside the polished brass voice tube to the pilothouse quietly impatient with the captain's hesitance when Starke motioned to him. Blair crossed the flying bridge to their enigmatic commander, "Yes, sir."

Starke allowed himself another look past the ship's foremast and bowsprit then lowered his binoculars, "You've my permission to swing across *Rafael Riego's* wake to vary our relative position. Don't be excessive and lose ground, but let's not make it easy for them. They might try jury-rigging a torpedo and dropping it astern. I'll be in my cabin, so watch for anything unusual, act as you believe prudent, and call if needed."

Blair realized dwelling on Starke's inaction distracted from proposing this before told, so dejectedly replied, "Yes, sir."

Starke weighed any additional burden on their stokers and steam plant by leaving the wake against the possibility of striking a torpedo cast astern, although both were slight. Most filibusters lacked the expertise, material, and time to construct such a weapon but *Rafael Riego* supposedly carried artillery experts and rumors of purpose-built torpedoes shipped to Cuba by other filibuster expeditions were appearing in some newspapers. Since any damage could end their strange pursuit it seemed prudent to avoid the risk.

The ensign left in charge was relieved and elated his commander was no longer there; while his counterpart, Martyn, would have fretted the loss of a security blanket. Which officer required closer monitoring was a tossup. Martyn was prone to hesitate or call for his commander before acting, but giving Blair the slightest leeway invited action. The corners of Starke's mouth lifted in what passed for a smile. Even the small discretion given probably left Blair working through how to best board *Rafael Riego*; but he would act, the standoff could last hours, and Starke had other tasks.

Yamashita greeted him as he entered the day cabin and asked if he required anything before returning to his pantry with Thaddeus in tow. The feline's partiality for the steward meant Arrecife Alacranes fishing yielded another fresh meal. Starke sat and began updating his personal log at the wood table. The boatswain pipes that signaled sick and officer calls while he was on the flying bridge announced ten-thirty sweepers and morning drill completion while he worked. When needing a break, he set the log aside, retrieved his pipe, and then ignited a fresh bowl. The tobacco sputtered then glowed as air passed down through moist, brown, shreds, then out the black stem whose scared lip evidenced periods of anxiety and heavy weather. Starke leaned back and found it hard to believe *Calypso* was at sea; except for the triple-expansion engine's steady rumble transmitted through her deck and slight roll each time *Rafael Riego*'s wake was crossed. The day was slightly hot for the season but exceptionally pleasant except for the filibuster conundrum. Starke disciplined himself to relax during lulls and, taking another puff, hoped those on the filibuster off *Calypso*'s bow would not.

There was a knock on the door and Watson entered, "Good morning, captain. I was just on the flying bridge. Dunbar and Owen are preparing noon sights and Blair's willing something to happen on our friend."

"I suspected as much, please take a seat, XO."

"Thanks, captain. Officer's call's over. Osbourne and O'Leary report our plant's performing well, but the distiller could do better. Martyn and Weaver are replacing two boat falls that twisted. Conrad will bring you the binnacle list later. The crew's healthy, but that's no surprise since we've not closed land or visited tropical ports; and there've been unusually few accidents."

"Very well, XO; and your thoughts on our friend?"

"Blair wants to break out cutlasses and boarding pikes, fire a broadside, then board in the smoke; but I'm curious why you've not used international code to request boarding, or require they identify themselves."

"I considered both, but changing our behavior could provoke a reaction; and it must be on our terms when the time comes. Besides, we've no evidence to justify boarding a ship flying Mexico's ensign, especially if our suspicions prove incorrect."

"But she's registered in Brazil."

"We've only reports of that and she just left Mexico so her registry may have changed. The Mexican flag also offers better cover since any incident could worsen things on the border or risk American investments. We'll enjoy the weather for now and let them sweat until dark."

"I suppose my inclination is to act before they've a chance to lose us, captain."

"Ever hunted rabbits, XO?"

"Jack rabbits."

"Where I grew up it was cotton tails. They mostly stay put when you walk through their territory, but grow anxious if you pause. Wait and they'll break cover, then it's down to their speed, your shooting, and who's more startled."

"Yes, sir, but . . ."

"I'm concerned about tonight, but let them stew until then. *Vanguard* might show up or something else happen. By the way, are you still writing Captain Albert's daughter?"

"Ah . . . yes, sir."

"Good. She seems a lively and intelligent young lady."

Caught off guard, the executive officer mumbled, "I think so captain; with your permission."

"Of course, I plan to return to the flying bridge after eating."

Chapter Seven
Francisco de Montejo

Starke returned following Yamashita's poached red snapper and rice. Martyn's port section assumed the afternoon watch, with *Calypso* two miles astern of *Rafael Riego* and cutting slowly across her wake in no predictable pattern. Arrecife Alacranes had disappeared astern, there was a clear horizon under white clouds, and birds cut lazy circles above patches of passing seaweed. From the flying bridge, he saw the reason Martyn sent for him, a faint disruption on the horizon that was intermittently blocked by the bark's foremast or subsumed by thick, black smoke rolling over the sea to leeward from *Rafael Riego*'s funnels. To Starke, dense smoke was confirmation the tug burned different coal trying to pass the reef unnoticed but his primary interest was the possibility of a westbound ship.

At the chart table, Starke considered whether the newcomer might prove useful and suspected it would be a few minutes before *Rafael Riego* noticed since *Calypso* had an alert man in the foretop charged only with lookout duties. He studied the chart, thinking most traffic would follow the more heavily traveled shipping lane north of Arrecife Alacranes. This was likely a small merchant bound for Veracruz from Cuba's north coast or Yucatan Channel. It could also be a warship since Consul-general Lee would have received his letter and passed some contents to Weyler; but Spain's overstretched and penurious navy was not known for alacrity, and Mexico's corvette based in Veracruz, *Zaragoza*, was circumnavigating the globe. Other nations were in Caribbean, so it might be British, French, Austrian, German, or a South American coming west from the Yucatan Channel.

As they closed, Starke watched the increasingly distinct smoke column place this new player slightly north on a near reciprocal course to *Rafael Riego* and *Calypso*. With a closing speed approaching thirty knots, they would be close aboard sooner than the inexperienced might think, so he scanned the entire horizon before his binoculars rested on *Rafael Riego*'s fantail. Two men emerged from the deckhouse then walked to the stern where they were joined by another pair and began removing battens, rolling back a tarpaulin, and lifting cargo hatch covers. Crates were soon being manhandled to the main deck, then dragged and pushed forward. Starke sent for Watson when the first pair returned to the tug's pilothouse.

Calypso's executive officer entered her pilothouse as sweepers and commence work were piped, checked the chart, then climbed to the flying bridge; pausing momentarily halfway up the ladder to absorb the sea, its smells, and warm breeze as the bark plowed through humid air at fourteen knots. Starke was at the port side, beyond the brass voice tubes, his figure split at the waist by a canvas windscreen below and sea above. Walking to him, Watson began, "Captain, you sent for me."

"Yes, XO. Change afternoon drill to general quarters. Use the thirty minutes grace to set it quietly. Get the magazine keys and issue service rounds."

"Yes, sir. Are we boarding, captain?"

"No, but something's up and we've time to prepare without advertising. After that, let's see what develops."

Watson snapped a quick salute, "Aye, aye, sir."

Starke returned it before resuming his watch on *Rafael Riego* and the third ship, just beginning to take shape. On *Rafael Riego*, Captain Buff's thoughts roughly paralleled Starke's, except he half-expected the third ship was *Vanguard*. If so, *Rafael Riego* was cornered.

Hearing a noise behind him, Captain Buff lowered his paired-telescopes as Valencia and another passenger entered. Both looked grim and single-action Colt pistols in thick canvas holsters hung from heavy cartridge belts. These were not from the tug's arms locker so they obviously breached the cargo. Captain Buff's thick neck compressed into broad shoulders, "What's this, Manuel?"

"Preparations, captain."

"What preparations?"

"To fight our way through. If *Calypso* comes alongside we'll use machine guns and if they board we'll take hostages."

"So it's mutiny and piracy?"

The passenger, until this moment just a rough-looking but nondescript member of twenty-odd insurrecto recruits, lifted his holster flap then rested his palm on the old Colt Army's worn wood grips. Captain Buff could drop the swarthy dilettante with one punch, but held off. The fool clearly thought merely possessing a gun assured compliance and ended dissent, but Captain Buff had seen enough combat and bar fights to know holding a weapon was not using it. Of greater concern were the obvious zealot's intense, dark eyes that belied his professorial tone, "Irrelevant; this cargo will go through. Besides, they're only waiting for night to sink us without witnesses."

Captain Buff's frustration, exasperation, and anger soared; powerful fists brushed his trouser seams. The anarchists were two blows from unconsciousness; but also unpredictable and probably backed by others. Besides, it seemed the game was over with *Calypso* astern, an unknown ship approaching, and

Vanguard probably coming up fast. Captain Buff's hair-trigger temper could be damped by a well-honed survival instinct; and remembering a warrior's coldness in Starke's eyes off the Florida Keys, he knew it would this time.

The master deliberately turned his broad back to them when crates were dragged across the forecastle, saw what was happening, and then turned to look aft. He raised the paired-telescopes, rechecked the rapidly closing ship astern, lowered them, then spoke to Valencia and Salvaggi, "I assume you dragged those crates forward in full view of *Calypso* and are aware of the ship ahead?"

The two men glanced at each other as Captain Buff continued in a low, steady voice, "She's too far north for Porto Progresso, and south for Veracruz, so there's a damn fair chance she's a cutter or warship."

While the pair debated in harsh whispers, Captain Buff walked past to the narrow deck outside the pilothouse to look over the uncovered fantail hatch, surrounded by equipment, towards *Calypso*. When he returned, Valencia ventured, "They'll think we're rearranging cargo."

Captain Buff dropped his paired-telescopes' lanyard forcefully over a hook below the center window in disgust then turned on the pair with a neck consisting of three flesh rolls forming a collar between jaws and shoulders. After staring at both, with teeth clenched, his voice rose menacingly, "Then you stupid bastards can explain why *Calypso*'s set general quarters?"

Valencia snatched a set of paired-telescopes, moved to the spot Captain Buff just vacated, and trained them on *Calypso*. Her sailors were moving purposely about the main deck and a group forward was removing the canvas tarp covering her forward mount. He spent several minutes quietly staring before reentering the pilothouse; just as Salvaggi ducked below, leaving Captain Buff writing in the deck log. The master finished his entry, turned, crooked a finger to summon Valencia to the chart table then pointed to the open book while handing him a freshly dipped pen. Without emotion, in a tone that brooked no argument, he said, "Señor Valencia, you will sign this entry. Your fellow mutineer provided his after some propaganda of the deed nonsense; whatever in hell that meant."

Valencia's stomach clenched as he read, "On September 11, 1896, approximately 110 nautical miles southeast of Arrecife Alacranes, the owners' agent, Mr. Manuel Valencia y Gomis, and passenger, Mr. Niccolo Salvaggi, took command of *Rafael Riego* over the objections of her legal master, Fachtna Harler, known as Captain Buff."

The ship closing *Rafael Riego* and *Calypso* from the east was completely unaware and saw only two ships that would pass relatively close on an otherwise deserted sea. She was the small, flush-decked Spanish gunboat *Francisco de Montejo*, whose ram bow was slicing neatly through nearly calm water for Veracruz by way of Arrecife Alacranes. The third ship of the *Hernan Cortés* class, named for conquistadors, her 156-foot steel hull had a beam of twenty-two feet, draft of seven, and displaced 295 tons. Looking through the small pilothouse's open windows, Teniente de Navio Emiliano Mendoza y Aguilar watched two smoke columns off his port bow through Zeiss binoculars, a gift from his father. Neither ship was close enough to identify so he let the glasses hang from a strap around his neck. The day was good and weather clear but neither matched his mood, and they allowed time to brood. Except for an inopportune Havana visit, *Francisco de Montejo* would be patrolling off Puerto Rico; not on a speculative filibuster mission. His gunboat brought dispatches to Cuba's captain general and was coaling for the return to San Juan when Consul-general Lee provided information that matched Spanish reports about *Rafael Riego*. Captain General Weyler immediately directed his naval commanders to sortie *Francisco de Montejo* after the filibuster. Since the Gulf of Mexico was vast and mission vague, Mendoza calculated his best and sole opportunity to intercept the tug would be off Veracruz as she left. The admiral accepted his plan, knowing the odds laughable, because it could be done, sounded logical, and he viewed the exercise as a gesture anyway.

Francisco de Montejo left Havana two days earlier and steamed steadily west before raising the two ships. Mendoza resented orders sending a coastal gunboat far into the Gulf of Mexico on a gratuitous mission during hurricane season. *Francisco de Montejo* could steam 3,000 miles with her sixty-seven tons of coal, if a good quality. However, Navy stocks in the West Indies were mediocre at best, which cut distance and speed so the same triple-expansion engine making almost fifteen knots on sea trials seldom achieved thirteen; with ten normal for any distance. Since filibusters favored oceangoing tugs that equaled or exceeded this there was little chance of running one down on calm seas, let alone rough ones. Another reason Mendoza wanted any meeting to occur just after the filibuster cleared Veracruz was a rumor *Rafael Riego* was willing to fight. If true, she would not have any time to mount serious weapons before they met. *Francisco de Montejo*'s two 57mm Hotchkiss quick-firing guns were equal to the task, but their two 22mm twin-barreled Nordenfelt guns had an unreliable lever-firing mechanism. If *Rafael Riego* mounted some of the Hotchkiss guns, she would have a straightforward, lightweight weapon effective to 1,000 yards with three-pound shells that traveled far beyond. His rapid firing Nordenfelts' smaller shells could pierce thin-skinned ships to something like 1,500 yards, but close in, where he would be to board, Maxim machine guns would be better suited, and *Rafael Riego* reportedly carried those as well.

Mendoza was experienced and tested. He saw combat in coastal actions during the Melillan Campaign against Morocco, partly caused by the taking of a Spanish merchant ship and selling her crew as slaves. That unanticipated conflict prevented his joining *Nautilus*, under Captain Fernando Villaamil, a well-known officer and family friend, for her circumnavigation, but gave him the newly built *Francisco de Montejo* as his first command. After taking delivery from the builder a year before, he steamed her from Scotland to Cadiz along the British, French, and Spanish coasts. Although intended to operate in the Mediterranean out of Cartagena, the fleet's latest addition was diverted to the West Indies station where her type was urgently needed. Every available small ship was being sent while more were building, bought, and leased; although how the nation would pay for additional ships, much less maintenance and operation, was left unsaid. Crewing was also a problem since experienced sailors were far scarcer than the poorly paid conscripts transfusing Spain's army in Cuba and the Philippines.

Mendoza watched as decreasing range revealed a large tug several miles distant on near reciprocal course, with a large bark astern. Although looking for one ship, taking a quick look would not delay his passage significantly and the log entry might prove useful when he returned empty-handed. *Francisco de Montejo* came smoothly to port, aiming far enough ahead of the leading ship so he could come right to pass down its port side within hailing range. His apprehension grew as he saw they were traveling at a fair turn of speed; perhaps in company or one pursuing the other. Shifting binoculars to the tug, Mendoza saw two legs emerge from the smoke column's base, sent the crew to action stations, and watched the large

Spanish battle ensign soar to the mainmast truck.

As *Francisco de Montejo* and *Rafael Riego* consumed the sea between, Salvaggi was on the forecastle with two others working furiously to rig a dynamite gun that could fire over the tug's bullnose. He considered their Hotchkiss guns, but calculated the recoil would cause problems, securing them time consuming, and the effort obvious to the warship astern. Two Maxim guns on tripods were also uncrated, sited with the muzzles peeking over the forecastle bulwarks, ammunition belts positioned, and water-filled cooling canisters attached. Meanwhile, anarchists carrying Colt handguns in canvas holsters and cartridge belts locked dissenters into the large berthing compartment; then stationed armed men in pilothouse and engine room.

Salvaggi directed everything while Valencia studied the approaching ship, trying to convince himself it was a small coastal freighter, then a large white-hulled yacht, before deciding to wait for Captain Buff's verdict. As it grew larger and more distinct before turning rapidly to port, Valencia no longer needed confirmation. The broadside view revealed a slightly curved stem, overhanging transom, single raked stack, whaleboats swinging in davits, and two thin masts. At the same time, a dark bundle shot to the mainmast truck and broke to reveal Spain's red ensign with a single broad yellow band behind the royal coat of arms. Captain Buff lowered his paired-telescopes, turned to the young anarchist, observing, "The Spaniard's flying her battle flag, señor. You've been sold out. Best yield to *Calypso*. American courtrooms are healthier than a Havana wall."

Two miles astern of *Rafael Riego*, Starke watched the third ship close on the filibuster, unable to determine nationality and whether it was a warship or large yacht, but the white hull, fine lines, overhanging stern, and ram bow meant she was no merchant ship. Through binoculars, he scrutinized her hull for sponsons, gun mounts, and locomotive torpedo ports or mounts. On *Calypso*, every general quarters station reported manned and ready. The executive officer was with the stern 4-inch mount and repair party. O'Leary reported engineering standing by and Conrad sent word their wardroom operating theater was ready. Osbourne had the deck, and stood beside Starke, with Ensign Martyn conning from the pilothouse below the flying bridge. Behind the ensign and helmsman, Dunbar and Chief Owen were at the chart table, plotting and taking notes.

Starke watched the graceful white ship close *Rafael Riego* then come smoothly about as Spain's red and yellow banner unfurled against a blue sky seeded with white clouds rising from gray underbellies. Letting binoculars dangle from their neck lanyard, he retrieved his pipe, unconsciously rasped its wooden bowl with a scraper, then turned casually to the chief engineer, "Ready to maneuver, Mr. Osbourne?"

"Yes, sir. Engineering's standing by to answer all bells."

"Very well, put us on a northeast course and hoist our battle flags."

Calypso heeled starboard as she came to port at nearly fourteen knots, causing the interval between *Calypso* and *Rafael Riego* to open. Three large American ensigns rose to their mastheads above furled sails. Continuing to fuss with his pipe, Starke looked to Osbourne, "Open the tug four miles, then turn east and slow. I want to avoid interfering with the Spaniard, but remain near enough to act. Keep our broadside to the tug and main battery ready but center-lined. With one under a Spanish ensign and the other Mexico's, we'll keep clear for now."

More to himself than Osbourne, Starke added quietly under his breath, "And hope the Don knows what he's about." He then bit the unlit pipe stem and adjusted his cap visor the binoculars had pushed upward slightly. Once satisfied, he set the pipe aside. The gunboat appeared slower than the filibuster so its commander took a position for boarding that was slightly ahead of *Rafael Riego* then a quick flash and dirty-gray smoke burst from the gunboat's forward mount. The round splashed off the tug's bow as the report reached *Calypso*. Both ships went nearly dead in the water, with the small gunboat less than 100 yards off *Rafael Riego*'s port bow and lowering a whaleboat while its forward mount covered the tug. This exposed her starboard side to *Rafael Riego* but was necessary to hold position, ensure the field of fire was not blocked by foremast stays, and avoid being rammed. It seemed the boarding was going smoothly.

Starke was considering whether he may have been unnecessarily cautious and intelligence reports exaggerated as the whaleboat closed the tug; and how to best meet with the Spaniard to confirm *Rafael Riego*'s registry and whether any Americans were on board. Suddenly, *Rafael Riego*'s Mexican flag came down at the run and was immediately replaced with the flag flying from *Calypso*'s three masts while he was mulling protocol.

A perplexed Osbourne asked, "Captain, why raise that flag knowing we'll see it?"

Starke saw several reasons, so he responded without lowering the binoculars, "Mr. Osbourne, turn southeast, keep our batteries clear, and don't let the gunboat drift between us and the tug. Have Mister Dunbar log the new colors and time."

Calypso steadied on her new course then slowed. She was nearly four miles north and slightly east of *Rafael Riego* with the gunboat was just off the tug's port bow. Starke thought the spectacle resembled a bullfight, with *Rafael Riego* playing the bull and Spanish gunboat the matador. For this tercio, however, the picador flew the bull's colors. The filibuster had unsettled the Spaniard and left the gunboat unsure of *Calypso*'s intentions, but Starke had few immediate options. The tug was obviously under false colors, but the latest flag may have been raised to justify future claims there were American citizens on board and force *Calypso*'s assistance. It also gave *Calypso* the right to board, so it was possible the sudden change of ensigns was a ruse to clear the gunboat then run east again; hoping *Calypso* would temporarily shield *Rafael Riego* in the same way Admiral Benham protected American merchant ships from Brazilian warships blockading Rio de Janeiro.

Starke began to think *Rafael Riego* was using the flag as a ruse, preparing to bolt once the whaleboat crossing under oars was far enough away to require time to retrieve. The ships appeared to drift, with *Rafael Riego*'s profile shortening and her bow angling towards the gunboat, when *Francisco de Montejo*'s stack belched thick, black smoke, indicating her commander was responding. *Rafael Riego* followed, then, as the gunboat gathered way, its starboard midship vanished behind a broad water column clawing up the hull and pouring over her deck as though a moored torpedo detonated; then the muted explosion reached *Calypso*. The column hung several seconds in the air then collapsed as its detonation heeled the Spaniard to port and left her slowly rocking slowly while the surface calmed. At the same time a machine gun's sharp staccato reached *Calypso*'s flying bridge. Starke could only imagine the confusion, shock, and surprise of being struck by a dynamite gun. The filibuster apparently jury-rigged one in its bow, so the ability to point and train was nonexistent, but it had fired on a national ship so no matter registry or flag *Rafael Riego* had turned pirate and *Calypso* must assist.

Chapter Eight
Commence Action

Rafael Riego firing on a Spanish gunboat swept away legal niceties. Grasping the brass voice tube's funnel, Starke twisted it towards him then spoke deliberately and clearly to the pilothouse, "This is the captain, Mr. Dunbar, log: While flying American flag, *Rafael Riego* fired on Spanish gunboat causing unknown damage. This ship is engaging pirate. Then enter our position."

Dunbar acknowledged while Starke made a last, quick sweep of the horizon. *Calypso*'s 4-inch rifles outranged any weapons the tug might jury-rig, and she was equally fast, so the attack may have been calculated to mortally damage or sink the gunboat, prevent boarding, and force *Calypso* to choose rescue or pursuit. The dynamite gun's first dart-like shell must have bounced off the Spaniard and was the smaller artillery version. A heavier naval type would have finished her and another round might still. The gunboat needed to get clear and return fire but was laced with machine gun bullets. Her commander might also think *Calypso* was in league with her assailant so Starke could not rely on being seen as an ally; especially since Spain believed the American navy gave tacit support to filibusters before the *Virginius* affair, some years before. Starke chose to allay suspicions and succor the gunboat by attacking *Rafael Riego* immediately. He released *Calypso*'s main batteries and starboard 3-pounder when in range; despite risk of hitting the gunboat or blowing up the tug close aboard. He also resolved to end the machine-gunning, which could only be done by the bark's Gatlings, and closing to under 2,000 yards. He pointed *Calypso* slightly east of the gunboat and increased speed to shorten the range, block *Rafael Riego*'s escape east, and keep his main batteries clear of masts and superstructure. With black smoke pouring from her stack and their ship maneuvering, gun captains were cautioned to avoid hitting the Spaniard, but clouds of gun smoke and the ships' proximity meant the gunboat risked a stray shell. Starke might have held off firing longer except for confidence in their two gun captains.

As he surveyed the crippled gunboat through binoculars, and Chief Owen called out ranges, *Calypso*'s forward 4-inch mount belched flame with flat crack accompanied by the sensation of something striking the starboard side. The noise hurt his ears, and he hoped gun crews blocked theirs with cotton. The gun captains were deliberate and their crews well-drilled but Starke knew the corrosive effect of combat's urgent unreality as he saw a dark shape speed across blue sky, land 500 yards short, skip over *Rafael Riego,* then detonate beyond; a perfect first round. It must have screamed past just above the tug's fantail. A second followed that appeared to distract those manning the dynamite gun. It went slightly high, passed between her two masts, barely missed the stacks, struck the sea beyond, sank immediately, and detonated; causing a mushroom-shaped geyser of white water. Although tug and gunboat remained engaged, the sounds reaching the bark came from small arms and machine guns because the dynamite gun fired without noise or smoke and the gunboat's main battery, an exposed open mount, was abandoned to the lead hailstorm clawing her main deck and bridge. Rifle fire from Spanish sailors on the gunboat and in the boarding party responded with greater courage than effect.

Calypso's third 4-inch round screamed over *Rafael Riego* at funnel level, skipped across the sea, then detonated. Starke noted the forward mount was shooting a touch high. *Rafael Riego* still fired gamely at her closest adversary, hoping for a fatal strike. Starke suspected filibuster and gunboat were locked together at pointblank range. The tug's improvised dynamite gun was unable to depress its muzzle enough to hit the gunboat, but opening the range and maneuvering to accomplish this might end all hope of escaping east. Breaking away from the crippled gunboat would also diminish the machine gun fire preventing her opponent from using deck guns. The gunboat's situation was no less palatable. Another near miss would split more hull seams and she could not continue absorbing the relentless machine gun fire as her crew passed through the surreal delay between the dynamite gun's cough, a round landing, and several seconds wait before five pounds of nitro-gelatin detonated. If she tried to steam off, however, *Rafael Riego* might gain a better opportunity to hit her and would escape.

This might have continued until one or both sank but *Calypso* steaming to block *Rafael Riego's* path east forced the filibuster to extricate herself and try to escape, or finish off the gunboat. Starke decided not to steer for the engaged ships, knowing this risked Spanish lives and some might accuse him of shyness, but calculated he could do little if *Rafael Riego* was intent on sinking the gunboat at the cost of her own demise. Check fire was ordered and, as the wounded Spaniard slid past the forward mount's sights, Starke watched Blair from a flying bridge permeated by gunpowder's acrid smell as the ensign's discipline triumphed over ardor and the mount went silent.

Starke blinked, his eyelids gritty from small powder grains, then lifted an empty pipe and clamped it between his teeth without thought. When *Calypso* was far enough down her track to unmask the aft 4-inch mount its first round exploded close under *Rafael Riego*'s fantail, drenching those working there. Several feet left would have disabled the filibuster and a few more could have been fatal. It was enough. *Rafael Riego* saw the trap closing, decided there might be time pass ahead of *Calypso*, and began to disengage. This left Starke seconds to choose between pursuing the filibuster and assisting the small gunboat already listing heavily to starboard. *Calypso* sailors cheered as *Rafael Riego*'s shape lengthened, her two stacks billowed black smoke, and she began gathering way. Steadying on a due east course south of the gunboat she continued hammering the Spaniard with machine gun fire until well away. As the gunboat's boarding party rowed back to assist, their shipmates savaged by *Rafael Riego* rallied when the fusillade slackened, increased small arms fire, and re-manned gun mounts. More by chance than anything else, one of their main battery's last rounds clipped the aft corner of *Rafael Riego*'s deckhouse and detonated in the air alongside.

The Spanish warship, attacked by *Rafael Riego* under an American flag and within sight of *Calypso*, might sink in minutes, leaving survivors with the full whaleboat, what could be lowered, and floating debris. Should that occur without *Calypso*'s safe haven, Starke expected the fortunate left floating would drown immediately and the remainder face voracious sharks. The crew was probably around fifty and he nearly bit through the unlit pipe stem without realizing.

Calypso was making full speed with the listing gunboat just forward of her starboard beam and *Rafael Riego* off the port bow when Starke turned due east, placing his ship on a parallel course about two miles north of the filibuster. As the gunboat fell astern, slowly settling with an increasing starboard list, Weaver looked to the flying bridge where his commander concentrated on the tug. Nature or nurture, it was not the first time he saw a veteran campaigner's detachment in Starke; but never a brawler's zeal, even today. It was simultaneously reassuring and ominous. He heard yelling as they passed the ravaged gunboat, knew Starke would not stop, and released two of the large, white life rings nestled in brackets on either side of the fantail. Watching them bob in the churning wake as *Calypso*'s stern squatted slightly from acceleration even his poor Spanish understood they were cheering and shouting encouragement.

Calypso remained astern of *Rafael Riego* and about a mile north as they steamed due east at top speed. Boilers fed with bituminous coal for power sent smoke rolling from stacks while engineers concentrated on black needles quivering on the white faces of round gages. It was now their race since *Calypso* was designed to engage off either side, not ahead or astern. Once bowsprit, rigging, and superstructure no longer masked her batteries that would change, but until then Starke must yaw and lose ground to fire. Sailors on the main deck, and especially the forecastle, crouched behind bulwarks too thin to shield them from machine gun bursts stitching across the sea and sporadically leaving thumb-sized indentations or splintered gouges on the hull.

Starke left the race to his chief engineer, Lieutenant (j.g.) Adrian Osborne, and studied *Rafael Riego*'s fantail through binoculars. He could see one group struggle and argue as they wrestled a long tube; apparently manhandling the forecastle dynamite gun aft or mounting a second to use on *Calypso*. A single round from a naval or coast artillery type could sink a ship but the tug carried a small horse artillery version. These lacked range and had a complex firing mechanism consisting of a small black powder charge to generate compressed air that forced its long, finned-projectile through a smoothbore tube. Starke guessed the jury-rigged mount would be fixed, or nearly so, which meant the greatest risk for *Calypso* was coming too close and almost directly astern of the tug; although the damage done to the steel gunboat from a near-miss was not lost on anyone.

Rafael Riego and *Calypso* raced east knowing the outcome turned on speed and stokers' stamina, barring some casualty. They were almost evenly matched for the short term but time passed the advantage to *Calypso*. Once Starke chose to abandon the gunboat, *Rafael Riego* had almost no chance. Too much daylight remained, there was no shoal water for cover, and the bark appeared a knot or two faster. With more stokers, she would slowly gain a little each hour the pursuit continued. The filibuster would be overhauled, the bark's main batteries unmasked, and tug torn apart by 4-inch rifles. This would not change even if the tug held out until nightfall since *Calypso* carried powerful searchlights; but having fired on the gunboat, *Rafael Riego* was committed to stay the course, avoid breaking down, and hope *Calypso* suffered an engine casualty or strayed into the dynamite gun's range and narrow field of fire.

Starke calculated he would be in position well before dark, but stern chases were fought by mile, yard, then foot; and won by perseverance and avoiding mistakes. He checked the helmsman, was confident a tight course was being steered using minute helm changes, and then called an engineer cadet to the flying bridge. He wanted someone to let the black gang know what was happening and everything depended on them. Later, as the excited cadet vanished down the ladder, Starke fondled his pipe, placed it in his mouth, then returned to *Rafael Riego* steaming hard off the starboard bow, a little over two miles away; her long wake paralleling *Calypso's*.

Action could not resume soon enough for Blair or his gun captain. Both stood near the forward 4-inch gun, willing the rigging to clear. The ensign would periodically walk aft to the pedestal-mounted Hotchkiss 3-pounder below the pilothouse. That gun continued to slowly aim and fire, but iron sights made gunlaying difficult and it was hard to tell if rounds not falling short were on target or over. Above, with his hands on the rail, Starke bit down on the unlit pipe, weighing alternatives. When *Calypso* overhauled *Rafael Riego*, he wanted to avoid risking the Spaniard's fate and saw no reason to expect a peaceful boarding even if the filibuster appeared to yield. In the meantime, they would probably try mounting one or more Hotchkiss guns and, although difficult to work a field piece from a ship's deck, a lucky shot was possible. Starke stroked his sparse beard concealing a jaw so tight it was slightly white, and wavered between closing the tug if she asked for quarter, or remain at a safe distance and shoot her to pieces. Either way, the next move was *Rafael Riego's*.

Stokers in *Calypso's* boiler room understood the contest playing out above rested on their sore shoulders, aching backs, and tired limbs. Osbourne was passing information from the flying bridge to O'Leary; who moved from fire to engine room, encouraging, tweaking, and ordering fading engineers to the topside ladder. Lead stokers Dylan Jones and Delmar Kemp set the example by exhorting their men to work fast, smooth, and proper. Already unbearably hot and humid temperatures raced up past triple digits as shovels sent dusty coal lumps through boiler fire-holes to spread across the glowing bed. A galvanized water tub placed between boilers enabled the fire room's black gang to thrust head or handkerchief through coal dust surface scum to the relatively clean, warm water beneath. When it became too filthy, the contents were dumped to the bilges and replaced with fresh. Stokers rotated every twenty or thirty minutes; and those passing out, or about to, were ordered to a shaded spot on the main deck to recover and drink the clear, tepid water waiting for them. Many, with mind and body in conflict, stayed only until they could force themselves back to the moist, hot spaces, permeated by hot boilers and loud machinery.

Near the aft 4-inch mount, Watson curbed a gun crew eager to outdo their forward rivals. Its gun captain, Beauregard Kirby, was from a West Virginia mountain family that hunted for whatever could not be coaxed from a rocky hill-farm. Firearms came naturally and he found it inconceivable to be paid for studying them, shooting, and travel. A snap shot back home often decided whether it was meat or beans for supper so he instinctively took advantage of a fluke swell that briefly offered his first clear opening. The aft 4-inch rifle recoiled with an eardrum-shattering crack that shook the ship and drowned out the 3-pounder's slow, deliberate detonations. The first round landed over, and a second short, but Kirby had the sea's rhythm so his third crashed through the aft funnel's base to explode just off *Rafael Riego*'s starboard side. Hot air and smoke forced up through the debris contributed more damage until the mangled stack was supported only by stays. Less than a minute later, it toppled over the starboard side, towed briefly in a confused water spray, and then broke free when the last stay parted with a sharp crack.

As the funnel rolled over, bobbed briefly astern, and sank, black smoke, steam, and debris transformed the filibuster's two merging smoke-columns into a broad-based cloud billowing out from behind the forward stack's single plume. Although the aft funnel did not drag long alongside, it was enough to cause the helmsman to overcorrect; rotating *Rafael Riego*'s stern towards *Calypso* and pointing her bow at the

Yucatan Peninsula, fifty miles south. She kept to this new course, at reduced speed, and *Calypso* turned with her. Ensign Dunbar and Chief Owen estimated thirty-five miles to shoal water and with *Rafael Riego* running at eight to ten knots they would reach it before evening. Since *Calypso* now had an overwhelming speed advantage, Starke resolved to end this chase long before then. Within minutes, the bark was on a parallel course off the tug's port quarter where it could easily block any turn east without coming within range of the dynamite gun. It also partially masked the bark's main battery, so fifteen minutes later a flash on *Rafael Riego*'s fantail preceded the dull, flat crack of a Hotchkiss field piece. Starke did not see the round land, but it served notice the filibuster succeeded in mounting a field gun. As *Calypso*'s Hotchkiss and Gatling guns continued firing, Starke observed the fall of shot through binoculars then unusual activity on the tug. A few people were emerging on deck and grouping near her pilothouse while a larger crowd on the fantail grew increasingly animated until some jumped, or were forced, overboard.

Seeing this, he eased *Calypso* into *Rafael Riego*'s wake, slowed to bare steerageway, ordered the ready lifeboat lowered, then had it set adrift. While completing this, a large white water burst erupted midway between the ships. Someone on the newly mounted stern dynamite gun must have seen *Calypso* drift across his iron sights, succumbed to temptation, and fired. Estimating range at sea was difficult, even for those experienced, and the weapon was only effective to 900 yards, so the dart-like round landed well short of the intended target. The explosion briefly distracted sailors launching the boat, but the sea painter was soon released and it was adrift on calm seas. As *Calypso* turned slightly to assist, her 4-inch guns were unmasked and fired simultaneously.

Thirty-five pound shells screamed over the tug, plunged into the sea off its bow, and created two water columns; then the gunners' brief window snapped shut when the bark came to port and resumed the chase. As *Calypso* gained speed, it left behind a wake dotted by bobbing heads struggling to remain afloat amongst other debris or clinging to what flotsam could support them. As the bark slid past, with bow wave and wake adding to their misery, the castaways looked up at sailors along her deck, pointing astern to the whaleboat while shouting direction and encouragement.

As *Calypso* closed *Rafael Riego*'s port quarter to just over a mile, Starke saw a small black flag replace American colors and had it logged; knowing the severely injured tug running for the distant shallows just rejected quarter or surrender. Wounded, perhaps dying, *Rafael Riego* made several attempts to suddenly slow and surprise *Calypso* with the stern dynamite gun. Starke parried by turning or slowing to maintain the interval, while continuing to block her escape east. Finally, with its fire falling off to the occasional machine gun burst or Hotchkiss round, *Rafael Riego* committed herself to ram or bring the forward dynamite gun to bear by turning towards her tormentor. As she heeled and came about, the black smoke pouring from her deckhouse roof was carried off to the west and stripped away all concealment. Judging her intentions, Starke put *Calypso* in a 360 degree turn, unmasking both 4-inch mounts and starboard side batteries. While Chief Owen called out ranges using the stadimeter, every gun fired. Both 4-inch rifles managed two rounds, the 3-pounder somewhat more, and rattling Gatlings filled the topside with off-white gun smoke floating thickly over cascading spent brass that bounced and rolled across deck planks.

Starke saw the fusillade strike the tug, tearing away parts, causing one figure to jerk then drop overboard, and *Rafael*

Riego stagger. She immediately turned starboard and slowed, assuming a southeast course with *Calypso* taking one parallel and astern. Through binoculars, Starke watched the black, expanding smoke cloud boiling from her deckhouse, immediately aft of the missing funnel, and suspected it meant the fire room was hit. Yellow flames followed, encircling the missing funnel's base and mixing with smoke, turning it black, white, and gray. In seconds, the superstructure aft fragmented and fantail crumpled as an explosion in her hold suddenly unleashed pressure that was unable to instantly vent into the adjacent engine room so it rent the steel deck overhead, surged through passageways, and blew open hatches and doors. The initial blast fed off a string of sympathetic detonations seeking every avenue of release with containments holding only fractions of a second. The main deck was pealed back aft of the forward fire room, her hull spread, and main mast spun over the side while the dying tug's deck equipment, boats, guns, and a handful of bodies were launched into sea and sky.

From midship aft, a rising cloud of steam, smoke, and debris enveloped *Rafael Riego* then broadened its base before developing a distinct trunk below an anvil-shaped head, offset slightly downwind. Massive convulsions continued flowing over *Calypso* as the dark base expanded and partly visible forward stack emitted a dark, black burst of coal dust, followed by grayish-white smoke as exploding munitions crushed her boiler, ripped the fire room apart, and instantly killed those still in it. Partly gutted, with the aft third of her steel hull open to the sea, *Rafael Riego* began settling stern first. The bow rose slowly until her abused keel separated and mangled aft hull section slid below the blue water. Unencumbered, the largely intact forward portion returned briefly to an even keel before rolling starboard; exposing a hull streaked with marine growth. It lay on its side for several minutes, then vanished amidst fountains of water, eruptions, and mist as submerging compartments vented trapped air. The bullnose and bent foremast were last to slip away, leaving nothing but flotsam populating an expanding surface disturbance that soon faded.

Despite high spirits from the chase, a second sinking left *Calypso*'s incredulous crew stunned. The entire ship went silent, except for the engine's low, steady rumble. Starke turned to Osbourne and both officers stared into the other's eyes for several seconds without speaking. Starke retrieved his pipe to steady himself and occupy his hands, then carefully said, "Mr. Osbourne, close that debris, but don't drift over it. When we're at the edge, launch the whaleboat. I doubt many survived, but those that have will require attention. Review the log and make any notation you see fit before signing; and pass my appreciation to your engineers for an outstanding effort."

Lieutenant Osbourne glanced at his captain, who stood looking over the grave with an unlit pipe in his mouth, head lowered, and hands lightly grasping the railing. Beyond, the Caribbean already began healing with an arriving flight of expectant seagulls searching out and pecking at floating tidbits.

Chapter Nine
Rescue

Calypso's slow-moving white whaleboat sought survivors or remains on the Gulf's blue shroud as *Rafael Riego*'s shattered carcass settled 300 feet below, scattering residue from surface to seabed. While fish foraged this rich detritus, causing some floating bits to twitch, several flights of birds fed well.

Starke wanted survivors at the site found and recovered, but could not remain when others might be floating in the filibuster's vanished wake; especially as he doubted any lived through the explosion. Those not instantly concussed and fragmented were most likely entombed in her bow section. People did sometimes survive so he took *Calypso* near the debris where her height and numbers looking would aid the search; and the hull offer a thin shield from surfacing fragments. Starke monitored these efforts through binoculars from the flying bridge, keeping an eye on the single whaleboat put at risk for recovery and close inspection. The white craft rowed through the flotsam bobbing in a gently rolling, blue-green sea to clusters of birds, or spots pointed out by the executive officer through his speaking trumpet. Intermittently, it slowed, looked, then continued on or stopped. When it did halt, one or two on board would leave their oar to retch, while the more inured or less sensitive kept on task.

Calypso was steaming slowly west within the hour, retracing *Rafael Riego*'s track, with two relatively intact, canvas-wrapped bodies laid out for burial at the starboard gangway. Starke knew the task could not be long delayed due to afternoon heat and crew beginning to avoid that part of the main deck. Elsewhere, unemployed sailors lined the rails or clung to rigging, scanning for life or debris sufficient to support it, but discovered only two floating seaweed patches. *Calypso* reached the approximate area where their whaleboat was set adrift by late afternoon, but found nothing. Starke brought the bark to bare steerageway then called for silence unless something was spotted. The quiet was broken only by panting boilers, humming ventilator fans, and running rigging shifting from *Calypso*'s slow, easy roll. The unnatural stillness grew oppressive as burning coal and escaping steam fumes permeated weather decks, pilothouse, and flying bridge.

Starke asked Dunbar and Owen to recalculate the track twice before calling Chief Weaver to the flying bridge. The boatswain's roughhewn, weathered face soon cleared the top step. He briefly considered the tight-planked deck encircled by off-white canvas windscreens, walked to Starke, saluted, and began, "You sent for me, captain?"

"Yes, chief. What's your thinking on the whaleboat?"

Weaver considered the question before responding, "Well, captain, there's bits and pieces in the water, so we're on the tug's wake, but no sign of our whaleboat and it should be nearby. There's not much wind, boat plugs were in place, and its anchor bent to the Samson post with a long line. That would have slowed drift so it should be nearby, awash or capsized, unless it was picked up. If under sail, they should be in sight."

"What equipment, chief?"

"Lifeboat provisions: water, hardtack, oars, boat compass, and sails."

"Very well. We'll circle south then steer for the gunboat. No need for a survey before we're back in Key West; it might still turn up."

"Aye, aye, captain."

Calypso turned south towards Puerto Progresso, increased speed and covered nearly ten miles before setting a northwest course for the gunboat's last known position. Just before dusk, the masthead lookout reported smoke on the horizon and they altered course for it. They found *Vanguard* several hundred yards off the listing Spaniard's starboard quarter with sailors wearing two nations' uniforms absorbed in saving the gunboat. Starke had Watson ready the remaining whaleboat for lowering and prepare a steam pinnace. The whaleboat was launched as the ship coasted to a halt off the gunboat's port side; rocking slowly as speed bled away. Once loaded, it cast off and made for the Spaniard carrying their executive officer, chief engineer, and surgeon.

That evening, *Calypso*'s crew assembled on her starboard side for the burial service read by Paymaster Wiggs then solemnly watched each bundle slide from the platform, arc out and down, to enter feet first. A white sheet supplanted national ensigns, since the bodies' origins, loyalties, and beliefs were unknown, but one bundle would have preferred a red and black flag with no religious reading. Later, from his cabin window, Starke clearly saw *Vanguard's* navigation lights as she imperceptibly slid forward less than three miles away, with the listing gunboat floating uneasily between. Leaving the thick glass pane, he returned to a cluttered table, recopied scribbled notes into his personal log, and retired late.

The executive officer learned the *Hernan Cortés* class gunboat was *Francisco de Montejo*, commanded by Teniente de Navio Emiliano Mendoza y Aguilar; an officer Watson characterized as courteous and energetic. One who, despite tenuous circumstances, greeted him wearing the Spanish Navy's open blue blouse, white waistcoat, and cravat.

Temporarily discarding a lifetime's customs, he asked about *Rafael Riego* immediately. Watson briefly described their chase and her destruction. Mendoza expressed no compassion for the tug's explosive demise, lack of survivors, or missing whaleboat since *Francisco de Montejo* had four killed and six wounded out fifty-four. Sailors on her forward mount fell to machine gun fire, others were hurt by the dynamite gun, and two scalded when a steam valve unseated. Mendoza reported hearing a loud cough from the filibuster's forecastle while his boarding party crossed, began opening the distance, then felt something strike the hull. A massive explosion off the starboard side came seconds later. Fortunately, the projectile struck her reinforced hull, bounced, then exploded yards away near the surface, so its energy mostly diverted into the impressive water column. He was convinced it would have been fatal except for bouncing; but still sprung plates, opened seams, and caused other damage. *Rafael Riego*'s machine guns began killing and wounding before there was time to recover.

Watson offered *Calypso*'s sickbay, on Conrad's suggestion, and provided deck and engineering volunteers under O'Leary to help with repairs, keep dewatering pumps going, and release *Vanguard*'s cuttermen. Osborne reported the gunboat's engineering plant survived mostly unscathed but the underwater explosion damaged her hull and several machine gun rounds penetrated. Deck and superstructure were badly shot up but Osborne supported Mendoza's evaluation most equipment could be quickly restored to partial service with the serious damage consisting of four sprung plates, leaking heavily, and possible shaft or rudder misalignment.

Vanguard's executive officer, Second Lieutenant Earnest Buck led the cuttermen assisting *Francisco de Montejo*. He told Watson they reached Arrecife Alacranes just shy of five o'clock, found no ships and guessed the tug's speed was faster than estimated. Hunter assumed *Calypso* chased the filibuster slightly south and east, so he struck out in that direction, steaming southeast then east. While scouting for *Calypso* and *Rafael Riego* they investigated a smoke column and found *Francisco de Montejo* in extremis. Hunter then faced a dilemma, much like Starke's, requiring immediate and decisive action. It was clear the Spaniards were in danger and, from their captain, that *Calypso* was last seen in a running fight with *Rafael Riego*. He decided to stand by the battered gunboat and was proven correct but a different outcome could have ended his career ignominiously.

During the night, when not called to the pilothouse, Starke slept fitfully, reconsidered the engagement, or looked out his cabin window to confirm the gunboat still floated. After waking early, he moved about the cabin with a solid porcelain coffee mug on a crooked finger, its hot, dark contents sliding back and forth with the ship's slow roll. He sipped deliberately while gazing through his window at the growing eastern twilight preceding the rising Caribbean sun. It looked as though benevolent weather would continue, so he took time to enjoy Yamashita's eggs, rice, and toast.

Late that morning, he went to *Francisco de Montejo*. Teniente de Navio, Emiliano Mendoza y Aguilar and First Lieutenant Boyd Hunter greeted him with requisite honors before the trio went to its small, ornately paneled wardroom. After taking seats at the elaborately carved walnut table running athwartship, tempranillo wine was poured from a cut-crystal decanter into matching, tulip-shaped glasses. Their host was not large, but refined and proper, with short hair, high forehead, neatly trimmed mutton-chop whiskers, and manicured mustache. Dark, hooded eyes, positioned solidly under heavy eyebrows, momentarily evaluated his guests, then he smiled and raised his glass, "May I convey Spain's appreciation, and my own, for the filibuster *Rafael Riego*'s destruction, and assistance given this ship and Spain."

Realizing well-intentioned words might play differently at the Department, or in the New York press, Starke interjected, "I must clarify, sir. Law and custom obligated *Calypso* to engage a pirate using my nation's flag to attack your command; as you would have."

Hunter added, "Captain Starke's correct, captain. However, you may wish to include in your report that *Vanguard* followed her from Veracruz, suspecting our laws were being violated. We could not board *Rafael Riego* on suspicion alone to confirm registry or cargo, but firing on you changed that."

Lifting his glass by the stem, then moving it slightly to encourage the slow rotation of a red wine aged in oak casks, Mendoza responded, "Boarding in Spanish waters would have been my preference, but *Rafael Riego*'s speed left no choice but act or allow artillery to reach the insurrectos. I admit to being concerned about the role *Calypso* might play when they changed flags but rigging a dynamite gun was unexpected. I cannot express my relief when *Calypso* fired, then pursued and sank the assassin. Filibuster or pirate, Spanish sailors were murdered and *Vanguard's* help may have saved this ship, so my nation is in your debt, as am I."

Mendoza graciously revised his toast then resumed the Spanish custom of addressing business only after more casual topics. Starke listened intently as he described patrols between Puerto Rico and Cuba, the Havana visit that sent him after *Rafael Riego*, and possibility a new Philippine rebellion had begun in August. Starke noted everything, especially his host's observations on Cuba, for a naval intelligence office letter. According to Mendoza, Puerto Rico was mostly loyal and tranquil. In Cuba, the new captain general was pressing rebels hard and sending incompetent or corrupt officers home.

His reconcentration policy seemed to be working in two provinces; except supplies of food, clothing, and shelter for rural Cubans forced into fortified towns and cities were lacking. Starke politely pressed him on Havana, a city he knew and where his family's shipping firms had offices. Along with details on baseball, bullfights, and Hotel Inglaterra, Mendoza confirmed a navy yard remained at the Arsenal, although officially closed ten years earlier when funding vanished, and its small machine shop and foundry would provide *Francisco de Montejo* with voyage repairs and conduct a preliminary survey. However, its small marine railway was unable to take the gunboat, so Mendoza anticipated orders to a larger yard for docking and repair. Starke also learned a large floating dry-dock was coming to Havana; something Mendoza thought long overdue considering the Spanish warships in Cuba with fouled hulls. He then took a sip of wine and smiled; adding that could mean an American shipyard, with New York City a strong contender. In which case, he looked forward to an evening at Delmonico's restaurant and several plays.

Once serious discussion began, Starke agreed to stand by *Francisco de Montejo* as far as Havana and tend her casualties for the voyage. Hunter would take *Vanguard* southeast, searching for the missing whaleboat, then southwest for Puerto Progresso before returning to Key West; and offered his entire cement supply to seal the gunboat's sprung hull plates. Mendoza pointed out custom and climate required burial of his dead, so shortly after the Americans returned to their ships, bark and cutter stood by silently as *Francisco de Montejo* conducted a Catholic funeral. Afterwards, smoke from *Vanguard's* slightly raked, single stack signaled her departure, with Hunter waving to Starke as she began gathering way and using twin screws to tighten the turn. He carried a preliminary letter and coded cable for Captain Albert, should *Vanguard* enter Key West first. The white hull shortened as she settled on course until only her port quarter was visible beneath a vertically striped ensign streaming astern from the mainmast truck.

Starke's attention returned to the gunboat where Mendoza's crew and American sailors completed *Francisco de Montejo*'s temporary repairs. Cement flowed into leaking voids and cofferdams; wooden plugs were driven into bullet-holes or temporary plates bolted over them; and necessary topside equipment returned to working order then preserved with paint and grease. Material *Francisco de Montejo* carried, along with items from *Vanguard* and *Calypso*, was used to repair the blown valve and other systems in the boiler and engine rooms. When shaft and rudder tests proved satisfactory early that evening, Mendoza believed he could make Havana, or a closer port if not.

Calypso prepared to get underway with *Francisco de Montejo* immediately after evening sights. Dunbar already consulted with Mendoza to lay out the best track. They would make for Bahia Honda, forty miles west of Havana, then follow the coast to the city. This took them across the Yucatan Channel shipping lane then along a reef system stretching from the island's western tip to Bahia Honda. Running the coast was less easy because Faro de Roncali lighthouse, overlooking the Yucatan Channel at Cuba's western tip, would be too far south, and navigation aids along the Pinar del Río coast to Bahia Honda must be considered nonexistent, unreliable, or suspect. The rich western province was ideal for tobacco and sugar, with subtropical weather and flat valleys, but its wealth, and smaller African population, made independence less attractive for the same reasons it became essential to Gómez's plan to destroy Cuba's economy while increasing

Spain's costs. To this end, he dispatched the insurrectos' Stonewall Jackson, Lieutenant General José Antonio de la Caridad Maceo y Grajales; called The Bronze Titan in the American press and El Leon Mayor by the Spanish. Fighting became continuous after January when his small army of cavalry and infantry arrived; and Weyler's response was a fortified trocha crossing the island between the Pinar del Río and Havana provinces designed to end Maceo's ability to communicate, resupply, and maneuver. Nothing was immune in the province, including navigation aids, so the ships would remain well off the string of reefs and islets between Cape San Antonio and Bahia Honda.

Once *Calypso* sailors returned, *Francisco de Montejo* steamed east with *Calypso* two miles astern. They later altered course to east by north once Dunbar and Owen's calculations from reducing evening star sights matched Starke's. The gunboat was also keeping to the agreed eight knots over ground, if *Calypso*'s functioning, but suspect, patent log payed out over the stern could be trusted. Navigation had been taken over by the bark, with course, speed, and location passed using *The International Code of Signals*, which allowed Mendoza and his crew to concentrate on repairs and inspecting damage. If all went well, the two-day trip would end September 14, 1896, off Havana.

The clear, tropical, and ethereal evening began with rays from the setting sun astern exploding the horizon's clouds into a rainbow of colors; without the green flash several hopefuls waited for on the fantail. Despite its beauty, Starke knew the humid, deceptive weather was typical for a late Caribbean rainy season. High winds, vicious seas, downpours, tropical storms, and hurricanes would come with little warning, especially during August and September, so he slept in the sea cabin and was often awakened; usually during Martyn's watch when *Francisco de Montejo*'s stern-light vanished during bouts of heavy rain that began late in the evening then intensified.

As seas built and their ship grew lively, pilothouse watches were buoyed by the perverse relief of seeing what the shallow-draft gunboat's crew endured. In his sickbay, Surgeon Conrad was awake, reading Anna Green's *The Doctor, His Wife, and the Clock* when *Calypso* suddenly heeled well over, then righted; rattling securely shelved bottles along whitewashed walls and swinging patients' bunks suspended from the overhead. Stepping topside, he stood in the passageway, braced himself on a doorframe, cracked the lee side outer door, and watched the small gunboat plow through the night, fighting to hold course after each plunge, roll, slide, or combination. Thinking he was a long way from Michigan, Conrad gave *Francisco de Montejo*'s dancing stern light a parting glance then returned to his patients, satisfied he persuaded Watson to transfer them to *Calypso* and expecting to remain awake most of that night.

Starke eked out three straight hours of sleep towards morning then rose to shoot stars on the flying bridge with Watson, Dunbar, and Owen. Everything was gray, the horizon empty, and *Calypso*'s small consort recovering. Their calculations had them crossing the Yucatan Channel around noon Sunday; and when they began the afternoon weather was warm, humid, and somewhat alleviated by the light breeze crossing *Calypso*'s deck. Steaming easily through blue-green water, her triple-expansion engine's low vibrations and ventilation fans' constant hum were conspicuous. Boiler exhaust left her stack almost leisurely, cleared main and mizzen masts; then spread, dispersed, and settled astern. *Calypso* was alone on the Caribbean, except for the small gunboat's stern, stack, masts, and smoke two miles ahead;

leading them to Havana.

Sunday meant inspection and today, captain's mast. The less enjoyable event's guests of honor were five Irish sailors with contrary opinions regarding a New York City ward boss. Having thoroughly debated the issue, the only consensus reached was to square off and settle it. For good or ill, Ensign Martyn happened by, did not accept it was a private affair, and placed all parties on report. Starke knew mast only postponed the reckoning, but his punishment ensured similar incidents would not occur on board and this one would not resume ashore for some time. He also knew Chief Weaver could be relied on to further sour their future by assigning especially onerous extra duty tasks saved for such occasions.

Church service followed mast, with Paymaster Wiggs leveraging *Proverbs*, to caution pride precedes fall, before leading several hymns. After the service finished, a group drifted aft to recline near the taffrail; where they listened or sang to Coxswain Clement Melvin's mandolin, accompanied by a harmonica and penny whistle. Melvin was a first-rate coxswain who played mandolin or banjo with talent, discipline, and persistence; prompting Chief Weaver to undertake an unusual act of favoritism by arranging for secure storage of his instruments. Once these sessions became a Sunday custom, those preferring to "pound their ear" without music, gravitated to the forecastle where they sprawled in a warm sun while caressed by the gentle wind passing over them.

Additional idlers and the off-watch spread out along either side of the deckhouse to repair uniforms, weave lanyards, carve small items, or gossip. This weather deck population increased as more sailors escaped from below, where the solitary enticement was shade made possible by *Calypso*'s wood sheathing, windows, deck prisms, and portholes.

Although the bark's ventilation system struggled to inhale enough air, even with windsails rigged forward of her masts, there were few complaints above or below deck with *Francisco de Montejo* off their bow in a beam sea, masts swinging with metronome precision; except when caught by an unusual swell that caused her to roll heavily to port.

Ensign Blair opened every pilothouse window and door, before shifting to the flying bridge where there was a breeze, but even more sun. He could also better hear the entertainment aft; at least when stack noises failed to dampen notes and voices. Bursts of laughter also drifted forward, as Melvin's mandolin and accompanying instruments produced passable renditions of *Farewell Spanish Ladies, Brighton Camp, Annie Laurie,* and other favorites. The atmosphere seemed odd after the running fight less than two days earlier and its aftermath, but Blair soaked in the mood; his eyes constantly passing along the horizon. Periodically, he turned his binoculars on the gunboat and saw their companion similarly engaged, despite the deadly attack and constant threat of sinking. Less often, the glasses went to some anomaly his eyes picked up until satisfied one was a ship. After remaining silent a few minutes, to see how long before the lookout reported it, he decided it was not soon enough for a sailor placed high above and resolved to speak with Weaver. He also used the interval to confirm its constant bearing and decreasing range before sending word to Starke an inbound visitor would pass close aboard their port side. Ships more often sailed through the Yucatan Channel than across it, but Blair saw no threat. He also hoped Starke would remain in the day cabin; but few ships appeared during this passage so it was almost certain his captain would come to the flying bridge.

Blair's message gave Starke the opportunity to break from a

draft report of *Calypso's* actions and decision to escort *Francisco de Montejo* to Havana's entrance. He briefly considered entering to drop off her burned and wounded but decided official and public reactions from *Calypso* arriving with a battered Spanish gunboat were unpredictable. On his way to the flying bridge, he spotted Thaddeus lurking or napping by the pantry; Yamashita's small kitchen and workroom where the steward attacked every task with tightly disciplined energy. He also passed three sailors squatting on the deck. As they began to rise, Starke quickly said, "As you were men," since they were braiding elaborate lanyards to replace the plain straps issued for boatswain pipes and pocket knives. Responding, "Thank you, sir," both quickly resumed braiding. On the flying bridge, he found Naval Cadet Terrence Timme, intent on the approaching ship as Ensign Blair saluted, "Captain, she appears to be a fast liner, holding course and speed. We're doing the same, as is *Francisco de Montejo*."

"Very well, Mr. Blair, get a name for the log if you don't have to maneuver."

Starke was standing quietly near the ensign, letting Blair deal with the visitor about to pass down the Spanish gunboat's port side about three or four miles north. Despite being too far off to dip her flag, Timme had the watch prepare to respond rather than be called out by Blair. Starke was almost certain it was *City of Washington*, traveling to Veracruz from Havana. From there, she would continue to Panama then return to New York. A familiar sight along her route, the 300-foot liner displaced near 2,500 tons and was equipped with a seldom used sail rig. While she passed north of *Calypso*, through binoculars Starke clearly saw the single high funnel used to gain natural fire room draft without resorting to blowers, wheelhouse forward of several boats slung in davits, white superstructure, and solid, black hull with straight stem and pronounced counter.

Starke said nothing, but waited until Blair reported, "I read *City of Washington*, captain."

"Very well, Mr. Blair, log it; and I'll be here awhile."

Blair's, "Yes, sir," lacked enthusiasm.

While Melvin coaxed melodious tunes from his mandolin, Landsman Mallory Hawk sat with his long legs stretched out and back against the warm, wooden bulwark. He wore his working clothes; an old service dress uniform that would be used until discarding was the only option. After adjusting the tunic blousing, he turned to Kearney, "Melvin's in fine tune."

Kearney retrieved a pipe from his jumper and began preparing a bowl, "That he is; and on a pleasant afternoon such as this, with a full pipe."

"You knew the captain as a cadet?"

"True enough. I went ashore in Alexandria with him after John Bull shelled it. There was rioting and we had to fight our way out through rubble and corpses."

"I heard he was smoking a pipe during our fight."

"Perhaps, but the captain knew that was target practice, Mallory, not a fight."

With that, Kearney snugged his back into the bulwark, lit the pipe, pulled a stained gray hat over his eyes, and began slowly drawing tobacco smoke. Hawk watched, relaxed, and listened. At the other bulwark, Kemp, the massive stoker, was nodding off, while just forward of them, he noticed the captain's steward cracking a door to check fishing conditions then, deciding they were poor, closing it; but not before the ship's cat slipped through to make his topside rounds, evaluating places and people for the most inviting spot.

Calypso crossed the Yucatan Channel with most traffic remaining on the horizon and Starke unwilling to leave the gunboat to investigate anything; which frustrated Blair and assuaged Martyn. Osbourne, during one of his pilothouse visits, felt obliged to remind Blair the explosion's effects on the gunboat's hull could not be fully determined without docking so Starke was obliged to stand by until she passed safely below Havana's Castillo de los Tres Reyes Magos del Morro, popularly known as the Morro. Two miles ahead, Mendoza's engineers struggled to make the ten knots required for eight over ground.

Late afternoon showers and high winds became so heavy at times that *Francisco de Montejo* lit running lights and the forward windows of *Calypso*'s pilothouse had water enough flowing over them to obscure everything ahead but the foremast. Main deck activity ceased with the first deluge and other activities faltered as seas picked up. The bark slowed slightly, but pressed ahead with less drama than the gunboat rolling and plunging off her bow. The weather came from the east, lasted about two hours, then began clearing; so evening twilight was perfect to shoot stars and a solid fix placed them nearly on the intended track; which safely cleared the many cays and reefs of Cuba's northwest coast. Dunbar predicted Cayo Jutías would be raised around ten-thirty in the morning, with Bahia Honda passing to starboard about six that evening. From there, it was an easy pilot up the coast past Puerto de Cabanas and Puerto de Mariel, to Morro fortress lighthouse. With any luck, *Francisco de Montejo* would be off the port by ten-thirty that evening.

Better than eight knots was required against an opposing current before reaching the Yucatan Channel, but afterwards the flow became an ally that pushed them north and sped their advance up Cuba's north coast. As Pinar del Río slipped past *Calypso*'s starboard side throughout the afternoon, Dunbar and Owen predicted they would remain ahead of track; putting less strain on the gunboat. Off this north shore lay black coral reefs, a profusion of cays, and the long navigable channel separating them from white sand beaches. Like the Florida Keys, these diminutive islands perched on reefs and were blanketed with mangroves and the occasional swamp. The province's steep limestone hills were sometimes visible in the distance, looking like gray lumps looming over flatlands where plantations were attacked by one side and defended or abandoned by the other. If not for dark plumes from burning crops, buildings, or villages, it was difficult to imagine war lay just beyond the beaches.

The next day brought additional short, sharp storms that left wood decks steaming and limited topside work. Chief Weaver used the respite to send those standing lookout watches aloft for impromptu training, especially the sailor Blair reported. Watson sent their four cadets, who listened as Seaman Kearney explained depths of less than a yard appeared as brown or dark patches surrounded by light green water that darkened until becoming a deep blue after the reef or shelf ended; and emphasizing any surface other than blue or dark green required caution with *Calypso*'s draft. Watson allowed others to go aloft for the stunning view so several off-duty engineers, including Jones and Kemp, made the climb, as did Surgeon Conrad.

Beyond Puerto de Mariel, the terrain inland flattened with *Calypso* remaining astern of the gunboat as it began closing the coast. Despite approaching darkness, both ships finally eased to a stop in calm seas three miles off Havana's entrance; and the pilot boat, stationed just seaward of the gray Morro, came about and made for them. *Calypso* closed her charge and used searchlights to illuminate the clear night as badly wounded Spanish sailors on stretchers were lowered in a steam pinnace and returned to *Francisco de Montejo*.

After hearing Conrad's complaints, Starke reconsidered taking *Calypso* under the gray Morro fortress across from and above Havana's whitewashed buildings, but decided against it a second time since the Spanish wounded would still be transferred to Machina Wharf by boat. Besides, warships only entered other nations' ports after requesting permission with adequate notice, then faced a barrage of administrative and courtesy protocols. He also thought it prudent to avoid giving Consul-general Lee the opportunity to request *Calypso* stay in Havana once there for a legitimate and innocuous reason. He recalled the stout gentleman's visit to his family's Washington mansion. The ex-Confederate cavalry general and Virginia governor left a favorable impression, but not enough for Starke to want *Calypso* placed at his disposal. Besides, Mendoza already faced a difficult challenge explaining his return with a crippled command; and an American gunboat's unannounced night arrival would rile correspondents pawing through a dumping ground of truth and rumor in a city where most residents and the local press were already antagonistic towards the States.

Once the steam pinnace transferred its wounded, the pilot boat cautiously nudged alongside *Francisco de Montejo* and a harbor pilot boarded through her midship gangway. Almost immediately, white frothing water surged from under the gunboat's counter as its gray shape altered, gathered speed, then, with funnel sparks floating into the warm darkness, made for a dark break in the coast between the high Morro and much lower city lights.

With the Spanish gunboat entering harbor, Starke knew Washington, and particularly Captain Albert, must quickly receive a status then full report. Since the Havana cable office was unusable, being closed overnight, riddled with informants, and controlled by Spanish censors skilled at their trade; he decided to make a fast crossing and reach Key West the next morning. Looking ruefully at flickering city lights beyond white breakers that marked a dark sea crashing against gray-black rocks, he wondered how his correspondent friend, Darwin Tyson, and Cassandra Evans fared at Hotel Inglaterra, across from the central park. She had most likely retired and Tyson was coaxing information from those in the lobby or bar; perhaps Consul-general Lee since he lived there.

Calypso had both main boilers on line in case the gunboat required towing, so they were available to cross the ninety miles and enter Key West at first light. Dunbar stood by Owen at the chart table after giving Martyn course and speed. Starke nodded and *Calypso* quickly gathered enough way for a crisp turn, then, after heading north, walked their speed up; with engineers balancing feedwater, steam pressure, and fire.

Looking astern from the narrow channel under a forbidding Morro, Mendoza glanced aft as *Calypso*'s masts and running lights shifted smartly, then faded. After a formal parting wish for *Calypso*'s good fortune, he prepared for the starboard turn to take *Francisco de Montejo* into the large harbor's center, north of Regla's lights and south of the waterfront where Machina Wharf's conspicuous three-legged derrick towered over an ominous set of buildings that included the naval commander's offices.

Chapter Ten
Standing into Danger

Late next morning, Captain Albert was gazing through his Washington office windows and light rain to Lafayette Square, just beyond the Executive Mansion, when Starke's coded cable arrived in a sealed brown envelope. It was the first *Rafael Riego* pursuit status since the Veracruz consul sent *Vanguard's* message to State that she was in pursuit with *Calypso* covering Arrecife Alacranes. Newcomb also sent a note from Consul-general Lee reporting a small Spanish gunboat that brought the regular courier from Puerto Rico, suddenly left port in a cloud of rumors.

People in the Building and Executive Mansion were pressuring for news about *Rafael Riego* and the envelope left on his desk meant one or both ships reached port, probably Key West. The filibuster might be turned over to port authorities but he thought it more likely *Rafael Riego* eluded her pursuers. Either way, *Calypso* could return to her mission. Sitting down, he began to decode, slowly at first, then faster until he finished, sat back, and reread what was penciled on lined paper beside a standard message form: "*Rafael Riego* fired on Spanish gunboat southeast of Arrecife Alacranes then sunk by *Calypso*. This ship and *Vanguard* aided same. *Calypso* escorted damaged gunboat to Havana and returned Key West."

Albert cursed the Navy accountants who made information subservient to cost; an equally common complaint with his correspondent contacts. It would be at least three days before a full report arrived by courier. Until then, he could telegraph for clarification, which often raised other questions, or rely on newspapers' dubious accuracy. Since it appeared *Calypso* sank *Rafael Riego*, Starke, and he by extension, were entangled in two alleged filibusters' destruction. Looking outside at water rolling off the window awning, he wished the new telephones could reach beyond city limits. His Eagle pencil slowly drummed the notepad. The project to disrupt filibusters could end because Jefferson Starke's son possessed more of father's buccaneer proclivities than he thought; but Albert refused to believe trusting the lieutenant wrong. In any case, he moved immediately to break the news first and avoid the "second liar" trap which regularly cost political capital in the Building; something he worked hard to accumulate. After hand printing copies, he sent them by clerk to Assistant Secretary McAdoo, Captain Fischer at Treasury, Newcomb at State, and Spencer at Justice. A second man delivered one to Secretary of the Navy Herbert, along with a superfluous suggestion it be added to the day's meeting on increasing North Atlantic Squadron ships assigned filibuster duty. Once these copies were away, he carried another to the Bureau of Navigation chief's second floor, east wing office to schedule a meeting through the admiral's chief clerk, William Chardavoyne.

When Albert entered, that gentleman lifted eyes strained from reading correspondence neatly aligned in piles across his desk, as did two special duty ensigns assigned to the office. Chardavoyne saw Albert's expression and immediately knew he wanted unscheduled time with the chief. These intrusions were always the top priority for those requesting them; and the chief clerk's desk sited to deflect or manage them. Albert was never an offender, planned well, and was already on the schedule later that day so he immediately agreed to pass

Calypso's decoded message to Rear Admiral Ramsay.

Returning to his cluttered desk under the dangling electrolier, Albert considered what mischief Havana or Key West correspondents might create, and external interest the *Rafael Riego* affair might attract. Carefully leaning back in the rolling chair, he took solace in the national election and free-silver debate absorbing press scrutiny, with Navy articles confined to brief notices on battleship contracts awarded and increasing numbers of American citizens enlisting. Even Cuba was receiving less coverage than preliminary negotiations for a Fitzsimmons-Corbett boxing match.

Despite his anxiety, or because of it, he grinned, pulled a well-browned meerschaum pipe from its rack and scraped away some residue; then carefully filled the bowl before lightly tamping the brown shreds. The fight would have received enough attention on its own, but Fitzsimmons lost an earlier one refereed by Wyatt Earp that many thought rigged; and suffragettes were demanding women spectators be allowed. Unlike most, Albert's partiality to the manly art was limited to promoting morale and settling the odd quarrel on ships; but he stood firm on respectable women attending matches and the rest as a matter of public order. Abigail was not interested in the sport but opposed him on principle so Casa Albert's current temperature was below weather bureau predictions.

As the flame passed slowly over bowl center, his thoughts shifted to *Calypso* sailors in Key West's welcoming bars. The combination would prove fertile for reporters since a sailor's skill concocting stories often exceeded their own. He was considering how to go about separating them when called to Ramsay's office. Apprehensive, he balanced the smoldering pipe in the ashtray then walked down the familiar off-white corridor with its checkerboard marble floor bounded by black borders. At a recessed pine and mahogany door with overhead transom window and heavy frame, he knocked, grasped its brass door knob with embossed anchor, twisted, then went in. The cadets looked up as Chardavoyne stood, disappeared into the inner office to announce him, and then quickly reemerged to hold the door open, saying, "The admiral will see you now, captain."

Ramsay was very thin with white hair and mustache at odds with dark eyebrows. He rose from behind his desk, gesturing Albert to the same wood-framed, pleated-leather chair he occupied in February when gaining approval to offer *Calypso* to Starke. It was still between the tall bookcase and substantial oak desk blanketed with books, reports, correspondence and other items; but this time Albert did not know what would come. However, the die was cast, his interrogator possessed all available information, and Starke's future, along with his own, already decided. Ramsay wasted nothing on preliminaries, "So Lieutenant Starke's sunk a second alleged filibuster?"

Albert was uncharacteristically tongue-tied and both silently held each other's gaze for several seconds, before Ramsay prompted, "Well, Captain Albert?"

"His full report is expected Monday, admiral; and telegrams sent to confirm one or two points. It appears *Rafael Riego* fired on a Spanish gunboat attempting to board her, was engaged by *Calypso*, and blew up. The Judge Advocate General thinks his actions do not appear illegal if the report confirms what we've been told."

Ramsay considered this, studied the decoded cable, then looked straight at Albert, "I need that report when it arrives, but what are your intentions?"

Better prepared, Albert began, "Assuming Starke meets with no immediate legal complications; I propose sending

Calypso to Jamaica. The press claims government agents, Spain's or ours, sabotaged one of the Junta's largest filibusters, *Laurada*. Other reports have her master arrested, the ship unharmed, and that she was never there but in Wilmington."

The admiral uncharacteristically interrupted, "Why not cable Kingston's consul?"

"That is being done, but before we receive an answer, the conflicting reports provide a reason for *Calypso* to leave Key West immediately. She'll go through the Yucatan Channel to Jamaica then return by Old Bahama Channel to Port Royal for coal and maintenance. The crew can have liberty in Kingston and Nassau, away from the press. We'll announce Kingston as her first destination then ask for a number of Caribbean port visits and let the Junta guess where she's headed. If there's an inquiry, modified orders can be cabled to Starke in Kingston, but *Calypso* needs to be at sea. The North Atlantic Squadron is mostly above Charleston at the moment so *Newark* is the only ship covering the Straits of Florida to Port Tampa. *Vanguard*'s still somewhere in the Gulf, but once the Revenue Cutter Service examines Hunter's report she might be assigned to a district unless Captain Fischer can prevent it."

"That's what you're proposing to the Secretary?"

"With your approval, admiral."

"It's your plan, but also press for sending two additional ships south and prepare to testify before some congressional committee. Sinking alleged filibusters does not sit well, so there may be an attempt to cast Starke as a renegade. After all, most Members support the Junta and several remember his father, or the rumors. In any case, tread carefully."

Seeing their discussion at an end, Albert rose as Ramsay mused, "Sidney, check the Bahamas and Jamaica for yellow fever; let's not risk half her crew."

"Yes, sir, I'll have State confirm it with our consuls."

Although he was encouraged the bureau chief used his first name, Ramsay made it clear Starke's neck was not the only one facing the chop. Albert met with Secretary of the Navy Herbert later that day in his second floor office; at the head of a broad marble staircase that continued up beneath the rotunda's stained-glass dome to the fourth and fifth floor Navy Library. Many were convinced it was the Building's, or even Washington's, best office. Under the vaulted ceilings with large brass electroliers; a beautifully carved desk, large table, comfortable chairs, busts, and vibrant oriental rugs rested on a mixed-wood marquetry floor. Its opulence befitted a cabinet member two steps below the president.

As the captain entered and advanced past a floor globe, Secretary Herbert stood beside his desk, near one of two black marble fireplaces, motioning him to a chair. Albert was familiar with Herbert's well-groomed flowing white mustache and goatee, precisely mounted on a smoothly cultured face. Constrained in a dark suit, his somewhat rotund shape reflected a life spent largely practicing law or in Congress, but the left arm swinging loose at his side since the war spoke to another time. He resigned a Confederate colonel's commission after being badly wounded during the Wilderness battle. In Congress after the war he earned a reputation for being honest, fair, and direct; although not overly expressive which Albert suspected was the reason Herbert never married.

Shaking Albert's hand, the smooth, cultured voice began, "I believe we were to discuss increasing filibuster patrols but your note suggests *Calypso* takes precedence."

Albert agreed, despite the missed opportunity to advance his other interest and was considering that when Herbert asked, "Have we anything more on *Calypso*?"

"There'll be nothing official until the report arrives, Mr. Secretary, and God knows what Key West correspondents will create."

"A group religiously disposed to fiction. Forward the report directly when it arrives; and what do you propose in the meantime?"

"With your approval, Mr. Secretary, send *Calypso* through the Yucatan Channel for Jamaica to keep correspondents from her crew and let filibusters know she's at large. Conflicting press accounts regarding *Laurada* provide the rationale. Her movements after Jamaica would be secret, but include coming north through Old Bahama Channel, possibly a Nassau port call, then Port Royal for coal and maintenance."

"Removing her from the gentlemen of the press seems appropriate; one ship bagging a brace of alleged filibusters offers too many possibilities."

"Yes, sir, besides, *Calypso*'s the only ship exclusively assigned to disrupt filibustering; although the others rotating through Key West help. Revenue Cutter Service headquarters will keep *Vanguard* for now but there's always pressure to send her to a district."

"I share Admiral Ramsay's desire for more ships on filibuster patrol, but Commodore Bunce must drill them as a squadron. It must operate as one should it be called upon to face Spain or some other nation. The Cuban situation, our past affairs with Chile and Brazil, not to mention recent issues with Great Britain, clearly show we must stand ready. President Cleveland's against war with Spain, but avoiding it cannot disrupt what must be accomplished to prepare for one."

"I understand, Mr. Secretary, which is why *Calypso* needs to be at sea."

"Then I will agree to your plan, subject to change after reading the full report. You'll meet with other Departments involved about *Rafael Riego*?"

"Yes, sir; before the week ends."

"Very well then, captain. Prepare your orders, keep me updated, and reschedule to discuss where we stand on ships assigned filibuster patrol. I would also like a list of private ships and yachts that might be converted to fill our patrol boat shortage. In the meantime, I'll look into including filibuster tasks in the torpedo boat maneuvers planned off Florida and speak with Treasury about *Vanguard* but cannot promise anything."

Albert left the Secretary's outer office, walked the corridor, and passed through his wood door; identical to every other one occupying indentations flanking the corridor's off-white walls. Although Starke's full report was not expected before the following Monday, he left the Building on Friday, three days later, wearing a dark-blue sack suit and bowler to meet the group that considered Pinkertons' *Rafael Riego* intelligence; in the same second floor room of the nondescript red-brick building. Albert left his streetcar and quickly completed the brief walk; eager to get on with it and hurried by a light rain. After entering the small door squeezed between storefronts, he climbed the steep stairs then passed through a small office to the conference room largely formed by the building's single turret.

One person sat at the table reviewing notes while another, who must have just arrived, slid his umbrella into a stand that was the lower part of coat and hat rack. Albert hung his coat then walked past the large, circular oak table, remembered its wood chairs quickly grew uncomfortable, and chose to stand at the curved wall's double-pane windows until they started. Looking out on the street, he observed the intermittent mist-rain soak people, horses, and a stray dog. Overhead, the fan's blades were stilled in deference to the weather.

This assembly included Captain Gibson Fischer, Clarence Newcomb, Arliss Spencer, and a well-dressed young man whose air was studied and confident. Once seated, Spencer introduced him as Maximilian Falk y Machado. The American came from a love match between an Austrian engineer and Spanish woman from Cadiz who met in Cuba then left for the States. Although raised and schooled in New York, he visited Europe regularly, possessed familiarity with Cuba, and was a well-connected lawyer. Working for Justice, Falk discretely contributed to various filibuster prosecutions and liaised with Congress on Spain and Cuba. Albert quickly noticed Spencer kept a taut leash on his protégé who exhibited a curious combination of passion, discipline, knowledge, and diplomacy.

Since *Calypso*'s cablegram brought them together, Spencer invited Albert to lead off. The captain extracted a pipe from his jacket, thinking the space afforded by civilian attire was a definite advantage, set it in a black stone ashtray, folded his hands over a small open notebook, then began, "Gentlemen, you've Starke's cable and a full report's due. From what we know, *Rafael Riego* raised our flag, attacked a Spanish gunboat, and was destroyed by *Calypso*. *Vanguard* found the damaged gunboat, stood by, and helped keep her afloat; then left for Puerto Progresso to search for a missing lifeboat and make inquiries. Until particulars are known and confirmed, the Secretary's agrees *Calypso* should leave Key West so Starke's been sent sailing orders for Jamaica to investigate reports of a large filibuster wrecked or aground at Port Antonio."

Spencer looked at Albert then, heading off Falk, inquired, "*Laurada*?"

"Yes."

With that Captain Fischer, equally uncomfortable in mufti, added, "One hopes she's another Junta loss. A large and well-known offender: iron hull, 230 feet long, eighteen-foot draft, and clipper bow. Also been around some, built for the fruit trade in '64, took a load of Blacks to Liberia, and carries tramp cargoes when not filibustering."

Falk added, "She was seized in Charleston and the master indicted but returned to sea under his replacement."

Fischer resumed, "*Vanguard* cabled this morning. She touched a fever port and was placed in Key West's quarantine anchorage; which conveniently keeps reporters away from the crew. They saw nothing before anchoring off Puerto Progresso, but a Mexican pilot schooner turned over *Calypso*'s missing whaleboat and *Rafael Riego*'s log. Local authorities claim two unidentified bodies found in the boat were buried; but had no knowledge of other survivors or personal effects. The rest fled or are ignored. Hunter's sending a full report and the whaleboat was returned to *Calypso*. Starke reviewed the logbook but asked the Revenue Cutter Service to retain custody."

Falk observed, "Good; derails any claim it was doctored."

Spencer continued, "Ordering *Calypso* from Key West appears sound, but what about this Jamaica excursion?"

After working with Mexico, and Falk joining the group, Newcomb no longer felt the novice and was waiting for an opening, "The British embassy is arranging *Calypso*'s visit and our consul in Kingston, Mr. Rickford, is investigating *Laurada*. Consul-general Lee's also making discreet inquiries regarding the Spanish gunboat."

"One thing more," Spencer said in a low voice, "Pinkerton's worried about their sources. With two expeditions lost to the same cruiser, the Junta believes *John Gwinn Williams* and *Rafael Riego* were betrayed and want to unmask the perpetrators."

As he fondled the pipe, Albert thought aloud, "*John Gwinn Williams* was a chance meeting and boiler explosion, but *Rafael Riego* must have loosed a fox in the chicken coop."

Falk responded, "Perhaps too much, Captain. Starke may be

called to testify before a congressional committee, if only to hobble *Calypso*. Quesada, the Junta's man in Washington, is probably working it as we speak so it's safe to expect some action from their Raleigh Hotel suite, or Front Street headquarters in New York."

Seeing he gained the room's attention, Falk exploited the opportunity, "As you may know, my mother's Spanish. She corresponds regularly and I've Madrid and Havana contacts. Spanish press aside, they feel the insurrection's cost in people and money is making politics increasingly unstable and the government less inclined to negotiate since almost every faction see Cuba as a province. They fail to understand why Junta proselytizing and their expeditions cannot be ended. Spain has declared martial law and they see no reason why United States can't do the same. Consider our response if Louisiana was fighting for independence with weapons, supplies, and fighters from Mexico, Spain, or France. Meanwhile, those in Cuba say no loyalist or insurrectionist has any illusions regarding what the loser can expect and believe filibuster expeditions keep this insurrection alive. I doubt the Junta will complain about these two losses openly, and be linked with piracy and anarchy, but their extreme factions appear to now argue the current stalemate might have ended with *Rafael Riego*'s artillery. This strengthens the case made by those advocating more aggressive action. Consequently, we must take care; another event like *Rafael Riego* could prove catastrophic."

Chapter Eleven
Jamaica Bound

Calypso left *Francisco de Montejo* below the Morro, steamed hard through a calm night then ghosted up Key West's South East Channel with the rising sun. For the next week, she lay off the white Marine Hospital preparing for this morning's return to sea. Starke's mechanical calendar, displaying "WED SEP 22 96", stared at him from the top of his oak secretary desk. The sorting slot designated "OUT" by an engraved brass plate contained official correspondence along with two personal letters he just finished, sealed, and prepared for the final mail run. The one to his uncle was difficult, necessary, and short but Katherine's offered a temporary break. Reclining slightly in his chair, Starke selected a lightly browned meerschaum pipe from the wood stand, thinking two letters to Albert's daughters would also be posted if overhearing Watson and Osbourne through an open window was any indication.

While anchored northwest of the hospital's masonry seawall and dock, Starke and Watson concentrated on readying *Calypso*. She not only coaled off a barge and re-provisioned but carried out an ambitious agenda of training, maintenance, and repair. Her hull was scrubbed then touched up, especially where saltwater scoured paint away near the stem, then rigging was inspected, and gun mounts blackened. Boats were lowered and secured to one of two out-swung booms for their wood to soak and swell in salt water. On wash days, canvas hammocks, underwear, towels, and uniforms blossomed across the rigging. Crew enthusiasm and attention to detail, even for activities seen as onerous or not pressing, seemed excellent, perhaps because at each day's close, off-watch and idlers were free to address personal tasks, read books from the ship's library, or drift to the fantail for music. Watson was clearly trying to provide compensation for sailors kept on board since only the top liberty class was allowed to enjoy Key West's shore attractions; which resulted in several revelers having their class reduced.

Rising, he walked to a cabin window and mulled going on deck to escape the stifling interior. Temperatures would lower as they entered October but summer still retained its grip on the thermometer, and walking outside welcome despite the heat. Having the captain out and about prematurely, however, could disrupt preparations to leave port or give the impression he lacked confidence. Releasing faint blue smoke, Starke rued the necessary isolation that stifled his proclivity to join the common effort, despite a reclusive manner. Watson, Osbourne, Weaver, and others were molding a cohesive team so not disrupting them was obligation and priority. *Calypso*'s crew of nearly 150, filling a 245-foot hull with men from disparate nations, languages, and cultures was becoming a community. Although common in navy and merchant ships, the enormity of forming a crew from the hodgepodge muster list Starke reviewed in Norfolk continued to concern him; along with being their commander and no longer a wardroom officer.

Starke attributed a great deal of this success to Albert's support and their careful crew selection. Watson had also proven consistent and fair; traits which lessened potential discord while promoting crew morale and ship loyalty. This was demonstrated over the last week when several liberty party incidents saw sailors aiding others with whom they seldom associated, despite risking class reduction, extra duty, or another penance. Less disruptive indications included the executive officer receiving few requests to change messes and Weaver hearing sailors refer to *Calypso* as a home, which told other crews the ship was a good one.

Scraping the pipe over a carved beechwood ashtray, Starke gently tapped the bowl against its rim. He suspected *Francisco de Montejo*'s commander spent the last week dealing with less pleasant demands than maintaining daily routine off Key West. After *Rafael Riego* assaulted the gunboat, Teniente de Navio Emiliano Mendoza y Aguilar not only fought and saved his ship, but completed repairs at sea then brought her safely to Havana. Starke could not predict the Spanish admiral's response, but wished Mendoza well. His own position was little better. After a few months at sea under orders to disrupt Junta filibustering expeditions, support presidential proclamations, and enforce American law; *Calypso* was party to *John Gwinn Williams'* foundering and brought about *Rafael Riego*'s spectacular demise. While convinced his actions were legal, reasoned, and justified; two alleged filibusters destroyed would not sit well with a press that openly supported the Junta and its quest for Cuban recognition. Spain, who regularly raised official and informal complaints, would take a more favorable view; as would business interests that feared a Spanish war would be costly, damage the recovering economy, threaten trade, and risk overseas investment. Shipping firms were especially on edge since they never regained the enviable position held before Confederate raiders like *Alabama* and *Florida* took their ships or rendered them uninsurable; to the benefit of competitors like Great Britain.

Starke accepted there was little more he could do. After

anchoring and reporting *Calypso*'s arrival, he cabled a coded status to Albert then sent a detailed report to Washington by courier. That would have required an officer take the steamer to Port Tampa or Cedar Key, then several railroads, further straining *Calypso*'s thin wardroom for an unknown duration, but Forsyth supplied a man from his modest staff. Starke suspected it was considered a plum assignment by station inmates and bestowed on a deserving subordinate. Similar thoughts were shared by several on *Calypso*. Even Watson, Osbourne, and Weaver subtly expressed their readiness, if called upon, to make the trip. Stifling a grin, Starke commended their initiative, without inquiring if the willingness to endure the onerous boat and train trip was motivated more by a family and two young ladies than duty.

After taking a more comfortable leather chair to consider his uncle's last letter, Starke filled the bowl and tamped down moist tobacco dredged from a pliable leather pouch. His career may have been irreparably damaged, but the possibility forced his first real understanding of the burden waiting once outside the Navy. The letter from his uncle acknowledged age forced accommodation and the Starke firm must adapt. Their vacated West Point shipyard recently sold for a thin profit, negotiations with Katherine's brother to sell the Cuban properties were progressing, and even a small Newport yacht went to new owners over the summer. His uncle wanted an opinion on hiring a general manager and taking the company public to protect Constance. It was unsettling, but no surprise since they already spoke about the small plantation he owned through his mother and a substantial Starke inheritance at some point.

After several slow draws of slightly tart tobacco, Starke admitted similar events might soon be repeated with his father's firm in Rio de Janeiro; although they corresponded less frequently. Relighting his pipe then tossing the match to his ashtray, Starke felt family obligations closing in; which led to his aunt's intermittent but persistent matrimonial campaign. Katherine and Cassandra were obviously favorites but should they not work out he was confident others would take their places. Considering this ongoing dilemma invariably distracted and drained him so Starke decided the crew would survive his early presence.

He surveyed the anchorage from *Calypso*'s pilothouse, before crossing to the chart table where penciled bearings confirmed their position. Surgeon Conrad had been emphatic they anchor in deeper water flowing through the North West Channel, southwest of the Middle Ground, because it did not pass along the city's waterfront. Starke agreed, despite a harder bottom and stronger current that required more attentive anchor watches and increased swinging. Through an open door, he considered two nearby buoys to the north. Their fading paint was nearly obscured by mottled bird droppings, except along the base where lapping seawater scoured away their leavings. Occasionally, a seagull would land, pause, then fly off, or find a spot on the hot steel to sun. Northeast, beyond the buoys, *Calypso*'s steam pinnace, marked by a white canopy, cast off from the station's steel pier in front of its stucco depot and administration building. That would be the final run, which took letters ashore and was returning with the last mail. With luck, it carried boiler parts the station paymaster assured O'Leary would arrive before *Calypso*'s departure.

Stark watched the pinnace until it eased against *Calypso*'s accommodation ladder's lower platform, unloaded freight and passengers, then moved under dangling boat falls. Weaver soon had it raised then lowered onto boat chocks and secured for sea with gripes. Once the small boiler and condenser cooled, they would be cleaned and running boats between ship and station at an end. They might be essential for errands, business, and liberty, but created constant problems and involved so many only executive officers were given overall responsibility. Starke knew Watson was relieved that running boats resumed painlessly during *Calypso's* second visit and no major incidents occurred during the week. Boat crews and sailors immediately restarted routines developed during the long stretch at anchor after arriving with *John Gwinn Williams'* survivors and corpses. Word would pass of the pinnace's impending arrival when its faint smoke plume left the naval station pier and departure from the ship by a series of warning bells. While one pinnace made runs, the second remained at the starboard boat boom to be thoroughly cleaned, clinkers removed, hand-picked coal loaded, and maintenance completed on the hull, fittings, and thin-stacked boiler of polished brass. The white canvas canopy, stretching from bow to stern, would also be cleaned and rope lacing binding it to the metal frame adjusted. Sun and rain relief was the reward, even if smoke, steam, and oil fumes were occasionally trapped beneath when the wind was right.

Starke's attention passed to the naval station's Quarters A and B, a two-story structure with white siding shared by the station commander and paymaster. Sited just south of the administration building, its ornate porches overlooked the ship channel seawall and its parlor provided a sanctuary to discuss plans, opportunities, and risks. The previous evening's session was in a room furnished with bamboo chairs from China and stocked with excellent bourbon. Unlike other visits, this was to consider orders cabled from Washington directing *Calypso* to leave for Jamaica and be replaced by a cruiser to better augment local patrols.

The two men enjoyed an easy relationship during *Calypso's*

Key West stays, despite dissimilar rank, age, demeanor, and appearance. Starke was of average height, lean but well-muscled, and carried himself with confidence. His short, neatly trimmed beard might have added sophistication, except it was insufficient to conceal an angular and slightly scarred face. Deep-set, faded blue eyes below arching eyebrows surveyed all within range, unless locked on something of interest. His nose was slightly large for a moderately gaunt face, but not objectionably so, and overhung a mouth with thin lips that remained slightly compressed unless speaking. His overall build, countenance and carriage conveyed a serious outlook, commitment to consistency, and reluctance to lose control; although a hint of independence existed in several thin locks of dark hair falling across his forehead in subtle rebellion. Forsyth was older, and may have enjoyed a similar build when a masters mate during the war, or sailing merchant ships, but now outweighed Starke. His disproportionately large head had a receding hairline and the oversize graying goatee utterly failed to conceal the absence of any distinct chin. Consequently, every facial feature sloped uninterrupted from his mouth to the thick neck rising from broad, curved shoulders and rotund, but still powerful, torso.

Placing his glass on the lace doily protecting a small table between their chairs, Forsyth began, "Sending you after *Laurada* seems plausible. She's a large filibuster sometimes put to use as a mother ship and press reports have her wrecked, broke, and still in the states. However, sending a ship to Jamaica, when it's British territory with cable office and consul in Kingston, seems like Albert wants you out of Key West."

Lowering his drink and looking over the table, Starke responded, "Unless aground or disabled, there's no chance she'd stay in Port Antonio anyway. Kingston's my first stop and, even if communication is poor from there to Port

Antonio, *Laurada* will know when I leave. Besides, *Vanguard's* a better choice and Hunter has more legal authority."

"Albert is a keen politician and I'll wager he sees *Calypso* anchored across from our story-starved correspondents. For the same reason, I doubt *Vanguard* remains much longer at the quarantine anchorage since she's not reported any disease."

Starke slowly twirled translucent, brown bourbon about his glass, before lowering it to observe, "I suspect you're right. *Calypso's* been here a week, *Vanguard* brought *Rafael Riego's* logbook soon after, and the press can be avoided only so long."

"True. *Rafael Riego* might be kept from the mainland crowd for a time, but locals have private arrangements; like Judge Alvarez with *The New York Herald*. There're also rumors surfacing in the San Carlos Club that *Calypso* intentionally sank both filibusters. It's the same on the waterfront. Captain Buff may have been unpopular but he was one of their own."

Starke recalled dinner at Duval Street's San Carlos Club with its Havana architecture of white and gold, black arches, many windows, and wrought iron railings. He regretted their host, Herminio Gonzales, might be upset but Key West was not Cuba and running weapons illegal so he mused, "The Collector of Customs and Special Deputy Collector of Customs said the same; also that police are worried about our crews making rounds of local bars."

Forsyth nodded, "Since everyone agrees your Jamaica cruise is fortuitous, what's the plan?"

Starke spread a chart on the varnished floor, weighted its corners with several objects, including two bourbon glasses, then used his pipe stem as a pointer, "Albert's orders to focus on Straits of Florida and routes east of Cuba stand, although the new ones alter that somewhat by requiring *Calypso* take the Yucatan Channel to Kingston, then Windward Passage after leaving Jamaica. Otherwise, there's leeway, including a stop in Nassau."

After a sip of bourbon, Starke continued, "*Calypso* will leave Key West, round Cabo San Antonio, and enter the Yucatan Channel. After leaving it, I could follow Cuba's southeast coast towards the Windward Passage then cross to Jamaica or continue further west along the shipping route to Colon; before cutting due east for Jamaica. The second keeps *Calypso* east of shipping to Santiago or other Cuban ports so, without knowing our track, the Junta can't be certain where she's at before arriving in Kingston. It also avoids any claim an American warship is patrolling Cuban waters. False rumors can also be started before leaving Kingston to ensure the Junta hears *Calypso*'s bound for Port Royal, our Gulf ports, and Veracruz."

Thinking aloud, Forsyth nodded and weighed the proposal against his experience, "Make sure Cabo Catoche gets a wide berth, there're bad shoals just north of there. Cabo San Antonio can be closed to about seven miles. You can expect heavy Yucatan Channel traffic south of Jamaica, mostly bound for Veracruz, but also those northbound under sail for Gulf of Mexico ports."

"Exactly, and my navigator's track lets us run the latitude east to Point Negril on Jamaica's western tip where some French company built a lighthouse in the last year or two. After that, we follow the coast to Kingston."

As the night ended, Forsyth refilled then drained his glass before smiling at Starke, "If you land at Port Antonio, tell me what you find. Boston Fruit Company's expanding and their banana boats carry cargo and tourists. Can't say I remember it as the paradise they claim; just another picturesque Caribbean port that's entirely different ashore and blessed with a cornucopia of tropical diseases."

Forsyth added as Starke left, "We'll have tugs standing by tomorrow. Signal if you need anything."

Remembering that last exchange, Starke climbed to the flying bridge from the pilothouse. At the forward canvas windscreen, he paused to absorb a morning sun rousing smells of ship and sea. As he turned to go to his cabin, the executive officer reached the top of the ladder, obviously burdened by something unpleasant, quickly saluted, and began, "Morning, captain,"

"Good morning, XO, is there a problem?"

"Pilot, sir; local custom says the one that brought a ship in always takes it out and ours is at the sea buoy waiting for a liner. They've asked we delay departure."

Starke, studied the ship's ensign, showing a steady breeze from the north, "I see; and your thoughts?"

Watson quickly responded, "Get underway as planned, captain. We've been through two channels and you're familiar with the port."

Starke recalled Chief Weaver approaching him about sailing out and he agreed the experience was needed. Doing so now meant it might be less smooth than he would like, and the Key West audience would probably include filibusters weighing their chances, but the wind was favorable and tugs standing by; something that might not exist in the future. The crew was greener than desired but they sailed the ship to Arrecife Alacranes and experience came from doing. Starke was pondering specifics when he noticed Watson studying him; probably thinking why the hesitation and whether it had anything to do with offending port authorities. Starke raised his eyes to harbor-furled sails then, after an admittedly theatrical pause, responded though tightly pursed lips, "Signal the naval station we'll get underway as scheduled; then get Dunbar, Osbourne, and Weaver. Let's take her out under sail, XO."

Calypso's signal reached Forsyth at his desk in the administration building where the commander dabbed light sweat with a limp, stained handkerchief and contemplated a uniform change. He expected *Calypso* to leave as planned, with or without a pilot, so the three station tugs were raising steam and preparing to get underway. When they were halfway down channel he pulled recently acquired binoculars from a desk drawer, took his cap from a coat-hook by the door, then stepped into a brilliant sun turning the pier's steel surface into a mirrored hotplate while enhancing the pungent bouquet drifting south from the commercial port. Mixing with near constant odors of paint, coal, grease, and harbor water, today's steady breeze also bore the smell of sponges piled on City Wharf and a small steamer unloading leaf tobacco to a warehouse.

Glancing at the bustling port that continued into Man o' War harbor, he looked over the small marine railway to a curving shoreline densely populated with piers, wharfs, offices, and warehouses; then turned his attention south, where station tugs were making good time under gray-white smoke plumes. Channel traffic was light, only a sponge schooner outbound under sail, wing-on-wing, with a boom swung to either side as she took advantage of a soldier's wind from astern and slight southern current. Her once white hull showed a working sponger's dirt and damage. Small dinghies were lashed down on her main deck and a large punt swung from davit arms extending over a flat stern. Since nothing was towed, he guessed she was bound for Cedar Key then some favored Gulf Coast fishing hole.

Fort Taylor, to the southeast and just beyond the white Marine Hospital, rose from the sea at the end of a causeway tethering it to the island. Two bastions were incorporated into casemented brick walls with three gun levels. After sweeping south to the horizon over a sprinkling of buoys, Forsyth panned west where the similar seascape beyond *Calypso* included several small keys and sandy shallows. The actual horizon seemed a lively seam between clear blue sky and translucent blue-green sea that sparkled and flashed, with a scattering of small whitecaps out to it. Sensing a movement beside him, he paused, lowered the glasses, acknowledged the station boatswain, and resumed scanning.

With wind and current from the north and *Calypso's* port anchor down, Forsyth could see the bark's starboard bow and most of that side; displaying the fine, elegant lines that set her apart from more utilitarian visitors. These were accentuated by a dull black hull, slightly raked straw-yellow stack between fore and main masts, and space at either end to accommodate a 4-inch rifle. The bark-rigged *Calypso's* fore and main masts carried square sails, and her mizzen fore-and-aft; which stood out against the straw-yellow masts contrasting with black bowsprit, top masts, yards, booms, and gaffs. The ship's awnings and wind sails were already stowed for sea and boats secured under round bar davits aft. Above the main deck, yards were squared and sails harbor furled. During the last week, as *Calypso* swung at anchor, Forsyth would sometimes catch her full profile from his office window and it spoke to an era fading fast with the old Navy's black-hulled steam sloops. Only their unlimited range, aesthetics, and ability to turn out deep-water sailors commended these anachronisms to a navy that might be called on to fight modern European or South American warships.

After the leading tug reached *Calypso* and went alongside, Forsyth watched its master in animated conversation with someone leaning over a bulwark, then back away rather than make up. Following this, the other two tugs stood by to the bark's north, between a pair of buoys, while the third broke off to steam southwest towards the hospital pier, reverse course, then go dead in the water. While it loitered, figures climbed *Calypso's* ratlines then edged out over her deck on footropes as they clung to spars. After the main and foremast's off-white sails were loosed and partway shaken out, most returned to the deck, leaving only topmen aloft. Her stack smoke almost immediately increased, but not enough for the main engine, then her port anchor chain suddenly straightened, shot briefly from the water, and sank. It was the steam windlass was dragging *Calypso* to short stay.

Black bulwarks partly masked an anchor party above her port hawse, so Forsyth only glimpsed upper torsos and heads as they alternately worked and waited. Watching through binoculars, he saw the starboard anchor readied for letting go; something he did not expect. When the tugs continued standing off, he lowered his binoculars and turned to the man beside him, "Boats, our tugs should be made up and her engine turning. What's your thinking?"

Hampered by a Mail Pouch Tobacco chew, the boatswain launched a shimmering brown projectile laden with tobacco juice several feet beyond the pier before replying, "Chief Weaver said *Calypso's* captain could sail her out any time he wanted and their XO's near as capable. Weaver's no braggart, but I thought it was just talk when he included the engineer. Expect we're near to finding out, sir."

Forsyth lifted the binoculars and studied the ship, responding, "You may be right Boats. But, still . . ."

Leaving anchorage under sail was basic shiphandling, although steam tugs routinely assisted in harbor or tight quarters. Unless facing exceptionally strong current at odds with the wind, it began downwind from the anchor by heaving round on windlass or capstan until reaching short stay. The anchor would then be tripped and brought on board. With wind from dead ahead and ship drifting backwards, sail and rudder would be used to reverse direction if needed. After that, the ship would maneuver and trim sails to gain the position and steerageway to get on course and remain.

Annapolis school ships were sail-powered, and most Navy ships still carried a suite, but steel cruisers only spread canvas on long voyages to extend range or reduce engine load, since their tonnage, size, and amount spread made anything but straight courses extremely difficult or impossible. Starke did mention one evening that *Calypso* was built to perform under steam or sail; but she was still a compromise and Key West lacked maneuvering room.

Studying the anchorage through binoculars, Forsyth decided buoys north of the ship posed no issue, since wind and current came from that direction, but extensive shoal water lay to her west; especially a small shallow area just southwest of the anchorage, with Buoy 4 floating east and slightly north of it. That and another buoy would be the primary concern since leaving under sail required the ship to fall back south when free, turn completely around, then gain enough way to safely pass between them; heading southeast. With the buoys clear and enough steerageway for control, it only required a turn south off Fort Taylor to enter the ship channel. After that, it was a question of making sufficient speed under sail to counteract any current and remain in it. Looking up, Forsyth watched the naval station ensign stream from its tall flagpole. Starke would have a favorable wind but it and the Florida Current often made harbor flows and depths capricious.

All things considered, it was feasible with a good crew, but any unwelcome interference by other ships or unplanned events could make it tight. As Forsyth's binoculars again ranged the horizon, then traced the ship channel up to the port, he found only the small sponge schooner; well past the anchorage, entering the South West Channel, and heeled to port with her patched rig swung to that side. *Calypso*'s lack of smoke and loosed off-white sails flowing in slow, undulating curves from their yards as she approached short stay boldly announced Starke's intent to experienced onlookers. These seamen, like Forsyth, were doubtless weighing his chances, since large sailing ships were usually towed or made up tugs alongside.

Forsyth let the binoculars hang from a strap encircling his neck. Starke stationed the tugs to be available if needed, so the risk was unnecessary, not unreasonable. His first impulse was to require *Calypso* leave under steam or use tugs, but he had no authority and, in fairness, would enjoy the challenge himself. Captains considered risk, made a decision, and then owned the result; even when something unpredictable or overlooked interfered. After their evenings together, he did not consider Starke shy or reckless but possessing an innate and practiced ability to balance caution and prudence with action and result. Even so, *Calypso* was attempting a maneuver Key West's seasoned masters and pilots considered only when unavoidable. Starke had not mentioned it so Forsyth suspected this demonstration was sparked by a suspiciously absent pilot and intent to display the élan and capability of a ship some locals thought sank two filibusters; as she set out on another hunt. Gently stroking his goatee, Forsyth felt the binoculars tug his neck as he walked to the pier's edge, trailed by the boatswain. What happened would be a minor event to be embellished then woven into local waterfront gossip. If Starke did well, *Calypso* would be seen as a formidable opponent but should it go badly, equal leverage would be applied in the opposite direction. Either way, Starke was committed.

An impromptu gathering on the steel pier's head watched her starboard side shorten and bow begin pointing towards them as the station boatswain, confident in his expertise, risked launching another spittle round before observing, "Set her spars to kick the stern around. She looks to be using anchor, rudder, and current to increase the angle before weighing; and will need it."

Forsyth knew chewing was popular with men and rural women across the nation so he tolerated it ashore if the projectiles landed in spittoon or harbor. However, catching sight of this one just clearing the dark pier before striking the water reinforced his distaste for the habit on ships. Returning to the binoculars, he added, "Yards are trimmed and braced well. There … a jib and staysail's going up."

"If *Calypso's* setting those sails, she's underway, sir."

While Forsyth responded, *Calypso's* sternway became apparent, the national ensign shifted, and her bowsprit pointed almost directly at the naval station pier. She continued swinging until the starboard bow vanished, port bow became visible, and then entire side. Another jib and the mainmast staysail were run up as commander and boatswain watched her swing starboard. They knew it was now critical to use rudder and square sails with skill and confidence. The turn must be slowed while coaxing out enough forward movement; even as the current relentlessly carried her towards the small shoal and surrounding water, only a few feet deeper than the bark's draft. On her forecastle, men fished the port anchor and readied it for letting go.

Forsyth was about to observe Starke had delayed too long when the yards on *Calypso's* main and fore masts swung to positions that would drive her forward, just as upper and lower mizzen sails were raised. At his side, ignoring the pungent smells and searing sun's reflection off the steel pier, the boatswain, cleared his throat, "Picking up speed, but she best gain steerageway now, or soon as."

Before Forsyth replied, *Calypso* ceased swinging then began slipping forward under sail, her rudder starting to bite. Calculating aloud, he observed, "She'd best take Buoy 4 close aboard to port, then aim for Buoy 8."

"That's all she can do, sir. No other choice. Needs to get more way or call for tugs."

Forsyth checked. The two tugs north of *Calypso* were rapidly taking station close astern as the third steamed slowly towards Buoy 8, but was keeping clear. The commander made a mental note to praise their masters' handling of an unexpected situation.

With wind blowing uninterrupted past the waterfront and down channel, Forsyth and his boatswain watched *Calypso* heel a shade to starboard with sails drawing well, then gain momentum enough to bring her bow slightly upwind towards Buoy 4, canceling the southern set. He was unable to judge separation as the buoy passed down her port side, but once clear, *Calypso's* stern swung immediately past the obstacle as she turned a touch south towards Buoy 8, trimming sails for the new course.

Just before Buoy 8, *Calypso* eased into a slight starboard turn, entered the channel, then quickly steadied on a course south and west, through two rows of channel buoys. Fort Taylor passed down the port side as three tugs loosed several short blasts from steam whistles then turned for the naval station. With nothing more to see, Forsyth walked to the administration building, trailed by his boatswain who extracted a dark, spongy tobacco wad from his mouth, snapped it over one of the pier's cleats, and grinned, "Don't suppose the ship engineer took her out, sir?"

With wind from astern, or port quarter, depending on course, *Calypso* continued picking up speed passing down South West Channel. Using the lighthouse for a stern bearing and shooting sextant angles to prominent points, the quartermasters plotted her progress on a chart; then compared it with passing buoys, spots where the sea washed over rocks or coral, and water color. Dunbar listened, calculated, checked their progress outside the pilothouse, and recommended course adjustments.

Calypso cleared the Middle Ground under full sail then entered deep water beyond Spartan Shoal where the Key West pilot boat, *Jon Gett*, rolled slightly on easy swells, anticipating customers. With none on offer, the sloop's crew and pilots watched the elegant black bark with three levels of off-white sails ghost into the Caribbean, secure its stocked anchors for sea, and set the underway watch.

Watson came to the flying bridge after the anchors were secured, complimented Osbourne on conning the ship, reviewed the chart with Dunbar, then left to meet Martyn about one of his seamen. Starke slowly scanned the horizon before following his executive officer below. It was completely clear to the sparkling seam between blue sky and greenish-blue sea, except for a smoke smudge to the northwest and shrinking stern of a small, white schooner with worn sails. The sponger caused some concern as they came down South West Channel but turned west when her shallow draft allowed and cleared before *Calypso* sailed past.

Calypso pushed twenty miles into the Gulf under sail, giving her crew time to eat, before Starke ordered fore, main, and royals furled; leaving topsails, mizzen, jib and staysails. Fires were spread in both propulsion boilers and once the engine room reported ready to answer all bells the familiar vibration of large pistons spinning a single shaft came up through her deck planks. When the screw bit, only staysails remained up to steady *Calypso*'s passage through the Gulf. She came to a new heading, roughly west by southwest, just north of the powerful current flowing east to become the Gulf Stream then made for the Yucatan Channel on an easy sea with few whitecaps.

Chapter Twelve
Hurricane

Naval Cadet Hamilton Caldwell prepared for the approaching midwatch with a personal logbook entry. He would return to the Naval Academy in two years and his class standing assigned based on its contents, a comprehensive examination, performance, and academic standing. The result would determine whether a commission would be offered after six years and, if not sent home, establish his seniority among other classmates throughout a career.

Caldwell's disposition was a logical, analytic, and romantic blend so he made preparations during the second academic year to graduate with or without a commission. After considering the Revenue Cutter Service or, like Philo McGiffin, a foreign navy if faced with a degree and severance pay, he settled on reading law then joining his father's New York City office and perhaps the naval militia. With pragmatism satisfied, romantic inclinations had free reign and a summer under sail on *Monongahela* gave life to Preble, Hull, and Decatur. *Calypso* caught his interest after hearing instructors caution graduates about selecting her for their final two years at sea; which prompted a letter asking his father make discrete Navy Department inquiries. From that, he learned of her privateer roots and young lieutenant commanding who supposedly joined the disastrous Montana campaign as a civilian packer, went ashore into Alexandria's chaos, sailed merchant ships, and claimed a father who stepped from a Marryat novel. His romantic inclinations gained ascendency and he requested her, despite firm advice that *Boston* or *Maine* was more desirable. When *Maine* seemed inevitable, a second letter went to the influential father who enthusiastically supported a ship that might scuttle his son's commissioning. Visits were made, favors called in, and Caldwell joined *Calypso* in Norfolk soon after graduation. The bark exceeded expectations. Besides the dramatic first few months, her executive officer, Watson, proved a reserved, but vigorous mentor, fair disciplinarian, and first-rate seaman. Unfortunately, in his eyes, the fledgling wardroom included Caldwell's division officer, Ensign Blair. Caldwell found him intelligent, competent, often pompous, and an incurable romantic who dominated the gun division and starboard underway watch. Watson, thankfully, assigned him to the port section, which offered relief from Blair during every other watch at sea.

While stowing his log, someone approached Caldwell's berth deck stateroom near the stern, then quietly knocked on the thin wood door. It was Martyn making his way to the pilothouse and stopping to make sure his assistant was up. Blair would never condescend to that, but pound loud enough to let the entire wardroom think his junior was in deep sleep; which was never true, and everyone quickly divined this behavior was not so much malicious as perverse humor. After closing the door, Caldwell followed Martyn through a dark, subdued world dominated by the pulsating engine, humming ventilation fans, and constant rasp of saltwater against hull sheathing. On the way, they passed tightly packed and close berthing areas where sailors slept in hammocks slung from numbered hooks and ate meals at mess tables now raised to the overhead. Signs of life, other than the ship's sounds and movements, consisted of snoring variations, intermittent twitching of the canvas sausages, and packed humanity's bouquet.

They climbed to the main deck then passed from deckhouse to tropical night through a door just off the stairs. As they walked towards another ladder then pilothouse, Caldwell felt immersed by a warm Caribbean breeze bringing smells of sea, hot steam, and coal smoke. The celestial dome rested on a horizon devoid of lights or looms, with planets lost in thousands of stars garnishing the night sky. Below the deck edge were bow and midship wakes, created as the hull sliced through a montage of evolving gray, black, and white hues that shimmered near the ship then faded to black in the distance. Pausing at the top of the ladder, he looked astern past stack and masts to glittering blue-white phosphorescence lighting *Calypso's* expanding wake as she plowed through millions of minute organisms.

Martyn and Caldwell acknowledged their quartermaster as they entered the pilothouse, read night orders, then listened to Blair describe what passed and what to expect on watch. Since boilers shifted daily at noon, and turning south for the Yucatan Channel would come after their watch, traffic and weather would normally have been the greatest concerns; but the night order book emphasized the barometer and waking their captain should it change. After relieving, Martyn had the forward windows swung in and latched to the overhead, giving the night breeze full access as Caldwell adjusted the duty binoculars Naval Cadet Terrence Timme turned over. His fellow naval cadet was short, with effeminate features topped by thin, wispy hair ruffled by the slightest breeze, and little facial hair. When not on watch, he was Martyn's deck assistant under Chief Weaver's tutelage. Although extremely intelligent, he possessed an impressive temper that must be severely tried as he obviously chaffed under Blair's starboard watch dictatorship.

Caldwell was grateful Starke ensured watch officers had binoculars rather than paired-telescopes, but, as he made adjustments using stars and sea, wanted his own that would remain adjusted for him. Finally satisfied, he let them hang from his neck; scanning the horizon unaided until an anomaly caught his attention. Periodically, he or Martyn checked the magnetic steering compass or asked their helmsman to mark his head, confirming they were on course. Between tasks, he listened to water moving alongside the hull, accompanied by a regular sucking, surf-like sound as *Calypso's* bow rose from the sea then settled down into it. Smoke could be felt and heard as it passed through the stack before drifting astern to vanish in the dark night. Engine vibrations worked up through framing to the pilothouse deck while the running rigging outside moved in the breeze, a canvas staysail filled and emptied with a crack, and the forward 4-inch rifle's canvas cover flapped when a stray gust stole under it.

Studying the mount's amorphous shape, Caldwell found it difficult to believe it was firing on *Rafael Riego* two weeks before. After four years in school or on summer cruise, life had been surreal since Norfolk. He helped commission a warship, hunted filibusters, saw violent death, sailed the Caribbean, and would soon be in Kingston, the Jamaica of Nelson, Morgan, and others. There was also leaving Key West under sail. Academy school ships made it a point to return in that manner, often struggling up through the bay then into the broad Severn River estuary, but Key West was different. The captain took a risk Caldwell failed to understand at the time, but it changed the atmosphere. When Watson announced they would sail out, *Calypso's* doomsayers emerged, including an older sailor who raised his concerns with Doran Kearney, one of the ship's top seamen. Caldwell overheard Kearney respond, "Belay the nonsense, bucko. Captain Starke'll take her out and more. I sailed with him when he was a cadet. You'll not be lacking action, so best get used to it." Starke remained a properly distant figure after the flawless exit but the crew was increasingly loyal.

Calypso steamed steadily for Jamaica with the at-sea routine beginning before sunrise. Turn-to and sweepers were passed by mouth and boatswain pipes since there was no bugler then running lights were extinguished at sunrise. Sailors' hammocks came down from hooks then rolled and passed through a measuring ring before stowing. Breakfast was at eight, then sick call. Just before nine-thirty quarters, Watson would have officers assemble to put out approved day orders and make adjustments. Dinner came at noon, a second officers' call late afternoon, then quarters and supper. Training took place during specified morning and afternoon periods and, unless maintenance or repair prevented, concentrated on seamanship since it was hurricane season. Sailing skills were honed by sending upper masts up and down, working yards, bending on sails, reefing them, stripping them, and raising storm canvas. Boilers shifted at noon and ashes hoisted throughout the day. Sweepers sounded repeatedly while watches completed two or four-hour stints. Running lights were relit at sunset, foretop lookouts shifted to the flying bridge, and crew hammocks rigged. Then the cycle repeated.

As *Calypso* approached the Yucatan Channel, Dunbar calculated sunrise and sunset, took sights at morning twilight, noon, and evening twilight to obtain fixes. Using this, he completed noon reports and prepared the night order book. He also ensured running lights were lit and extinguished with equal precision. *Calypso* was proving a fast steamer; making almost twelve knots on one boiler along a track laid out to avoid powerful currents flowing east along Cuba's ravaged

Pinar del Río province. After turning south into the Yucatan Channel, he gained a visual fix from Cabo San Antonio lighthouse, then followed the Colon shipping route until reaching Negril Point's latitude, where *Calypso* turned due east, intending to run that latitude to Jamaica.

Traffic varied, but the heaviest was near Cabo San Antonio where the sea lanes funneled between Cuba's western tip and Mexico's Yucatan Peninsula. During night watches, some ships passed near enough to make out red, green, or white running lights, but most were marked by an indistinct cluster, or loom if more distant. Masthead lookouts were relied on throughout the day to spot ships. Those passing close aboard were identified and logged. Most were open-deck sailboats working fishing grounds and the rest a mix of small steamers, schooners, barks, and one full-rigged ship. When they passed close by, *Calypso* would alter or hold course, depending on situation.

During early morning on the day Negril Point would be raised, Starke was in his day cabin after a night spent in the pilothouse or adjacent sea cabin until the midwatch settled in. When things seemed quiet, he went below to refresh and change, but nodded off in a leather chair for most of an hour after advancing the desk calendar to "FRI SEP 25 96". He was wakened from deep sleep by Dunbar and Martyn's messenger, who reported the brass barometer's readings, which rose earlier, were steadily dropping. Starke climbed to the pilothouse through an oppressive night knowing the changing pressure confirmed heavy weather's approach. There had been an extraordinary stillness accompanying the unstable barometer, excessively moist and warm atmosphere, scent of approaching rain, and increasing swells. Birds, fish, and other creatures were acting strange or vanished. Even Thaddeus abandoned his insatiable quest for food, spent the afternoon scouting, then went to ground in a small locker near the keel where he curled into a ball and refused to leave, eat, or groom. Caribbean hurricanes and storms roughly handled Starke in the past, and one was enough to recognize their harbingers.

In the dark pilothouse, Starke, Martyn, Caldwell, Owen, and others heard Dunbar's evaluation then the executive officer, Osbourne, and Weaver sent for. Crowding around the chart table fixed to the aft wall under a flickering light, Starke began, "As Mr. Dunbar observed we're probably looking at a hurricane. It'll come from dead ahead or somewhere off the port bow and likely beat us to Negril Point so let's see where we stand."

Being junior, Chief Weaver started ticking off items using powerful, stubby fingers with overlapping scars, "Storm canvas was left bent to the yards after yesterday's drill for an airing, captain, but we'd best strip canvas to cut top hamper then make certain nothing aloft comes adrift. Boats need more securing and running rigging checked for chaffing. Best rig another anchor preventer, heavy weather lifelines, and netting. I doubt we've time to strike upper masts and jibboom; so it's best not to risk it. I'll ensure oilskins get lashed with line; buttons never hold."

Starke considered this, "I agree, chief. When we call all hands, strip the main yards; but keep topsails, storm staysails, jibs, and mizzen. If we lose power, the topsails, aft staysails and mizzen should help keep us pointed upwind."

Caldwell risked interjecting, "A sea anchor, chief?"

Watson resisted pointing out cadets did not offer advice, but instead responded, "Our large screw has greater drag than two small ones. Combining that with a sea anchor could put us in the trough if a mistake is made or the engine fails."

Caldwell realized his transgression and backed slightly

from the table as Stark turned towards him, "Thanks, XO, and an excellent question, Mr. Caldwell. Ensure the explanation makes it to your personal log. Is there anything else, chief?"

"No, sir, if there is, I'll get with Mr. Martyn."

"Mr. Dunbar."

The lanky, sandy-haired navigator looked up at Starke, "We'll have a man dedicated to the EOT." There was no need to mention this, being routine for major storms, but it allowed time to exchange the brass dividers spread in his right hand for notes resting on the chart then continue, "Storm card's built to estimate the eye with barometer readings, wind direction, and force. It should be ten to twelve points off the wind, which should veer east to north. If it stops veering, we're directly in the storm's path. Considering the swells, I recommend steering southwest. Continuing east will take us deep into the worst of it. We should get as far west as possible then steer for Negril Point or Kingston. Southwest also takes us clear of land but not far off course."

Caldwell stifled an impulse to ask why he did not recommend coming about, putting the wind on their starboard quarter, and run until the barometer began rising; a textbook answer. Starke observed Watson's glance and naval cadet's reluctance so he interjected, "I agree with turning southwest, Mr. Dunbar; and Mr. Martyn may do so now. I suspect Mr. Caldwell's curious why we're not running to avoid a head sea's pounding?"

As Caldwell struggled to decide if this was good or bad attention, Starke supplied an answer, "While lying to works for steamers heading away from the eye, even those with a few auxiliary sails, *Calypso's* lower freeboard, steam plant, and sail rig must be considered. If limited to sails, the best approach would be to stream a sea anchor and wait it out. Under steam alone, Mr. Dunbar would recommend placing the wind on the starboard quarter and run, but that gives up our advantage of having steam and sails while taking us further from Jamaica. Besides we can't underestimate the waves with a stern that won't take heavy beating."

Starke, to Caldwell's relief, then addressed the group more broadly, "My intent is to steer southwest using just enough power to meet the seas head on and drift under aft staysails and reefed mizzen. We'll adjust shaft turns to control headway, maintain position, minimize rolling, and reduce pounding. Expect the wind to come over the port bow, since most hurricanes start south or northeast of Jamaica. While I doubt avoiding coasts or shoal water will play a role, Mr. Dunbar will be alert for that, as will all watchstanders. We'll make for Negril Point or Kingston once the storm passes."

Turning, Starke continued, "Engineering, Mr. Osbourne."

Osbourne was wedged between chart table and wall. Without abandoning this secure position, he pushed the service cap up his forehead then calmly drawled, "As reported captain, both boilers are on line. May not be used but gives us back-up. We'll double up watching feedwater. The ship will be lively and if a single water tube fails the boiler must come off line. Same as with spars, rolling's worst. There'll be seasickness and perhaps some injuries so the black gang will rest and sleep on station. We'll take coal from upper bunkers first and watch for shifting. Like the pilothouse, one man will be on the EOT. We've been making feedwater and dumping it to freshwater tanks; but those that are partly filled can be topped up with sea water to damp roll or add ballast. O'Leary has the engine and auxiliary rooms. I'll stay with the boilers."

"Very well Mr. Osbourne. XO?"

Watson was last so he could weigh everything to that point and catch anything overlooked. He began, "With your permission Captain, we'll wake the crew and begin work at the end of this watch then, weather permitting, breakfast as usual to allow a short break. Idlers will be available for use on deck or assist the master-at-arms look for anything not properly secured. We've not had the weather to shake out everything that could get loose so Paymaster Wiggs will inspect the supply storerooms and assist the surgeon with his. I'll take officer staterooms; they're probably the worst."

Watson's last words struck home with cadets struggling to appear nonchalant. Starke reminded himself to take a last look at his day cabin, despite Yamashita's diligence, before ending with, "Gentlemen, that should do for now. Report to the XO for what you need. I'll be here or in my cabin."

The watch immediately began tasks that could be worked in darkness or twilight then "all hands" went at four, when watches normally relieved. Navigator Dunbar shot morning stars with Chief Owen, calculated their position, plotted it on the chart, and drew a line from the previous evening's fix; then figured set and drift. With that, barometer readings, and other information, the card made up earlier would estimate storm center.

Dawn came with a brilliant sun, more red than orange, lighting a morning pregnant with rain, increasing swells, and an unsteady but falling barometer. *Calypso* was steaming roughly southwest, adjusting course and speed to steady her deck for those working. A faster pace would take them further from the brunt of the storm but Starke was certain it would not be enough to avoid a beating and could delay preparations or risk accidents.

Chief Weaver's mast captains began stripping canvas. Several square sails were unbent from their yard, lowered, rolled, and snaked into a storeroom, accompanied by light canvas jibs and staysails. *Calypso's* military conversion included two sail rooms. One contained sailmaker equipment, spare sails, and canvas; the other her light and storm sails. Stowing unwieldy canvas required most of the deck force and more, so the gun division rigged heavy weather lifelines and storm netting under Seaman Kearney's direction. While netting was unrolled along the main deck, he paused to look aloft as topmen loosened a sail. They were bent double over the yard, with each pull dragging torsos forward as if diving over it, feet still on foot ropes, and backsides rising in the air before falling back. Advancing years robbed Kearney of the speed and agility to work high above deck, where everything was on the double, but left the experience to be more valuable elsewhere. Even so, he felt the loss watching a mast captain near the foremast excoriating a mixed group of landsmen and reluctant volunteers who forgot to start lines by jerking them, not just pulling. He spotted a frustrated Landsman Hawk, among them, someone Kearney knew would become a first-rate petty officer if he remained past his enlistment.

The mandolin virtuoso, Coxswain Melvin, walking aft with boat plugs waved to Kearney, who nodded in reply. Melvin had been directed to inspect boats and davits, ensure everything was properly stowed, and all storm lashings secure. The two gun captains, Grier and Kirby, supervised brushing an additional layer of grease on the 4-inch mounts before securing their canvas tarps with thick lines. Gun division seamen not working the mounts, lifelines, or rigging stowed Gatling and 3-pounder guns below deck then emptied ready-service magazines near the mounts. Lead stokers Jones and Kemp worked to secure loose equipment, clear paths between coal bunkers and boilers, and ensure equipment was on station while water tenders oversaw their preparations. Machinists in another compartment coaxed their equipment to distill more water for the fresh and feedwater water tanks;

and constantly sounded them.

Paymaster Wiggs' domain included galley, bread-room, dry provision storerooms, and spirit room for wet provisions. As storekeepers, commissary men, and stewards worked, he encouraged, inspected, and sometimes ordered complete re-stowing. When supplies were moved from bread and clothing storerooms' walls or shelving, he checked their sheet tin lining. Wiggs, Conrad, and the apothecary then went through sick bay and their medical storerooms; mostly forward and low in the ship. Afterwards, Wiggs advised the surgeon draw additional instruments, medicine, and items they might later need to augment that normally kept on hand. Assistant Surgeon Conrad followed this advice then sat at his sickbay desk anchored to the deck near six box-like berths suspended from the overhead, anticipating his first hurricane with excitement and apprehension.

Leaving the pilothouse while the crew breakfasted, Starke found Yamashita had rigged his day cabin for heavy weather. Everything was clean, stowed, and secure; except the desk. Chair lanyards were doubled, bookshelf bars fixed, and window port-lids bolted. Minutes later, the table's spider corralled hot coffee, toast, and sliced ham followed by oats boiled with salt and butter then laced with molasses. He ate slow and well as noon approached; enjoying what was probably his last substantial meal for some time. As Starke ate, *Calypso's* slow and gentle seesawing, from shouldering through swells, took longer. He was about to send for Watson when the executive officer entered to report preparations nearly finished so he lifted his cap from a wall hook and left with him for a last walk-through. This informal, but thorough, inspection was completed without disturbing tasks requiring that last bit of attention. They examined storerooms, staterooms, and galley before passing through the berthing, medical, and administrative spaces. After these were complete, magazines were checked and main deck walked. Stark returned Kearney and Melvin's salutes and nodded as he passed; saying nothing that might delay progress or cause shipmates to think them captain's favorites.

As the Caribbean sun approached its zenith behind a veil of light clouds, the gray sea and sky off their port bow darkened then became a rapidly advancing black wall. Large rain drops began striking the main deck's salt-bleached wood, leaving dark stains as Chief Weaver sent two sailors to tighten a poorly coiled line wedged between several others on a bulwark pin rail. Seeing the officers approach, he crossed the deck, saluted the captain, then reported, "We're secure topside XO; with your permission, sir, I'll send the men below for oilskins."

After Watson nodded, Weaver motioned to a waiting petty officer who left to pass the word then join the others retrieving their slickers, or waterproofs; a sailcloth overcoat glazed with wax and linseed oil. This slightly yellow canvas apparel, encircled by marline at key points, soon repopulated *Calypso's* main deck and pilothouse. Unless inundated, waterproofs were usually effective keeping rain out but superb at keeping sweat in so Starke bought a lighter, rubberized officer's coat in Washington with ventilation panels under the arms and back flap. Yamashita hung it from a peg near the day cabin door earlier, but Starke opted to wait until after inspection. Once Watson and Weaver left to retrieve their slickers, Starke stopped by the cabin for his.

Ushered in by increasing rain, with swells becoming waves, the wall of dark clouds grew taller as it relentlessly closed *Calypso*. Starke scanned what little horizon remained for shipping then a largely deserted main deck for poorly made-up lines because securing them during a storm risked lives.

The most noticeable difference, besides absent sailors, was rope netting strung along bulwark crowns like boarding nets. Instead of repelling the enemy, however, these four-foot high, light brown and gray nets might keep a sailor from washing overboard when not, albeit painfully, halted by the bulwarks. They were the last hope for anyone carried across the deck since only large steam ships such as *Maine* could attempt a recovery in heavy weather; and that risked lives and damage on what was usually a futile gesture.

Leaving the forward pilothouse window, Starke crossed to the small shelf reserved for his use and retrieved a worn briar pipe; inexpensive and expendable. Once between his teeth, he pondered the relief lighting it might bring, but the smoking lamp was out and he followed his own, and Navy, rules. Returning to the forward window, he admitted it made little difference, avoiding damage or casualties would demand his full attention; and everyone not incapacitated by seasickness. Looking over the jibboom to dark clouds rising from the water, he concentrated on how to ensure oncoming seas met the ship's bow at an angle and speed that kept shipping water and hull pounding down while avoiding the excessive rolls that risked spars and boilers. They would also need to avoid becoming trapped in the trough to capsize or swamp. *Calypso*, with her fantail stern, also risked damage aft if pooped; another reason he was grateful Osbourne and O'Leary had charge of steam engineering. Over the next hours or days, *Calypso*'s survival would depend on generating steam for main engine and dynamos. *Calypso* became a sailing ship without it; to be handled entirely different with far greater risk. Losing auxiliary steam also meant relying on a hand bilge pump that would never keep up since planking worked excessively in storms and seawater washing over the deck entered bilges through hatches, doors, and vents. This made the ship less buoyant and, with water sloshing from side-to-side, less stable. The steering engine also needed steam and without it they might be forced to use the exposed aft helm station.

Starke watched the tempest advance rapidly over a building gray sea until, without preliminaries, it enveloped *Calypso* and transformed the universe. Color succumbed to various shades of black, gray, and white. Swells and waves became ranks of increasingly large boomers *Calypso* plowed into; her bow lifting with each, riding up through its crest, then twisting down into the trough, heeling well to starboard until submerging bow and anchors brought an explosion of frothing white water shooting up, out, and away. What remained, cascaded against her deckhouse then raced down the main deck's starboard side, shooting overboard through every opening. For what remained of the morning, then afternoon and evening, this heavy weather built, periodically subsided to gather strength, and returned with increased ferocity. The pilothouse watch wedged themselves in corners, if able, or fought the plunging, gyrating deck to remain upright by rotating weight, ankles, and knees. Sailors on the helm and lee helm were lashed in place. Anyone distracted or caught off balance was carried across the space in hesitant hops until striking the lee wall, or thrown to the deck in a tangle before sliding to the low side.

Ensign Blair relieved Martyn at noon, while Starke and Watson agreed one or the other would always be in the pilothouse. Confident in Watson's abilities, Starke took a turn below deck through an odorous, disorienting, confined world where the smallest tasks proved exhausting. Standing or moving required at least one arm dedicated to gripping something solid, and all four limbs to cushion slides into walls, bulkheads, doors, or other fixed objects. Many sailors lay in a stupor, unwilling to move and impervious to pleading or threats. The rest braced themselves where they worked or, like Thaddeus, found a personal refuge. One group gathered anxiously by weather deck doors, in slickers tied with line, waiting for the call. On the berth deck, he watched *Calypso's* lee portholes submerge, solid water rush past their glass, then a glimpse of foam, waves, and gray-black clouds. He particularly wanted to visit the engineering spaces. They were low in the ship where there was less movement but the disturbed bilges' noxious gas twisted the strongest stomach while high, humid temperatures sucked away energy then will. Working in the fire room, now well past 120 degrees, men barely endured until bodies rebelled and vanquished flesh slumped down a bulkhead to the deck or suddenly collapsed. Those still able removed them to the berth deck or sick bay then rejoined the fight.

Their chief engineer stood alongside Starke, seemingly oblivious to the fire room's noise, humidity, and heat, despite a generous physique. Surprised, but grateful his captain came down during a storm, he nodded towards the large Negro supervising stokers shoveling coal through the stokeholes' heavy iron shutters that slammed open briefly then crashed shut on the glowing bed inside. A dirty red bandana was knotted around his head, just above the eyes, to catch sweat rivulets emerging from curly black hair, while perspiration glistened over ebony skin covering pronounced muscles.

Osbourne gained the man's attention though a commanding tone, far different from his wardroom drawl, "Stoker Kemp."

"Sir, yes, sir."

"A moment."

It was the first Kemp noticed their commanding officer left a storm to join the chief engineer in the fire room. A quick check revealed the boiler front was in hand; and his only known transgression was an episode on the Port Royal pier that left an Irish deck seaman nursing a broken nose. That was some time back, however, and no longer of interest to the officers or injured party. Like the others, Kemp spoke mostly through water tenders, less frequently the machinist chief, occasionally Ensign O'Leary, and hardly ever with ship's engineer. Above the lowest petty officer, it was mostly some technical issue or request, but Kemp set out over the lively deck, replying, "Sir, yes, sir."

He moved carefully, taking care to avoid the shifting steel deck-plates showing every intention of throwing him against a hot boiler face or piping. It struck him how Starke's faded blue eyes tracked his progress across the boiler flat and their steadiness when he stood in front of the man. Smiling, Osbourne announced, "Captain, this lead stoker Delmar Kemp."

Kemp almost recoiled as the captain's right arm unhesitatingly emerged but without realizing it removed his heavy glove and grasped the outstretched hand. Feeling wet coal dust sandwiched between their palms, his natural reaction was to pull back, but a solid grasp resisted.

"Mr. Osbourne and Mr. O'Leary tell me you and Jones are doing well and steam's more important than ever right now. Mr. Osbourne says you're from Virginia?"

"Sir, yes, sir. A farm near Lexington, captain."

"My mother's family had a plantation downriver from West Point. I think we're a long way from the fields today."

With that, Kemp glimpsed a slight smile through the sparse beard as his hand was released. Grinning, he responded, "Yes, sir, captain, a long way, sir."

Their brief exchange altered his perception of *Calypso's* commander; until then a vague figure. Starke seemed to lack frills and the unhesitatingly firm handshake confirmed stories about him sailing as a merchant ship mate. Back at the boiler face, Kemp replaced the stiff glove, decided some rumors about their captain might be true, and relieved a spent stoker.

Starke felt almost cold as he returned to the pilothouse where rain hammered into hard sheets by the wind was battering their ship. Each violent assault was separated by a momentary pause as though the storm needed to regroup before another furious strike. His waterproof was pulled tight to avoid leaks but several rivulets started under the collar. Ignoring these, he studied wind and sea, visualized the Beaufort Scale that classified weather, and estimated the storm a severe gale, or level nine, and worsening. Building waves separated by deep troughs and crowned with spindrift struck her port side and bow like breakers pummeling a rocky shore; and the horizon vanished completely when the ship was low and waves at their zenith. Each time *Calypso's* stem axed down through a wave, white spray blasted outward from under her plunging bow, frothed aft alongside, joined the midship wakes, and was quickly absorbed off the stern. Bowsprit and jibboom remained mostly above the water, but the largest heels submerged her starboard side then flooded the main deck before overboarding through slotted openings above the sheer strake. Less often, the bulwark's entire outboard side went under to the netting, inundating everything, as roll and pitch colluded to completely bury the main deck forward of midship. Three widely spaced rogue waves tested *Calypso's* limit by submerging bowsprit, jibboom, and then forecastle; scooping up ten or more feet of churning seawater. Starke was relieved to see everything emerge intact as the resulting bore raced aft down the deck, encircling larger fittings, engulfing others, crashing against bulkheads, and sweeping the very few sailors topside from their feet.

Calypso's storm sails added power as the wind blew steadily across the ship from port bow to starboard quarter, but their greatest value lay in damping rolls; causing *Calypso* to sway full starboard, hesitate at the vertical, then go slightly to port. Every inch of the heavy storm canvas bowed outboard like steel breastplates, leaving the port running rigging rod-like and starboard curving outboard as a screaming wind smashed against and through lines, stays, and shrouds. Constant groans from her twisting keel, hull frames, and wood sheathing were intermittently subsumed in a staggering shudder when the stem crashed through a recalcitrant wave. The engine's steady throb carried through the hull, assuring those remaining sensate that steam still powered three pistons forcing the ship forward; but even that was regularly supplanted by a demented scream as the screw lifted from the sea, raced free, then reentered. The pilothouse occupants heard and felt all; amazed their perch did not carry away, even during three rogue waves' brutal onslaughts.

They survived by balancing sails, helm, and engine to head into the seas, maintain steering, hold the wind just off her port bow, and achieve the best ride. Realizing any helmsman could instantly lose everything, each sailor doing his trick at the wheel fought doggedly to steer within a quarter compass point; even when their rudder lifted from the sea and lost bite, pulling the ship one way or another as it submerged. Raising aft staysails helped, but those wrestling *Calypso's* large brass helm required frequent relief.

Attempts to maintain a constant southwest course ended as day and evening were spent adjusting to the continuously veering wind; which meant they were avoiding the eye. Watson was in the pilothouse when the bark lost headway and began falling off, even with forward storm sails ready and those midship and aft set and drawing. He stood by an alarmed Martyn then suggested the ensign put their helm down hard and increase speed. He later explained the maneuver allowed her aft sails to force the ship back into the wind, like a weather vane, and Martyn passed that knowledge to Blair.

During late afternoon and evening, the storm's eye passed north of *Calypso*; racing for the Yucatan Channel with 110 to 130 mile per hour winds whipping the sea into a dark, violent caldron. Although the ride remained tempestuous after its passing, wind and rain lessened then scattered stars appeared. Aware night orders never replaced experience, and his responsibility absolute, Starke remained in the pilothouse most of the storm, except for brief snatches of sleep in his sea cabin and the tour below deck.

By the time Stark, Watson, Dunbar, and Owen took their sextants to the flying bridge for morning stars, a light wind came in gusts, the entire sky had cleared, and the vibrant Caribbean dawn was incomparable. After calculations were complete, results compared, and position fixed; the brass helm spun and *Calypso* heeled slightly starboard, climbed an oncoming wave, and steadied on course to Kingston. Seaman Kearney was the first sailor back in the foretop, satiated from a large breakfast and accompanied by Landsman Hawk. After explaining several eye-splicing tricks, he looked over the edge at their commander standing outside the port-side pilothouse door, near the collapsible bridge-wing railing, his abused, unlit pipe cradled in the right hand and waterproof draped over the left forearm.

Chapter Thirteen
Catastrophe

Captain Albert woke to a pleasant morning the day after *Calypso* left Key West for Jamaica and lingered several minutes at the Building window following his morning ritual of sipping coffee from a worn, white china cup with fading gilt eagle. Returning to the oak desk, he sat down and leaned back; a precarious maneuver in the swivel chair, made feasible only because a Persian rug constrained its five casters. His arthritic knees responded with several sharp pains, unusual for September.

The Morning Times featured a story about state troops with Gatling guns in Leadville to end a violent miners' strike. That imbroglio, the coming national election, and Ottoman Empire turmoil pushed Cuba stories to the back pages and reduced *Calypso's* encounter with the late *Rafael Riego* to a simple rescue. He also suspected telling the filibuster's story without linking the Junta to anarchism played a supporting role, but was satisfied nevertheless. After triaging papers spread across the desk, he felt ready to begin the day's work, paused to glance up at the white glass and tarnished brass lamp above his desk, lifted a briar pipe from the mahogany rack, then dredged its veteran bowl though a new tobacco pouch from Abigail. While enjoying the first draw's satisfying bite, he spotted a light yellow-brown message form jutting from the wood correspondence box beside his mechanical calendar. It was Forsyth's telegram stating, "*Calypso* departed this forenoon under sail. No steam, no tugs."

Albert grinned as light gray smoke gathered around the lamp. Abigail was right, Starke had a brushstroke of the buccaneer despite an attentively respectable, almost stiff, demeanor. The question was whether those traits would lead him down the path of Sir Henry Morgan or Calico Jack Rackham. Partly overlapping that telegram was Consul-general Lee's cable to State. The senior Spanish admiral in Havana asked for Starke to support a board convened to consider *Francisco de Montejo*'s handling off Arrecife Alacranes. The attached handwritten note advised State, Justice, and Navy that the President favored this request, with reservations. The thrust appeared to be that agreeing might benefit negotiations but any perception of being overly friendly with Spain before the election was unwelcome.

He suspected the Junta's Washington office, unofficially labeled the Cuban Legation, operating from a leased Raleigh Hotel suite less than a half-dozen blocks east of the Building, was an equal consideration. The Junta was headquartered in New York City but this effective operation was run by Quesada who, along with Horatio Rubens in New York, considered their Expeditionary Section's filibusters the revolution's lifeline. Albert occasionally sparred with them and respected their legal, political, and propaganda skills. He thought this player's quiet acquiescence probably indicated they wanted the *Rafael Riego* expedition's anarchist roots buried as much or more than the newspapers and administration. Otherwise Quesada would have used it to end, hamper, or discredit a project that just cost them two expeditions. The Justice troubleshooter Maximilian Falk predicted they would instead move against it by using Congress and administration allies to press for *Calypso's* transfer to the European Squadron and eastern Mediterranean duty; or ensnare Albert and Starke in committee testimony. Falk's offer of assistance to derail these ploys had been immediately accepted.

He recommended they concentrate first on schemes to exile *Calypso* to the Mediterranean, since congressional testimony was further off and the Junta would move slowly to avoid exposing their anarchist faction. He also warned the Junta held a solid hand. Newspapers were filled with true and questionable accounts of Ottoman atrocities against Armenians, Christians, and others. Pressure from missionary lobbies already had the protected cruiser *Cincinnati* and gunboat *Bancroft* steaming for the eastern Mediterranean so *Calypso* might seem a logical addition. The outgoing administration was also pressured by Junta supporters, public, and Congress while the press churned out a varying mix of fact, fiction, and fantasy. Most newspapers favored independence and allotted little acreage for Spanish truth or propaganda so the Junta and its supporters' energetic campaign for support prospered while Spain's minister, Dupuy de Lôme, was forced to respond, contract the Pinkerton agency, and file formal protests in Washington and through Spain's consuls at various ports. Other overseas nations added a third complication since they grew agitated whenever colonial stability was threatened. Newcomb already relayed rumors about Spain's Minister of State attempting to enlist European support for an international demand the States limit Junta activities, prevent filibuster expeditions, and declare martial law if necessary. Newcomb claimed the scheme was gathering momentum when British support ended for reasons unrelated to Cuba.

Albert also anticipated relationships cultivated in the Building and city would grow less reliable as the Cleveland administration wound down and the odds about even a new administration would end his special assistant to the Secretary position. With *Calypso* away from Key West and *Rafael Riego* fading, Secretary Herbert was also shifting attention from Albert's project to commissioning the battleship *Indiana* in New York and a blossoming torpedo boat controversy. The Chief Naval Constructor Hichborn and Engineer-in-Chief Melville wanted torpedo boat contracts awarded to Bath Iron Works and Union Iron Works while Captain Sampson's Bureau of Ordnance preferred the Herreshoff Manufacturing Company design. When three states became involved, one of the constant bureau clashes went public, spawned legal challenges, and involved the attorney general.

Even so, Albert's maneuvers to prevent missionary lobbies encouraged by the Junta from exiling *Calypso* to the Mediterranean made headway with Ramsay, the Secretary, and others after he argued unchecked filibusters could cause war with Spain while adding a weak gunboat to ships already steaming for the Ottoman Empire would have little effect there or with missionary groups demanding a fleet. Parrying Junta efforts to separate Starke from *Calypso* was achieved by ordering the bark to a Norfolk area shipyard rather than Port Royal. This made Starke and his ship easily available by rail and was supported by the Bureau of Construction and Repair, Bureau of Steam Engineering, and Bureau of Ordnance who welcomed an opportunity to examine the engine, boiler, and other equipment *Calypso* had been testing at sea. Since the shipyards could not take her before December, and Falk predicted nothing would happen in Congress before then, *Calypso* remained free to operate against filibusters under Starke. Junta supporters might later push to decommission *Calypso* while in the yards, a common practice for major repairs, but doing so after the recent conversion would raise awkward questions in a Congress that closely watched its purse. Falk predicted neither political party wanted a debate that might open Junta supporters and jingoes to charges their manipulations caused unnecessary costs; especially with Speaker Reed resisting war with Spain over Cuba.

Albert obtained Ramsay's support during a meeting to consider recommending the Secretary add ships to filibuster patrols. His bureau chief's predisposition was to place three off south Florida in December, despite Albert preferring to station whatever they might obtain off New York, north Florida, and the Chesapeake. Ramsay seemed preoccupied throughout the meeting, perhaps because his assistant, Captain Francis Cook, was leaving to command the new armored cruiser *Brooklyn*. Captain Albert thought he might be in the running to replace Cook, had qualms about taking the post, and could not refuse; but it never came up and Ramsay ended by deciding to recommend the ships be sent to south Florida.

Albert sat in his office afterwards, took a draw from his pipe, expelled, and studied light gray smoke ascending past the suspended ceiling lamp. The decision was no surprise and he knew from experience nothing was final until it was; and positions impossible to argue one month might sail through without question the next. This Building axiom was especially true with filibusters since Junta public relations were resourceful and constantly trying to constrain his project.

Starke was apparently disrupting Junta operations faster than anticipated but the Junta lacked any appetite for open debate over how *Rafael Riego*'s shattered corpse came to rust on the Gulf floor; or its story would be spread across the front pages. Instead, he found articles suggesting a filibuster expedition left port, possibly Veracruz, and vanished; accompanied by rumors it was in the Gulf of Mexico biding time until it could deliver a submersible torpedo boat. Albert suspected the story was planted in Key West or Tampa then given credence by clever semi-denials in New York. Several articles resulted that claimed a small, submersible torpedo boat left the Chesapeake in crates during September that was propelled by compressed air, carried a detachable torpedo, and mounted a dynamite gun. Albert read the Office of Naval Intelligence analysis Starke completed before taking command and aware several nations, including Spain, were exploring these boats. The Navy was also preparing to build its own within months; which proved enough expertise existed in the States to increase Spain's discomfort. Albert's pipe faded away as he decided it was time to serve notice on the Junta and Spain that *Calypso* was hunting filibuster expeditions and not surveying or testing boilers, engine, and guns.

While Albert was with his family that evening, the Royal Blue Line train from New York descended from high ground northeast of Washington for the wye, slowing as it rolled down the street brushing aside dogs, pedestrians, bicycles, and horse-drawn vehicles. After reversing direction at the wye it backed past sidings and through switchyards to the New Jersey Avenue Station. Observing through a Saxony blue parlor car's leaded glass windows, Constance Starke, Katherine Ledford, and Cynthia Jefferson relaxed in gold-trimmed blue upholstered chairs encircled by varnished mahogany walls under a royal blue ceiling. Cynthia always accompanied her mistress, who was not overly demanding when traveling, so the return was more pleasure excursion than work. Midway through the trip, the trio went to the dining car, took a booth and enjoyed roast duck served by a white-uniformed waiter. There were few Negroes or obvious Colored passengers and no difficulty being served north of Washington, although several southern states now segregated the races on trains and even Virginia was drifting that way.

Cynthia considered the woman she served while Mrs. Starke gathered incidental possessions from an overhead rack. Elegant, attractive, and seldom lacking composure, her mistress was more polished, but no less proper and demanding than when she arrived from Oxen Grove as a young girl. Constance's fairness, passion for education, and tolerance had not diminished over the years despite the last being well-concealed, especially around unbelievers. At the same time, she claimed several acquaintances Cynthia thought improper for a lady.

Cynthia's parents stayed on to help Oxen Grove recover after the war and were often paid in kind since money was scarce. The Jefferson home was a solid house built on high ground in the old quarters overlooking the York River where she paddled, splashed, and eventually learned to swim under watchful eyes. Her earliest memories were debates between her father and a White man called Master Tobias about crops, pigs, and horses. Slavery or its aftermath was not discussed in the home; except her mother's stories about the Oakley's bible school which taught reading and, to those showing an aptitude, sums. Cynthia shared a cramped one-room schoolhouse with poor White children who also received no formal education before the war. Cynthia thought little about this until the beautiful spring day she resisted going. The result was a passionate rebuke, describing education being excluded by law to the enslaved and not accessible to any but those able to afford private schools or tutors. She finished the benevolent harangue by declaring learning was the way up and only thing no one could ever take. Her mother's passion, and seeing education as once-forbidden fruit, ended Cynthia believing it an imposition and fueled her appetite.

Cynthia lived at Oxen Grove until early adolescence and was optimistic, like many of her race born after the war and slavery's demise, but claimed no unique relationship with the Starke family other than being employers she lived with for many years. She still remembered her father's grief, concern, and long discussions with Tobias Oakley before being sent north, scared and despondent, to a woman known only from brief visits. Mrs. Starke not only proved kind but matched her mother's insistence on reading, writing, and learning sums. Other maternal aspects were assumed by the formidable Negro cook, Martella Young, who proved as much an indomitable disciplinarian as loving.

The nephew, Jacob Starke, was Young's obvious favorite and also sent north from Oxen Grove. He arrived with his mother during the war but was raised by the Starkes after she died before its end and his father expatriated. He was older and different from boys at home, reserved, polite, and cautiously adventurous. Although he was often away at military school, a subdued teenage attraction and passion flickered then faded with maturity until she was convinced it was only because he was older but not too much so.

She always accompanied the Starkes to Oxen Grove but the pleasure passed with her father and country life became alien as the city grew familiar. Cynthia was considering this when noise and jolts announced their eight o'clock arrival at the train shed. She immediately spotted Immanuel Starke and Katherine's brother, Edward Curtis, standing back from those clustering near the tracks, waiting for conductors to place metal stools below three of the elaborate platforms framing every car's doorways. Rising, she fell in behind the women as they joined a column of passengers shuffling down aisles then onto the station platform. The men greeted them and, once their baggage was on a handcart, Immanuel Starke led their party through the waiting room and canopied main entrance. Outside, the Starkes' groom and Cynthia's ersatz uncle,

Darius Sutton, waited in his perch on the black landau, rocking slightly from its impatient team. When they walked through the door he quickly led a yellow Herdic cab in sweeping U-turns to the entrance where porters loaded them. Cynthia took her seat in the cab with most of the luggage while the others sat in the black landau. Sutton confirmed his passengers were settled in red leather seats, drove up New Jersey Avenue to Massachusetts Avenue, turned north at Dupont Circle, then continued to the Starke mansion where Martella Young waited with hot chocolate.

Immanuel and Constance spoke throughout the trip, Edward occasionally joined in, and Katherine said little after the carriage jolted slightly then began rolling. She looked back at the Baltimore & Ohio's station and Government Printing Office when they turned, but mostly watched passing buildings frame carriages, pedestrians, and handful of bicycles in the fading light. Slowly twisting her mourning ring, it was hard to accept seven months passed since she and her brother arrived from Brydian Grange by way of New York City at the same station on a similar evening then driven to the mansion by Sutton in the black landau trailed by a Herdic cab.

Recalling it was also the first time she met Jacob Starke, Katherine sensed the onset of another bout of despondency, the malady periodically plaguing her since adolescence. She attributed it to homesickness from passing through a foreign city aggravated by the unintended, disconcerting, and impossible relationship with Starke. It could never advance beyond correspondence but she clearly felt his absence, her ambivalence, and life passing. The company of someone she once found stiff and unpolished seemed easier to endure than the unquenchable wanting now eroding her studied abhorrence of opportunistic men seeking a young widow's fortune. Equally confusing, she could not understand how his lack of interest fueled an allure that spiked suddenly when Constance arranged for Jacob to escort the unmarried Times reporter Cassandra Evans to a mansion dinner party; and shamelessly went to him in the library after he returned from taking Evans to Georgetown. Katherine not only found herself uncharacteristically forward but sought conversation then shocked herself by proposing they correspond. She anticipated rejection but he agreed and later replied to an exploratory letter. The custom established with her late husband immediately reasserted itself except the content grew more personal; perhaps because Jacob could never be more than a comfortably distant voice. She was guarded, formal, and unsettled when he was present but craved his letters; especially as she discovered him to be more intelligent, inquiring, and liberal than first thought. Katherine had grown to love her husband but marriage was less unsettling when he was away and she suspected it may have been one of his attractions. Her friends avoided understandings with naval officers because they could be away years at a time after marriage. She initially thought a husband's physical demands repulsive then, finding she was barren and still desiring them, grew disgusted with herself. She thought that conundrum died with Philip and HMS *Victoria* but it reignited with Jacob during *Calypso's* Norfolk commissioning; an event she reluctantly attended with the Starkes. He was scrupulously formal and proper, something demanded from her male acquaintances, but she attributed it to her barrenness, independent income, and desire to return home. Recent Newport sessions with Constance convinced Katherine it was his nature, which did little to ward off the familiar physical unease and emotional agitation experienced during their evening together at Old Point Comfort's Hygeia Hotel.

He was there with the Starkes, and by default her, for

dinner and dancing. Katherine was convinced the moral slide that began in the Starkes' library reached a precipice that evening when Constance slipped her hand through Immanuel's crooked arm and she, without thinking, did the same with Jacob. Touching roused sensations that escalated throughout supper then became unbearable while they danced. Jacob not only proved accomplished but she reveled in holding and being held as they glided over the waxed parquet floor open to a dark bay under star-filled heavens.

When the Starkes retired arm-in-arm to their room, though not visibly fatigued, their nephew invited her for a stroll on the short observation pier jutting into the bay. It was the first interest shown beyond exchanging letters despite injudicious remarks made earlier about swimming nearly naked with her brother and his friends in Brydian Grange pond; then by herself in the nude after she began developing. She grew increasingly anxious and frustrated when he failed to respond then began despising herself. Katherine was not flirtatious, and since being widowed had disciplined and dressed to avoid any hint of desire or invitation, but keenly accepted his unanticipated suggestion they walk the pier. Strolling into the night above the dark bay with water lapping a sand beach, she struggled to appear casual, if not indifferent, while resisting an uncomfortable desire for improper attention. She barely managed to control herself but he did not appear similarly afflicted, never flattered or pursued, and showed no inclination for an amorous relationship. Churning emotions aside, she was grateful since Jacob would not fare well in her society and she could not exist in his. Katherine was decided not to leave her Brydian Grange home a second time, especially for the States, and his approaching her father, who still referred to Americans as colonists, was ludicrous. Even so, her resistance continued to weaken as she discovered more and developed acceptance of, if not a taste for, his masculine attributes. This left her struggling to retain morals and dignity while he remained infuriatingly proper then left her to spend most of the voyage to Newport in a canvas deck chair staring at the passing ocean and vacillating between physical frustration and self-loathing.

Newport's season proved no better. Constance was as proper as her mother and perhaps more pious but a confidante willing to discuss topics never entertained at home. These talks helped dampen, unravel, or understand her emotions but eroded resolve, especially when Constance let drop that she and Immanuel were open to an understanding between their nephew and the barren English widow despite an obvious desire for children.

This self-analysis ceased when the carriages left Florida Avenue and Katherine saw the Romanesque mansion. Its trees, shrubs, and lawn reflected early autumn but otherwise little changed over summer. As the landau rolled easily down the street she clearly saw the broad lawns surrounding and small grass strip fronting the red-stone, four-story building with three rounded corners and tall turret substituting for the fourth. The stable was partly visible in the rear, as was a greenhouse abutting the mansion, across a concrete pad from the carriage house on its west corner. Sutton expertly handled long, sweat-darkened leather reins to guide Gemini and Castores to a curbside mounting block dwarfed by the massive whitish-gray stone porch flanked by curving marble steps rising to a main entrance. The anxious bays halted instantly when reined in; knowing it signaled release from the encasing harness and blinders, a walk to cool down, then currycombing and grain. Noise on Castores' left caught his attention and held it until the Herdic cab pulled alongside, briefly stopped, then clattered off to unload in the rear. The

Starke butler, Joshua Altman, observed the party climb to a pair of large oak doors, opened one, then greeted Mrs. Starke and others in turn. Exiting the short passage separating butler's office and cloak room, Constance surveyed the paneled two-story entrance hall with curved staircases below Tiffany stained-glass windows on the far wall.

The household recognized their arrival ended summer's casual atmosphere. The Washington season would commence in the morning when Constance Starke emptied the hall's silver salver of accumulating cards. This entailed guests, social visits, formal dinners, and possibly a ball, although the last was drifting out of fashion. Meanwhile, the staff unloaded luggage, cared for horses, and finished work before retiring to their third floor rooms.

As the household slid beneath silk or cotton sheets for the night, *Calypso* was recovering and the tempest that pummeled her south of Jamaica was now a powerful hurricane careening north. Birthed in the Lesser Antilles three days before, it crashed into the Gulf of Mexico between the Yucatan Peninsula and Cabo de San Antonio on the morning of September 28, 1896, hurling heavy rain driven by powerful winds against that lighthouse then leaving Pinar del Río province with enough flooding to delay transport ships carrying veteran Spanish troops. The fast-moving hurricane then curved gently east overnight, spared Key West, and crashed ashore near Cedar Key in the early morning.

That city, port, and railroad terminus was struck without warning while greeting the new day so only a scattering of early risers witnessed the storm charge in from the Gulf. They saw much the same as *Calypso's* crew, except the center passed close by and Cedar Key was no ship, but small populated islands just offshore. The rolling wall of dark clouds and sky delivered inexorable wind and rain from one direction then paused briefly before hammering the city from a new bearing. Residents were overwhelmed even before three mammoth waves crashed through in succession. Foundations collapsed, windows shattered, roofs vanished, and whatever lay in their path was damaged, destroyed, or mauled. Dozens of small spongers anchored off Depot Key and surrounding islets were not spared so most succumbed without trace. One small white schooner dragged anchor until its flukes snagged, taking her bow under long enough for the storm surge to crash over gunwales, rip off hatches, and send what remained to the bottom. Protruding masts marked her grave until another sponger, adrift and driven by the wind, stove in its hull snapping them off then went down just inshore. No trace of either remained above water the next morning. After destroying spongers and devastating buildings, piers, and railroads, the storm gained speed and roared across Florida before turning inland to claw up the Atlantic coast between ocean and mountains. Within two days, Jacksonville, Savannah, Port Royal, and Charleston were thrashed, Norfolk spared, and Richmond mangled as the hurricane raced towards the capital.

Washington's Tuesday morning began much like Monday, when Katherine enjoyed a pleasant ride through Rock Creek Park with Edward, and *The Morning Times* promised similar weather. Katherine entered the library where she accosted Jacob Starke after the dinner party then initiated their correspondence. His uncle sat in the leather chair instead, facing the fireplace, sipping a brandy, and reading *The Evening Star*. She intended to thumb through *The Morning Times* before it went to the household but usually avoided the room when he was there. Although smaller than Brydian Grange's library, Immanuel made a point of welcoming family; unlike her father, Jacob, and late husband who treated these rooms as sanctuaries and disliked anyone joining them except by invitation or on urgent business.

Although Immanuel preferred his library and Constance the parlor, these habits developed naturally and the patriarch was never upset by company; perhaps because it was of no real consequence since he dominated any room. Nearing sixty, he was stoutly built with full beard and demeanor suggesting readiness for instant action. Even thinning hair and preference for muted clothing failed to diminish this. Katherine also suspected the beard concealed a pleasant smile, since she found him considerate, kind, and scrupulously fair, although seldom jovial or trivial. After observation and speaking with Constance, she almost understood the woman's steadfast affection despite an all-consuming dedication to business which often kept him away.

He looked up as she entered, "Good evening, Katherine. I assume you're here for *The Evening Times*."

"Only if you're finished."

"Of course, I'm reading *The Evening Star*."

Katherine took the Democratic paper to a second chair near the fireplace and began reading. The front page reported a British squadron pressuring China to act against an official who condoned outrages inflicted on a mission station then provoked a massacre. It reminded her Jacob was a freethinker who saw little nobility in most missionary enterprises; another reason to avoid further entanglement. While reading, she sensed Immanuel staring at water thickly coating the window. It had been a light rain when she entered and the wind was also increasing. Immanuel observed, "*The Evening Star* says we're due for heavy rains but the big storm is still in Georgia."

He just finished *The Evening Star* article about a storm off Florida's west coast when rain striking the window increased further. The story caught his notice only because it could affect shipping and *Calypso* might have run into it. *The Evening Times* reported nothing, but that was unremarkable since it was a smaller edition put out primarily to update the morning offering, compete with afternoon papers, claim twenty-four hour coverage, and serve streetcar commuters.

Katherine replied before returning to her reading. An article about Negro migrations within the country was interesting because of those she knew from *Calypso* and the mansion; while another listed the new man beliefs and traits demanded by Americans of her sex claiming to be new women. After comparing them with bluestockings, she turned to a third article on new fall gowns then several paragraphs describing the Rubens Club; a group of heavier New York City women trying to force or encourage manufacturers to offer clothes that fit. Katherine was nearly finished when she saw the American Navy announced three Catholic chaplains had been appointed. It seemed these were the first to join the twenty-four Navy chaplains for a number of years and she was reminded that Jacob, the freethinker, oversaw *Calypso's* religious instruction.

Katherine retired near ten o'clock after visiting with Constance in the parlor. Heavy rain and gusting wind were shaking walls, roof, and windows. She drifted off beneath warm covers, unaware of a rapidly advancing black mass consuming the already dark and turbulent night sky. Roaring northwest past the mansion, its punishing downpour and screaming winds, accompanied by continuous lightning and thunder, woke anyone asleep. Immanuel and their butler gathered the inmates and the entire household was soon sheltering in the basement; except Darius and another man who remained in the stable to calm Gemini and Castores.

Katherine stayed near Edward, struggling to appear calm but fighting an overwhelming urge to flee, waiting for the structure to collapse, and feeling trapped by the thick stone and concrete masonry surrounding her. The incredible wind and rain sounds grew more terrifying with intermittent crashes and muted detonations when large objects struck nearby ground. Someone would occasionally take a quick look through a basement window but nothing could be seen and the vibrating panes risked being struck or blown in. Electricity and gas finally went, adding yellowish, surreal quality when Martella Young lit kerosene storm lamps. Immanuel and Altman went upstairs intermittently to check for damage after exceptional crashes while the others, cut off from the world, found a spot and waited; whether around the basement's large kitchen table, in one of the more comfortable chairs, or wrapped in blankets on the tile floor.

Washington endured this barrage until nearly one o'clock in the morning when the wind lessened and the tempest turned towards the Great Lakes to exact more damage before dying away. For over two hours, the city endured a steady, sixty mile an hour, debris-laden wind that shifted southeast to east with gusts surpassing 125 miles an hour. Hundreds of trees were severely damaged, uprooted, or snapped off ten to fifteen feet above ground. The Washington Arsenal's were especially hard hit as were those on the mall leading to the Capitol. A power station went offline, darkening some neighborhoods and the entire city left strewn with broken poles, collapsed lines, and wires sparking where they touched bare ground, pavement, and structures. Damaged storage tanks crippled the water plant. Although telegraph lines within city limits were underground, the poles beyond went down and contact with the outside severed. Streets were left filled by debris or blocked by fallen trees with enough crumpled copper sheets and broken glass to ravage bicycle tires for weeks. The Metropolitan Company streetcar car shed was destroyed along with a five-story building under construction on Pennsylvania Avenue. The Smithson Institute building was badly damaged, a Presbyterian Church's steeple toppled, and host of other structures mangled. The Treasury Building and President's Grounds were battered and statuary disfigured but the Executive Mansion required only minor inside repairs from glass and roof damage. Trees surrounding Washington Circle were casualties, including large elms near the mansion's north entrance and its flagpole. The Building lost a roof section over State's offices when it lifted then scattered. The port was particularly hard hit. Buildings were damaged or destroyed and Wheatley's Lumber Yard stock scattered. Ships like *Newport News*, underway for Norfolk, rode it out but those moored at piers or anchored fared poorly. Gale-force winds joined a high tide to break already taut mooring lines and drag anchors. *Martha Washington* and other large ships wrecked with most small boats sunk or crushed by the drifting ships causing havoc on piers and wharfs. One large ship finally jammed against a bridge. The small Georgetown port upstream suffered equal devastation with the anchored four-masted schooner *John W. Linnell* driven aground near a tug and barge that sank just off the piers.

Katherine longed for Brydian Grange since first setting foot in New York City and a night expecting Starke mansion to collapse into the basement reinforced this beyond all argument despite it coming through in good shape. There would be yard cleanup, small roof sections to patch, chimneys to re-point, lightning rod repair, brickwork, and a tree to extract from the stable yard fence but the property was recently built on high ground so there were few large trees nearby and no flooding.

Albert's red-brick row house, almost due south, did well

because it was shielded somewhat by surrounding buildings, but was not left unscathed. Roof and water damage resulted from a large tree limb striking the rear eves so Abigail sent her husband to work then started cleanup aided by Isabella, Olivia, and their maid. Meanwhile, Albert walked to the Building through streets clogged with debris, some animal carcasses, and abandoned carriages. Fallen trees were so numerous he learned the city was letting residents saw them in place for firewood. The police were also out patrolling or guarding damaged buildings to discourage looting.

Albert failed to enjoy his morning ritual once inside the Building since the coffee was tasteless, city battered, and capital isolated. What information came from the north was sketchy but almost nothing emerged from the south beyond a few rumors from Norfolk, Port Royal, and Key West. *Calypso's* cable reporting arrival in Kingston beat the storm to the Building so he finished his coffee and arranged an audience with the Secretary through the naval aide, Lieutenant Commander Buckingham.

Chapter Fourteen
Course Correction

Washington remained isolated into October until telegraph lines north were repaired and the first news was disheartening. Baltimore's port flooded and several structures damaged, which peaked Building concern about southern ports. As more lines were restored and reliable reports trickled in, it appeared the storm bypassed Norfolk; Port Royal, including its new dry-dock, weathered it; and Key West reported no serious damage. The Navy emerged relatively unscathed but what little came from several large Atlantic ports meant others were not so fortunate. Cedar Key was dead silent.

The storm slowed Albert's efforts regarding two lost filibusters, Junta machinations, Havana's request, and an election campaign with both parties avoiding Cuba. He did manage to confer with Ramsay and the Secretary then schedule another Building meeting to reveal the proposed response. The same conference room where his filibuster project was introduced would be used but fewer would attend since Starke was at sea with *Calypso*, Hunter off Florida's west coast with *Vanguard*, and Fields trapped by the seaboard devastation. Captain Fischer agreed to come from Treasury, as did Spencer and Falk from Justice. Newcomb would again represent State's Diplomatic Bureau.

Albert approached the small conference room early then entered through the pine and mahogany door below a partly open transom window. To reach his chair, he slipped past its rectangular table of darkening oak, shaped like the room with little clearance for the plain, cane-backed parlor chairs surrounding it. The heavily used space included a tall window at one end, single entrance door on the opposite wall, and dark pine floor. The dull walls were coated by thick layers of off-white paint and decorated with the same brown-framed ship photographs as their March meeting. A tall pitcher and half-dozen glasses filled the white cotton placemat at table center and heavy ashtrays waited at either end.

Albert shuffled along the wall to his seat below the window, sat, and then placed notebook and pencils on the table. While waiting, he rotated an Eagle pencil spanning both hands until stopping at the trademark. It was made in Cedar Key and he wondered if its maker survived. What reports emerged from the area indicated little remained of port, buildings, factories, or cedar trees. After twisting in his chair to confirm the clear sky beyond the window, he added some items to his notebook and paged through it until nine-thirty when he heard people approaching. One knocked twice, then Fischer, Spencer, and Falk entered. It seemed two of them met at the east entrance then climbed the marble stairway together. Newcomb arrived soon after. There were greetings and light gossip, mostly about the storm, and everyone took seats at the table. Albert sat at its head, beneath the window, with State and Treasury to his left and Justice the right. Smiling as Fischer retrieved his pipe, Albert did the same and, before beginning, dredged its bowl between his new tobacco pouch's stiff leather sides, gently tamped down moist brown shreds, then passed a flame over its center. Tossing his match into an ash tray, he began, "I'll summarize what's taken place before describing Navy's next move. Since March, *Calypso's* been commissioned, completed shakedown, and disrupted the

Junta effort to supply insurrectionists from the States, with somewhat more notoriety than anticipated."

With that, Captain Fischer, wearing a uniform similar to Albert's, pulled a worn pipe stem from a full, graying beard that began under a weather-beaten nose, grinned slightly, then added, "I'm betting the Junta considers *Calypso* a bit more than notorious after losing two expeditions to her."

Spencer ran a left hand over his short hair, lowered it, resisted an urge to twirl the large mustache then added, "Based on Starke's report, *Calypso's* within the law, but only just. *John Gwinn Williams* was less problematic since her master's actions caused the boiler explosion and the owners satisfied with their insurance money. *Rafael Riego's* less safe since *Calypso* took her under fire and brought about the explosion."

Before Spencer began laying a legal foundation, Fischer lowered his pipe, looked over the table at the nondescript Justice official in brown three-piece suit with banker collar, "As far as I'm concerned, *Rafael Riego* became a pirate when she fired on the gunboat. *Calypso's* also become quite popular within the Service because they know it could have been one of our cutters. *Vanguard* was first to assist and Hunter's report claims the Don was within a gnat's backside of sinking. Most cuttermen in the Atlantic and Gulf share my thinking that it was just damn good shooting."

Spencer laughed uneasily and looked briefly through the pipe smoke to Fischer before saying, "I could offer a precise legal opinion but it would be a poor repetition of your sentiments."

Albert could see Newcomb from State wanted to speak. As always, his appearance remained unchanged, no matter the season; a three-piece suit over billowing white cotton shirt, less comfortable wing collar, and black bow tie. The same large gold rings graced thick, soft fingers. Above a carefully trimmed mustache arcing over his goatee was brown-blond hair, meticulously center-parted and shinning from Macassar oil. Albert knew Starke disliked the man, unfairly in his opinion because Newcomb proved useful with *Rafael Riego* and more willing to involve himself since March. The senior Diplomatic Bureau clerk assigned to Cuba favorably briefed State's Second and Third Assistant Secretaries several times about *Rafael Riego* and proved steadfast, despite knowing he was State's scapegoat should the filibuster project pluck the wrong diplomatic feather.

Looking across the table, then to Albert, Newcomb began, "Gentlemen. Although State has no substantive role, I've made inquiries and it appears no party, including the Junta, intends to come forward regarding *Rafael Riego*. Mexico's upset about the location but has no issue with the demise of foreign anarchists using their flag and is probably using the incident against their anarchists. Thompson, our minister in Brazil, reports they deny *Rafael Riego* was ever registered there. Besides the anarchist aspect, he believes they wish to improve relations and suspects Starke's father having some role. Spain's pleased two filibusters were sunk, upset a gunboat was nearly lost, and prefers the affair pass quietly; so they do not plan to formally protest *Rafael Riego* flying our flag or an American warship nearby. We've no official contact with the Junta but it seems the *Rafael Riego* expedition caused a great deal of dissension there before it failed. Their primary concern is to avoid it becoming widely known one of their expeditions led by anarchists fought an American ship. Consequently, State recommends allowing the affair to fade."

Falk, taking a cue from Spencer, added, "Some sources claim *Calypso's* become a phantom with filibuster crews. Although one expedition pays about the same as a Navy captain earns in three months, it's rumored she sinks filibusters on sight. Before her, only Spanish gunboats raised the possibility of not living to spend these takings and their patrols have not been excessively zealous. Besides, Spain's not executed an American filibuster for some years and Junta lawyers have almost eliminated risk of prison here. *Calypso*, on the other hand, has sunk two filibusters, caused casualties, and established her movements as unpredictable."

Albert lowered his pipe, "That's correct and the Junta's working to remove Starke, *Calypso*, or both."

Newcomb sat back in his chair, "How?"

"By bringing him to Washington to testify about *Rafael Riego* then use his absence to justify replacement with a less effective commander; or having *Calypso* sent from the Caribbean."

Falk rejoined the conversation, "Our European Squadron's the most likely choice since Armenians seized the Ottoman Bank in August and there's speculation the Sultan may be overthrown. With the press providing a constant diet of massacres, sending another ship would seem reasonable and gain the missionary lobby's approval."

Albert recalled discussion of *Calypso* and *Vanguard* being transferred to the Bering Sea for seal protection duty, another popular cause, just as Newcomb looked about the table, "Or the Asiatic Squadron; it needs ships and exiling *Calypso* to the western Pacific would be permanent since our old ones don't return. Spain's also been fighting in the Philippines since last month. They claim it's a Tagalog uprising. If not, they're facing two major colonial wars and can't deal with one so the conservative government and even the regency could fall. Germany and Japan could view this as an opportunity, while Britain, France, and the monarchies are inclined to support Spain's queen."

Falk displayed intense concentration as he continued, "I

doubt the administration wants Starke removed, but Captain Albert's correct, Junta supporters may attempt to have him ordered here until Congress is back in session, perhaps early December. That would find less resistance than orchestrating ship movements and he could be buried in some office."

With this, Albert raised his hand, "Admiral Ramsay controls officer assignments and assures me he'll not reassign Starke, the Secretary agrees, and Speaker Reed can be relied on to deal with House committees."

Spencer remained silent since Falk had the bit in his teeth, "Reed's position is clear and the House Foreign Affairs Committee wants to avoid war with Spain. Republicans are unlikely to lose the House this election but the Senate Foreign Relations Committee's more pro-independence and will change regardless of which party wins. Chairman Hitt will probably keep his spot, but Shafroth's left for the Silver Party and whether Pearson or Quigg will . . . ."

Spencer admired his colleague's knowledge and intensity but decided a gentle tug on the leash appropriate so he interjected, "I believe, Captain Albert, Maximilian's working up to offering you his assistance with Congress."

Albert accepted, "That's appreciated. September's the last month of the first financial quarter so I'm expecting just enough funds for *Calypso* to enter a shipyard in December. Starke's no political creature so avoiding his testifying would be best but he'll be available after *Calypso* enters the Norfolk or Newport News yard."

Newcomb used the opportunity to raise his Havana request, "Consul-general Lee forwarded a note received from Spanish naval authorities and the captain general. They're asking for Lieutenant Starke's testimony in the *Francisco de Montejo* inquiry. The President and Secretary Olney wish to avoid incidents before inauguration so State does not favor official involvement. However, should Starke participate in an unofficial capacity he could explain *Calypso's* presence and mitigate damaging conjecture from entering the official record should the gunboat commander see advantage emphasizing that *Rafael Riego* appeared with *Calypso*. The Spanish press might portray her as an accomplice and ours claim the Navy's aiding filibusters. Either could bring about war or end talks with their government."

Spencer and Falk inundated Newcomb with questions while Albert and Fischer listened and drew slowly on their pipes. Propriety, law, and mechanics were debated, especially the reaction if Starke's Havana trip was viewed as siding with Spain. After every conceivable aspect was covered they began revisiting specific points. Albert attempted to show more interest in recharging his pipe but noticed the debate glossed over risk to Starke's career and reputation. Captain Fischer appeared to view it as enlightening, if not entertaining, which piqued Albert since they agreed earlier that *Vanguard* and Hunter, having arrived at scene later, were not involved.

As his pipe bowl finished and three drained participants sat back in uncomfortable chairs, Albert played his hand, "I'll raise the question with the Secretary and Admiral Ramsay. *Calypso* cannot enter Havana, but could remain a week or so in Key West while Starke crosses as a private person on leave. There's a regular liner and his family owns property in Cuba so the testimony can be incidental to a business trip."

Falk added, "With a transcript of the inquiry's report, or his portion, we might possibly arrange a closed session with the congressional committees."

Spencer followed up, "Fields will provide assistance and coordinate with Clark, the United States District Attorney for Florida's Southern District."

Albert rested his pipe in a black ashtray and nodded. Just

because they agreed, and Newcomb obviously had his Secretary's backing, Albert was uncertain how Ramsay and Starke would react. The Spanish request had been studied but not agreed to so he would approach the intelligence office to help make the case; thinking Wainwright might be prevailed upon to support the venture.

Cradling the warm pipe in one hand, Albert looked around the table, "Gentlemen, let's turn to *Calypso's* current assignment."

Fischer frowned, "Ah, yes, *Laurada*."

Newcomb leaned slightly over the table, "State received a cable that British officials arrested two Cubans in Kingston for ignoring quarantine. They apparently left a ship there, had suspicious documents, and tried to cable insurgents. Our consul was unable to learn what these papers contain but thinks the men might try to claim American citizenship."

Fischer set his pipe down, "Interesting, but *Laurada* may not be the ship."

"That's correct, captain."

Albert lowered his pipe, "We've a confusing picture. *Calypso's* steaming north from Port Antonio after reporting no sign of *Laurada* or anything similar. She'll sweep north through the Old Bahama Channel to the Cay Sal Bank then northeast through the Santaren Channel. *Laurada* was said to have left for Port Antonio in early August and reported sunk there but another source has her damaged and the master, Murphy, under arrest. He was apparently detained in Jamaica and returned to the States a week later with some of the crew claiming *Laurada* was filibustering and abandoned them in Port Antonio when they refused to join. The ship had returned to the States by then and released by the Attorney General on the seventeenth. There are reports she was at Wilmington in early September under a new master since Murphy was charged. She's since been reported afloat in one place and sunk in another so there were concerns two similar ships were operating under one name but *Calypso's* visit ended that thinking and left us with conflicting accounts."

Fischer added, "That matches our information. *Hamilton* trailed *Laurada* for a time. She's apparently bound for Halifax and should dock tomorrow; then sail for Europe or the Mediterranean with a legitimate cargo. Its common practice for filibusters but the Junta or her owners might think *Calypso's* hunting her and this keeps the ship from joining *John Gwinn Williams* and *Rafael Riego*."

The meeting ended soon after, with participants leaving the Building forced to navigate through city recovering from the storm. As Albert closed the door and began walking down the hall he expected the bark's December stay in Norfolk would also occasion a visit by at least one of two *Calypso* officers corresponding with his daughters.

Chapter Fifteen
Unanticipated Duties

Calypso survived her first hurricane, raised Jamaica, and then made for Kingston. The British port closed to foreign warships earlier that year but had reopened and both cruisers enforcing the ban had departed so fewer salutes and official calls were required. The British fleet that once sailed from the harbor had been replaced by the North American and West Indian Squadron out of Bermuda and Halifax, but its navy yard and hospital remained under a commodore reporting to the island's major general. Only the station ship HMS *Urgent*, a converted Crimean War troop transport, and her two small tenders watched *Calypso* enter.

Starke anchored, completed salutes and official calls, cabled the Department to report their arrival then grappled with the shore leave regulations required. *Calypso's* crew deserved it so eligible sailors were allowed liberty, but it expired before dark at the surgeon's request. He believed yellow fever and other tropical diseases worsened after sunset and was preparing for them by visiting the Royal Navy Hospital; a long brick and stone building with encircling verandas overlooking the bay. Conrad was correct, or the season past, because they left port without tropical complaints. Instead, two sailors experienced venereal disease's excruciating symptoms and treatment while several shipmates waited to see if they were next.

Watson and the American consul, Mr. Eckford, approached local officials regarding *Laurada,* but learned little beyond confirming her master was detained then packed off to the States. The consul also mentioned Cuban insurgents or sympathizers from another ship broke quarantine, were arrested, and documents confiscated the British authorities would not let him examine. His review of arrival and departure records suggested several filibuster expeditions used Kingston and, more often, Port Antonio. Since communication between these port cities included a regular mail coach and coastal steamer, filibusters in either could be warned by contacts in the other within days, despite difficult terrain between.

Starke left Kingston for Port Antonio, where he anchored, lowered their steam pinnace, and sent Watson ashore to speak with customs officials. *Laurada* was not there, rumors about her contradictory, and the port had no active yellow fever cases so he returned after a brief visit and *Calypso* departed for the Bahama Islands. She traveled the Cuban coast without colors while sweeping north through Old Bahama Channel to create rumors amongst small fishing boats that an unknown cruiser was prowling. Once anchored off Nassau, sailors in the top liberty class went ashore under the same rules Conrad set in Kingston, with similar results. Starke also hung false name-boards where they could be read by informants in bumboats and through glasses from shore. After Nassau, *Calypso* continued north along Florida's east coast to Port Royal where she coaled, took on stores, and replaced six boiler tubes.

A second hurricane crossed Florida, west to east, in early October but passed north of *Calypso* and the ship weathered it easily. Afterwards, she steamed or sailed off the east coast between Port Royal and Jupiter Inlet with periodic sorties into the Straits of Florida or Old Bahama Channel. When they passed Watson's last ship, *Winston A. Capps*, now a Cay Sal Bank wreck left to scavengers and the sea, he stared briefly at her disintegrating remains through binoculars then returned to work. *Calypso* trailed, spotted, and stopped suspicious ships flying the American flag. None were filibusters. The Spanish took part of a cargo the American tug *Dauntless* was offloading in the San Juan River delta late in the month, although a dynamite gun made it through. However, two months of hard patrolling allowed Watson, Osbourne, and Weaver to train and the sailors accumulate experience so *Calypso* had a tight, professional crew when Starke received orders placing him on leave for a week and clearance to visit Havana.

The State Department prevailed over Navy reticence about Starke giving evidence at the Spanish Navy's *Francisco de Montejo* inquiry although he was to travel on leave in civilian clothes. Starke's uncle enthusiastically provided a rationale since negotiations for sale of his Cuban holdings to British investors, represented by Katherine's brother Edward Curtis, were nearly complete so his nephew and heir could wrap them up in Havana. There was extraordinary risk buying an unused sugar mill and plantation during the insurrection but substantial profit when fighting ended and the properties were sold or operated. Starke suspected Curtis obtained a bargain price but his uncle was astute and no doubt cleared a satisfactory amount since they were obtained for very little after the last insurrection. Selling them off also fit his uncle's desire to close or shed risky assets.

Starke's feelings were ambivalent. Havana was a city he enjoyed, completing the transaction would help repay years of kindness, and his correspondent friend Darwin Tyson was there. However, it meant abandoning *Calypso* and seeing Katherine, however briefly. The young widow would accompany her brother, leave with him on the French Transatlantic Line to Saint-Nazaire, and then continue to the

Curtis family's London house by rail and channel ferry.

Calypso steamed for Key West and anchored in the now familiar spot to wait out her commander's Havana interlude. Starke's anxiety increased when he saw *Montgomery*. The steel-hulled cruiser under Commander Davis relieved *Newark* in July. She was attached to the North Atlantic Squadron, and *Calypso* the Special Service Squadron, but the senior officer of Navy ships meeting acquired limited authority to control the junior's operations and visible shipboard routine. *Montgomery* was an unprotected "peace" cruiser with auxiliary schooner rig, capable of near twenty knots, and a desirable command. Davis was an experienced officer whose outstanding record and influence allowed him to commission her in 1894 and carry out what the press claimed was a clandestine filibuster hunt off the Honduran coast. He was also an admiral's son and brother-in-law to the powerful interventionist senator Henry Cabot Lodge. Starke was loosely acquainted through his aunt, who shared several social circles with Davis' wife, but knew little of him. Building rumors suggested his tour as Chief Intelligence Officer began poorly with that Assistant Secretary then worsened during the Chilean crisis. Fewer officers sought billets or submitted letters during his tenure and he was alleged to be one of many officers possessing exceptional recall of any slight and ruthless to perceived adversaries. Starke's primary concern had been steering *Calypso* clear of incidents or disputes whenever their ships met. Relations were good, but he worried that could change with Watson taking command for over a week. *Calypso's* orders were crafted to shield her from outside interference but Watson carried *Winston A. Capps* baggage that might haunt him and he lacked Starke's social connections.

The executive officer had more than earned an opportunity to make what he might of temporary command so Starke boarded the Plant steamer *Olivette* at the Commercial Company Wharf in early December and settled in for the overnight run to Havana. Several lines from Europe and North America's east coast served the Cuban port but only Plant Line steamships shuttled constantly between Florida and Cuba. Leaving Port Tampa for Key West, then Havana, the line's two ships, *Olivette* and *Mascotte*, made the thirty-six hour run three times a week from November to May; then one less during summer months due to seasonal diseases driving a marked drop in passengers. Both were purpose-built in quick succession by William Camp & Sons Ship and Engine Building Company. Their black hulls were trimmed in white, with a rounded pilothouse, single stack, two pole masts, and white lifeboats along the upper deck. The somewhat similar designs served different roles. At 291 feet, *Olivette* was just over eighty feet longer with raised forecastle. This accommodated increased winter traffic and fit her summer Boston-to-Halifax route while the smaller *Mascotte* easily handled summer months with fewer passengers.

Olivette was closing Cuba by early morning under clear blue skies cutting easily through placid seas. The regular flash coming from the blue-gray coast slightly off the bow was Morro lighthouse so Starke knew it was less than twenty-five miles to the mouth of a narrow passage into Havana's harbor and a pilot boat loitering under the old fortress. In the pilothouse, *Olivette's* master and mate shielded their eyes from the blinding orange sun reflecting off a light chop as they scanned for the schooner that would bring a harbor pilot to guide *Olivette* to anchor or a mooring buoy; and officials for the initial customs and health inspections.

Starke finished breakfast and was reclining in a canvas deckchair outside his starboard side cabin enjoying a pipe and watching the coastline pass since it would be some time before passengers could disembark. The light civilian attire bought in Key West was a welcome change from the uniforms worn almost exclusively since March, as was the brief respite from direct responsibility for his ship. As *Olivette* carried him further from Key West, knowing Watson was left in charge contributed to shedding the command burden he shouldered since commissioning. While watching the coast and liner's long wake he visualized Watson, Osbourne, Weaver, and others carrying out the daily routine. Hopefully, his cabin steward Yamashita had taken the strong suggestion to spend time ashore while his captain was in Cuba; although Starke briefly considered taking him to Havana. There was also Albert's letter advising that orders to the Newport News shipyard in late December or early January were coming. The short yard period would be welcomed by the crew. Weaver would see his family, Osbourne could chase down boiler problems vexing him, and others would have shore leave. Starke disliked the timing since Cuban campaigns were initiated during winter, which increased fighting and filibustering, but Albert leveraged *Calypso's* indisposition and convinced Commodore Bunce to assign three of his North Atlantic Squadron ships to filibustering duties in early December.

Starke gazed through pipe smoke and *Olivette's* lifelines to the blurred coast across a stunning morning sea and found it discomforting to think the glorious Caribbean dawn promised a new day of attack and reprisal beyond Havana's fortifications. Although fighting was only kept at bay by barbed wire, outposts, and strongpoints ringing the city, he looked forward to this short visit. The Starke company representative, and its reliable ship chandler Aron Sharett, already made arrangements. Starke lifted his pipe, drew in some biting smoke then smiled. The voluble chandler recommended Hotel Mascotte on Oficios Street, a former mansion near the naval headquarters with a harbor view, but he insisted on Hotel Inglaterra from habit and by design. This favored destination for well-heeled northern tourists that overlooked Parque Central now furnished lodging for diplomats, including Consul-general Lee, and served as the correspondents' primary haunt; although only those with plump expense accounts could room there. Sharett argued his choice might compromise a low profile. Starke agreed, but calculated it also put him in the rumor mill and supported claims he was there on private business. Tyson was also lodging there and Starke already cabled him; partly because he looked forward to seeing his old friend and *The Sun* correspondent but also because it would be impossible to surreptitiously enter Havana with Tyson there. Attempting to avoid that first-rate sleuth would leave a strong scent of story when his nose was in the air sniffing for leads; and underestimating the man's persistence and capability was never advisable.

As he recharged his pipe and watched small fishing boat sails dance between *Olivette's* lifelines and Cuban coast, Starke considered November's elections. William McKinley won the presidency, despite internal Republican turmoil, because populists split from Democrats. Starke did not vote or support any party but knew a civilian tide within the Department would ebb and flow despite civil service reform. Almost everyone from Secretary to shipyard laborer changed in the past and a number would now. Captain Albert's could be one of the upper-level positions transitioning during spring and summer, which might end *Calypso's* mission or independence.

Katherine and her brother would arrive later. Her most recent letter was emphatic about returning to Brydian Grange while alluding to a growing closeness with his family and envy for rights enjoyed by American women of her social class. Katherine's current interest was the Welsh immigrant Martha Hughes Cannon who was just elected Utah state senator; one of her opponent's several wives, a physician with several degrees, and suffrage advocate. She also recounted an afternoon with his aunt's old friend Clarissa Barton who visited Starke mansion after returning from the Ottoman Empire where she negotiated for Armenians and organized efforts to help all in need. Katherine thought it incredible a woman of her years, other than royalty, could be so involved, respected, and active at home and abroad. The letter's more personal lines, however, wavered between anticipation of their reunion and severing all contact.

Starke left his chair and climbed to the boat deck as the Morro neared since *Olivette's* forecastle obscured passengers' view ahead. After emerging on the open upper-deck behind her pilothouse, he glanced at five white boats on either side, pairs of ventilators, and aft deckhouse then went to the railing. He regretted leaving his binoculars on *Calypso* while using a palm to shield his eyes from the blinding trapezoid of morning sun reflecting from the sea. To starboard, rippling waves topped by small white crests that marked water close aboard faded with distance then vanished before reaching an increasingly distinct coast. Over the starboard bow he could see the shore step down to sea level then suddenly rise up to the Morro with its lighthouse marking the narrow entrance to a large bay adjoining several small interior ones.

He felt *Olivette* heel slightly as the helmsman adjusted course to cut through small fishing boats. Several passed close aboard then fell astern. It was a familiar ritual for Starke after entering Havana several times from the west or northwest. A coastline notch soon became the narrow channel passing under the Morro with its walls and ramparts proud on the high eastern bank and, depending on the sun, appearing gray or light tan. On low ground below and west of the channel lay Havana where buildings were emerging from the gray blur then showing color as the liner continued closing. The same schooner that welcomed *Francisco de Montejo* in September was lying-to under the Morro. She suddenly sheeted home tanbark sails, gathered momentum, turned, and made for *Olivette's* starboard side where a short pilot ladder was rigged from the boarding port. Four uniformed men scrambled aboard as the schooner eased gently alongside. The pilot was taken forward to the master while two customs officers and a health official left for the dining room to begin screening. With its boarding party away, the schooner hauled off and was left in *Olivette's* wake as the liner's triple-expansion engine increased turns and single screw thrust the much larger ship forward.

The pilot steered for the narrow channel's far side, close under the Morro's ramparts, then began a starboard turn just before crossing mid-channel, placing the liner on the narrow passage's axis. This took them under the Morro then Fortaleza de San Carlos de la Cabaña on the high bluffs. Starke also watched the small San Salvador de la Punta Fortress, where filibusters Lopez and Crittenden were executed forty years before, pass down the starboard side as they glided forward and the coast curved inward to become the channel's west bank. Along it was a low seawall with empty cannon embrasures that fronted the Plaza del Armas and adjacent Palacio de los Capitanes Generales before ending at another small fortress. The peninsula behind these ramparts contained Havana, where buildings varying in size and shape were broken up by several parks. *Olivette* then began her turn starboard as the channel opened into a broad bay, started bleeding off speed, and slipped past the customs house, waterfront, and Machina Wharf's soaring derrick. Her goal was a black mid-harbor mooring buoy caked with droppings. Only Spanish Transatlantic Line ships docked because their arriving passengers usually included a thousand fresh troops and each departure retrieved pitiful contingents of exhausted, wounded, and sick. Passenger liners moored or anchored in the stream were serviced by a restive lighter and bumboat flotilla now waiting for *Olivette* to snatch the mooring buoy, pass a heavy shackle, pay out anchor chain, adjust its length to keep her stern clear of other ships, then reset chain stoppers.

Olivette's buoy lay northeast of the customs house piers and quarter way across the bay towards Santa Catalina peninsula where Regla, a town at its base, contained coaling piers, two rail terminals, the bull ring, an active smuggling population, and other attractions. Few large steamers were in port, but there were several sailing ships; bevies of small craft pierside, anchored, or underway; and ferries south of *Olivette's* mooring that crossed between the Muelle de Luz and Regla.

Starke's transition from *Olivette* to Hotel Inglaterra began with a lighter carrying him through the harbor; releasing noxious, pungent vapors as it sliced open the dark water's seal. After landing below Machina Wharf's towering derrick he walked through an archway into the customs house to register himself and baggage. The Spanish navy would not be greeting him since he was outwardly on personal business and his interview not until the following week, but they must have spoken with the customs officials who passed him rapidly through. Other entering passengers, and particularly correspondents, were meticulously searched while fielding a barrage of questions. A Starke shipping firm representative met him on the other side and took his luggage to the hotel, freeing Starke to engage one of the Cuban carriages foreigners called volantas. Although larger hotels ran shuttles along with lighters, he preferred the two-wheeled vehicle drawn by small horses with its driver astride one animal because their view forward was less restricted and they fitted in better than the victoria carriages that also hovered near the customs house exit.

Under a clear sky with little wind and bright sun he saw the navy building beyond the post office across from the customs house as they joined traffic passing along the waterfront's wood and steel piers jammed with lighters, boats, and small cargo schooners. Rolling through the city, Starke recalled it long since expanded beyond the old wall as its population climbed past 250,000, consuming the low peninsula then continuing west. Large commercial, religious, and government buildings were constructed of muted brick or stone but most close-packed houses surrounding them were painted yellow, pink, green, blue, or white. Larger structures were built around central courtyards and most topped by red-tile roofs. The streets were paved and unpaved with important avenues served by horse-drawn streetcars and side streets bleeding raw sewage. There was also a telephone system, Red Telefónica de la Habana, S.A. and three-year-old aqueduct supplying drinking water.

Starke climbed down from the volanta's black leather seat at the hotel then stood back from its large red wheel and panting horses to pay the driver. As his recent transportation moved off, he looked across Paseo del Prado's tree-filled median to Parque Central, directly opposite the Inglaterra. It consisted of paved walkways, ornate street lamps, and monuments separated by well-maintained grass and low shrubs. One stature honored Isabella II while a nearby large stone urn contained flowers and was likely a memorial. There were few trees, and its paved sections were cluttered with utilitarian park benches, tables, and chairs. Large buildings encircling the park included several hotels.

Hotel Inglaterra was unchanged from Starke's past visits. It was built with two floors in 1873 and a third added in 1886. Besides overlooking the park, it was across a side street from the enormous theater, Teatro Tacón, which included a cafe popular with foreigners. The hotel exterior's ground floor consisted of a terrace with large gasoliers suspended at the precise center of each arch and its name carved into a small curved facade rising from the roofline above the entrance. Second and third floor rooms opened through louvered double-doors to small porches girded by intricate, cast-iron railings that overlooked the street. Large ventilation grids filled the space between each door's frame and the next story.

Starke entered a large lobby of high arches and intricately carved ceilings beyond the hotel's open doors, momentarily paused, and then walked across a tile floor to the desk. He registered and received a large room facing Parque Central. It was one of eighty with high ceilings, no electric fixtures, common bathrooms, and large chamber pot population. Although tempted to take refreshment at a terrace table, Starke knew business must complete before afternoon or late that evening. Only the inexperienced would enter siesta without being settled because the city's residents, like those in all hot climes, began early, avoided midday heat, then worked late into the evening. Besides, he wished to avoid the reporter coveys milling about lobby, bar, and terrace.

Chapter Sixteen
Havana

Darwin Tyson reached Starke's door soon after siesta began and despite his time in Havana the only noticeable change was a slight tan and light cotton suit. He was still thin, bony, slightly balding, and clean-shaven; with eyes that took in everything and remained constantly alert for the next story. Starke's grinning visitor vigorously pumped his hand, "Let's find a table, Jacob. My flask's gone dry waiting on you."

As they passed through the lobby to an unoccupied street-side table Starke felt several correspondents watch their progress; probably marking him as the latest competitor. Tyson ordered rum once they were seated in wicker chairs at a small iron table and Starke requested the medicinal Spanish gin drink served in a balloon glass with fruit and quinine-laden tonic water. The correspondent moved swiftly after laying his fine straw hat on the table, "Never expected you here without *Calypso* so something's afoot."

Starke studied his glass as thin horses clopped sluggishly by in the street and people threaded past to nearby tables, "If I said my uncle's business, would you believe it?"

Tyson lifted his drink, "Out of friendship, form, and courtesy; but the Navy doesn't cut loose ship commanders to visit Havana, especially one with a reputation for sinking filibusters. Is the administration going to coordinate with Spain?"

"No, but since you've the scent; remember *Rafael Riego*

attacking the Spanish gunboat?"

"Yes, *Francisco de Montejo*, you were fortunate our election sucked up headlines and anarchist rumors surfaced. Editors resist having their public positions threatened so they'll run like Lucifer's lit their butts from anything linking the Junta with anarchists."

"That aside, my uncle needs someone to close a deal with British investors buying his sugar mill and plantation, but I'm here unofficially to make a statement at the inquiry into the gunboat's actions. I suspect some want a head to roll while others are opposing it or favor another candidate."

Looking half-convinced, Tyson smiled, "You still may read something different in the New York papers. It depends on which, but I'm guessing a secret mission to collude with the Spanish Navy or scouting for our Havana invasion. You'll find the local jackals create stories from whole cloth."

One of these defamed creatures apparently caught his attention, since Tyson lifted a glass in the man's direction before continuing with, "It seems you're already noticed."

Starke loaded his pipe and slowly moved a lit match over it, "What I've said is true and would check out but your lot seems well-represented."

"I've been here since after the election. Some are on assignment, others freelancing, and most passing through to Key West, Tampa, or Jacksonville where it's safer to continue reporting from Cuba. Captain General Campos provided passes to go with the army, but few took advantage. Weyler doesn't, which pleases the less energetic. Unlike you, most don't speak the language and rely on interpreters so they seldom look beyond Cuban victories or Spanish outrages. Before leaving New York I visited the Junta office where Horatio Rubens holds court for local reporters. It's nicknamed the Peanut Club because they keep a supply of nuts to feed the press along with propaganda. No one's completely free of bias, but real and rumored Spanish atrocities get covered while the insurrectionists' are overlooked or downplayed; and the same filter's applied on defeats and victories."

After downing half the glass' contents Tyson made a low circular motion with it before observing, "Real stories exist; but Inglaterra lobby lizards only make the obligatory execution across the channel. I suppose it's their rite of passage but I see no reason to watch some poor bastard shot. Sometimes they'll make the odd excursion with a translator who's probably an informer, favors the Junta, and produces whatever his customer desires."

After finishing, Tyson apparently felt it necessary to lift his thumb from the scales, "Don't get me wrong, Jacob. Ona Melton was caught on *Competitor*. Dawley's in prison and just before *Calypso* arrived in Key West the *Equator-Democrat*'s Charles Govin was executed by machete. A handful, like Harry Scovel and George Rea, are out there. I could also introduce you to William Bowen who works for the *World* and says he was an assistant surgeon in the Navy. Besides, we all tread carefully between Cuba Libre and Weyler since cables are censored and stories sent by boat could mean deportation if printed and considered too offensive. I'm better insulated because *The Sun* doesn't use bylines but Weyler sees no daylight between paper and correspondent."

"So how do you see it?"

"The island's poorly managed during the best times but some want independence and others don't. The majority are pacificos praying for peace. Insurrectionists mostly control the eastern provinces, except fortified cities, but aren't popular in the west, especially Pinar del Río. Weyler's firmed up three trochas across the island with La Trocha de Mariel-Majana designed to cut off Pinar del Río and trap Maceo. It's nearly complete so he's sending fresh troops there to go after him. That's why there're not many Spanish transports in port."

"Beating Maceo won't be easy."

"He's not shy about engaging Spanish troops, unlike some others. Our press calls him the Bronze Titan and the Spanish El Leon Mayor. He's part African, what they call a Mambí. Was an insult until Mambises earned a reputation for being the best fighters and now relish it. Even Weyler's personal troops are Black. Many Junta leaders, however, fear Cuba replicating Haiti under Maceo so there's a split between fighters and politicos. General Gómez backs him and the brother completely but must still deal with factions wanting him replaced."

"What about the Spanish?"

"Except for officers, and there's plenty, most regular army soldiers were drafted or enlisted in Spain. Voluntarios are those who join here and resemble our state militias but within them is a smaller group that scouts and hunts insurrectionists, called guerrilleros. They're from the island, fight like insurrectionists, expect no quarter if captured, and give none. It's an open secret the army's poorly supplied, hasn't been paid for months, and entrepreneurial officers are making the most of their office. Which reminds, be careful about your fencing. A lot of loyalists dislike the States and sword duels are fashionable. They're apparently arranged so few are killed, but you can never rely on niceties and I believe it violates Navy regulations."

Starke was listening, sipping, and watching people walk past, "My father's sword is safe on *Calypso*. What about Miss Evans?"

His friend's ebullient mood vanished, "Did well before catching whatever it was. The doctors weren't certain. She was vaccinated for smallpox and it didn't seem to be malaria, yellow fever, dengue fever, or cholera. Consumption was also ruled out. It could have been some unnamed tropical fever since the island's a cesspool of them. Spain's lost more soldiers to disease than combat and their surgeons expect typhus will strike troops or reconcentrados any time. That's why our Surgeon General Wyman's pushing for strict quarantine enforcement when anyone enters from Cuba. Anyway, Cassandra survived, was cleared, and took *Seneca* to New York where she's recovering."

Tyson looked from the shaded table into sunlight flowing over hotel and park as the tropical day brightened further. Starke sipped from his quinine drink, partly intended to protect against malaria, adding, "You've got to admire her pluck for stepping into this."

"You know she clung to that damn Brussels carpet bag even when delirious, then staggered up *Seneca*'s brow with it. There're not many women down here. Lily Curry was in Havana for a time. She reports and translates for *The Sun*; also writes books as Cecil Charles. I remember her being involved in some Chicago divorce scandal. Speaks the language and knew Martí. Kate Masterson from the *World* was here. Don't know her as well, except she's billed as a new woman. It's easier to attend executions than speak with prisoners but they mingled with women bringing food to relatives in La Cabaña's prison and came out with stories.

Tyson's use of Evans' first name and apparent familiarity made Starke wonder if his friend's aversion to anything beyond dalliances with her sex had weakened but instead asked, "What about Weyler? Gunboat commander thinks he's succeeding."

"Havana and the large cities held by Spanish troops aren't at risk but everywhere else is open to minor attacks on people and property; not much beyond brigandry but anyone not protected by the army or insurrectos risks their neck. Weyler hopes to isolate insurrectionists from supporters and victims."

Tyson looked across the street as a well-dressed man of African lineage stepped from a victoria to enter the park, "It's a stalemate one side can't win and the other can't abandon. Only Maceo engages in anything like battle. The rest might harass a column, raid small towns, or show up at some farm or plantation to take what they want then destroy what's left. Wealthier plantations pay protection money; what insurrectos refer to as taxes. Fighting age Cubans who don't join or support them are denounced as traitors. The penalty is hanging or a firing squad, but they're mostly just macheted. Rural Cubans began fleeing to fortified areas before Weyler's reconcentrado policy then ordered to after October. The loyalists consider anyone outside without a pass rebels and the insurrectionists declare those carrying one a traitor. Spain believes reconcentration is the only alternative to leaving but can't support or pay its soldiers, let alone feed and house thousands. Some Spanish officers are using personal funds to help or turning a blind eye to those returning to farm, but many ignore what they can't change."

Tyson, as always, came across as clear, insightful, relatively unbiased, and lacking gratuitous optimism. Starke felt light sweat on his back and warm wicker as he leaned back in the chair then dredged a pipe through his leather tobacco pouch. Tyson extracted one Turkish cigarette from a gold-trimmed jade case, tapped it against the face, and lit up.

Starke had no commitments over the approaching weekend, slept surprisingly well, and woke early to people and street traffic. Rising quickly, he pulled back the curtains and looked into a park surrounded by large buildings then over the city and across its ship channel to Havana's largest fortresses. Once dressed, he joined Tyson in the lobby then walked across the street for breakfast at Saloon Brunet, a cafe in the Teatro Tacón. Afterwards, he hired a small victoria to refresh his memory of the city. It carried the two friends along the waterfront to Machina Wharf then down Calle Oficios, before driving Aguiar Street past the consul-general's office where Starke would report Monday. The route also took them by navy headquarters, the post and telegraph offices, Mascotte Hotel, Plaza del Armas, Captain General's Palace, and Casino Español, where winter balls were held. For their return, the driver threaded his way through the crowded Calle del Obispo with its many shops. Starke purposely avoided the Arsenal's near dormant shipyard.

The next day, a baseball game began just after Sunday mass. Tyson claimed these were so popular the government refused to forbid them; although festivals and other large events were restricted or prohibited. The only other diversion, besides Manrique Street's cockfights, was a weekly three o'clock bullfight held across the bay in Regla since the Havana bullring closed. Tyson recommended a baseball for Starke's first Sunday because it avoided the ferry, seemed neutral ground, and his hosts would probably offer to arrange bullfight tickets anyway since senior officials, especially peninsulares, were regulars.

Starke did not see Lee at the Inglaterra that weekend but met with him early Monday morning in the Casa Nueva at 92 Aguiar Street where the ex-Confederate cavalry general and Virginia governor dominated his office. As he rose from the desk, Starke saw the dark, vested suit accentuated his bulk and almost rotund figure topped with thick silver-gray hair and matching mustache. Approaching with outstretched hand, he smiled, "Lieutenant, or rather captain since you've *Calypso*, it's good to see you. I trust your aunt and uncle are in good health?"

Lee was confirmed in April and arrived in June but Democrats lost their November election so his position was only secure until the March inauguration. After that, the new administration would keep him in place or send their man through confirmation. Motioning Starke to a chair, Lee retreated to his, which squeaked in protest under the bulk, "I would have attended *Calypso's* commissioning but was traveling. Read your *Rafael Riego* report. Anything else, I should know before moving out?"

"Only that some fairly solid anarchist rumors exist, sir."

"Your opinion of *Francisco de Montejo*'s handling?"

"I suspect Teniente Mendoza's orders were similar to mine. *Rafael Riego* was a large tug easily identified by her two stacks and the gunboat slower. His only choice was to board or watch *Rafael Riego* outrun him. Her raising our flag in sight of *Calypso* complicated matters."

"*Rafael Riego* fired on the Spaniard and was dealt with as a pirate. I suggest you make every effort during the interview to prevent or dispel any suggestion *Calypso* was in company with the filibuster or coordinating with *Francisco de Montejo*. You acted according to international law and custom to aid a national ship under attack by a pirate."

"That is essentially accurate, sir."

"Excellent. One more thing, I believe you speak the language?"

"Yes, sir; I'm near fluent in Spanish and German, although my Academy French only approaches adequate."

"Excellent. The Junta's not recognized, so neutrality laws don't apply, but Spain's long-term position is untenable. Our press and public favoring independence doesn't go down well with the Spanish generally and many believe the fighting has been prolonged by our support. Most junior army officers are agitated and support Captain General Weyler but I've no insight regarding the navy. Whatever the rights and wrongs, my first duty is protecting American citizens and property so anything that improves relations helps; which is why I supported Captain General Weyler's request."

With that settled, Lee pivoted to a new topic, "How large is *Calypso's* marine detachment?"

Caught off-guard, Starke answered, "There isn't one, sir. Captain Albert and I saw no benefit with the small crew. Commandant Heywood might have insisted but was pulling marines from other duties to fill new ships and prepare for a Central American flare-up. *Calypso's* landing party is well-armed with Remington-Lee rifles and Gatling guns but not yet exercised to the extent desirable."

"I've pushed for our ships to restart port visits around Cuba and requested one stationed where it could be in Havana immediately if American citizens or property were threatened; but haven't made a great deal of progress."

This did not surprise Starke after watching Albert's struggle to obtain far smaller ships than Lee would need; but sensed *Calypso* was a potential candidate and parried, "How would Spain respond?"

"Not well, certainly, but that's for the future; our immediate concern is your engagement with their naval authorities. I've arranged it during Wednesday's siesta to limit attention and will meet you there. We'll go to a restaurant that evening if you're free."

With that, Starke's time elapsed, they shook hands, and he left the consul poring over papers extracted from a pile staged for the next visitor. Outside, Starke decided to pass along the waterfront and see what ships were in port so he hailed a victoria cab and instructed the driver. He was back at the Inglaterra just before siesta, went to his room, opened the balcony door for a breeze, made some notes, read, and later spent an evening with Tyson.

Starke had nothing scheduled the next day so he began with breakfast, spent part of the morning on a park bench across the street, read newspapers in the lobby during siesta, then finished with his friend at El Palacio de Cristal restaurant. Tyson arrived late because he was delayed at the cable office forcing through a minor story about Spanish infantry surprising insurrecto cavalry near San Pedro de Hernandez. The censor proved troublesome because it was not written as a major victory. Tyson viewed it as something to justify his expense account and might not have pursued it that far except Spanish infantry catching insurrecto cavalry unawares was novel. His sources claimed the cavalry commander rallied his men, who charged the infantry with machetes and drove them to a nearby wall where there was cover but no escape. Forced to regroup, the soldiers began volley firing. This common practice was poor use of the excellent Spanish Mauser but conscripts going to Cuba had no opportunity for practice due to ammunition cost. In any case, the cavalry commander and his aide fell. The infantry advanced, confirmed they were dead, and retreated when more insurrectos arrived. Tyson's account caused Starke to spend the night vacillating between lying awake in the heat and an uneasy sleep punctuated by visions of exhausted troopers firing unfamiliar Springfield carbines in Montana.

Starke met Lee at the naval commander's building that Wednesday and was deposed, or the Spanish equivalent, by three senior navy officers and recorder. The controlled, but anxious, Teniente Emiliano Mendoza y Aguilar was also in the spacious room arranged and equipped for such inquiries, or more severe proceedings. The cool atmosphere thawed somewhat when the senior officer informed Starke, in French, that their recorder spoke English and would translate his statement; provoking Starke to reply he appreciated the courtesy but preferred answering questions in Spanish and hoped to review the original and translation for signature.

He was questioned on timing and navigational details, with one officer repeatedly asking why *Calypso* was off Arrecife Alacranes and a Revenue Service Cutter arrived so soon after. Starke knew local authorities were warned of *Rafael Riego* and told something of the American plan so appearing to conceal this activity would defeat the reason he was sent; but foreign inquiries were not appropriate venues to advertise Albert's operation. After considering how Washington and Madrid would receive his answer, he restated known facts. *Calypso* and *Vanguard* were in the southern Gulf of Mexico looking for a possible filibuster reported in Veracruz and the Arrecife Alacranes rendezvous was to start a sweep east in company. He emphasized that Navy ships and revenue cutters were patrolling to enforce policies, statutes, and proclamations that forbid filibustering. When asked if he observed any violations of law, customs, or agreement by *Francisco de Montejo*, Starke replied he did not and before the senior officer began his next question added that *Rafael Riego* had flown two national flags in succession so the attempted boarding was legitimate, the gunboat's warning shot landed well-clear of the tug, and flag-hoist communications could not be established before the filibuster fired. Since the Spanish officers appeared willing to listen without interruption, he described the dynamite gun's effect and how their damaged gunboat closed its assailant; firing until her gun crews were wounded or driven away by machine guns then continued to respond with rifles. He emphasized the gunboat's batteries re-manned immediately after firing slackened and despite their ship's condition managed to hit the fleeing *Rafael Riego*. His testimony concluded with a tailored flourish, "Continuing after *Rafael*

Riego with *Francisco de Montejo* facing death was undertaken with the greatest reluctance but no other choice was possible after witnessing her assassin's cowardly assault and *Francisco de Montejo*'s gallantry."

The interview concluded with the most relieved party being *Francisco de Montejo*'s commander, whose ship was at the Arsenal's vestigial navy yard. Consul-general Lee was also satisfied since every indication was *Rafael Riego* would soon enter diplomatic oblivion. Starke was asked to remain another week while statements were prepared for review and signature. Lee did not allow any protest so they left the building near siesta's close with the city returning to life under a hot sun and clear skies. Once in the street, Lee chuckled, "You can use time away from *Calypso* and there's your other business. If you've trained your second it should present no problem so I'll cable Washington "

That night they enjoyed a late dinner where the consul-general's observations mirrored Tyson's. Starke also learned Lee's idea of time away from *Calypso* included assisting with several sensitive translations and completing an evaluation of local shipping and naval capabilities.

Over the next few days he met Tyson each evening for supper. Since his friend was on *The Sun*'s account and Starke possessed independent income, they patronized the best restaurants, usually El Louvre or El Palacio de Cristal. These evenings included leisurely dinners and refreshing libations; amidst pipe, cigar, and cigarette smoke. The days were spent shopping and lounging, with light work capped by a military band playing under tropical heavens in Parque Central every second evening. Havana's cosmopolitan population and plethora of colorful Spanish uniforms made sections seem like Paris despite troops and fortifications isolating it from an island hotly disputed by loyalists and insurrectionists. This surreal atmosphere, especially surrounded by starving reconcentrados, was an ominous change from previous visits.

Chapter Seventeen
Pinar del Rio

With the interview complete, Starke began arrangements to transfer title of his family's Pinar del Río sugar mill and plantation near Artemisa; a city thirty-five miles from Havana by rail, nine miles southwest of Guanajay, and south of the mountains. The surrounding flat, fertile lowlands, filled with royal palm trees rising from reddish soil, were known for disease-ridden summers and profitable businesses; before crops were destroyed, buildings burnt, and life made more precarious by the insurrection.

Gómez and Weyler saw the wealthy province's loyalty as a major reason the previous war for independence failed. Consequently, Gómez sent Maceo there with an army and Weyler chose Pinar del Río to commence a province-by-province pacification that would move gather momentum as it moved east. To choke off supplies and trap Maceo, the newest, and most sophisticated of three fortified lines segmenting the island was almost complete and in operation so Weyler was committing fresh troops to defeat the Cuban general.

This made Starke's trip to the properties longer and more dangerous since it could no longer be accomplished by rail alone and required a train to Artemisa then horseback to the plantation and mill. Fewer trains were running to the city from Havana and those tightly controlled because Artemisa bulged the Mariel-Majana Trocha near its midpoint and was the military headquarters. Consequently, Lee's help was needed to assuage Spanish qualms about an American officer visiting the installation or being killed during one of the frequent insurrecto raids. Starke would have let that be an end to it except his uncle cabled that Curtis was determined to visit the property his syndicate was investing in and Britain was also represented in Havana should the Americans not assist. If Starke hoped Lee might prevent the excursion, he was disappointed. State's representative not only viewed the request as legitimate but pointed out Starke was in Cuba at the captain general's request so refusal would be awkward and the trip might provide reliable information about the trocha and situation beyond Havana's fortifications. Weyler was equally unhelpful. He readily agreed, not only because Starke was an invited guest and Spanish hospitality demanded it, but saw the risk as acceptable for any military officer and some benefit might come from advertising the massive project. The military pass also included Tyson since Lee became aware the men were friends after his evening with *Calypso's* commander and Spanish authorities considered *The Sun* correspondent more reputable than most plaguing their city.

Spanish and English copies of his *Francisco de Montejo* statement arrived the Friday before their excursion and were perfectly timed because Starke's weekend plans vanished when Tyson became unexpectedly engaged. While Starke reviewed, corrected, added clarifications, and adjusted phrasing, Tyson learned it was probably General Maceo shot from his horse during the reported skirmish and was trying to confirm it by sifting through conflicting accounts. Because Maceo was often wounded, regularly reported killed, and the latest stories ran the gamut from poisoning by his own physician to assassination during a truce, *The Sun* correspondent wanted incontrovertible proof. Tyson's relentless digging and checking finally convinced him the minor story filed a week before accurately described Maceo's death and a major insurrecto loss.

Starke met Tyson for dinner after the correspondent returned from the censor and cable offices. On their way, Starke asked about the story. Tyson shrugged, sipped from his flask, and flatly observed the Inglaterra rumor mill would ensure his report of an exceptional general falling during a minor engagement would be overshadowed by more useful and creative accounts until truth resurfaced.

Once Starke's statements were signed and submitted he was approached and embraced by a much relieved Teniente Mendoza, then invited for supper, drinks, and cigars at a fashionable restaurant. Starke learned during their evening that *Francisco de Montejo* was at the Arsenal shipyard where completing her temporary repairs had been abnormally frustrating. The Spaniard deplored the state of the same yard that gave Spain fifty ships of the line, including *Santísima Trinidad*, and was once one of their largest, now struggling to repair a gunboat. However, he proved a gracious host who mostly avoided discussing the insurrection but did observe many navy officers who saw Cuba as a lost cause were also convinced American interference, funds, and filibusters played a major role in Compañía Trasatlántica Española shuttling thousands of fresh troops to Cuba and returning with wounded, sick, and dispirited survivors. He also confirmed Lee's observation that many army officers backed Weyler wholeheartedly because he took the field with them, ended repeated rebel pardons, and rooted out the lethargic, incompetent, and self-enriching. Mendoza was less familiar with reconcentrados, since he operated out of Puerto Rico, but could not see how they would be cared for. Like most officers, he was adamant the insurrectos lay down arms before negotiations or Spain would be abandoning her loyalists. He also lamented the Spanish, like every nation that sent armies to the Caribbean, were shocked at thousands dying without seeing a foe. Trapped between the dishonor of leaving and a depleted treasury, he worried the government would fall if pushed much further, liberals would take power, and the situation worsen. Starke thought his stoic pessimism rivaled Tyson's but enjoyed the evening. Afterwards, they shared a carriage that stopped first at the Arsenal where *Francisco de Montejo* was preparing to leave for Puerto Rico the next morning. Both men invited the other to visit their homes, and Starke wished Mendoza a safe voyage.

Starke began his next day at the waterfront watching *Francisco de Montejo* back into the broad bay then thread through harbor traffic until she reached the turn north. After coming to port, the gunboat picked up some speed in the channel but Mendoza was careful to prevent wake damage and hesitant to press the wounded ship during her first underway since limping in. Standing on the small gunboat's bridge, he looked forward to Puerto Rico and thanked Providence *Francisco de Montejo* was not patrolling Cuba. The Spanish navy had nowhere near the numbers needed and was so penurious that maintenance and training were thought an extravagance. He was not alone. Rear Admiral Pascual Cervera y Topete resigned as Minister of the Navy after political intriguing crippled his attempts to reform and rebuild the armada. Once clear of the mouth, Mendoza turned east then set a course to pass south of Cay Sal Bank. After steaming between it and Cuba, he came southeast, remaining clear of the island's irregular coast, and passed down Old Bahama Channel past Haiti to San Juan.

The Ward Line's *City of Washington* closed Havana's entrance on Tuesday evening then boarded a pilot, customs agents, and health official before passing cautiously through the narrow channel and turning starboard into the bay. The 300-foot, 2,500-ton liner would remain overnight at an anchor buoy off Machina Wharf then continue to Veracruz and Panama before returning on the leg back to New York City. A pair of boilers exhausted through her single stack aft of the wheelhouse between two slightly raked masts that could raise canvas in an emergency. Boats under davits lined a white superstructure above her black hull with its straight stem slicing easily through calm water.

Among passengers clustered along the deck and above her distinct counter were Katherine Ledford and brother, Edward Curtis. She shielded her eyes and watched the fortresses, seawall, parks, and buildings slip past; completing a transformation that began at New York's Pier 14. *City of Washington* steamed down that northern port's approaches to the Atlantic then plowed south through nondescript seas with rows of white caps under light gray clouds with dirty bottoms. After clearing Cape Hatteras in unusually fair weather, the ocean turned to bright greens and blues, waves grew less pronounced and the ship seemed to slip through the Atlantic rather fight it. Clear skies took on a crystalline quality, becoming more vibrant and sharply focused. At one point, the ship was paced by a large shark swimming south with skin glistening where seawater washed over an exposed back. Whimsical dolphins would appear, race alongside, and then dive under the bow before streaking off. Further south, flying fish joined in during the day and greenish-white phosphorescence lit the wake at night.

Disquieting thoughts agitated Katherine when *City of Washington* entered Havana's narrow passage and she looked up at the foreboding gray ramparts on high ground to the east then studied the passing waterfront consisting of a bustling street filled with vender stalls that ran behind quays and piers alive with small craft. Beyond was an imposing wall of commercial and government buildings obscuring the eclectic mix of cathedrals, parks, buildings, and houses with red-tile roofs visible from the ship channel. She persuaded her brother to bring her although he had planned to return north then leave for home from New York. Instead, they traveled together and would depart from Havana when his business concluded. Katherine now confronted a city that always fascinated her since it forever altered their family.

Oliver Barrington Curtis' somber portrait above the main staircase looked down on Brydian Grange visitors for 130 years despite his reputation as a romantic and incorrigible rake. The young army captain with blue eyes, high forehead, pulled back hair, and fine features never returned from Havana. He came overland as one of Pocock and Keppel's officers with the 34th Regiment of Foot to die of yellow fever after laying siege to the Morro. Katherine felt she was looking out over his forgotten grave; abandoned when Britain returned the island a year later. He frequented childhood daydreams and possibly influenced her accepting Philip's marriage proposal since the cousin somewhat favored him. The wealth and station she enjoyed was also down to him because the baronetcy diverted to her father's line when he left no legitimate issue.

Brother and sister soon made their way to the liner's cargo port where a steam launch came alongside to collect visitors for customs and baggage registry. Katherine grew more uneasy as it chugged through pungent harbor water towards a gigantic derrick. Starke cabled her brother they would meet in the Inglaterra lobby the day after registering and she brooded about seeing him. The voyage also convinced her that *Calypso* and the Caribbean fit Starke better than Washington;

and far more than Britain. Thinking she was too forward on paper, when he was at a safe distance, Katherine sensed Oliver Barrington Curtis' spirit haunting her emotions.

After leaving the customs house, a large carriage pulled by ill-used horses carried them to the off-white, three-story hotel beside the massive theater and across from a military band's evening concert in the park. Walking under the central archway and large glass gasolier, they entered a vibrant, ornate lobby with more arches and colorfully tiled walls. Her room was between Starke and Curtis because the brother requested accommodations near the American. While alone, and waiting for luggage, Katherine walked through its exterior door opening over Paseo del Prado then stood at the compact balcony's black metal railing, listening to music and watching people, carts, and carriages pass below.

Katherine seldom traveled before coming to the States so her bible was Campbell Davidson's *Hints to Lady Travelers: at home and abroad*. Based on its advice, she bought a steamer trunk, carried a smaller travel bag for the cabin, and saved worn linens while in the States, especially undergarments, to be reused then discarded at sea. Most of her wardrobe was shipped home through New York but she brought a single evening gown for unanticipated formal events, her traveling suit, and enough clothes to last until visiting Havana's shops. She also carried several letters of credit, minimal cash, and soda crackers for seasickness.

After her luggage arrived and everything was put in place, Katherine freed herself from the traveling suit with its light corset, changed to nightclothes, and entered a brass bed under light mosquito netting. Combined with the room's porch, fittings, and marble trim, it stoked a sense of the exotic and reawakened exuberance not experienced since long before her coming out. The heat made her mourning ring itch so she removed it for the first time since Philip's death and gently set it aside.

Starke's primary reason for being in Havana played out with little drama and he hoped the second, a favor to his uncle, would do the same. He began by meeting Edward Curtis and his widowed sister in the lobby. The men chose light linen sack suits over white cotton shirts with rolled collars, soft straw hats, and heavy canes for defense. Katherine's lightweight travel suit seemed uncomfortable but fashionable to Starke. After a cool and proper greeting, she remained calm and poised, except for fingering her parasol's ivory handle. Tyson was absent working the Maceo story but assured Starke he would not miss their evening excursion to El Palacio de Cristal restaurant on the corner of Consulado and San José Streets, about two blocks away.

The trio crossed San Rafel Street to Saloon Brunet, a restaurant in Teatro Tacón, for breakfast. Over coffee and pastry, Starke confirmed their French liner, departing from Veracruz, would stop in Havana then leave for St. Nazaire on the twenty-second. Starke would leave for Key West in three days on *Mascotte* so there was a short window to complete the transaction. He employed this to dissuade Katherine's brother from visiting the properties but Curtis was convinced he must personally estimate the rebuilding effort and explained most Cuban centrales lacked capital before fighting began and Spain was impoverished so investors from the United States, Great Britain, and other nations would compete for them once peace returned. The Starke mill and plantation offered his syndicate an opportunity to secure a foothold then construct a modern mill and acquire additional acreage; so he was also looking to establish local contacts.

Starke accepted this at face value but lacked any desire for gratuitous adventure and thought that might also be a motive.

Curtis mentioned an acquaintance, Lieutenant Churchill, saw action with Spanish troops the previous year which led Starke to suspect the younger Englishman might harbor a latent desire to imitate his friend. However, Curtis was adamant, Tyson eager to travel outside Havana, Lee supported the foray, and Starke felt reluctant to emphasize risk in front of Katherine.

Starke, Tyson, and Curtis spent most of the day preparing to leave early Thursday and return late Friday afternoon since an overnight trip was unavoidable. Tyson was already outfitted for such an opportunity so Starke borrowed several items, bought high-topped leather boots, and obtained inexpensive clothing for discarding afterwards. Curtis purchased an expensive outfit before leaving the States but added some small items during an Obispo Street shopping excursion with his sister.

The trip began at the Havana railway station west of Castillo de Santo Domingo de Atarés on the day's first Cardenas and Jucaro Railway run. Scheduled rail service to Artemisa was limited to morning and evening trips escorted by an armored train. Their transport consisted of lightweight cars pulled by a diminutive American-built locomotive belching black smoke and dripping water. Sitting in wicker seats facing forward, with steam and smoke wafting through vents and open windows, they watched a mostly depopulated land pass. Small army or voluntario detachments were visible at every town and bridge with reconcentrado encampments surrounding some outposts. Their accompanying train included three armored cars to fight off insurrectos and one flatcar equipped to repair track damage.

As the trains entered Pinar del Rio, Nuevas Filipinas in the last century, its fertile red soil and picturesque landscape daubed with palm trees seemed more a romantic canvas than real. They were slowing for Artemisa when the Mariel to Majana trocha appeared. This most modern and sophisticated of three fortified lines girding the island included barbwire fencing between forts, blockhouses, fortified guard posts, a 200-yard swath cleared for shooting, and narrow gauge railway to move troops, supplies, and construction material along it. As their train began braking for the station Starke saw makeshift reconcentrado huts constructed inside fortifications surrounding the city with no sign of sanitary measures.

He suspected many people met during past visits to the centrale were probably camped there, dead and buried, or killing each other. In addition, the short narrow gauge mill railroad from Artemisa to the properties no longer functioned while the red-dirt road it paralleled was unused, overgrown, and so perilous it required horses with an armed escort; so their rail journey ended with the train jerking and squealing to a stop on rusted rails with shiny crowns in front of the modest wood-framed station and covered platform. Artemisa lay just north of the railbed and to the south stood a water-tower then white picket fence holding back trees and vegetation.

An unenthusiastic second lieutenant, or subteniente, greeted them with assiduous courtesy as they stepped down. He wore the Guayabera tropical uniform made from light-blue, striped rayadillo. A tunic fastened with large brass buttons was worn over trousers and most soldiers chose the broad-brimmed jipijapa straw hat. The enlisted were also equipped with a leather harness and Model 1893 Spanish Mauser rifle for infantry or Model 1895 carbine for cavalry, although some irregular or militia units still carried black-powder single-shot Remington rolling blocks.

The officer provided three small horses and answered every question put to him as they mounted then rode to meet a half-dozen voluntarios before passing unmolested through several heavily guarded perimeter checkpoints. A short distance beyond they turned from the main road that was little more than a broad path to continue single file down a narrow trail through encroaching vegetation. It was the road Starke recalled as paralleling a railroad spur to the mill so both would have been busy this time of year with preparations for the zafra, or sugar cane harvest. He could just make out the old railbed, slightly higher than surrounding ground, with its single rusting track running along an overgrown crest. The subteniente was obviously avoiding it to remain less vulnerable to ambush or snipers.

Starke often rode to relax, and had no opportunity for some months, so he cleared his mind and adjusted to the late morning heat, inescapable humidity, and mount's steady motion. As their party advanced at a slow walk, leaving small clouds of red dust, he observed their escort closely watch the lush growth growing under various palm varieties just off the road; carbines at the ready. He occasionally looked back at Curtis and Tyson who seemed uncomfortable as they constantly wiped away sweat he ignored unless a rivulet threatened his eyes. The unnatural quiet was disturbed only by his two companions' subdued exchanges, sporadic sounds from the mounts, creaking leather, and gentle slapping of machetes against saddles.

Their destination first appeared as a handful of abandoned slat-sided railcars that once carried cane to the mill then took away its refined product. Beyond these carcasses was a tall red-brick stack surrounded by rusted, blackened, and twisted corrugated tin sheets. Once the small mill's roof, they were now shrouds for its derelict machinery and charcoaled remains of walls and rafters. Surrounding outbuildings inhabited by foliage and small wildlife stood with doors or windows ajar. One large structure, with double doors and iron stack, contained two fire-tube boilers with peeling black paint, shredded insulation, and orange rust coating exposed metal and piping. Nearby was the decomposed pile of milled cane that once fed them. Many grass tufts breached hard-packed red earth between buildings and a line of arches and partial walls on a rise covered by tall grass marked remnants of the main house. The subteniente allowed brief dismounts to examine a specific item, foundation, or area as their sweating horses walked carefully through this desolation; but kept his command saddled to discourage attack.

They were soon returning to Artemisa since small detachments outside fortifications after dark courted ambush. Starke questioned their subteniente about the damage while riding back. Although in Havana when the attack occurred, their guide heard the manager allowed workers to stay on when operations ceased despite the risk but was unable, or refused, to pay insurrecto taxes. It was attacked soon after and survivors fled to fortified areas around the city where reconcentration made any attempt to return twice as dangerous. He could not speak to particular individuals, but assumed most elderly, women, and children were in the camps and their young men with an insurrecto, voluntario, or guerrillero group; depending on necessity, loyalty, or scores to settle.

Tyson slacked his mount's reins during their return since the animal had only to follow the horse ahead and avoid the one behind, which seemed to enjoy nipping when the interval closed. After extracting a worn notebook, wilted and pliable from heat and humidity, he began penciling in semi-decipherable notes. Starke observed his friend's silver flask remained holstered in the tan, cloth jacket; where it invariably stayed during dangerous or tense situations. Tyson's thirst always vanished when others steadied their nerves with spirits.

The subteniente dismissed his voluntarios in Artemisa, except for a senior man willing to introduce Curtis around the city then he, Starke, and Tyson boarded the narrow gauge train leaving to resupply a trocha fort some miles south. After several jerks, its engine and tender pulled the half dozen open cars laden with soldiers and supplies out of General Juan Arolas' headquarters; swaying and squealing down the dedicated line. As they picked up speed, sweating men wearing light-blue uniforms, leather equipment harnesses, and straw hats kept bolt-action Mauser rifles at the ready, scanned the passing right-of-way for ambush signs, ignored the heat, and welcomed the thick, pungent breeze created by the moving train.

At Lee's request, and to compile a letter to the Office of Naval Intelligence, Starke studied the fortifications as they traveled down a swath cleared to effective rifle range. The trocha's scale was incredible, especially considering it was one of three designed, built, manned, and supplied by a bankrupt nation. The large whitewashed structures were forts. Between them were new or converted blockhouses linked by fortified guard posts and waist-high stone walls. Unending miles of barbed wire was fixed to lines of posts and enhanced by artillery coverage and electric lights; with areas susceptible to night crossings seeded with land torpedoes attached to tripwires. Starke saw hundreds of soldiers and voluntarios along its length: on guard, working, or resting. From what he observed and the subteniente's response to questions, Starke estimated many thousands were committed to defend static fortifications, provide mobile backup forces, and cover losses. Their guide also mentioned that building material mostly came from the States to reduce cost.

Curtis was waiting when they returned to Artemisa; the train now carrying sick soldiers, a few wounded, and the odd officer running a headquarters errand. After thanking their host and protector, the men overnighted on the train station's wood benches since hotels were full, mattresses might be populated with pests, and they did not want to miss the morning train. Tyson's silver flask and cigarette case reappeared, Starke's pipe was unlimbered, and Curtis lit a cigar before describing his afternoon. As Starke anticipated, reconcentrados lived in hastily constructed, improvised huts, or unused buildings, usually old warehouses or storage sheds. Sanitation was haphazard and a local doctor claimed diseases common to such situations were becoming rampant. Curtis found he was constantly approached by starving young children with swelled bellies, and some adults, asking for anything he would part with. Having emptied his pockets, Curtis tapped Starke and Tyson during the night for what money they carried then sent it to the doctor before leaving. Their Havana return mirrored the journey south except for rushing to a bathhouse where they steamed, showered, and shaved while their clothes burned; even Curtis' Brooks Brothers outfit.

Chapter Eighteen
Hotel Inglaterra

Starke met Tyson in the Inglaterra lobby the evening before he returned to Key West and *Calypso*. They spoke several minutes then rose from their chairs when Curtis and his sister arrived. Starke found Katherine aloof, nothing like her letters, and they were never left alone. He felt an attraction slowly grow as they wrote but seeing her float over the tile floor in a light cotton visiting dress added base and urgent sensations. He immediately recognized them as the discomfiting feelings that rose after his aunt's dinner party when she entered the library wearing an erotic black dress and later on the Hygeia Hotel pier where he barely managed to resist embracing her.

Balancing propriety and the tropical evening, Katherine's white dress had sleeves coming nearly to her wrists, a hemline cut just above the floor, and material imparting a smooth, sheer, silk-like transparency that pushed decency's limits. Possessing some familiarity with women's fashions, despite an absence of sisters, Starke guessed the corset less confining than most, but enough to mold the figure to the desired S-shape before continuing out and over her hips with a front tab dropping below the waist. Her undergarments accentuated this by causing slight straining across pearl buttons and other spots. The ensemble was completed by light cotton gloves, lace parasol, and soft straw boater.

He sat anxious and awkward beside Tyson and facing her in their carriage to the El Louvre restaurant. As their victoria rolled past parks, colorful homes with red-tiles showing at the eaves, and grand public edifices, Starke considered the woman who corresponded with him for the last half-year. He felt an irresistible allure spurred by her apparel and thick hair no longer confined in a tight bun but curled smoothly into a tawny pompadour pierced by a pearl-tipped hatpin anchoring the boater. The fashionable style, new to her, enhanced an oval face with longish nose and large faded-blue eyes set in a countenance marked by taut facial muscles stretching skin across pronounced cheekbones and jawline curving upward from a slight chin dimple. As he recalled from Washington and Norfolk, her lips, below a barely visible depression under the nose, consisted of a thin upper one tightly compressed against the more prominent lower. These parted only for speaking, and no more than necessary, like the occasional, almost stillborn, smile crossing her face when appropriate or horizontal furrows that slightly creased the forehead when considering some point or situation. Her poise remained unchanged and suggested intense self-control contrived to not only avoid inappropriate movement or suggestion but convey indifference. She deferred more than usual to her brother throughout the evening, as though he shielded her, and seemed distant, unlike the letters cached in his desk on *Calypso*. The mourning ring's familiar bulge in her glove was also absent, which was equally odd since Katherine never wore a great deal of jewelry but always that. He attributed it to heat or fear of theft.

Starke wanted to see her alone despite the seemingly aloof demeanor but Katherine left for her room soon after returning to the Inglaterra; leaving the men sitting around a small cafe table. While she was there, Curtis and Tyson contrasted the British view of Cuba with the States' while Starke listened. He was unable to concentrate until she excused herself then struggled to resist following her to plead an undefinable case. After she retired, Starke's companions returned to Curtis' description of Artemisa's reconcentrado encampment. His voluntario guide took him to a larger one where several men familiar with the plantation and mill, or their families, were rumored to be. His graphic description on the return trip kept Tyson filling a notebook and left Starke pondering how Cassandra Evans withstood excursions to these camps and buildings near Havana, but not how she came to be ill.

Tyson leaned forward once Curtis followed his sister, "I've a favor to ask, Jacob. Foreign ships fall under Spanish authority in port so *Olivette* and *Mascotte* allow Havana officials to search passengers and luggage even after they've passed through customs and boarded. Britain and France, to their credit, refuse but I can't wait for one of their ships. I'll be returning to New York soon and don't want my notes confiscated so I'm asking you to take them."

Tyson never involved Starke in his work and this was no small favor. He, or the Navy, might be tarred as *The Sun*'s courier or worse. Seeing him hesitate, Tyson added, "I understand, Jacob, but hear me out."

"I'm listening, Darwin."

"Use whatever information's in my notebooks for your Office of Naval Intelligence correspondence then send them to me at the paper."

Tyson was confident Starke would never betray his trust by opening the notebooks so allowing him to mine them meant an exceptionally detailed report and legitimate reason to accept his proposal. Starke carefully considered Tyson's proposition. The Chief Intelligence Officer, Wainwright, was not someone whose professional betterment Starke would take a risk for but he was also in Havana to obtain information so he agreed. Relieved, Tyson lit another Turkish cigarette,

"I'll bring them to your room later; now about your love life."

Starke was caught off-guard as Tyson pressed relentlessly on, "I assume Katherine's the distant cousin Aunt Constance's trying to harness you to."

"Yes."

"You claim she's an intelligent correspondent, and your eyes don't stray far when she's near."

Starke finished lighting his pipe, "That obvious? Anyway, I doubt there's any interest on her part beyond corresponding."

"I disagree and she seems to possess poise, beauty, and intelligence. That's a tough row to hoe. I'd guess most men take advantage and, as your aunt often points out, women see her as a threat. She may be a baronet's daughter who's had social skills drilled into her since birth but I suspect you'd find another widow Ledford much like her brother."

Tyson paused for a quick puff, adding, "She's also of the same church, close enough anyway, so you'll not have the problem of mixed religions. Think twice before bolting on this one, Jacob."

Starke lifted his glass to peer through its remnants, "You forget, Darwin, I leave for the States tomorrow and she returns to Britain in a few days."

Tyson smiled, flipped the silver flask's cap, then looked over it at Starke, "Your aunt is going to propose candidates until you've taken a wife, or consort to use her expression, and few will equal widow Ledford. The intrepid Miss Evans might suffice but not sure how you'd fare with a new woman type."

Starke silently agreed with Tyson, especially concerning his aunt's arguments; which he began taking more seriously after learning Starke Shipping and Shipbuilding would pass to him, and likely his father's Southern Caribbean and Atlantic Shipping Company as well. Before that disclosure, he thought the subject premature and her counsel mischievous banter, but also knew the age had come when its inevitability crept in. Starke looked across the table at his friend with some amusement. Aunt Constance was unlikely to discard years of experience and habits should he marry and equally certain she saw Tyson's redemption possible only under firm female guidance.

After Tyson matched two pipe bowls with several Turkish cigarettes they climbed the stairs to their rooms. Tyson was knocking on Starke's door within minutes carrying something like a dozen small dark notebooks; most badly worn but identical to the one he took Artemisa. The correspondent exchanged a few words then left. Starke locked the door, disrobed, and slipped beneath the brass bed's mosquito netting. His nightdress was left draped over a chair since he was alone and tired on a warm night.

Katherine was properly attired in the adjacent room but thrashing against the confining netting. Jacob's proximity and impending departure, perhaps for good, fed an emotional maelstrom she struggled to master. Its intensity continued building after their reunion in the tropical city and demanded every fiber of practiced self-discipline to check, until, during the evening's engagement, it mutated from uncomfortable to unbearable. She excused herself early and escaped to her room where she considered slipping an invitation under his door. Several friends, married and single, embraced the practice at country house parties but she spurned these trysts as low and sinful so self-disgust quenched the impulse. An assignation with Jacob would also be an affront to her friend, Constance Starke, and knowing her brother was asleep next door kept Katherine awake imagining what he would think of his sister. Restless and sweating lightly, Katherine Louisa Ledford also resisted a rakish ancestor's audacious spirit as she compared Havana to Brydian Grange, felt the exotic Caribbean playing havoc with her principles, and started to regret not sliding a note under Starke's door. Anxious and moist, Katherine felt as little control over her body as it had over the tropical night. She remained in a semiconscious state, often staring at the dark wood door, willing and fearing he would enter to bed her; before realizing the influence of gothic romance novels devoured as an adolescent was seeping back, along with the spirit of a young army officer and rake she admired during the years he was safely confined to the portrait above Brydian Grange staircase.

Half-awake, twisting and sweating, she recalled how Philip's gentle attentions grew more desirable; then contrasted them with this primeval, infinitely more sinful, desire for a man who was not her husband and never could be. She grew more disgusted when she admitted those emotions might not differ if Jacob was married; although she would never act on them. Instead, she rolled on her side, curled up, and tried to banish each succeeding vision.

She heard quiet knocking at Jacob's door followed by low voices when convinced it could not get more unsettling. Her first thought was Cassandra Evans; bold, attractive, and intelligent. Katherine considered her someone who would relentlessly pursue what she wanted before remembering Tyson say she was recuperating in New York. Failing to recall other women in Havana, her thoughts turned to those men engaged for the evening. She knew his sex had needs from her life with Philip. Even Edward visited her school friend who, unable or unwilling to find a suitable match, offered the service for a living; an ongoing liaison the family conspicuously ignored.

Katherine was relieved to hear Tyson's unmistakable voice and quick departure. As the door closed and his footsteps passed by she thought the visit strange after hearing her brother's door shut earlier; meaning all three had retired. Tyson seemed a curious soul and his relationship with Jacob and the Starke family curious. Constance Starke ostensibly deplored Tyson but treated him as the family rascal. He would fall near the actors' rung on Britain's social ladder, despite being a successful correspondent for a prominent New York paper, but seemed blessed with an uncanny capacity to assess situations and people despite constant self-medication. It made Katherine feel exposed since Darwin Tyson clearly saw her quandary yet said nothing

Katherine and Starke's beds were near an adjoining wall to accommodate large commodes so occupants could sometimes hear louder sounds next door. She heard him call out orders and warnings while half asleep, rose without thinking, wrapped the sheer peignoir over her night dress, and was suddenly knocking on his door. Starke was flailing about in tangled netting trying to shepherd Alexandria's survivors to four American warships anchored offshore before British ironclads resumed their bombardment. The refugees in this too-familiar dream were no longer mixed nationalities fleeing the Mediterranean port but reconcentrados. His arms, waist, and legs were entangled in boarding nets and he was calling to *Apalachicola's* captain, Commander Albert, when a staccato of hesitant knocks banished the nightmare. His first thought was Yamashita or the messenger calling him to the pilothouse so he responded with feigned detachment before realizing he was at the Inglaterra, pulled a nightshirt over his bare frame, walked quickly to the door, and opened it.

The distraught woman facing him was the last person anticipated and before a word was spoken Katherine impulsively thrust forward, threw protecting arms around him, laid her head against his chest, and murmured something about his being all right. Holding her for the first time, Starke realized she was not tall, but blessed with a firm, supple, physique that felt hot, moist, and alive. She looked up, her face a kaleidoscope of embarrassment, frustration, determination, and surprise. He kissed and caressed her with unapologetic urgency. During pleasant Key West evenings, with *Calypso* secure at her anchorage, Starke imagined how she would feel in his arms but dismissed the notion as improper and her deportment in Havana suggested no interest beyond corresponding, which he anticipated would end soon after she returned home.

Instead, Katherine was grappling and kissing. He responded with no less urgency and ardor. Neither remembered how they disrobed, nor falling into an already disturbed bed, but it was quickly done as the scent, sweat, and low murmurs of their exertions in the warm room accelerated rather than dissuaded from a shared purpose. She remembered through a frenzied haze how Philip ended lovemaking; as if afraid the woman he loved would break and had been violated. She would settle back in their bed, hesitant to touch her satiated husband once the necessary act for conception was complete. Although she anticipated the same from Starke, he continued until her own vigorous demands took control, propriety succumbed to primeval, and the lady erupted in bucking contractions; leaving them startled, sweat-soaked, and limp. While entwined, Katherine realized the raucous tryst occurred with Edward's room just beyond her own, two doors down the hall, but felt only drained pleasure and comfort while wrapped in and around Starke's warm body.

The spent lovers slowly grew awkward and confused. Starke lay entangled thinking he should propose but worried it might be taken as insincere and obligatory. He gently stroked the disheveled, damp mass of hair cascading across his bed and chest. He wanted to marry this woman and, more shocking, see her heavy with their child. As this unexpected sensation washed over him, Katherine was suddenly up, dressed, and quietly slipping through the door. Although equally overwhelmed, she saw her impulsive visit and wanton behavior a gratuitous seduction practiced only by the lowest of her sex and decided to leave before Jacob threw a disheveled harlot into the hallway for Edward to find. At the same time, she longed to rejoin him in bed forever so her departure consumed every ounce of willpower and self-discipline. Katherine loathed theatrics, had no expectation Jacob would follow to propose, an offer that must be declined, and yet still ached he did not.

Starke believed this sudden activity driven by modesty and desire to suppress any display before he formally approached Edward and her father. He resolved to do that before boarding *Mascotte* at noon so, unlike Katherine, slept soundly for what little night remained. After withdrawing from Starke, the lady spent the early hours adjusting to, then accepting, her newly acquired fallen woman status, or at least one with a past. Starke paused by her door the next morning as he left to breakfast with Tyson at Saloon Brunet before a courtesy visit to Consul-general Lee. Katherine crept softly past his door several times on morning errands and considered knocking but could not excuse her behavior. Starke found no sign of her after returning to the Inglaterra and needed to confirm the luggage for *Mascotte's* hold was delivered to the customs house. Edward finally went to Katherine's room and brought her to the lobby where Starke was preparing to leave for Key West. From the stairs, she saw Starke and Tyson standing near a chair arrangement on the vaulted lobby's tiled floor. Coming down, she slipped one arm through her brother's for support as the two men turned. Katherine looked at Jacob, holding his pipe, then to the slight bulge in Tyson's jacket, giving away the silver flask. She released her brother at the foot of the stairs, braced herself, and then trailed him across the room.

Convinced fallen women could still maintain a lady's poise, Katherine summoned her last reserve of self-discipline to look Jacob directly in the eye without expression but could not control the warm blush brought on by his knowing how completely she submitted to nature's basest aspects. The eyes seemed to attempt some connection but she saw only revulsion; unaware Starke was struggling to decide whether to approach her or the brother first about marrying. When Tyson and Curtis were a few paces away, speaking of something Starke no longer cared about, he whispered, "I love you, Katherine," to the woman he spent months corresponding with and bedded the night before. Stunned, she turned away, leaving him confused and unable to continue.

Her brother sensed his sister's growing unease throughout the trip from New York accelerate in Havana. She also felt excessively warm on the stairs and he noticed her body twitch and composure change when Starke whispered something. He thought it a good pairing, even if their father would resist marriage to an American, but later, as her hand rested lightly on his arm without comment, dismissed the thought as impulsive since Constance Starke's subtle hints had never taken root.

Starke boarded the smaller Plant Line ship *Mascotte* without significant complications or delays then entered cabin five on the promenade deck's starboard side, about midway between her smoking room and social hall. His steamer trunk, filled with clothes and personal items, was accompanied by a small leather valise containing papers and Tyson's notebooks. It was obvious the Spanish Navy, Consul-general Lee, or both ensured he passed through customs relatively unmolested. As Tyson predicted a dark-haired female that could have been Cuban, some naturalized Americans, and two correspondents received meticulous attention. The third, a loud, swarthy Chicago journalist who felt obliged to offer up belligerency and indignation provoked a painstaking search by uniformed agents in the custom house and again on *Mascotte*.

Since *Mascotte* would make Key West by eight that evening and leave for Port Tampa the next day, Starke cabled Watson he would keep the cabin and join *Calypso* on Sunday morning. As the crossing ended with *Mascotte* slipping up Key West's ship channel to the city wharf, he saw *Calypso* anchored in a slightly different location, near the white and straw-yellow cruiser *Montgomery*. Starke was concerned this meant *Calypso's* executive officer did not fare well with Commander Davis but later found *Montgomery's* captain had only praise for Watson, who not only avoided complaints during his temporary command but perfectly mirrored *Montgomery's* activities from flag raising to liberty, airing linen, and boating. *Calypso's* executive officer also shifted anchorages without flaw although Starke thought the evolution unwarranted and possibly a test by Davis.

Chapter Nineteen
Jacksonville

Captain Albert looked to the electrolier over his desk in the Building then passed a flickering flame over the browned meerschaum pipe bowl, leaned back in the swivel chair, and looked through a tall window. January's blue-gray sky, with scattered dark-bottomed white clouds pushed by gusting winds emphasized Washington's cold-wave. He scanned papers and items spread across the desk and enjoyed an extended draw despite the mechanical calendar reminding him the filibuster project and billet could be ending. McKinley would be inaugurated in March, an inundation of Republican appointees would follow, and he was remiss in lining up a new assignment should his position end with them. He would also lose a powerful ally and mentor during April's first week with Rear Admiral Ramsay's mandatory retirement. There were indications he remained in line for *Maine* as a final sea tour, and still wanted her, but was familiar with the Building and built a viable role on the Secretary's staff. Returning to sea would have been less disruptive two years before but Washington was now home to Abigail, Olivia, and Isabella. He also suspected his lady's premonition, based on letters between *Calypso* and their row-house, that one or both daughters would soon leave was accurate.

The second-class battleship *Maine* decision must be made soon because her initial commander, Captain Crowninshield, was due to be relieved and become the next Bureau of

Navigation chief; but her suitors had grown in number. The oddball, hard luck ship competed with *Texas* for the better of her type's two worst but was a prestigious command already in commission so whoever relieved would avoid passing through the technical, administrative, and political wrangling necessary to take new and overhauled ships out of a yard.

Albert attempted to strengthen the bid by increasing his familiarity with *Maine* through professional journals and several visits. He found the large commanding officer accommodations inviting but other attributes less impressive. The first Navy-designed battleship had topside mounts, cranes, ladders, equipment, and other fittings jammed into any space available with this ad hoc approach continuing below deck. The delay manufacturing her armor resulted in an extremely long construction period so designs moved on and she lacked the latest battleships' protection or armored cruisers' speed; resulting in her second-class battleship designation, along with *Texas*. Even so, *Maine* never suffered lack of employment and tended to receive unique assignments since only four first-class American battleships were at sea.

Another smooth draw on the pipe left gray smoke curling towards the ceiling as Albert enjoyed its aroma. He was a strong candidate as the junior line captain in a small field, had a solid record, and possessed Building credibility. He was also recently assigned to the group reviewing Lieutenant Kimball's Spanish war plan and competing Naval War College proposal; with the committee due to write its own by April. His filibuster project was also viewed as successful; playing a key role in the Democratic administration's efforts to avoid war before Republicans took office and proving useful when polite diplomatic blows were exchanged between nations.

Spain's diplomatic mission repeatedly protested Junta filibuster expeditions from the States while their Madrid counterparts returned the favor regarding destruction of American property and treatment of its citizens in Cuba. Albert's efforts, especially after his ferret halted at least two Junta expeditions and avenged an anarchist assault on their gunboat, supported this diplomacy while disrupting the jingoes, Junta, and their supporters. His success augmenting Navy rotations through Key West with three ships patrolling Florida's Atlantic coast was equally valuable, while a close working relationship with the Revenue Cutter Service through Captain Fischer raised their priority for intercepting filibusters in the Atlantic and Gulf of Mexico. The cutter *George S. Boutwell* was operating off Florida's east coast while their consistently aggressive *Vanguard* worked the Gulf. This coordination across departments may have contributed to *Commodore* sinking south of St. Augustine, the *Three Friends* and *Dauntless* driven from Cuba's coast by the Spanish, and the last two tied up in litigation with several others.

Not everything went Albert's way. The *Three Friends'* verdict was appealed by arguing the Cuban government represented by the Junta was not recognized under the neutrality statute and therefore it was not applicable. In addition, the reassignment of three Navy ships cooled the relationship he painstakingly built with the North Atlantic Squadron when they received orders from the Secretary before its commander. Fortunately, he was able to recover and obtain agreement on where they should be placed. The small cruiser *Montgomery* would operate from Pensacola, the dynamite cruiser *Vesuvius* off Jacksonville, and *Montgomery's* sister ship *Detroit* would assume the Key West slot. A fourth cruiser, *Raleigh*, tagged for a coast defense convention in Tampa, would add her weight while transiting. Albert also had *Calypso* patrolling offshore between Norfolk and Nassau to add depth during the Cuban dry season. That decision was necessary but frustrating since it meant sending his ferret south would not happen when conflict intensified and expeditions increased between November and April. It also delayed the planned sortie to Nassau, Puerto Rico, Jamaica, and Key West he wanted to finish before summer rain, heat, and pestilence made Caribbean port visits more costly. Newspapers were already reporting fever, consumption, and smallpox cases rising in Havana along with war's traditional maladies of typhus and typhoid fever.

Albert also wanted *Calypso* back at sea to forestall any effort to immobilize her by summoning Starke to testify before a congressional committee about *John Gwinn Williams* and *Rafael Riego*. Falk had done well delaying it but Albert saw no reason to rely completely on the young man despite his success persuading Reed to prevent scheduling it before June. In addition to the Speaker's opposition to jingo war schemes and a virtuoso ability to orchestrate debate and get results using House rules, the Raleigh Hotel's influential Cuban Legation was keeping to ground. Falk attributed this to their inability to bring up *John Gwinn Williams* or *Rafael Riego* without conceding both were filibusters and the *Rafael Riego* expedition an anarchist enterprise. Even so, Albert believed keeping *Calypso* at sea complemented Falk's machinations and offered insurance. After ruminating, Albert emptied his meerschaum pipe, returned it to the rack beside his white porcelain coffee cup, and reached for the day's cables.

While he read, *Calypso* was closing an uneven blue thickening on the horizon that was the Florida coast and St. Johns River mouth. Going upriver took time and grounding common so *Calypso* would anchor northeast of massive stone jetties cutting through a sand bar at its mouth. From there she could threaten the Junta in Jacksonville and Fernandina without constraint since the long channel upriver to

Jacksonville between flat marshes or lowlands was charted as eighteen feet, leaving only a foot or two under the keel with a shifting sand bottom.

Her steam pinnaces could also make day-trips upriver, sailors eligible for liberty might visit Mayport Mills, and Starke would telegraph the Department. Mail could be posted, including his awkward letter to Katherine, another to his aunt and uncle, and a third to Philo McGiffin, the Academy friend he last saw in the Far East. Because McGiffin graduated after Starke, he fell under a statute limiting the number of graduates receiving commissions to fleet vacancies so most received a degree and separation pay. McGiffin used his to reach China, where he was examined, served in the Beiyang Fleet, and taught at Tianjin Naval Academy. He returned on leave before Starke took up *Calypso*; after being wounded on the German-built Chinese battleship *Chen Yuen* during a major naval engagement off the Yalu River. Starke wanted to visit while in Washington but did not, although he read McGiffin's account in *The Century Magazine* and several smaller articles. His last letter, held in Key West until Starke returned, was written in an unsteady hand suggesting he was not healing and perhaps worsening.

As *Calypso* settled to her anchor, the accommodation ladder rigged, and boat booms swung out, Starke watched both pinnaces lowered and leave for the gray stone jetties. They were paired for this first trip so one could assist or tow the other if necessary and, being out of sight, regulations required a senior boat officer. Watson took the first run to make inquiries about Jacksonville filibusters since the north Florida port was home to several, favored Cuban independence, and boasted an active Junta organization. Blair asked Watson for the second pinnace, coxswained by Melvin. Their surgeon joined in to buy medical supplies and, Starke suspected, the latest Conan Doyle mystery. With Watson and Blair away, the navigator, Ensign Dunbar, and deck division officer, Ensign Martyn, would carry out the daily routine. Starke watched the steam pinnaces until they passed behind the north jetty's two miles of massive, jumbled rocks, ringed with small white-capped breakers along an uneven base, and then went to his cabin.

Starke later sensed a presence near his desk while reviewing draft reports, shifted in his chair, and caught Thaddeus mid-floor, padding quietly from the pantry door. The ship's gray and white feline paused when the man turned towards him, completed a cursory survey, then retraced his steps to rejoin Yamashita preparing dinner. Starke glanced at the desk calendar set to "WED JAN 20 97", then out an open cabin window to clear skies. Every indicator suggested their mild weather with brief showers would remain. East of the anchored ship was the Atlantic's distant horizon; a sharp line separating dark blue water from a much lighter sky. Although Fernandina lay up the coast to the northwest, due west was sand beach fronting green foliage that contained what seemed a plantation. The southwest was dominated by dark, stone jetties whose recent completion allowed large vessels to reach Jacksonville and ended days spent waiting for enough water to cross the bar. Scattered from beach to horizon were small fishing boats. Occasionally, a coastal freighter or tug, trailing gray-black smoke plumes would pass, and twice that morning inbound ships boarded a St. Johns River pilot from the loitering schooner then began their journey upriver.

He could hear Chief Weaver lending experience to sailors tuning mainmast shrouds through the open window and Seaman Kearney perched on an equipment box teaching Landsman Hawk to put a monkey fist on heaving lines. Less clear and audible, gun captains Grier and Kirby were with their 4-inch gun crews at either end. Cleaning, cycling, blacking, then lubricating their blooded rifles was now second nature; along with daily inspections supplemented by copious pointing, aiming, and loading drills. Live firing also took place when location, budget, and magazines suited. Wiggs was working through a hardcover account book in the paymaster's stateroom, his eyes following a ruler moving slowly down columns of precise, handwritten entries. Through the open porthole over his bunk came the hint of a breeze, strong sea scents, and constant suck-slap at the waterline. Chief Quartermaster Owen stood in the pilothouse near a battered wooden box containing his sextant; set aside to shoot angles to the shore then midday sun-line in a few hours. Quartermasters surrounding the chart table worked two large sheets of heavy paper that intermittently fluttered in unison with an open book's pages; given life by the light cross-breeze. A window on either side of the recently cleaned pilothouse was cracked for ventilation and to draw off heat while the others remained closed to prevent charts taking flight.

Osbourne kept a single main boiler on line to ensure *Calypso* could get underway quickly, provide steam for the dynamo, and distill freshwater. O'Leary was leaving the boiler flats, where Machinist Chief Emery Baasch was supervising their donkey boilers' periodic washout, to start his daily inspection of boilers, fire room, coal bunkers, and other spaces for the engineer's noon report. While in the fire room, he stood near their operating boiler as one of its heavy stokehole doors opened briefly, releasing a sudden blast of heat and flash of light to reveal a good fire. Few clinkers were forming and what flames showed, spurted from a flat bed of dark lumps mortared by brilliant yellow that underlay a pale haze floating low across the entire surface. This assured him the coal was properly laid. If spread too thick across the grate it would have been red. During each opening he saw a large flame leap from the haze, then die away amidst flickering forms and shadows cast by the firebox's steel walls and water tubes generating steam.

O'Leary detailed Jones, the off-watch lead stoker, to go with him while inspecting coal bunkers for temperature change, cleanliness, and security. *Calypso's* were mainly inboard of the carpenter's walk along the hull but two running athwartship were added during conversion when the cargo hold was sectioned. Every coal bunker was steel-lined with a flat central floor, no hard corners, and shaped to fit the location. Every bunker had a unique personality because their designers considered trimmers' efforts to extract and break coal into usable lumps, coal passers' exertions carting it off, and stokers' ability to feed each boiler's three stokeholes; but all included at least one chute from the main deck, access through a mechanical door at the base, an overhead hatch, temperature alarm, venting, drains, and at least one spray nozzle fed by the firemain.

Coal bunkers, empty, full, or in use, were checked by each watch since their apparently inert lumps of stored energy behaved differently, depending on source, storage time, moisture, and other factors. Ignoring this degraded performance and risked fire or explosion from coal or its dust; and the risk was so high that Navy regulations established specific shipboard responsibilities from the commander down. Osbourne and O'Leary ensured the black gang religiously followed all rules and, except during emergencies, everyone understood safe handling took priority over performance. Each bunker was meticulously maintained, full or empty, and swept clean. Corrosion inspections occurred every third month, with any discovered scraped away immediately and the area preserved with brown oxide. The black gang also kept to the bunkering plan so no coal went unused for long periods and part-empty bunkers were never topped off. Trimmers spread lumps in even layers while coaling then tamped each in place to avoid air pockets. Everyone watched for wet or damp lumps and a careful inspection completed after coaling to confirm main deck bunker plates were secure before cleanup and wash-down.

O'Leary and Jones inspected each bunker by checking temperatures, feeling bulkheads, and sniffing for burning or sulfurous odors. O'Leary called out discrepancies and Jones took notes for his oncoming watch to resolve. Everything was normal until they arrived at a port side aft bunker. Both paused then looked at each other as they matched temperature readings with earlier log entries. Osbourne and O'Leary monitored this bunker closely since the conversion due to its location, configuration, and venting; then increased vigilance after Key West when temperature readings rose slightly. Today's were not enough to trigger the alarm but showed a distinct spike and the smell was ominous. Bunker fires usually began with a hot spot buried deep in the coal where lack of oxygen slowed growth, but should the burning reach a bulkhead its heat could ignite flammable material in adjacent spaces and if it surfaced there could be a fire or dust explosion. Meanwhile, poisonous and explosive gasses were created that turned air unbreathable or deadly.

Spontaneous coal fires were a constant threat that was never eliminated, whether in mines, above ground piles, during shipping, in large coal sheds, or bunkers waiting to be used. Ships with large coal stores held in holds or bunkers for a long time were most at risk so these events plagued colliers, but no ship was immune. Neither O'Leary nor Jones faced one shipboard but both realized they had a hot spot and potential coal bunker fire. Jones, more than O'Leary, felt his gut twist since he fought several ashore when coal was piled too long waiting for transport or higher prices, and knew of sealed mines back home that still burned.

The ex-miner lost family and friends to underground fires so he needed no explanation when O'Leary said, "Assemble the trimmers. I'll inform the captain." The crew would soon face the hell of entering a bunker, digging through coal to the hot spot, then removing a glowing mass. Jones tucked a dirty notepad into his waistband and replied grimly, "Aye, aye, sir."

O'Leary located Osbourne, who reported it to the officer of the deck according to regulations. That unfortunate was Ensign Martyn so he accompanied the engineers to Starke's cabin struggling to appear in control. Although he listened to Osbourne and O'Leary debate proposed solutions on the way, his thoughts were dedicated to regretting it landed on him rather than Blair. He was responsible to the executive officer for boat operations and should have made that first run upriver with Watson but acquiesced because he liked Blair, despite the romantic inclination and caustic demeanor. Besides, he saw no benefit spending morning and afternoon on a lethargic river under Watson's eye with no guarantee good weather would hold. Remaining on board also promised a benign anchor watch and opportunity to make inroads on several administrative tasks. Now he must tell the enigmatic Starke their ship was in danger of burning.

Calypso's commander was completing the final draft of an intelligence letter compiled from Tyson's notebooks and his own Havana observations before starting to adapt a format used by steel-hulled ships to request dry-docking for the inspection and hull work Navy regulations required them to complete every six months. He already circled *Calypso* in a whaleboat and thought the March cleaning and maintenance of her coppered hull would improve speed; and taking the ship out of water would permit closer inspection of underwater plates. He planned to argue operational necessity required Newport News, Norfolk, or Port Royal, but his primary concern was to avoid New York, Philadelphia, or New Hampshire during late winter since the crew was acclimated to the Caribbean.

He was interrupted while considering the best wording to support this proposal once it encountered the bureau system and instantly realized it was a major problem since Osbourne and O'Leary accompanied the duty officer. Ensign Martyn appeared agitated, which was understandable since he was in charge of the ship, but general quarters had not sounded so Starke guessed there was time. Reaching for a pipe, he scoured the brown bowl's blackened interior, asking low and calm, "Well, Mr. Martyn?"

Finding comfort in formal jargon, the ensign responded, "Mr. O'Leary's discovered a hot spot in the aft coal bunker port side."

Every shipboard fire could be catastrophic, even overturned lamps accounted for major losses over the years, but coal bunker fires in wood hulls turned lethal fast so it was fortunate *Calypso* was anchored in benign weather near a populated shore. To gain time and present a calm exterior, Starke dredged the pipe through his increasingly supple leather pouch, "Very well, Mr. Martyn. What steps have been taken?"

"Mr. O'Leary is assembling trimmers at the bunker but no one's authorized to enter."

Starke looked at Osbourne, then Martyn, "Quite correct, but what else?"

Martyn knew his captain never inflicted personal whims or anger on officers or crew but the ensign still empathized with penitents eyeing the expectant rack since his captain was owed a proposed action from the officer charged with *Calypso's* safety. Martyn used the several seconds' grace Starke granted by lighting his pipe to consider what should have been worked out before entering. As the captain exhaled a cloud of pipe smoke Martyn began, "I judged setting fire quarters unnecessary considering bunker temperature, no sign of fire, and trimmers already going to station."

Starke took another draw then slowly released a light blue-gray cloud that drifted with air flowing between two cracked windows, "That avoided alarming the crew but you would have been equally correct to do so. What shares a bulkhead with that bunker?"

Realizing Starke already knew, Martyn answered, "A small medical storeroom with bulk alcohol is on one side, captain."

"And the plan?"

"No one enters without your permission and while the engineers prepare we'll clear adjacent spaces and station a watch."

"Also lower whaleboats, rig the portable fire pump, and let the crew know we'll set fire quarters before opening the bunker."

Turning to the chief engineer, Starke added, "Mr. Osbourne, I believe this bunker's one of those you and Mr. O'Leary were anxious about in Newport News?"

Osbourne's calm, slow drawl began, "Yes, sir. We'll follow standing orders and stop nonessential plant operations before setting fire quarters. Once everything's ready and you've given permission, we'll crack vents, check for poisonous gas, then enter and start probing."

O'Leary listened for anything missed, noting their chief engineer's capabilities were at odds with his appearance and demeanor. Osbourne had not only earned their black gang's absolute loyalty but achieved strict discipline while spurring senior members to question and even challenge him on technical matters. He also stood regular watches although Navy regulations relieved him of this duty unless the commanding officer stated it was necessary in writing.

Osbourne continued, "As we dig out the hot spot, safe coal will be sent to an empty bunker and anything questionable to the boiler or sea. What's burning goes over the side and the same for anything the boiler can't handle. Should the bunker need clearing faster everything goes over and the accountants can grouse later. We'll also line up the fireman to flood it but that risks a steam explosion so it's a last resort."

Starke was confident in his engineers and their black gang but would have immediately left for the scene on a merchant ship. Responsibility and accountability were equally inescapable on either but Navy captains worked through wardroom officers if they hoped to fight their ships successfully. He also needed to show his trust so, with great restraint, Starke shifted the pipe bowl cradled in his right hand to the left, "I agree with your plan, gentlemen, so let's be about it. Keep me informed and I'll join you to open the bunker. In the meantime, there's a letter to finish."

Starke heard the three talking in the passageway as they set out, and forced himself to draft the letter requesting a dry-docking some months off while a glowing red glob threatened to burn *Calypso* to the waterline. Despite naval protocol, he was grateful for the larger crew and dealing with a bunker rather than hold since colliers, especially windjammers, faced a near hopeless task. One iron-hulled ship was put aground, smoldered for two years then reentered the trade but *Calypso's* wood-sheathed hull and magazines ensured a rapid death if a fire took hold.

Martyn went aft to the accommodation ladder and began

dispatching messengers to alert the crew. Sailors were aware even small fires could quickly envelop the ship so it was best they knew exactly what was happening. When Osbourne sent word they were ready, he ordered fire quarters sounded by rapidly ringing the ship's bell followed by its location in distinct strokes. Minutes later, a relieved Martyn turned deck responsibilities over to the navigator, Ensign Dunbar, and left for his station.

Starke completed his dry-dock letter's initial draft before the bell sounded so he went on deck and paused above the accommodation ladder and boat boom to ensure the ship was prepared to be abandoned in an orderly fashion. Passing curious sailors, he saw the fire apparatus listed in the carpenter section of the *Equipment Book of Allowances* was staged or rigged. This included the handy-billy pump made up to three fifty-foot sections of cotton-covered rubber hose with brass fittings. Spanner wrenches were placed near a solid wood case containing six of four-dozen allotted fire grenades consisting of glass globes filled with saltwater and bicarbonate of soda. After speaking with Dunbar and Chief Weaver, he went below.

Access to the bunker interior would be through an overhead entry and escape hatch until enough contents were removed to also use its three-foot, hand-cranked door for retrieving coal. Like all bunkers, there was a loading tube to the main deck, air vents, and nozzles piped to the single firemain running along her keel. Under tons of coal, the bunker floor drain emptied into a discharge line roughly following the firemain. Their bilge and fire pumps could provide and expel saltwater so long as there was steam but it would be up to the handy-billy if they failed; something that did not bear contemplation.

He sensed apprehension in those standing near the heavy

hatch, especially among trimmers, and surreptitiously checked them. Tucked-in clothing offered some protection, as did dirty gray hats pulled down over ears. Everyone wore heavy gloves and thick boots. Those waiting to enter the bunker strapped miner's lights to their heads and covered nose and mouth with thick, wet rags. A wood-handled, portable electric light with its thick glass globe protected by a metal frame, and tightly coiled, long black cord, swung from the shoulder of one. After confirming a back-up hose was coupled to the firemain, the crew had been stationed, adjacent compartments cleared, and all coal dust removed, Osbourne requested permission to open the space. Once Starke agreed, O'Leary and Jones cracked exterior vents, checked for poisonous or explosive gas, unbolted the upper access hatch, and felt hot air rush past their faces.

After the explosion risk subsided, trimmers were lowered into a cramped, dark, dusty, and poorly lit bunker to begin sending coal to passers who took some lumps to an empty bunker and a few to the main boiler. Others had help on the main deck as they pulled coal back up through the loading chute then sent black lumps with smooth faces reflecting the sun's rays, plunging through clear, green water leaving a cloudy trail and gray surface blemish. Trimmers would remove a layer, probe for the hotspot, and then repeat the process. This continued several hours with men working in short shifts then recovering by sitting on deck in a sweaty heap hungrily sucking fresh air or collapsed against a dirty bulkhead below. Starke could do little but impede progress so he went to his day cabin, took twelve o'clock reports, and listened to berth deck cooks carrying tinned soup and coffee to the men.

Lieutenant Watson was returning from Jacksonville in the steam pinnace while the black gang dug. As it cleared the long jetties constructed of massive stone jumbles, he stood and steadied himself by grasping the frame that supported a vibrating white canvas canopy. He had watched Mayport Mills' piers, houses, churches, and hotel pass to starboard at the upstream entrance. Further up the river in Jacksonville he learned the village economy continuously cycled and was at a low point because rails from the city that once brought trains filled with tourists now carried handcars delivering mail. A tall, red-brick lighthouse rose above the little community and beyond it to the south, Ribault Bay was encircled by a cluster of local society's summer homes. Further south along the coast lay the Murray Hall Hotel ruins; charred remnants of a three-story structure whose central section once reached six, that burned six years before *Calypso's* arrival after pampering up to 350 guests during its four years in the trade.

Periodic glances astern as the jetties' mouth approached assured him there was no outbound traffic besides the second steam pinnace leaving a trail of light smoke drifting south and Coxswain Melvin proving he was equally accomplished with boat or mandolin. Once they turned northeast into open water, Watson's pinnace began shouldering ocean rollers pressing the starboard bow and when it lifted he saw both whaleboats riding to the bark's boom and more sailors on deck than should be. Something was amiss or Starke's plans changed but whatever the cause it was useless to demand more from his coxswain since their small steam engine, cheerfully clicking away, would go no faster.

He instead reviewed the results of their trip up the slow moving river that consumed most of a day. During the hurried visit, Watson sent mail to the post office, cabled the Navy Department to report their arrival, then spoke with Frank Clark, Assistant United States Attorney for South Florida. He intended to visit the St. Johns District Collector of

Customs but stayed with Clark because the Democrat appointee was one of a handful attempting to suppress the local filibuster trade.

According to Clark, Attorney General Harmon's December declaration that shipping arms without fighters to Cuba was legal under American law had restricted efforts to enforce proclamations or statutes by blurring an already murky boundary. This was clearly illustrated when the cutter *George S. Boutwell* pulled *Commodore* off a St. Johns River sandbar, was not allowed to board, attempted to trail the filibuster, then joined the search for survivors after she foundered. His informants speculated the expedition was lost in part due to Albert's work and *Calypso's* notoriety since the tug left hurriedly then took a different route to avoid *Newark* coming north from Key West and hearing rumors *Calypso* was off the coast. The result was *Commodore* grounding several times going downriver, not stopping to inspect for hull damage, and ultimately sinking off the Mosquito Inlet Lighthouse.

That filibuster's loss accompanied by sabotage claims, along with *Dauntless* and *Three Friends* placed under customs collector control, temporarily curtailed local Junta expeditions. However, Clark predicted the Junta's local organizer, Jose Alejandro Huau, would soon have a workaround with support from the Cuban Political Club, a social extension called the Cuban Circle, and leading citizens like Napoleon Broward. Huau was a naturalized citizen of French and Cuban descent, trained engineer, and veteran of several city council terms. He owned a cigar factory, tobacco store, and soda fountain but Cuban independence was his passion and he orchestrated a local culture of correspondents, adventurers, and businesses that openly ignored federal law and often profited by it. The opposition, besides Clark and some federal agents, was primarily Spain's vice consul in Jacksonville, Juan

Potous, and their state consul in Tampa. They were supported by the Pinkerton Detective Agency but Clark was unable to coordinate with either unless he wished to be labeled a Spanish partisan.

Watson was slightly discouraged when leaving Jacksonville but that changed to foreboding as the two pinnaces closed *Calypso* and her bulk increased. There was no distress or panic but the activity clearly exceeded any approved Day Orders. As his steam pinnace approached the accommodation ladder's lower platform, its coxswain replied to *Calypso's* hail then pointed the bow slightly astern of the half-submerged wood and steel framework. Watson kept silent despite growing impatience. He may be senior line officer of this miniature flotilla and second in command of the ship but coxswains controlled their boats unless relieved and that act entered in the boat log. Watson strictly enforced this. Ensign Blair, in the pinnace following, was a repeat offender but had no complaints on this run with Coxswain Melvin in charge of his boat and the executive officer close by.

Sending the bowhook forward, Watson's coxswain closed the platform, cut his engine, put the rudder over, and backed. The bow, seemingly feet from ramming, twisted smoothly alongside as the engine disengaged, leaving the pinnace stopped parallel to and less than a foot away. Boathooks immediately extended from bow and stern, caught the platform, and warped them in. Watson then stepped across with great care since accommodation ladders were steadied by hundreds and sometimes thousands of tons with a boat's unforgiving gunwale shearing up and down against them; eager for the opportunity to sever, break, or crush some human appendage. Watson intermittently witnessed the results, usually felt by visitors, inebriated sailors, officer types, and senior enlisted, but today his coxswain was chastising one of the boat crew volunteering to be an exception.

Ensign Dunbar met him at the top of the ladder, returned salutes, and reported they were at fire quarters after spending most of the day removing tons of coal as the black gang inched towards a hot spot. Starting for Starke's cabin, Watson overheard his pinnace being sent to the boat boom and Blair's hailed. Reaching the cabin door, he knocked, heard Starke respond, and entered to find Yamashita setting the silver-plated coffee urn with its black serving handle on the table. Starke turned to the steward, "Yamashita, another cup, please," then to his executive officer, "Welcome back, XO. Have some coffee."

Watson realized he was sweating despite their temperate weather as Starke added several spoons of sugar to a white porcelain cup, stirred until the brown crystals dissolved, then sat back in his chair, "I trust Ensign Dunbar explained O'Leary discovered a hot spot in the bunker he and Osbourne have worried over since Newport News."

"Yes, sir, and I saw the whaleboats lowered."

"I didn't think you'd object and told Martyn it was an excellent opportunity to soak their hulls in saltwater. Should the need arise, they're already launched and if not a good wetting helps preserve wood and swell seams."

Yamashita brought a cup and deftly filled it using the coffeepot's long handle before returning to his pantry. Watson offered what was learned in Jacksonville while they drank and when finished, Starke asked, "Did you spot either filibuster?"

"While our boats were waiting, some dockhands told Melvin where *Three Friends* was moored at a downstream pier so we passed close aboard coming out. She's a typical seagoing, single stack tug with rounded pilothouse, bow and side fenders, high bulwarks, and large cabin with a canvas awning rigged over the pilothouse deck's aft third. There's a main and fore mast with navigation lights, and two pairs of ventilators; one set behind the pilothouse and the other just forward of the stack. Rumor has it she's fast."

"So you'll recognize her in future; and *Dauntless*?"

"Didn't want to risk coming downriver after dark just to look for her, but she's also been libeled."

"How'd our surgeon fare?"

"Conrad's satisfied, sir. Picked up some mystery or other, and learned Doyle's out with a new serial, *Adventures of Abbey Grange*. He also bought a Bulls-Eye Number 2 Kodak camera, so Osbourne and O'Leary won't be far behind."

Starke twisted the cup in its saucer, grinned slightly, saying quietly, "I suppose not. Let's finish our coffee then go below and see if we spend tonight on the beach."

Watson's last captain would be with Osbourne and O'Leary questioning every move. Starke obviously wanted to but remained in command of the entire ship. An imprecise line separated allowing subordinates the freedom to carry out their duty and dereliction of it on the captain's part. Starke balanced this better than most so his officers would not hesitate to call, or he to respond; and that placed *Calypso* worlds apart from *Winston A. Capps*. It was one of several traits their enigmatic overlord possessed that attracted loyalty without his realizing it. Watson felt the pull when he was offered a second chance despite the *Winston A. Capps* letter designed to finish his career.

Starke and Watson entered what seemed a sweltering subterranean world permeated with steam and machinery smells. Black gang body odor and sweat was added to the mix as they approached men working with hands, shovels, carts, and sacks. The common enemy was a glowing mass buried in coal that searched for oxygen to ignite surrounding lumps while its heat allowed trimmers, passers, and volunteers only ten, perhaps fifteen, minutes before being pulled up through the bunker's overhead access like rag-dolls. Those forced to pry loose or fragment a recalcitrant lump wedged between or melded to another failed to last that long. Once out, most were half-carried, dripping sweat and black with coal dust, to a passageway where bandannas were removed, faces splashed from a tub, and slow sips of sugar water given. Surgeon Conrad joined his apothecary watching for headaches or vomiting, and prevented several from returning to the fight before marginally fit. Meanwhile, the surgeon, apothecary, and baymen also rotated below then topside for fresh air and to escape the stifling heat.

Seeing a familiar face returning to the fight with a long steel rod, Starke asked, "How's it going Jones?"

The ex-miner grinned, causing his mouth's pink and white interior to contrast with the sweat-drenched black and gray face surrounding it, "Hot as hell, sir; but not underground."

Osbourne noticed their arrival and ambled over as Jones continued to the lower bunker door. Black and sweat-streaked as his men, he wiped a wilted rag across his forehead, drawling, "It's getting hotter so I think we're close, captain. Main concern now is flaring or a coal dust explosion. O'Leary's topside working the chute with Martyn and setting up a pump to flood the bunker if the firemain fails, but don't think we'll need to."

The exhausted black gang removed enough coal by evening for a man to walk half erect around the bunker and sense its hot spot from heat penetrating thick shoe soles and heavy gloves. A young German trimmer in Kemp's section was first to spot a malevolent red glow in the blanketing coal. Kemp immediately dropped into the hot, dark chamber, dragging a fire hose. While the trimmer, flushed with adrenaline, pulled away lumps he sprayed around the spot then let water flow over it. The first seawater caused a warning hiss, adding steam to an already miserable atmosphere, before judicious application of more water turned the clump from glowing red to grayish. Meanwhile, what water reached the drains was pumped overboard; although the flow was intermittently stopped to clear pump strainers of coal.

Kemp was taken aback when his chief engineer's bulk appeared in the bunker then begin poking about with their trimmers working to remove the menace. Once satisfied, Osbourne called out to Starke it was a melded mass about three-feet long, two wide, and the same deep; with a hot central core. This nemesis was extracted in more than a dozen pieces showing various combustion stages. Some went to the boiler's firebox and others overboard as Osbourne balanced the risk of carrying a piece topside against it exploding on contact with the boiler fire bed. When the last remnant sputtered to the ocean floor, his black gang paused in relief and jubilation then went back to dislodging, digging, and redistributing coal. Although exhausted, they could not relax before the bunker was emptied since another hot spot might still lurk unobserved. When Osbourne reported the bunker clear, Starke returned to congratulate those involved then added, at the chief engineer's request, anyone off watch could sleep on station or topside overnight while recovering. Executive officers were always vexed when routine was disturbed, and Watson was no exception, but Starke thought it useful to not be completely predictable; so long as it was a rare event. The entire ship needed time to rally, re-stow coal, inspect the bunker, and write reports; so he also let them know *Calypso* would be anchored two additional days.

Throughout the clear night under a sky saturated with steady and flickering stars, *Calypso* slowly shifted position about the anchor in a figure-eight pattern. At times, the horizon vanished and shoreline turned to a dark shape, ill-defined and striped with the small white crests of waves rolling over its beach. A fixed white beam from the St. Johns lighthouse swept out over lights from ships and buildings near the river mouth. With danger past, surroundings pleasant, and ship secure, Starke slept well and true with two open windows allowing a gentle night breeze to pass over him, bearing traces of shore, sea, and coal smoke.

Calypso spent the next days anchored in sight of miniature breakers lapping against the north jetty or rolling over the crushed-shell beach towards low sand hills with Mount Cornelia's sixty-two foot mass rising above the lowlands. The roofs of Pilot Town, across the river from Mayport Mills, were also visible beyond the dunes' crest. The local association's schooner *Meta* periodically emerged from that cluster of houses and piers to greet incoming ships; replacing several schooners that once raced for customers.

Starke cabled the Department and Captain Albert, while Osbourne and O'Leary spent their first day examining the coal bunker and comparing notes for their Bureau of Steam Engineering report. They considered the traditional causes such as coal type, freshness, and handling, but also bunker design since some ships seldom had fires while others were plagued by them. Starke especially wanted the bunker design investigated since *Calypso* had no history of fires before conversion, the bunker plate seal checked out, the coal had not been stored overlong, and its handling appeared correct. Osbourne's draft report, however, could only conclude a pocket of coal acquired enough oxygen and moisture for spontaneous combustion and state he would continue the examination while the black gang increased their vigilance.

A steam pinnace made daily runs upriver during *Calypso's* extended stay, with Blair and Martyn trading off boat officer responsibilities. Chief Weaver also cajoled Martyn into asking Watson to schedule more small boat training. Rowing, sailing, and etiquette never quite came off to the chief's satisfaction; which was natural since boat operations established a warship's reputation. Starke thought it went well enough, could always be improved, and, watching them under canvas, wanted to join in; having sailed often during summers in Narraganset Bay.

The cutter *George S. Boutwell* and dynamite cruiser *Vesuvius* also made an appearance. Captain William Kilgore, commanding the cutter, was the Jacksonville filibusters' nemesis and occasional jailer. She was purpose-built for the southern coast and, although out of Charleston, often worked the St. Johns River. Her black, 200-ton iron hull was nearly 140 feet long with a twenty-three foot beam, useful seven-foot draft, and fine lines. Besides a unique semi-compound engine turning two screws, she was rigged as a two-masted auxiliary topsail schooner. Her bowsprit was short, with a small pilothouse aft of the foremast and forward of a tall, slender stack. Two boats were under midship davits and her white superstructure spread to the ship's sides for its aft third. She could also rig an immense canvas awning that covered the entire forecastle, with a second over her superstructure.

Kilgore, like all cutter commanders, balanced a maelstrom of legal restrictions and conflicting missions. He knew of *Calypso's* participation in the *John Gwinn Williams* and *Rafael Riego* incidents but had little sympathy for those smuggling military stores and insurrectos to Cuba. At the moment, it was even less, having just towed the serial offender *Commodore* off a sand bank while fielding filibuster owners' harassment complaints for boarding their ships. Starke suspected these were technically valid since Kilgore knew Jacksonville expeditions almost always loaded cargoes and passengers at the last moment from a secluded riverbank or off New River once they cleared with clean papers. Convinced these tactics made snaring one unlikely, like *Calypso*, he would try to frustrate and complicate these activities.

Vesuvius was another Albert achievement. The dynamite cruiser came south from her Philadelphia shipyard refit to patrol off Georgia and Florida; with Jacksonville and Fernandina receiving special attention. Excluding *Katahdin*, an experimental ram, the yacht-like *Vesuvius* was probably the fleet's oddest ship. At 250 feet and 950 tons, she was said to make twenty-one knots although reports indicated sixteen more realistic. Her nine-foot draft and twin screws might have been useful in shoal water but were offset by a long length and narrow beam that guaranteed awkward handling and excessive rolling, even in light swells. Her three 15-inch dynamite guns fired a 200 or 500 pound shell up to 4,000 yards that could be set to explode when it struck a target or after submerging alongside. This powerful battery vastly exceeded what *Rafael Riego* loosed on the Spanish gunboat but was not made operational since her 3-pounder guns were considered sufficient for filibusters.

Steaming south along the coast, she raised the black-hulled bark off the St. Johns River and her captain, Lieutenant Commander John Pillsbury, closed to investigate. He was Starke's senior, so *Calypso's* commander paid a courtesy call in his best service dress blue uniform. As *Vesuvius* stood by, one of *Calypso's* whaleboats was fitted out as the gig then rowed her captain across. After receiving honors, Starke followed Pillsbury to a bright deckhouse wardroom pierced by more windows than customary.

Pillsbury entered the Navy during the war, was known as a geographer, and recently commanded a coast survey ship. If physical appearance counted, Starke decided *Vesuvius* would come down hard on filibusters. The jutting jaw, large mustache, and pugnacious countenance suggested an adversary who did not lack energy or the will to act. Following another round of *John Gwinn Williams* and *Rafael Riego* questions, Starke passed on information obtained from the Assistant United States Attorney and Captain Kilgore. Pillsbury informed Starke that *Vesuvius*, like *Calypso*, was commissioned to deal with filibusters and ensure those operating out of Fernandina and Jacksonville felt the Navy's presence. He was satisfied with his command but admitted she might not be the best choice since maneuvering was awkward and a light hull forced her to shelter in the nearest port when heavy weather approached.

Starke felt the privilege Albert bestowed on him with *Calypso* as the gig slowly made its way back; and directed his coxswain to circle the black-hulled bark with tall straw-yellow masts before making for the accommodation ladder's lower platform. Watson was waiting at the starboard gangway to report Martyn just returned from Jacksonville with a Secretary of the Navy telegram that read, "Make for Newport News immediately to dock and service boilers."

The orders were obviously sent in response to the bunker fire report, but that could be repaired by the crew and Starke's letter requesting Port Royal, Newport News, or Norfolk had not yet been mailed. This also removed *Calypso* from filibuster patrol for at least two weeks of the Cuban fighting season so it could only mean Albert had something else in store for his ferret. Starke summoned Watson and Dunbar.

Once *Calypso*'s officers and cadets were seated at the large wardroom table, Starke pushed a pale yellow telegram over its green cloth to Osbourne, "Looks like you've a maintenance opportunity."

Then, looking around the table, added, "XO; please see to a

wish list of everything we'd like done at Newport News. While Mr. Dunbar's plotting our track, Mr. Martyn has permission to unrig the accommodation ladder, bring our boats aboard, and secure the boom. Once engineering has steam enough to answer all bells we'll head north; unless Mr. Osbourne prefers sailing her out."

About the Author

Michael T. Ribble was born in Lapeer, Michigan and raised on farms near Davison. He received a bachelor's degree in journalism after attending Central Michigan University and University of Colorado, Boulder. During high school and college he worked road construction, farmed in Colorado, helped build a feedlot, harvested sugar beets, was a summer camp counselor teaching marksmanship, and employed in a gas station/sporting goods store. Enlisting as a seaman recruit, he served in Guantanamo Bay, Cuba, followed by two minesweepers, a cruiser, destroyer, frigate, and other duty stations before retiring from active and reserve duty as a captain. After receiving a Master of Business Administration degree from Florida State University, he held various integrated logistics support, program analyst, and cost estimating positions in the nation's capital at Naval Sea Systems Command and Department of Homeland Security. He also participated in towing de-fueled nuclear submarines, taught naval science at Northwestern University, facilitated a national naval reserve policy board, and completed the United States Naval War College's continuing education program. He has crewed several annual sail races down Chesapeake Bay and served on steam and diesel ships as a Surface Warfare Officer. Articles and poetry written by Mr. Ribble have appeared in university publications, newspapers, and U.S. Naval Institute *Proceedings*.